Also by Kameron Hurley:

God's War

KAMERON HURLEY
INFIDEL

DEL REY

1 3 5 7 9 10 8 6 4 2

First published in the US in 2011 by Night Shade Books
First published in the UK in 2014 by Del Rey, an imprint of Ebury Publishing
A Random House Group Company

The Random House Group Limited Reg. No. 954009

Addresses for companies within the Random House Group can be found at:
www.randomhouse.co.uk

A CIP catalogue record for this book is available from the British Library

The Random House Group Limited supports the Forest Stewardship
Council® (FSC®), the leading international forest-certification organisation.
Our books carrying the FSC label are printed on FSC®-certified paper.
FSC is the only forest-certification scheme supported by the leading
environmental organisations, including Greenpeace.
Our paper procurement policy can be found at:
www.randomhouse.co.uk/environment

Printed and bound in Great Britain by Clays Ltd, St Ives PLC

ISBN 9780091952808

To buy books by your favourite authors and register for offers visit:
www.randomhouse.co.uk

For Joanna.
So long, and thanks for all the brutal women.

Fight in the cause of Allah those who fight you, but do not transgress limits; for Allah loveth not transgressors.

(Quran, 2.190)

Do not be deceived: "Bad company ruins good morals."

(Bible, Corinthians 15:33)

†.

The smog in Mushtallah tasted of tar and ashes; it tasted like the war. Mushtallah was nearly a thousand miles from the front, but the organic filter surrounding the city couldn't keep out the yeasty stink of spent bursts and burning flesh blowing in from the desert.

Nyx pulled on a pair of goggles and stepped over a dead raven. Dusty feathers, dog shit, and edible receipts clogged the gutters. Ahead of her, the pale, stupid-looking Ras Tiegan kid she was charged with keeping alive made her way down the crowded sidewalk, swinging her shopping bags ahead of her. Her name was Mercia, and she was daughter to the Ras Tiegan ambassador to Nasheen. The ambassador's kid covered her hair like most Ras Tiegans, though on choking days like this one, most everyone did. Mercia had big dark eyes and a flat nose like her mother's that gave her a distinctly foreign profile. The rest of her was awkward and gangly. Her hips were so bony she could have forced her way through the crowd without the bags. Rich Ras Tiegan girls were all too skinny.

Nyx moved around a tangle of women dancing outside a cantina blaring southern beat music. The tangy smell of oranges and saffron wafted out over the sidewalk. Nyx kept track of the time by counting the number of wasp, locust, and red beetle swarms buzzing by, delivering messages of a far higher caliber than she'd been entrusted with in years.

A bedraggled young vendor sat at the corner on a mat, holding up a "Paint your own prayer rug!" sign in one hand and a jar of zygotes covered in a sheen of ice flies in the other. Nyx's footsteps slowed as she passed. If she'd still been a bloodletting bel dame, she'd have chopped off the woman's head and collected the inevitable bounty on her. These days, women selling illegal genetic goods were policed solely by bel dames. There was a time when the vendor would have been spooked at Nyx's approach. Nyx had been better dressed, better armed, and better supported, once: running with her bel dame sisters instead of a cocky boy shifter and reformed venom addict. Now, instead of collecting blood debt, she was babysitting diplomats and cutting up petty debtors when the First Families paid her in hard currency. It felt more honest. But a lot less honorable.

The woman shoved the jar of zygotes at her.

"Ten hours of viability left," the woman babbled. "Good price in the pits for these!"

"Fuck off," Nyx said, "Or I'll call the bel dames."

Invoking their name produced the desired effect. The woman's eyes got wide. She jerked away from Nyx and collected up her illegal genetic material and her prayer rugs, then disappeared quickly and quietly down an alley.

Nyx looked up to see Mercia stepping into the doorway of a boutique selling conservative swimwear with tunics and hoods, oblivious of her spat with the vendor. Nyx slowed down. They were already in a better part of town than Nyx was used to—illegal merchants aside. With her whip at her hip and the hilt of a sword sticking up from a slit in the back of her burnous, she looked about like what she was: a bounty hunter, a mercenary, a body guard. Somebody hard up and dishonorable, like a woman just discharged from the front.

Nyx leaned against an unguarded bakkie—real risky, leaving them untended—to ease some of the pain in her back and knees. She wondered where she could get a hit of morphine this early in the day. She'd slept ten hours the night before, and thirteen the night before that. Too much sleep, even for a woman who bartered her organs for bread on occasion—one more reason she wasn't a bel dame anymore. Yet here she was, rubbing at her eyes before noon. She thought about going back and seeing her magician, Yahfia, and getting swept for cancers. Frequent trips to the magician kept her team relaxed. Eshe, her kid clerk, and Suha, her broken-nosed weapons tech, were a good crew, but they still had a lot of blind faith in magicians and bug tech. They thought that anybody who could afford to get patched up by a magician lived forever. Nyx knew better.

Nyx's charge walked out of the storefront. Mercia's pale face, flat features, and the cut of her clothes drew the stares of small children. A pack of adolescent girls in chain mail and boots snickered at her. The Queen was half Ras Tiegan, and since the brutal turn in Nasheen's war with Chenja five years before, the Queen and Ras Tieg weren't nearly as popular as they'd once been. The war hadn't been going well for Nasheen in almost a decade; there were boy shortages, rogue magicians, problems with the bel dame council, and one of Nasheen's primary munitions compounds had been bombed out the year before; a blister burst that would keep the area contaminated for half a century at least.

Bad for Nasheen—good for business.

Nyx watched the Ras Tiegan kid. She wondered what the hell the kid had found in there that required another three bags. Shit, probably. The foreign kids were all buying shit these days.

"Carry this, will you?" the kid said, holding out the bags.

Nyx crossed her arms and spit a bloody wad of sen on the sidewalk. She was trying to give up whiskey. Replacing it wholesale by upping her sen habit had seemed like a good idea. Better to dull pain than dull thought. The kid, though, said she was allergic to sen and didn't like the smell. Ras Tiegans were frail little roaches.

"I'm not a sherpa," Nyx said.

"A what?" the kid said. Daughters of diplomats took to languages like terrorists to water reservoirs, which meant the kid didn't have an accent. Nyx sometimes forgot that most Nasheenian slang was beyond her.

"I don't do shopping," Nyx said.

The kid looked put out. "My mother says you're to do what I say."

"Well, you and me can chat with your mother about that when we next see her," Nyx said. Nyx had acted babysitter to the daughters of diplomats enough times during the Queen's summits to know that the bugs would be silent for a good long while yet. Hopefully after the kid's mother deposited Nyx's fee.

"You need a sherpa, I'll hire a girl for you," Nyx said, and eyed the tail-end of the pack of girls in boots. Nyx wasn't so washed up yet that getting one of the girls into bed was all that ridiculous an idea. Young girls loved old bel dame stories.

"You're not very accommodating," the kid said. She sounded like some rich nose, one of the First Family women who lived up in the hills and sneered down at the sprawl of humanity they still called "the colonials," a thousand years after the last battered ship of planetless refugees was allowed onto the planet. Anybody who happened to bump into Umayma these days en route to somewhere else was either rerouted or left to orbit the planet and die a slow death by asphyxiation. Nyx had heard that when they still had the ability, the Families had the magicians blow up the ships. On those nights there was enough light in the sky to read by. That's what the old folks nattered about, anyway.

"My mother says you're the best in the business," Mercia said.

Nyx started moving down the street again, and the kid tagged after her. "No, just the cheapest," Nyx said. That was mostly true.

"But not easy to buy out?" the kid said slyly. Nyx had already considered pulling out the kid's sharp tongue. Probably be some monetary penalty for that, though.

"Sadly, no."

"My mother wouldn't have hired you if you were." The kid pulled out a berry-smelling sweet stick and started sucking at it like a coastal infant. How old was she? Ras Tiegan girls all looked younger than Nasheenians. She might have been eighteen or nineteen, but didn't look or act a day over fifteen.

"Takes some faith in your mother's smarts to trust that," Nyx said.

"She's a diplomat," the kid said, like that meant something.

"I've known some stupid diplomats." Hell, Nyx had *killed* some stupid diplomats. Countries like Heidia and Druce paid good money to diplomats who "lost" family members while on foreign assignments, especially in Nasheen and Chenja. The first illegal note she took during her short bel dame career was for a Heidian deputy ambassador's husband.

"My mother isn't one of the stupid ones."

Nyx watched a woman stepping out of a storefront ahead of them. The pitch to her walk as she came out told Nyx that she'd begun the movement from a standstill, loitering in the doorway, and the bag at her hip was holding something far heavier than the shoe brand it advertised.

Ahead of them, Nyx saw two more women standing alongside an otherwise unguarded bakkie. Never could say what made her watch some women closer than others. Maybe they tried too hard to look like they had nothing to do.

The bakkie was missing its tags. Missing tags meant the women were either bel dames or somebody doing black work. Generally, the sorts of people who illegally trafficked in bugs, people, and organs were gene pirates, mixing and matching blood codes and selling them illegally to the breeding programs in Nasheen and

Chenja. Nyx had run that kind of black work before. She knew enough about it to know she didn't want to have anything to do with the people running it.

As Nyx moved to get herself between the kid and the sidewalk, the women hanging around the bakkie too-casually turned their backs to her.

Nyx rolled her shoulders. The kid said something about a Ras Tiegan holiday where children wore funny hats.

Nyx saw a gap in the sidewalk traffic and grabbed the kid by the elbow. She steered her into the street.

Ravens' feathers stirred around their ankles. The kid tensed under her fingers and went real quiet. One of the benefits of working with kids used to kidnapping attempts was that they knew when to shut up.

With her other hand, Nyx reached behind her where she kept a scattergun strapped to her back. She was a bad shot, but a scattergun would hit just about anything in the general direction she aimed it.

As they walked into the street, Nyx felt a rush of dizziness, as if her head was floating somewhere over her right shoulder. A gray haze ate at the edges of her vision. She shook her head and blinked. Too old for this, she thought.

A cat-pulled cart rolled past. A rickshaw driver swore at her. Dust clotted the air. The cats stank. The kid started sneezing. Mercia's mother had said she was allergic to cats, too. And oranges. And cardamom. And a hundred other things. Nyx half-expected the kid to burst into hives at the sound of raised voices.

Nyx pushed the kid ahead of her and glanced at the cart window. She saw the reflection of the sidewalk behind her where the woman with the shoe bag was hastily stepping after them.

The kid dropped the slobbery sweet stick into the street.

"Suha," Nyx said. Saying Suha's name triggered the bug tucked into the whorl of cartilage at the entrance to her ear canal.

"Where are you?" Suha's voice had the tinny whine of the red beetle in the casing. "Eshe lost you back on south Mufuz."

Mufuz, near the cantina. Nyx remembered the stir of women hanging around outside, the smell of saffron and oranges. Saffron put shifter-dogs and foxes off the scent, and the smell of oranges confused the parrot and raven shifters—magicians, too. She should have noticed that. She was getting too tired and dizzy to think straight. Muddied heads in her business got chopped off.

Nyx chanced a look behind them, just over her right shoulder. Her head felt light again, as if attached to a string.

Hold it together, she thought. You don't make forty notes a day if your charge ends up dead. She tightened her grip on the kid.

"Nyxnissa—" the kid began, her voice low and cautious.

Nyx heard angry voices behind them, and moved.

She drew her scattergun as she turned. A hooded woman with a leashed cat in hand cried out and ducked. Several more women scurried out of the line of fire, leaving the woman with the shoe bag in the open. The woman crouched low and reached into the bag.

Nyx put herself between the woman and the kid and fired.

The woman on the ground pulled and rolled. Nyx ducked away and pushed the kid ahead of her, behind another rickshaw. She heard the shot. The back end of the rickshaw exploded.

"Move, move!" Nyx said, choking on yellow smoke. Pain blistered across her skin. She half-feared she was on fire, but the smoke in her nostrils didn't stink like scorched hair or flesh. She'd been set on fire enough times to know what it smelled like.

Nyx kept shoving the kid through the crowd. People were panicking now, screaming about terrorists and timed bursts as they flooded up the street. Nyx pushed the kid into the melee and tore off her burnous, leaving it to be trampled by the mob. The kid had dropped her bags.

Nyx needed to split from the kid, but Suha was holed up back at their storefront half a kilometer away, and there was no sign of Eshe. She didn't have anyone to pass the kid to.

Not for the first time, Nyx resented not having a bigger team.

Nyx put an arm around the kid's waist and hauled her back onto the sidewalk and into the doorway of a Heidian deli that stank of peppercorns and overcooked cabbage. Nyx went right on past the counter and through the kitchen, eliciting startled cries from squat, tawny Heidian immigrants. A big matron held up a bigger knife and swore at her in Heidian.

Nyx pressed right past her and kicked through the back door and into the reeking alley. She heard the breathy flapping of wings, and turned in time to see a black raven descend from the rooftop. Her vision swam. Her heart pounded in her chest as if she'd run five or ten kilometers. She gulped air. The kid wasn't even out of breath. Some vague part of her registered that something was wrong.

The raven alighted on a dumpster and shivered once, shook out a hail of feathers, and started to morph. Dusty feathers rolled down the alley.

Watching the tumbling feathers made Nyx's stomach roil.

She kept hold of the kid, who was saying something Nyx figured should make sense. Some other sound droned in Nyx's ears.

The raven shook off the rest of the feathers and flapped wings that were now mostly arms. It jumped off the dumpster lid and landed on two human feet while it took on the body of a teenage boy. The ends of his fingers still looked too long and bony. He was covered in a thin film of mucus.

Eshe was still getting used to morphing quickly, but he wouldn't be good at it for another couple years, about the time he got drafted for the front.

Whether or not the army made better use of raven scouts than Nyx did was debatable.

Nyx let go of Mercia's arm and pushed her toward Eshe. He wiped off the last of the mucus and feathers as his fingers finished taking on human proportions.

"Take her to the safe house," Nyx said. "Stay away from our regular front until I figure out who these women are."

"But you—" Eshe started, his eyes still black as a raven's, head cocked. Sometimes watching him shift put her off dinner.

"I'm going back and finding those—" Nyx was unsteady on her feet. She pressed a hand against the back wall of the deli to catch her balance. She closed her eyes, shook her head.

"Nyx, are you—" Eshe began again.

She opened her eyes and waved him away. "Get her out."

Eshe glanced at the girl. "You up for running?" he asked.

Mercia nodded.

Eshe started off down the alley, naked, and turned sharply left down another. Mercia took off after him—surprisingly fast for a soft diplomat's kid.

Nyx heard the door behind her bang open. She turned and fired her scattergun.

The woman at the door had pulled it half-closed, fast enough to catch most of the gun's spray on the door instead of her belly. She was young, slight, and fast. Her burnous was dusty, and she wore a dark tunic. Nyx wasn't sure how much damage the scattergun had done.

The woman launched herself at her. Nyx fired again and drew her sword. The woman fell into a roll and came up with a knife.

Screams sounded from inside the deli.

Nyx caught the first thrust of the knife with the gun, pushed it back. She thrust at the woman with her sword. The woman leapt back.

Bloody fucking fast for a mercenary, Nyx thought. Her head swam.

The knife lashed out at her again. Caught Nyx on the cheek. Nyx flinched, retreated. The woman grinned.

Cocky, Nyx thought.

Nyx let the woman push her back to the end of the alley. She parried most of the knife thrusts, but caught a couple on her forearms. There was nothing worse than a knife fight. Fuck around too long and you'd be in ribbons.

Nyx was within an arm's length of the wall. The knife flicked at her again. The woman's eyes were shiny—she must be new to the game—and sweat beaded her upper lip. Nyx caught the knife with her blade and pushed—hard. In the same motion, she threw her left hand out—the hand holding the gun—in a hard left hook.

The gun connected with the woman's temple. Her head lolled to one side. She stumbled. Her hands sagged. Then she crumpled like a drunken kitten.

Nyx raised her head and looked back toward the deli. There had been two of them. Where was the other one?

She slipped just into the next alley and kept her sword out. Sweat trickled into her eyes. She wiped it away, blinked furiously. She heard a noise in the alley, and chanced a look.

The second woman was up on the roof, taking in the full measure of the alley. She had a scattergun drawn. Nyx made herself flat against the wall, waited.

Nyx was a terrible shot from any range.

"Suha," she said softly. The name triggered the tailored red beetle in her ear. It opened the connection.

"What you got?"

"Two women. Possible assassins. Bagged one in the alley. I got another one on the roof of the deli behind me. You got my position?"

"Yeah."

"You still on point?"

"I'm moving to intercept. Eshe says you're in shit shape."

"I'm fine. But I've got a second shooter. I need you to intercept."

"On it. Got a description?"

Nyx gave her a description of the second shooter. When she looked back, the woman was no longer on the rooftop. "Lost visual on the roof of the deli," Nyx said. "Check the street outside."

"I'm six blocks away."

"Watch your ass. They're good. Young, but good."

"So am I," Suha said.

Nyx ducked back into the alley behind the deli and sheathed her sword. She crouched next to the woman and patted her down. The clothes were worn, dirty, but good quality. The burnous was organic, which wasn't cheap. She found two more knives and about five bucks in loose change—not an insubstantial amount of cash.

"Who the fuck are you?" Nyx muttered. A wave of dizziness passed over her again. She breathed deeply through her nose.

The woman began to stir. Nyx pulled out some sticky bands from the pack at her hip and bound the woman's hands behind her. As she pulled up the burnous, she saw a flash of red. She paused. Stared. A red letter was tucked into the back of the woman's trousers.

Nyx went very still for the space of a breath.

Then she pulled out the red letter and yanked it open. It was a bel dame's assassination note. The note wasn't written up for

Nyx or Mercia, but for some inland kid with a smoky face and big eyes. Only a bel dame would carry one of these notes. What the fuck was a bel dame doing hunting down the daughter to a diplomat without a red letter order to do it? Or was she running some kind of black work?

The woman was groaning now.

"Bel dame, huh?" Nyx said, and snorted. "Might be illegal to kill you . . . But a buck says you're running a black note."

Nyx shoved the note into her pocket. She stood and grabbed the bel dame by the hair.

"This'll hurt," Nyx said.

It took three whacks of Nyx's sword to take off the bel dame's head. Blood splattered her feet and swam in lazy rivulets down the alley. She tugged off the woman's organic burnous and wrapped the head with it. The body shuddered.

Bloody fucking bel dames, Nyx thought, and stumbled out the alley and across the next street.

Dust quickly covered the blood that coated her from hip to feet, but she still got cautious looks on the street. She turned down another alley and tried to catch her breath. She set down the head. Fuck, she needed a drink.

Nyx fell against the alley wall. She turned and pressed her forehead to it. Her stomach heaved. She vomited, tasted acid. Blue beetles lit out from beneath the wall, swarmed toward the steaming bile and blood splattered across her sandals.

She moved away from the wall and staggered. She needed to move before somebody else showed up. She needed to take this head to the bel dame office. Might be they'd pay her to bring in a bel dame running black work. She needed to check her account. She needed to bring home a nice girl. She needed a drink. She needed to call Rhys, she. . . .

Time stopped.

The world went dark.

"Nyx? Nyx?"

She was staring at the pale lavender sky from the floor of an alley. Eshe was staring down at her, a skinny little Ras Tiegan half-breed with a soft face and pouting mouth, too plain and unremarkable in looks for much of anything but disappearing into crowds.

He pressed a hand to her forehead, like he was trying to measure something.

"Whose head is that?" he asked.

Dark smears blotted out the boy's face. "I don't have time for this shit," Nyx slurred. She tried moving her arms. Everything felt heavy. Something stank like vomit.

"I think you need a magician," he said.

"What?" she said, but searching for the word took a long time, and even saying it seemed heavy, too difficult. "I think I'm a little tired," she said.

"I'll take you to Yahfia."

"The kid . . . ." Nyx said, and then stopped, unsure about what kid she meant. Some kid. Something important. Maybe it wasn't so important. "I need to call Rhys," she said.

"Who?" the kid said. "I'll get Yahfia."

"There was a little black dog," Nyx said.

"A what?"

Eshe started to look like someone she didn't know. What was a boy doing on the street unchaperoned? Shouldn't he be at the front?

"I just need to sleep, Fouad," Nyx murmured. "A little sleep, and maybe Kine can get me some whiskey . . ."

Something wasn't right. She saw a body in a tub, bloody, no eyes . . . Yes, that's right, Kine was dead. Her sister was dead. "Fouad," she told her brother, "Kine is dead. I think you're supposed to be at the front."

"I'm getting Yahfia," Fouad said. He stood, and that was fine, because she was tired of talking. She just wanted to lie there a little longer. Blackness clawed at her, but it felt good, like giving in to sleep after a long, hard day.

It didn't feel like dying at all.

2.

Yahfia's operating theater smelled of death and lavender, and there was something crawling up the far wall where Yahfia kept her jars of organs. The theater was a windowless room built into a storefront along one of the higher-end streets of Mushtallah. It had only been burned out once in four years. Most girls on this side of Mushtallah were training to be sappers and munitions experts. Nyx would have paid good money for a place that didn't attract bored teenage girls with a passion for fire.

Nyx licked at her thumb where a hister beetle had harvested a blood sample. Her head felt heavy now, just like the rest of her. The giant insects and organs inside the jars along the theater wall were all the more expensive sort, the type Nyx saw when she used to work with proper magicians in Faleen and on Palace Hill. Yahfia had done well for herself during the years she'd been back in country—better than Nyx; maybe better than anyone on Nyx's old crews.

"Sorry you had to wait so long," Yahfia said. "I had a bel dame come in ahead of you. Injured very severely by a deserter she was trying to bring in. Whole face taken off, can you believe it? She couldn't make it back to Bloodmount for care." She wiped her hands on her apron. Her green silk robe was stitched in gold and silver. Magicians did all right in Mushtallah.

"I used to be a bel dame once," Nyx said.

"So you've told me—many times," Yahfia said, and sighed. "I don't want trouble with bel dames, Nyx."

15

"Yeah, nobody does. So what the hell's wrong with me?" Nyx eased off the marble slab.

"Besides your deviant moral flexibility and severe phobia of emotional commitment?" Yahfia asked.

"I consider those virtues," Nyx said. She fastened the stays on her breast binding and buckled on her baldric.

"What made you finally come in?"

"Passed out today on a job. Eshe found me crawling around the alley looking for water. Felt a lot better after I got some water, but he started blubbering. Wanted me to come in. I humor him when I can."

Yahfia moved a couple of empty jars into the bowl of the freestanding sink and pumped water over them. "I can't blame him for being concerned. He's grown into quite the young man since you took him in."

"You say that like being a man's a good thing," Nyx said. "Men get carted off to the front to die. I'd rather he stayed eight forever, same as when I got him." She folded her arms. "You think it's cancer?" Getting cancer was like getting a cold. Everybody had a tumor or two taken out now and again. Most folks got malignant melanomas scraped off at least once a year.

She watched Yahfia. Yahfia was a head taller than Nyx, and that made her a tall woman, though she was slender in the hands and shoulders and thickening up in the hips. The age showed now in the set to her mouth, the spidery lines at the corners of her dark eyes. She had pretty eyes, big and long-lashed, like a girl dancer's.

"When was the last time you had your breasts out?" Yahfia asked.

"Couple years ago. Wanted to take them out all together, but I like my profile."

Yahfia smiled, but did not look at her. When a magician wouldn't look at you, it meant there was something about you she didn't like—or was afraid of. Never a good sign. Yahfia had never approved of her, certainly, but nobody did. Just because they didn't approve didn't mean they didn't like her.

"How old are you now, forty-five?" Yahfia asked.

"Thirty-eight," Nyx said. Saying it out loud made her feel even older.

A faint smile touched Yahfia's face. "I'm curious, Nyx. When did you go to prison and become exiled from the bel dame order?"

"I don't know. A while ago."

"How old were you?"

Nyx frowned. "Twenty-four."

"That was nearly fourteen years ago. Yet every time you come into my office, you introduce yourself to my staff as a bel dame."

Nyx shrugged. "It gets me in. I'm more concerned about what's wrong with me than about how I get an actual appointment."

"I didn't find any evidence of cancer," Yahfia said. "But there's certainly something wrong. I'm worried about the weight loss, and the dizziness."

Nyx grunted. "I need to eat more and lay off the alcohol, that's all." But she hadn't had a drink in two days, and she ate like a starving woman all the time now. Sometimes magicians weren't good for anything but replacing something you already knew was missing.

Yahfia turned away from the sink and wiped her slender hands again. Nyx had always liked magicians' hands. Yahfia did all of her body work for free in exchange for a little bit of paper forgery that Nyx had had the Queen take care of on Yahfia's behalf. Yahfia had been born with some boy parts. She was content to head to the front until she hit puberty . . . and started menstruating. Things were a little more complicated after that, and she'd fought most of her life to get her status changed. A tough thing to do unless you knew the right people in Mushtallah—people who owed you favors. And they had owed Nyx plenty back then.

"I have another magician I'd like you to see," Yahfia said. "She's far better than I, and works near the Orrizo. She may find something I've missed."

Nyx shrugged. "I got work."

"I thought you wanted to get out of red work."

Nyx shook out her dusty-red burnous and pulled it on. "If I'm not doing red work, I'm doing black work. We can't all be magicians."

"Or bel dames?"

Nyx grimaced.

"Is there something wrong with being respectably employed?" Yahfia asked.

Nyx walked over to the table at the end of the slab, took up and sheathed her sword. She lashed a dagger to her hip, holstered her scattergun, wound up and secured her whip, and stepped into and laced up her sandals, the ones with the razor blades hidden in the soles.

"Come on, you ever see me doing something respectable?" she said, and patted at the braids of her hair where she kept three poisoned needles.

"Might be an interesting career change. Rumor has it you've turned castration into an occupation."

"You go cutting one guy's cock off and you never hear the end of it," Nyx said. "I killed Raine six years ago. Nobody in the border towns has spoken straight to me since."

"Imagine that," Yahfia said lightly. Nyx was reminded that Yahfia had had her own cock cut off not so long before. Helped add legitimacy to the paper forgery. Best to leave that one alone.

"Huh," Nyx said.

Nyx walked to the door, said over her shoulder, "You need anything from Afifa Square? I got to return something to some folks there."

"No. I'm going to Amtullah tonight for a few days," she said. "Don't get yourself into trouble, Nyxnissa. Few people have patience for your sort."

"My coin's still good," Nyx said. "And I get people favors when they need them. You remember that." She opened the door.

"I do remember," Yahfia said. "It's why I still permit you in my theater. I do wish you'd appreciate that, instead of trying to bully my staff."

"I don't bully."

Yahfia waved a hand at her. "Go on. Get that magician's name and pattern from my secretary!"

Nyx closed the door.

Eshe stood in the waiting room. It was an airy, maroon-colored office ringed in stained-glass windows. All those outward-facing windows always freaked Nyx out. Eshe was rocking back on his heels and surreptitiously eyeing one of Yahfia's pretty little secretaries. The woman's plump body was partially concealed by the lattice of the privacy screen at the front desk. His mouth was hard and his face looked drawn. When he saw Nyx enter, his expression didn't improve.

"What did she say?" Eshe asked.

"Fit as a harem girl," Nyx said.

"You're a liar."

"I used to be good at it." Also a lie. She tousled his hair, though he was old for it. He ducked away from her, pursed his mouth, and looked out at the street. She didn't think his pouty, petulant-looking mouth would get any more attractive with age.

"Let's go," she said. "Suha's probably dropped Mercia off already and itching to get back to the keg." She still used the same affectionate term for her storefront in Mushtallah that she'd used for her storefront in Punjai, though it'd been ten years since she stopped selling beer kegs out of the one in Punjai.

"She didn't fix you up at all?" Eshe asked. He had big brown eyes, and when he looked at her, sometimes, she wondered what his mother had looked like. Nyx had caught Eshe trying to pick her pocket when he was eight years old. He'd run away from his state-sanctioned apprenticeship to a cat dealer when he was six and started dressing like a girl to avoid the patrols. Eshe was a breeder baby, one of a brood of eight or ten popped out by some career breeder. There were thousands of women in Nasheen who made a living breeding babies for the cause. Looking for her would have been pointless. Breeders didn't want to raise children. They wanted the state to feed them to the front. Where his half-breed blood came from was a matter of some contention. Nobody raised Ras Tiegan babies at the compounds, but he had found some sanctuary in the Ras Tiegan slums, and could speak the language passably well now.

"She said there's some other magician who could look me over."

"What's her name?"

Nyx shrugged. "Why don't you talk to the secretary and set it up?" Fourteen was plenty old enough for a boy to get tangled up with girls. Not that he didn't have any experience with that—he'd been a street kid, after all—but she was looking to find him somebody proper and half-virtuous before some bel dame came to collect him for the front, and there weren't a lot of those sorts of young women around in her line of work.

Eshe shot a look at the secretary. He fidgeted a bit before finally going over to speak with her. The secretary was all smiles. Boys outside the schools or the coast were rare, and though he was an obvious half-breed, most people fawned over him the way people fawned over babies—Nasheen's most precious resource.

His voice was changing. She heard it while he spoke with the woman. He was dressing less often like a girl, too. No more headscarves or belled trousers. He wore vests and somber-colored burnouses now, the sort Nyx only saw on old men. She hated it when he wore those stupid burnouses. He was getting old enough now that order keepers on the street were going to start asking him for his papers, too. She should have registered him for the draft two years before, but he was still passing for a girl then, and no one had come knocking on her door to get her to comply with the paperwork. Not yet. But shifter boys were especially conspicuous, and it was only a matter of time. Even if she discouraged him from shifting in public, the bags of feathers they packed out into the alley every week and the vast amounts of protein he consumed were going to give him away eventually. The war wanted shifters as badly as it wanted magicians.

Eshe chatted with the secretary and then walked back over, his face flush. Nyx tucked another wad of sen under her tongue. They left Yahfia's place together.

"Karida says the magician serves the noses up in the hills. She lives in a gated plaza near the Orrizo."

"I'm tired of hemorrhaging money."

"Karida says the magician works cheap for anybody Yahfia recommends."

"You two already swapping first names?"

"She has a girlfriend," he said.

"This is Nasheen. Everybody has a girlfriend."

They met up with Suha in the street. She sat in the driver's seat of their bakkie, smoking clove cigarettes.

Suha was a decade younger than Nyx, and still dressed like a woman at the front: long-sleeved, hip-hugging tunic bisected by a wide munitions utility belt; half-length trousers, dust-colored burnous, and standard-issue combat boots. She was a short, squat woman, more muscle than fat, with a protruding mouth, jutting chin, and mashed-up nose that had been broken more times than she could say. Eshe called her "the trout," which might have been funny if Nyx had ever seen a fish. Eshe said he had some sort of hazy memory of fish farms on the coast. Nyx suspected he was just using the word to show off.

"Mercia get back all right?" Nyx asked as she opened the door.

Suha blew smoke through her nose and tugged at her sleeves. The venom scars on her arms weren't visible with the long sleeves—she made an effort to hide them, especially around Eshe—but it was a nervous habit that reminded Nyx of a Chenjan woman tugging at her headscarf to make sure her hair was covered.

"Could have gone better," Suha said. "You should have been there."

"I can't be everywhere at once," Nyx said.

Eshe opened the front and squeezed into the little jump seat behind them. Nyx slid next to Suha.

"The diplomat fired us," Suha said. She put out the cigarette and stuffed a wad of sen between teeth and cheek. Her teeth were stained bloody crimson with it.

"She deposit my fee?" Nyx asked.

"Yeah. Says she heard we had trouble downtown today."

"Fucking diplomats. She should thank me for keeping her daughter alive."

"I called the bounty note office like you asked," Suha said.

She started the bakkie, and turned them out onto south Raban. From here, Nyx could just see the curved amber spire of the Orrizo in the distance—a monument to anonymous dead men.

"There's no record that anybody put out a note on you or Mercia."

Nyx chewed on that for a while. "So that bel dame *was* rogue. Interesting." And more than a little disconcerting. She was half-hoping she could just burn up the body in her freezer and be done with it.

"Only thing more dangerous than a bel dame is a rogue bel dame," Suha muttered. She hunched over the wheel and bunched up her mouth into a sour moue.

"You got that head in our freezer?"

"Yeah."

"May need to pay a visit to Bloodmount, then."

Eshe hopped up and down in his seat. "Bel dames? We get to see bel dames?"

Nyx sighed.

The awning above Nyx's storefront was battered and torn, and the unguent that kept the bugs away had long since worn off the slick surface. Locusts and sand flies clung beneath the awning during the day and crawled across the top at night. In the window just to the left of the door, Eshe had painted and hung a sign:

Nyxnissa so Dasheem
Personal Security
Blood Bonds
Bounty Reclamation &
Bel Dame Consulting Services

Nyx hadn't wanted to put in the part about bel dame consulting services, but she'd had a couple of kids come in from the front and ask her whether or not there was money in being a bel dame. More often, she had dodgy-looking young boys push in and ask her how to avoid getting caught by bel dames. She charged those ones half a note and told them to leave the country. Once a bel dame had your name, only death would stop her—and bel dames were notoriously hard to kill.

Nyx knew that better than anyone.

Suha unloaded gear and dry goods from the bakkie while Eshe

followed Nyx inside through the filtered smart door. Nyx had laid the place out a lot like her old storefront in Punjai, only this one was about twice as big. The wide, circular reception area they called the keg had an ablution bowl near the door and one padded bench along the far wall. Eshe's little desk guarded the entry from reception into the backroom where they kept their com and gear shop—they called it the hub—on the other side of a cheap, low-res filter. Nyx's office was to the right of the shop. She didn't bother keeping a filter over her door. Filters were expensive. She didn't run with a magician anymore who could do the maintenance for free, so she just kept the one filter over the entrance to the hub. The organic smart door had come with the lease. It was enough.

"What other contracts are on the boards?" she asked Eshe as she walked behind the slab of her desk. She and Suha had rescued the desk from behind a kill shelter on the south side of Amtullah during a low-spring rainstorm that flooded the streets long enough for them to float the desk out. The wood was synthetic, made from bug secretions instead of coastal timber, but the sort of people Nyx dealt with couldn't tell the difference. It made her look richer than she was.

Eshe pulled a battered, antique slide from the locked drawer of his desk and accessed a list of potential notes and clients that Suha had logged that morning. Nyx began taking off the most extraneous of her gear and set it out for cleaning. Her vision swam as Eshe spoke. She rubbed her eyes.

"So let's get this straight," Nyx said when he was done. "I can play babysitter to some First Family secretary, cut off a petty debtor's head, or . . . What was that other one?"

"Woman who owns a gambling pit in Ashad quarter wants you to evict some tenants."

"You've got to be kidding me."

Eshe shrugged.

How the fuck else was she going to pay the bills? Nyx felt suddenly lightheaded, and put her hand on her desktop to steady herself.

"Sign me up for the babysitting job," she said to Eshe. "I'll sort out the details tonight, all right? Go get cleaned up. It's fight night."

Eshe thumbed some notes into the misty slide and walked back into the keg. Nyx heard him crackle through the hub filter and batter around in the backroom with Suha. They started arguing about what kind of oil was best for rubbing down a double-barreled semi-organic Z1020 after disassembly.

Nyx pulled off her sandals. She hung her head between her knees. She closed her eyes and waited for her head to stop spinning.

She didn't want to go up the hill to the Orrizo and talk to some moneyed magician who looked at her like a broken anvil. She also didn't want to spend any more nights with her head between her knees. She wasn't doing herself or Eshe any favors, and Suha had a mother and three sisters to feed. For the first time in a decade, Nyx had money in the bank, gun and money caches for emergencies, and a team she was more than eighty percent certain wasn't fucking around on her. So why was she so sick and miserable?

Nyx sat up slowly and palmed open the sen box on the bottom left corner of her desk. A little sen with a morphine chaser cured just about everything.

When she was more coherent, Nyx accessed the day's accounts on her personal slide and paid a couple of bills. Mercia's mother had indeed deposited the promised fee. They'd all be able to eat for the next few weeks.

Winter days in Mushtallah were warm, but short. By the time she mostly squared her accounts it was already dark, and she had unshuttered both glow worm lamps; the one on her desk and the big cylinder near the door. She heard Eshe light the cheap lamps in the keg. Suha turned up the radio as a band of nighttime revelers passed through the alley on their way to a low-end brothel three streets over.

The local magicians were holding a boxing match later that night. Nyx figured she'd send out Eshe for food and then take him downtown after Suha packed up and went home to her mother. Payday nights were traditionally Nyx and Eshe's food and fight nights.

She leaned back in her chair and stretched. The chime on the reception area door sounded, which meant somebody had stepped onto the porch. She figured Suha had punched up a food delivery.

Nyx walked into the keg and slid her hand over the face of the door. The door went transparent—from her side, anyway—and she saw a girl on the stoop wearing a too-big burnous. Even with her face hidden deep within the heavy hood, Nyx knew it was Mercia. The kid had affected an awkward slouch, probably in an attempt to appear less like Mercia, but Nyx had spent all day staring at her ass-end, tracking her through crowds—she'd know that kid's bony little ass anywhere.

Nyx opened the door and stepped into the threshold to block Mercia from getting inside.

"Don't you put a foot in here," Nyx said. "Your mother likely has tags."

Mercia tilted her head up a little, so Nyx could just see the stubborn end of her pale chin. "No one followed me."

"I'm not hiring," Nyx said. "Cutting off heads isn't nearly as glamorous as it sounds."

"It's nothing like that. I wanted to apologize, about my mother."

"We all had them. Not worth apologizing."

"She shouldn't have fired you. That was . . ." Mercia hunched up again, as if retreating. "I had a woman once who wasn't as good as you."

"Hard to believe."

"I'm being very serious."

"If your mother's hiring in my pay range, I'm not surprised she's gotten some shitty service."

"Can I please come in? I don't like standing around in this part of the city."

"We're out of honey wine, and Ras Tiegans don't drink buni."

"Put something in it, and I might."

"A runaway and a lush? Your mother's going to enjoy feeding me to her security staff."

Nyx heard someone crackle through the hub filter behind her. Eshe said, "What's up front?"

Nyx stepped aside to let Mercia in. "We've got another bug for dinner."

Eshe's eyes got big. "We're ordering in?"

"Go pick something up. Suha's got petty cash."

Nyx sat Mercia down on the padded bench in the receiving room. The kid pulled back her hood. Her eyes were reddened from crying, but not bruised. Nyx didn't see any bruises on her bare arms or wrists either. Nobody had roughed her up—at home or on the street. Not tonight, anyway. So what was she running from?

"Does this apology come with some dinner money? You Ras Tiegan girls don't eat much, but I won't hold it against you."

Mercia shook her head. "I only wanted to say I'm sorry. She shouldn't have run you out like that. I saw what those women were. I don't think anybody else could have gotten out of that."

"Women are just women."

Mercia's forehead wrinkled. "Those women were bel dames."

That particular insight was surprising. How could a Ras Tiegan girl spot a bel dame? "You seen a bel dame before?"

"I've seen one of those ones before, at the Queen's palace. I told my mother I'd give a description to the authorities, but she didn't want to make a charge."

"You remember the bel dame's name?"

Mercia shook her head.

"But you know she's a bel dame?"

"Queen Zaynab introduced them as a group."

"Which one was it? One of the ones by the bakkie or the one with the bag?" Nyx asked.

"The one with the bag."

The one Nyx had killed.

"Was that the only one who looked familiar?" Nyx asked.

"That's the only one I remember," Mercia said.

Nyx leaned forward and put her elbows on her knees, clasped her hands. If bel dames wanted Mercia dead, it wasn't so much her business, but it was interesting. Ambassador sa Aldred had taken Nyx off watch, and the diplomat and her daughter would be heading back to Ras Tieg after the summit ended in a couple days. But a dead ambassador's kid might trigger a bigger incident—something rogue bel dames might like.

She looked over at Mercia. The skinny kid was watching her with sorrowful eyes, like she was worried about how Nyx was taking the news. It wasn't the sort of look Nyx expected from a girl being hunted.

"Your mother will hire you another bodyguard," Nyx said. "If she ups her fee, she can get one better than me. You'll be all right."

The half-lie tasted fine. There were a couple of retired bel dames who could make good bodyguards, if the ambassador was willing to pay the fee. Knowing the ambassador's pay rate, though, she probably wouldn't parse out that much for a replacement, and Mercia would be left with some snot-nosed kid just out of university who wouldn't stand a chance against three or more bel dames working a blood note. Just another soft, educated idiot.

Nyx sighed. Ever since Nyx took Eshe in she'd had a soft spot for kids with shitty mothers. I must be getting old, she thought.

"I know a few women I'd trust to watch after you," Nyx said. "I could make some calls, maybe convince them to work cheap."

Mercia wrinkled her brow. "Me? I'm not worried about *me*," she said.

"Why the hell not?" Nyx said.

"Because," Mercia said, very slowly, as if speaking to a soft, educated idiot, "those bel dames weren't after me. They were after *you*."

3.

The Tirhani Minister of Public Affairs was in a foul mood. In the three years Rhys had worked with her, he had come to know her moods better than those of his own wife. The Minister bore her moods more clearly in the severe lines of her face, the deepening crease of worry between her heavy brows. When her mood moved from severe to foul she would tighten and release her fist on her desk the way she was doing now—tighten and release, tighten and release—as if she were strangling kittens one by one and dropping them into a pail at her feet.

Rhys sat across from her at the center of the broad map of her office, a slide pulled open in his hands. A pattern of gilded palm fronds repeated along the border of the room, like the name of God in a prayer. The windows behind her were opaqued and filtered to keep out the sun. He could look just over the Minister's shoulder and see the whole of Tirhani's capital, Shirhazi, spread out across the flat plain below, crowded along the rim of the salty inland sea called Shahrdad. Tirhanis liked their buildings tall, and from this height, fourteen floors above the city, Rhys could share their enthusiasm. Being above this big city made him feel less small.

The Minister thumped her fist on her desk.

"These bloody black roaches think that covering up women's faces makes the lot of them more pious. Piety does not determine price. I won't part with the fruit of our labor for a brick man's fee. Do they think we are a country of stevedores?"

Rhys pulled his attention back to the Minister and the pleasantly cool room. The slick semi-transparent screen of his slide displayed his notes on the translation of Chenjan contracts relating to an exchange of goods and services with Tirhan. Like many of the documents Rhys had dealt with during his translation work with the Tirhani government, the actual goods and services were not specified, merely the terms of the amounts agreed upon, the delivery dates and times, the payment milestones, and generic legal jargon.

"Are you going to have your assistant consul politely decline their offer?" Rhys asked. "I'd like to have an idea of the tone you wish to present before I receive the document for review."

Though the goods were never named outright, Rhys suspected the Minister of Public Affairs was negotiating arms sales with Chenja, and had been for as long as he had worked for her. A third of the population of Shirhazi was employed in its weapons manufacturing plants. Most of Tirhan's economy was tied up in arms deals that fueled the centuries-old war between Chenja and Nasheen. It kept Tirhan's neighbors busy and made Tirhanis rich. It also required a significant ex-pat community of magicians to produce it. Shirhazi was a hodgepodge haven of refugee Chenjans and exiled magicians from Nasheen, Ras Tieg, even Mhoria. The Minister knew he knew her business, but they never discussed the movement of arms in such blunt terms. Some of this was merely the Tirhani custom of false modesty and false politeness. Rhys had spent much of his time as a child learning similar conversational rituals at the Chenjan court while on business with his father. He had picked up the Tirhani version easily. He found it much more comforting than brutal Nasheenian honesty.

The Minister's frown deepened. "You must decline their offer politely, but with a touch of disdain. This is the second time this new Minister has treated us as infidels during a negotiation. He must know his place before God. I will have my consul remove the offer completely, as a lesson. I will have him forward you our reply tonight, but do not trouble yourself about its delivery. I will have their minister stew himself to death while his people starve in the trenches.

"Would you like some tea?"

The segue was abrupt, and familiar. The Minister pulled a cup and saucer from her desk, a strainer, a tea bag. Business was concluded for the day.

Rhys rose. "Thank you, but I must humbly decline," he said.

"Oh, no, I insist you sit and have a drink," she said. She ladled a teaspoon of fire beetles into a water shaker and shook it up to heat the water. "I cannot allow you to part ways without a drink."

Tirhani false politeness.

"I respectfully decline. I am not thirsty. Thank you for this reception. I do look forward to hearing from your consul." Rhys bowed his head and waited. They had still not discussed the matter of payment.

"It is really too much," the Minister said, taking her cue. "You do too much for us."

"I am, as ever, pleased to offer my services to the benefit of this great country," Rhys said.

"And how much is it I may reward you for those services you've provided today?"

"It is nothing," Rhys said. "It is my pleasure."

He continued waiting.

"No, indeed, I insist. It is the least I can do."

"I am pleased to serve such a pleasant employer."

"I must redeem you. Come now."

"A day's work, twelve hours, correspondence with a Chenjan minister," Rhys said. "God willing, the price for such work is sixty notes." It was a price ten percent higher than he believed she would pay.

"That is too much," she said, and her expression soured further. "I could have had a boy from the Chenjan ghetto do the same, for far less."

"And you would have gotten work of an equal quality to the price you paid. You will not find a boy familiar with Chenjan politics and the workings of the minds of her war ministers begging for bugs at the corner."

"Yet I have had Chenjan men provide me with just such a service at half the cost."

"Half? Then they are beggars, and scoundrels, and it is no surprise that they are no longer in your employ. Instead, you have found my services more than adequate for several seasons."

"It is adequate only when it is fair. I'll pay you forty, no more."

"I do appreciate proper recompense for the valuable work I provide for Tirhan. If you wish my family and I to soil ourselves in the Chenjan ghetto, please pay me what you would a dock-worker, and excuse the state of my soiled bisht," he said, taking a handful of the gauzy outer robe he wore and holding it out to her. It was not, indeed, soiled, but it was a bit dusty. "I cannot ask for less than fifty-five."

"I, too, have mouths to feed, and a public to serve. Do you wish to bankrupt my country? Fifty notes will fill the bellies of half the children in the Chenjan ghetto."

"For fifty-two notes, I can feed my children and perhaps excuse the Minister's insults as to my ethnicity."

The Minister leaned back in her chair and regarded him. "You're very Chenjan," she said.

"It's why you hired me," he said.

The Minister pressed her hand to the upper left corner of her desk. Rhys felt the air fill with the soft chatter of wood mites. The mites in the desk vomited up the Minister's pay tickets. She wrote out a receipt for fifty-two and handed it to him.

Rhys accepted the receipt and bowed his head.

"Peace be with you," the Minister said, "and may God bless your house and family." She raised her teacup.

"And yours," Rhys said, "God is great."

He walked out of the Minister's cool office and into the grand hall of the Public Affairs Ministry. The building's gilt-domed mosque was on the top floor, two floors above him. He had gone to prayer before his meeting with the Minister, and now he took the stairs back to street level. It was a long descent, but he preferred it to the lifts, which were encased in an opaqued glass shaft that made him nervous. He knew too much about how easily a magician could alter the instructions given to the burr bugs that drove the lift up and down the height of the building. The convenience wasn't worth the risk.

As Rhys took the stairs, he passed several other magicians doing the same. Though Rhys had the ability to perceive another magician through look, manner, and gaze alone, magicians on official business in Tirhan were required to wear a yellow, ankle-length khameez with wide sleeves and greenish bisht over the top of it. The bisht was thin and gauzy, hemmed in yellow along the collar, and both garments were cool and light enough to make walking around in the heat bearable. Cool and modest as the garments were, however, they did mark him apart; removed him from the rest of the community. There were days, passing through the streets of Tirhan as people moved out of his path, that he wondered if this was how members of the First Families of Nasheen felt when they descended from the hilltops to mingle with the common folk. Tirhan was notoriously short on magicians and shape shifters, and their genetics and breeding programs had been working on a solution to their dearth of talented individuals for decades. It also meant their immigration policies were extremely favorable toward magicians and shape shifters, regardless of nationality. That had been a blessing six years before when he crossed the border.

Rhys walked across the cool marble inlay of the foyer and out the wide archway that opened onto the street. He passed through a low-res organic filter that kept out the heat and stepped onto the palm-lined pedestrian way. Bakkies weren't permitted within the city center, so Rhys had to walk to the edge of the center to catch a taxi. Above him, trains crawled along a suspended rail, spitting red beetle and roach casings from the back end. The trains were good for getting around inside the city and out to the factories, but Rhys lived in the suburbs. His wages were comfortable enough that he could afford a taxi.

As he walked, clerks, officials, and street cleaners and sweepers stepped out of his way. He passed the big tiered marble fountains and grassy knolls of the park at the city center. In the middle of the fountain stood a stone sculpture of a robed, veiled magician, her hand reaching toward the sky. Water cascaded from her palm and sloshed over the tiers below. Each slab was adorned with gold and silver gilt stone beetles and dragonflies, thorn bugs and owl flies. Stone dogs, foxes, ravens, and parrots crowded around the lip of the fountain. They had been coated with a skein of flesh beetles, so they appeared to shift and move.

Rhys had never liked the fountain. In Chenja, human representations presented as public art were banned. In Nasheen, they were merely discouraged. Idols left on display encouraged the worship of idols. Rhys often worried to see men and women approach the fountain and toss stones into the water as tokens in return for wishes granted, as if offering up prayers to . . . magicians. He supposed it was one more alien Tirhani gesture he would never get used to. Tirhan had grown up short on magicians. That idea was foreign enough.

Rhys lined up for a taxi at the edge of the center. The porter directing traffic insisted he come to the front of the line. Rhys no longer protested such treatment. The first few times he insisted on waiting in line—at the taxi ranks, at a restaurant, while out with his wife at a local art gallery—the porter, the clerks, and all of those waiting in line had grown anxious and expressed their concern—and later, outrage—at his refusal of their courtesy, particularly after they heard his Chenjan accent. Tirhanis would not have foreigners calling them impolite.

He stepped into the front passenger seat of the taxi, and four other men squeezed into the seat in the back. The driver refused a fifth who wanted to sit between him and Rhys.

"I am escorting a magician!" the driver yelled, and shut the door.

The driver was Rhys's age, probably in his early thirties, and he appeared to have been trying, unsuccessfully, to grow a beard for some time. It had grown in in patches. He kept it short, which eased the contrast between beard and hairless cheek.

The men in the back wore white khameezes, aghals, and sandals, and from the look of their manicured nails and neat beards, they were probably lower-level assistants or officials working in the financial district. They could have, perhaps, been lawyers or businessmen, but they seemed too young to have reached such heights, and interns would not have had the cash for a taxi fare.

The driver slowed the taxi as the traffic ahead of them came to a halt. Rhys looked out the window. He saw a toppled rickshaw thirty meters up the road. He closed his eyes and searched for a local swarm of wasps to sniff out the disturbance, but could sense none nearby. He gave up and opened his eyes.

"Pardon, Yah," the skinny man in the middle said, and leaned forward. Yah, or Yahni, was the polite prefix to a magician's name across Umayma, an old term dating back to the days when bel dames policed the world.

But Rhys had never been certified as a magician. The title was not earned, just assumed when he wore the robes.

Rhys did not correct him.

"You are married, yes?" the man asked.

"I am," Rhys said. He wore a silver ring on each of his ring fingers, the left to symbolize his engagement, the right to confirm his marriage.

"And how is it you drew this woman's interest? Was it that you were a magician?"

Rhys's wife was Chenjan, but she had been raised in Tirhan. He had had to learn his courting behaviors whole cloth. Not that he had much experience in courting before he came to Tirhan.

"It did help that I was a magician," he said.

The men nodded seriously.

They got off at the next street. Rhys and the taxi driver rode the rest of the way in silence. Just outside the hybrid oak park at the edge of Rhys's district, the driver came to a halt.

Rhys stepped out. "What shall I give you?" he asked.

"Praise be, it's an honor to ferry a magician."

"From the city center to the grove is generally a note and a half. Is this agreeable?"

"A note and a half? Do you wish to see me starve?"

"I am a fair man, not a fool."

They haggled. Rhys paid the driver a note sixty-five. He took the shortcut through the grove. It smelled of lemons and loam and the tangy sap of the hybrids. Bugs swarmed the treetops, none of them virulent. Clouds of wasps patrolled the streets, tailored to track and record the movements of nonresidents. At the end of the grove, he stepped out onto his street.

Rhys had wanted to live somewhere in the hills, but Shirhazi, at best, rolled. It did not have proper hills, not until it came to the base of the mountains, to the north. And by then the city had turned to scrubland and clover fields. So he settled for living in a three-storied house made of mud-brick and bug secretions sandwiched at the far end of a long row of similar houses. There was a roof garden, and a wide, open balcony on the second floor. There were no windows on the first floor, of course, but windows on the upper floors opened out onto the rear garden, and during the hottest part of the day, they could push them all open and catch a breeze off the inland sea.

They. Rhys had expected to remain alone in Tirhan, his narrow days interspersed with occasional visits to Khos and Inaya, his fellow exiles, to ease some of the loneliness. But it hadn't turned out that way. Nothing about his life in Tirhan had turned out the way he expected.

Rhys walked across the street, through the front gate, and onto his tiled front patio. He heard laughter from behind the house. He passed through the cobbled alley to the treed yard surrounded in an eight-foot-high privacy wall. His family's refuge.

His daughters played in the yard, attaching strings to giant ladybugs and hanging them from the wisteria bushes that bordered the backyard. Ladybugs were supposed to be lucky, and were a popular symbol of the Tirhani Martyr. It was said that after she was burned, her body was consumed by ladybugs. It was nearing the time of the Martyr's festival, when the whole of Shirhazi would fast for nine days and feast for nine nights down at the beachfront. It would be the first year he and Elahyiah felt the girls were old enough to join in the nighttime festivities. There would be fireworks and magicians. Elahyiah had friends running the food kiosks and performing in the theater groups. The girls had been talking about it for weeks.

He stood at the edge of the yard and watched them. The girls were two and four now, not old enough, in his opinion, to be left out in the yard with bugs in the sun, but he did not see Elahyiah or the housekeeper. The girls had shed their coats and played uncovered in the dirt.

"Laleh, Souri," he said. The girls lifted their heads. Souri, the younger, squealed and ran across the dirt in her bare feet. Souri had once eaten a spider and nearly died from it. Laleh was far more cautious, willing to follow but never lead.

Laleh hung back with the bugs under the scant shade of one of the thorny acacias.

"Where's your mother?" Rhys asked Souri.

Souri clung to his robe.

Rhys scooped her up and asked Laleh, "How long have you been out? Come inside. You're going to get cancer."

"Da," Souri said, and threw her little arms around his neck.

"Come," Rhys said to Laleh again, and held out his hand.

Laleh took a few tentative steps forward, head lowered. He often wondered where Laleh got her docility from. Certainly not from her mother.

They passed through the filter spanning the arched entryway of the porch and stepped across the cool tiles and into the house. A dozen succulents with broad green leaves crowded the porch, situated around a low, bubbling fountain lined in blue and green tiles. The main floor was one big room, loosely divided by hand-carved screens that Elahyiah's father had brought over from Chenja. The screens were her dowry; her family had little else to offer besides Elahyiah herself.

Elahyiah sat bent over her desk near the ceramic stove they sometimes lit during the cool winter evenings, consulting her Tirhani dictionary. She spent several nights a week improving her Tirhani with a group of women downtown. The women were all Chenjan refugees, or the children of refugees. She had emigrated to Tirhan when she was nine, and he thought she spoke the language well, but she was constantly worried about it. "When we met I believed you would think I was some uneducated Nasheenian, it was so poor," she once confided.

He had thought nothing of the kind. Elahyiah was nothing like a Nasheenian woman, though he had not felt the need to tell her why he knew that for a certainty.

Elahyiah turned when he entered. He saw that she had the long stare of deep immersion. It took her a moment to focus, to come back from wherever she had been in her head, and then she was looking at him, at the children—and she smiled.

"You left them outside uncovered," he said.

She blinked, and the smile faded. "It's only been a few minutes." She turned to look at the water clock next to the call box.

"Where's the housekeeper?"

"I sent her home. It was such a beautiful day."

That was Elahyiah—compassionate when she remembered to be, but not always practical. God, he loved her for the compassion, but . . ..

Rhys left the girls with her and walked into the kitchen. Dirty dishes littered the counter; half-eaten mangoes and a loaf of uncovered rye bread, plates smeared in peanut butter and toast and grasshopper heads.

"Elahyiah, you can't send her home before she's even finished the tea dishes."

When she did not reply, Rhys turned to look back into the study, and saw Elahyiah giggling over some bug with Souri.

"Elahyiah?" he said. "The tea dishes."

"Hm?" She raised her head, distracted. "That's just tea."

Rhys felt slow irritation building in his chest, disrupting his hard-fought calm. He closed his eyes. These are not important things, he reminded himself. It was a blessing that his days no longer consisted of cutting off heads and blowing up buildings. A blessing.

"Let's get the children slathered down and put to bed," Rhys said. "I'm not paying to have their skins replaced before they're twenty."

He went upstairs to the tidy bedroom and changed his clothes. The housekeeper had the unenviable job of trying to keep up with his distractible wife. She did her best to keep the children fed and the common rooms clean, but it often fell to him to keep the bedroom neat. He had become terribly fastidious about it. When he came back down, Elahyiah had managed to move the children halfway to the bathing room. They stood in the hallway talking idly about how fast bees could fly.

Together, he and Elahyiah got Souri and Laleh bathed and slathered in burn ointment and put to bed. It was a long, drawn-out process. Laleh, ever the dour, sensitive one, cried and protested. Elahyiah kept up a constant stream of chatter, spoke of Heidian philosophy and Tirhani verb structure, and Souri spun stories of dervishes and sand demons who lived in the garden and became imprisoned in the belly of a sand cat.

By the time they put the girls into their room, the suns had died and the blue dusk had long since fallen.

As Rhys stood at the door of the girls' bedroom, he realized all of them had gone without dinner.

Elahyiah remained inside the bedroom, telling the girls stories about Chenja and the war in her soft voice.

"I need to speak to you when you're done," he said.

"I'll be down in a bit, love," Elahyiah said.

A night without dinner would not kill them. If Elahyiah didn't remember to feed them in the morning, the housekeeper would.

Rhys walked back down to the disastrous kitchen. There were no clean knives. He rolled up his sleeves and threw out the rapidly rotting food—nothing left uncovered for long kept well—and opened the bug bin. He stacked the dishes in the bin and opened the access panel for the refuse beetles. They would lick the dishes clean in a quarter hour.

Rhys left the rest for the housekeeper and made himself a quick meal of stale rye bread, curried protein cakes, and a lone mango he found at the back of the ice box behind a very curdled jar of cats' milk. He opened the jar and threw it and its contents into the bug bin. The beetles hissed.

As he ate, standing next to the counter, he wrote some notes for Elahyiah on the live countertop. *Make sure the children eat breakfast. Don't send the housekeeper home early. Don't leave the girls outside uncovered.* He nearly wrote, *And remember to eat something, yourself,* but that was too much, like reminding her to wash her hair. Which she also often forgot. I'm not raising three children, he amended. How did such a brilliant woman lose so many details? Why did he have to play father to all three of them?

He finally went upstairs to find her.

The window was open. A cool breeze stirred gauzy curtains. Elahyiah stood at the door that led out onto their private balcony. Her hair was unbound; black curls tumbled down her shoulders. She wore only a loose shift.

She turned when he entered, smiled.

"I missed you," she said.

He moved toward her in the dark. "Elahyiah, the children—"

She brushed a hand across his mouth, delicate as a moth's touch. "Hush now, they're in bed. I missed you."

She kissed him.

They didn't make it to the bed. She straddled him in the dark, almost frantic, passionate, as if they would be caught and stoned like two unwed lovers.

The whole world, for a moment, was just this: Elahyiah, his wife. The spill of her hair. The warmth, the urgent desire. He didn't know where her sudden passion came from on these nights, when he was nearly exhausted and the house was in disarray. But her passion never ceased to move him.

Later, he got up to use the privy, and paused again as he entered the archway leading into their shared room. He watched her through the stir of the white curtain that separated their room from the hall. Elahyiah was already asleep. She looked small and dark; she had the fine features of a lizard; delicate as a dragonfly. Their girls had been born small—too small for him not to worry.

Both were growing up as fine-boned as their mother. She was peaceful and perfect in sleep, disarmed, completely vulnerable.

He loved her. He felt that in his bones, but some days, even when he lay next to her, when he looked at her as he did now, he could not help but feel, somewhere just under the surface of his love, of their sometimes strained contentment, that something that should have sustained him was missing. He supposed all marriages must be like this; great chunks of contentment, frustrated daily living, shot through with moments of absolute terror and doubt and disappointment. The world was large. It was no fault of his or hers, he supposed, to sometimes wonder if a mistake had been made.

And then as the wind fell and the curtain stilled he felt his restlessness still as well, and his wife was no longer a frail stranger across the hall who could not remember to eat her own dinner or keep an appointment, but the mother of his children, his gift from God, the passionate love of his life, because the love of one's life was never that which you wished for or hoped for or forgot or lost or mistook; it was the partner you spent your long days with, the woman God made for the partnering of all of your days.

The love of your life was never the woman you left behind.

He moved to step into the room, to lie next to her, but as he did he heard a faint sound from below, felt the stirring of some bug in a wire—old, familiar.

Rhys turned away from the bedroom and descended to the kitchen at the bottom of the house. From here, the sound of the call box was louder, though the stirring in his blood remained the same.

The box was soldered to the wall next to the desk. He picked up the receiver.

"Peace be with you," he said.

"And with you," the woman on the other end said. He knew

the voice. The connection was good; nothing hissed or chittered over the line. It meant the bugs that originated the call were expensive. Government.

It was the Tirhani Minister.

"I need you to take a train tonight to Beh Ayin," she said.

"This is . . . unexpected." He was thinking it would cost her two hundred notes.

"It's of great importance."

If she was being blunt, he would follow suit. "It will cost you," he said. He thought of the housekeeper, wondered how much it would cost to hire a second.

"I expected nothing less," the Minister said, but her tone was the same. No amusement, all business.

"Who am I meeting with?" he asked.

"I will have one of my people meet you in Beh Ayin. She'll give you more information. She lost our original translator. How's your Nasheenian?"

When was the last time he had spoken Nasheenian? Six years? Inaya and Khos preferred to speak to him in Tirhani. When the three of them lapsed into Nasheenian, it was generally brief, to explain a term, or triggered by some memory.

"You'll need to translate a negotiation," the Minister said, "and you need to be on your best behavior."

"Goods and services?"

"Very discreet goods and services. You understand?"

"If I did not, you would not employ me."

"There's a train to Beh Ayin in two hours. There's a ticket with your name at the call desk."

"Minister?"

"Yes?"

"What happened to the other translator?"

"Two hours," the Minister said, and hung up.

The bel dame reclamation office in Mushtallah was at the base of the city's fifth hill, unofficially referred to by bel dames and civilians alike as Bloodmount. Particularly pious Nasheenians paid exorbitant prices to take a brief, musty tour of the interior of the derelict that made up the center of the hill. All the hills of Mushtallah were artificial. Their rotting cores were made up of old refugee ships, derelicts from the mass exodus from the moons back at the beginning of the world. Nyx had never been down there—she didn't much care what came before her—but she heard most of it was sealed off. What was left was just a sterile tangle of old metal, bug secretions, and bone dust.

There had been talk a few years before of the bel dames selling their residences on Bloodmount. Some had gone so far as to set up an alternate site in Amtullah for training new bel dames, but whatever grief they had with the Queen or with themselves had been sorted out, best anybody could tell, and Bloodmount was back at full capacity again.

Nyx had brought the whole team to drop off the head. She was interested in keeping them all together right now, at least until she had some answers. They had packed up the rogue bel dame's head in the trunk, and Nyx had finished off a fifth of vodka for breakfast, since she'd sworn off whiskey. It took the edge off her nerves. The last thing she wanted when she walked into a boiling hive of bel dames was to go in jumpy.

As they proceeded around Palace Hill, Bloodmount came into

view. At the height of the hill, a single tower gleamed a burnished copper color. That was the only visible part of the ship above ground—a twisted metal spire where every bel dame took her oath to uphold the old laws of blood debt.

"You sure you want to do this today?" Suha muttered, and spit sen out the open window.

Nyx stared at the spire. The bel dame training schools, residences, and reclamation office ringed the base of the hill. From here, she couldn't see the organic filter that protected the hill, but she'd been through it enough to know that it was the most powerful one in Nasheen. Hard to do, with Palace Hill and its high security organics just up the street. And the inner filters were more precise, and more deadly. She didn't figure she'd get much past the first filter on this little jaunt.

"I'm sure," Nyx said. "Best case, we find out what the fuck's going on with this rogue bel dame. Worst case, they kill me and you're out of a job."

"I like my job," Suha said.

Eshe stayed quiet.

Suha drove to the big, burst-scarred main gate at the base of the hill. This neighborhood was mostly boxing gyms and cheap eateries. There were a few shabby text and radio program stores and some bodegas. Nyx stepped out of the bakkie and looked up in the tenement windows above the shops. Teenage girls—bel dame hopefuls and university students—sat around on the tiny balconies. High-pitched laughter trickled over the street. She caught a whiff of marijuana, opium, and the distinctive milky stink of too many teenage women. A couple of leggy girls stood on the stoop of a bodega across from the bakkie. They smoked clove and marijuana cigarettes and wore calf-length burnouses. They looked Nyx over with heavy-lidded eyes.

"Can I come?" Eshe asked, leaning out the window. A

couple of passing girls turned at his voice and stared outright. One of them stumbled. Her companion shrieked with laughter.

Nyx pushed his head back into the bakkie. "Stay with Suha. This isn't a good place for boys."

"Nyx—"

"You heard me. I'll lose com with you once I'm inside the filter," Nyx said. "I'm not back in two hours, you file a report with the order keepers." Not that it would do much good. Bel dames were outside government control. They policed themselves. How they dealt with Nyx and the rogue bel dame's head was no business of the Queen's, so far as they were concerned. Still, she liked the idea of somebody filing some obscure paperwork on her behalf.

Nyx motioned for Suha to pop the trunk, dug the burnous-wrapped bel dame's head out of the back and slung it over her shoulder. The burnous had eaten most of the blood, but it was still stained with amber-brown splotches.

She leaned into the driver's side window and nodded to the side street. "There's a good Ras Tiegan place two streets over called the Montrouge. Get the kid a soda and some curried dog."

Eshe grimaced.

"You watch yourself in there," Suha said.

"You watch yourself out *here*," Nyx said. She walked up to the front gate.

There was a young woman posted, just a kid, maybe twenty. Couldn't have served a day at the front. She had clear skin and shiny eyes, just like the cocky bel dame Nyx was bringing in. Definitely not a day at the front.

"Here to report a rogue bel dame," Nyx said.

"I gotta take your identification," the woman said. Nyx held out her hand.

The woman wiped Nyx's finger across her portable slide. Nyx felt a wisp of pressure as some tailored bug skein sucked up a blood sample.

Nyx watched the woman's reaction as the file came up. The girl didn't blink.

"You've got level one clearance. You can go as far as the reclamation office without being cleaned." She punched open the gate.

Nyx slipped inside. The gate clanged behind her. Old, old metal—the sort of stuff that came off derelicts. She walked across the courtyard, past the bakkie barns. A couple of tissue mechanics raised their heads as she passed. Otherwise, nothing stirred on the other side of the gate.

The bounty reclamation office was a single-story building of amber stone. Most of the original arches had been whittled away by small arms fire, and what remained had been badly reconstructed with concrete and crumbling brick. Only half of the bel dame oath was visible. The complete line, the heart of the bel dame oath, was "My life for a thousand." All that was clearly readable above the office now was "My life." Nyx thought that somehow appropriate, knowing what she did about bel dames.

She hesitated at the stoop. It'd been a while since she crossed this threshold.

"Well, shit," she said aloud, and moved the weight of the head to her other shoulder.

She walked into the musty interior of the office. It took a minute for her eyes to adjust. A kid clerk stood behind the counter, chin in hand, staring at some misty drama leaking out from the radio on the counter. She jerked her head up when she saw Nyx and turned off the radio. The images began to dissipate in the dry air.

Nyx thumped the burnous-wrapped head onto the counter.

The girl put on a haughty face to cover her surprise. It was fun to watch. Nyx figured she wasn't a day over sixteen.

"You have a note?" the girl asked, casually extending her hand.

"It's not a note," Nyx said.

The girl's posture changed, then, subtly—enough for Nyx to judge that she'd had some bel dame training already.

"I'm here to deliver a rogue bel dame," Nyx said.

The girl's eyes widened. She shifted away from the counter. "You killed a . . . bel dame?"

"More or less. You've got another thirty hours or so before the head goes bad. They put the bug in your head yet? We're hard to kill for a reason."

"The . . . bug?"

"Call whoever's in charge of black marks, all right? I'm filing a report."

Another woman walked in from the back. She was a gray-haired matron with a face like death and vinegar. One hand rested on the pistol at her hip. The barrel glowed green. It was some new organic model. Suha would know it.

"You left me a long time with your runt," Nyx said.

The matron crinkled her face into the semblance of a smile. "A surprise or two is good for her. Teaches her to pay attention."

The girl moved to shove her hands into her pockets. Hesitated. Left them free. One of the first rules of self-defense was to always keep your hands free—so you could grab a weapon, or use your hands as one.

"Go sort the dead notes in the back, Hind," the matron said to the kid.

Hind sidestepped behind the matron and ducked into the back.

The matron spread her palms on the table, cocked her head at Nyx. "I can see you've been in the business awhile. Most don't reach our age."

I'm only thirty-eight, Nyx wanted to say, but this old woman—this crone—was likely no more than forty.

"You handle black marks against bel dames?" Nyx asked.

"No. That's a council job. I already called her. She'll be coming down to chat."

"Council? The bel dame council?"

"Been a council job the last four or five years now, since the new gals got elected."

"Didn't know there was an election."

"They happen hard and fast around here. Usually 'cause somebody got cut up. Just elected two new ones. Shook things up. Been some . . . interesting times, last few years." She palmed the burnous. "So, what you bring us?"

Nyx heard at least two people take up positions outside the front door, blocking her escape. It felt good to have somebody make a fuss over her again, at least.

Then the door at Nyx's left opened—the door leading back into the bounty reclamation offices.

A familiar figure entered. Her hair was completely white now, tied back from a pinched, hallowed face. The years hadn't been kind. A long scar marked her from nose to ear on the left side of her face. Whoever had given it to her had taken half the ear as well. She wore loose black trousers and a tight, sleeveless tunic the color of sage. Her hands were fine boned, like her face, but heavily veined and wrinkled. You could always mark a woman's age by her hands, even among the First Families.

The matron at the counter nodded at her. "This is Fatima Kosan," she said. "Fatima handles all the black marks."

"I know who she is," Nyx said.

"They told me when you breached the gate," Fatima said coolly. "I requested a personal notification if you ever blooded the gate."

"How many people you kill to get that council seat?" Nyx asked.

"Enough," Fatima said lightly.

"I'm here to deliver a head. That's all. This honey pot tried to kill the daughter of the Ras Tiegan diplomat, Erian sa Aldred. Maybe me too."

Fatima approached the counter. She walked with a barely perceptible limp. Nyx figured the right knee had been replaced, maybe a year or two before.

Fatima pushed open the top of the burnous, a bold thing to do, considering Nyx and the head hadn't been through a filter. Nyx could have brought in any kind of Mushtallah-based contagion and killed the lot of them. But Fatima, best Nyx remembered, wasn't stupid. She just knew Nyx well.

"Make sure she's one of ours," Fatima told the matron, "and get her to the Plague Sisters."

Nyx pulled the red note from her dhoti. "Found this on her."

Fatima took the red note and examined it. "We'll have it tested. Where's the body?"

"Last I saw it, Mashad and East Efran, in the alley behind a Heidian deli. Don't know the name, but the food smelled right."

The matron took the head carefully, as if it were a child.

Fatima rested a hand on the counter, faced Nyx. Her eyes were soft and brown, but the hollows were deeply lined now.

"You looked better back when you were teaching me the laws of blood debt," Nyx said.

"Long time ago," Fatima agreed.

"Before you sent me to prison and tortured me?"

"Before you started doing black work, yes."

"You got the girls outside for a reason?" Nyx said, nodding to the front where she'd heard the bel dames take up position.

"Nyxnissa, if I wanted you killed, I'd have done it long ago. Your name has come up many times at the council . . . but the death vote never passed."

"Which way did you vote?"

Fatima showed her teeth. "We're no longer children, Nyxnissa. Let's not fight."

The matron returned from the back. "Blood test says the girl's ours," she said. She handed a coded note to Fatima. "Called Ara so Basmirah. One of Shadha's girls."

"Shadha?" Nyx said.

Fatima stared at the coded note. Nyx saw her mouth harden. Then she raised her gaze, and the slip in her expression smoothed.

"The council has encountered some conflicts of interest among its members."

"So she's rogue after all?" Nyx said. There was no more "conflicting interest" in Nasheen than bel dames policing a rogue bel dame.

"That term is a little extreme," Fatima said. "We have full control over the matter."

"Isn't that what Alharazad said before she killed half the council twenty years ago?"

"Thank you for bringing in the head," Fatima said, avoiding her look. "We'll get her reanimated and interrogate her. I assume you checked to make sure the diplomat's name wasn't on a red note?"

"Obviously."

"And—"

"And I checked for mine," Nyx said.

Fatima nodded, showed her teeth again. Was that supposed to be a smile? Nyx wondered if the facial scar had severed something essential in Fatima's face. Best she remembered, Fatima knew how to smile, when it suited her. "If nothing else, we'll discipline her for causing a public disturbance. You should come up to file a report."

"Why the fuck would I file a report?"

"Records. The council loves them. Indulge me." Fatima hesitated a moment, then, "What happened in Chenja was a misunderstanding." Her words came out quickly, like pulling a scab on some old wound. "The Queen saw fit to clarify your purpose for being in Chenja after the fact, but you must have understood my position at the time. It's another reason you aren't dead. In the future, it would be . . . prudent if you informed us of your private notes. It ensures that our interests are aligned."

So, Nyx thought, it had bothered Fatima that she tortured her back in Chenja. That was something.

"The Queen told you Rasheeda was working both sides back then?" Nyx asked.

"No note was put out on Rasheeda. She was reported dead six years ago. I assumed you'd killed her."

"I did, but I never burned the head," Nyx said. "I guess somebody could have had her reanimated within the thirty-hour window." Tended to happen, with rogue bel dames.

"You, of all people, should know better," Fatima said. "As it is here, there have been some changes."

"Like you getting elected?"

They were only an arm's length apart now. They could have reached out and strangled each other. Nyx thought about that for a while. "How many council members are rogue, now?" Nyx asked.

Fatima showed her teeth again in her half smile/half grimace. "Bel dames don't go rogue."

"Like Rasheeda didn't go rogue? Or this Ara girl? You remember who I am?"

"I remember. Which is why you should come upstairs and file that report."

Nyx could have filed a report in the office. Fatima didn't invite folks up into Bloodmount proper for paperwork. All told, Nyx was idly curious about why Fatima wanted to pull her away privately. She could kill her easily and legally enough here.

Nyx shrugged. "Your time."

Fatima's mouth twitched.

Nyx followed Fatima back into the courtyard. The two bel dames posted outside the door took up the rear. She was struck by how young they looked. Neither was a day over twenty, but they carried themselves with the assurance of bel dames—the cool expressions, squared shoulders. She noted that the pistols at their hips were the new kind—those organic hybrids with green glowing barrels.

Fatima led her up toward the primary filter at the base of the hill. Nyx passed through it with a soft pop and hiss. She smelled something strange on the other side, and realized the filter had eaten at the hair on her arms. She touched her scalp, and found that her braids were dry and frayed.

"Turned up your filter?" Nyx asked. Her skin prickled.

Fatima half turned, continued walking. "No. Perhaps it simply doesn't like you."

Nyx frowned. She didn't want to test any more filters.

Fatima turned off the paved road, toward the big stone residence where the bel dame and council offices resided.

"You come out for every call from the front desk?" Nyx said.

"I had your code flagged, as I said." Fatima pressed her hand to the faceplate on the front door. It opened, and they stepped into the cool foyer. The bel dames continued to keep pace with them. Nyx heard the soft *shush-shush* of water being piped through the walls, cooling the building.

Fatima motioned to the stairs. "My office is this way."

Nyx hesitated on the stairs. Offices for petty officials and bug pushers were downstairs. The bel dame council offices were upstairs.

"When were you actually elected?" Nyx asked.

"I joined the bel dame council last year," Fatima said. She started up the stairs.

Nyx followed Fatima into a wide circular foyer. She saw runners on either side of the door, and lifted her head to see the ass-end of a metal portcullis hidden in the deep recesses of the ceiling. The floor was blood-red brick. The bel dame council offices ringed the foyer. All of the doors were made of metal-studded bug secretions. She noted personal filters on each door, and faceplates. At the center of the room stood a ragged bel dame with a face like a smashed melon. She already had both hands on the hilts of her pistols when Nyx and Fatima entered.

Fatima keyed Nyx into her office. Inside, there was very little furniture. A low table, some rugs, cushions to sit on, a big standing cabinet. The way the table was angled, nobody would have to sit with their back to the door. Still, Nyx took her time finding a good place to sit.

She eased herself to the floor and pushed one of the cushions behind her. The windows were filtered slits, set just above head height. Every building on the hill was built like a fortress.

"It's quiet up here," Nyx said.

Fatima sat across from her at the table. "We're in the process of moving our operations," Fatima said.

Nyx didn't like sitting on the floor. It was one of the things she missed the least about being a bel dame. "Moving operations? Another bluff, like last time? Don't shit me, Fatima, bel dames have operated out of Mushtallah for over a thousand years."

Fatima shrugged. Nyx noted that she hadn't pulled out a slide or some organic paper for a blooded statement. She wished for a cigarette, some sen, a glass of whiskey—something to do with her hands. Sitting across from Fatima this way felt like being back in bel dame school. So she did what they did in school—laid her hands flat on the table. Fatima did the same.

"We still have partial residences in Amtullah, which we had begun to establish during the last move."

"You're clearing the whole quarter?"

"Select training facilities will remain, as well as the reclamation office. We'll continue taking our oaths in the tower, and Blood-mount is still sovereign. A consulate will remain."

"A consulate? You're not a foreign country."

"After a fashion. It seemed only polite to keep an emissary in Mushtallah, near the Queen's seat."

Nyx mulled over that for a while. She watched Fatima's dour face.

"You didn't bring me up here for a statement," Nyx said.

"No," Fatima said.

Nyx's fingers twitched. She considered stabbing Fatima with one of the poisoned needles stashed in her braids.

"I didn't expect the rogues to come after you," Fatima said. "But because they did, it does open some possibilities."

"Can we talk about it over a drink?" Nyx asked.

"No," Fatima said. "I know why the rogues want you dead. I thought about it myself, before things got . . . messy. You must understand the politics of bel dames using rogues to do their black work?"

"Yeah, I remember you and Rasheeda sending me to prison."

"You weren't rogue. Merely acting against our ethics. We don't sell out our country on the black market. It's dishonorable."

"Ferrying zygotes is hardly—"

"This isn't the time to discuss it," Fatima said sharply. "Old days. Old arguments. I speak of today."

Nyx thought about stabbing her with a needle again.

"Bringing in rogues is much trickier than merely disciplining a morally corrupt bel dame," Fatima said.

"Cause then you've got to admit you're dealing with a bel dame civil war?"

"Let's not go that far."

"What do you want, Fatima?"

Fatima's mouth twitched. Another attempt at a smile? "The question is, what do *you* want, Nyx?"

Nyx shook her head. "I can't do what you're asking."

"Who better?"

"Somebody who likes life a little less."

Nyx began to rise.

"Wait." Fatima held up her hand. "You haven't asked what I can offer you."

"What, money? Me and my team are doing all right. If you asked me up here for this you already know that."

"What's the one thing I can offer you that no one else can?"

"Prison?"

Fatima clucked her tongue. "Come now, anyone can get you that." She got to her feet. Nyx noted her favoring her knee, again. She walked to the big cabinet behind her and pressed her hand to the faceplate. The cabinet opened. She pulled out a high-profile document case made of shiny black resin. They were fireproof, waterproof, and generally impossible to open without the right blood code. She palmed it open and pulled out a slick sheet of organic paper. She laid the paper on the table in front of Nyx and took her time sitting down again.

Nyx grabbed the paper. She couldn't make out much. It was First Family nonsense on flowery monarchy script. Official documents like this were why she liked to keep somebody lettered on her team.

"What, you want me to wipe my ass with it?" Nyx said. She knew the bravado wouldn't fool Fatima into thinking she understood it, but it made her feel better.

"That's a six-year-old request from Queen Zaynab asking us to reinstate your bel dame status," Fatima said.

Nyx felt her gut clench. "I didn't think she bothered."

"She did. We've been . . . processing it."

"For six years?"

Fatima shrugged. "Rejected requests are forever rejected. Until it's rejected, it's still being . . . processed."

Nyx really wanted a drink. "What's your point?"

"I can make you a bel dame again."

"If I hunt down your rogues for you," Nyx said.

"Tell me about your life right now, Nyx."

"I have a good fucking life."

"Do you? Babysitting diplomats' daughters. Hunting down First Family servants who've stolen their cast iron. Paying miserable wages to a venom addict and harboring an all but illiterate boy shifter—"

"Suha's reformed, and the kid can read just fine."

Fatima raised a brow. "My point. What happened to your honor, Nyx?"

"Like you know what that is. Fuck you."

"Let me tell you something. I've worked twenty years to clean up the bel dame circle. I've hunted and bled a dozen petty rogues just like you. You're the only one we didn't reform or kill. Why is that?"

"You tell me."

"Somebody was protecting you. I don't know who it was, and I'm not sure I care to know. But whoever it was isn't protecting you anymore. I can offer you protection."

"If I hunt down the rogues."

"If you work for me."

Nyx shook her head. "Fuck you." She started to the door.

"Think about it. No one else is powerful enough to offer you protection anymore, Nyx. Not even the Queen."

We'll see about that, Nyx thought.

She pushed out into the foyer. The hulking bel dame guard was immediately at her side. Nyx jerked away reflexively.

"Hush, now, woman," the guard barked. "I'm just escorting you out."

Nyx left Bloodmount under escort, and walked back out through the primary filter and onto the girl-clotted street. She took a deep breath to clear her muggy head while she gnawed on Fatima's offer. Bel dame? Why would she want that again?

Because you used to be something, she thought, and snarled. A young girl at the corner jumped at her look and shrank back, frightened. She grabbed at her companion, and ducked into the nearest doorway.

Nyx used to be young, and fiery, and strong. She used to be able to cut off a head in forty-five seconds with a dull blade. She used to be able to drive a bakkie like a demon.

She stopped at the corner to catch her breath. Her head swam. She blinked a few times. Fuck, she used to be able to cross the fucking street without gasping for air. What the fuck was she now? Some diplomat's errand girl?

Better to be Fatima's errand girl?

She stumbled around the block to the Montrouge and found Eshe and Suha at a corner table—the ugly weapons tech and the plain-faced kid clerk with the bent spine—gnawing on fried plantains and curried rice. She remembered meeting up with other teams. Better teams.

Don't let her get to you, she thought. But it was too late for that. Honor. Sacrifice. Obligation. All the death she meted out used to mean something. When had it stopped meaning anything? When did it turn into worthless bloodletting, just like the front?

"How'd it go?" Suha asked.

"I don't know yet," Nyx said.

"I got some news you'll like, then."

Nyx sat next to her and ordered a whiskey straight. "Hit it," she said.

"Just checked the bounty boards again."

"Glad your contact's still talking. She owe you something big?"

"Big enough to get me high-end news."

"Tell me the name's not mine."

"Better. Somebody posted a bel dame note for Kasbah so Sabah."

"The Queen's head of security?"

"It came down half an hour after it was posted. Queen struck it, of course, but somebody in the bel dame council approved it before the Queen got wind of it."

"Only the council can issue a note."

Eshe whistled softly. "That's pretty gutsy."

"Fuck," Nyx muttered. "That's civil war. They're going after the *Queen*."

"The bel dames?" Eshe said. "That's stupid."

"Politics," Suha said.

Nyx shook her head. She was tired. "We need to go," she said. "This place isn't safe."

"When the fuck was Nasheen ever safe?" Suha said.

Nyx tried to get up, stumbled. Eshe jumped up to help her. She pushed him away. "I'm fine," she said. "We need to go. We're next."

5.

On clear days, when the smog wasn't so bad, Nyx and Eshe would drive out to one of the low hills outside Mushtallah. They would trap one end of a white burnous in the bakkie window and prop up the other end on two long poles and create their own shade. For a while they used old rifles as supports, but the sand and dirt jammed in the barrels afterward made Suha spit and mutter and bang around the hub like a woman possessed by gun-loving angels.

After they set up the shade, they watched the blue sun fire up over the black sky, its tail-end going lavender, then deep violet as the second sun—the big orange demon—overtook the horizon behind it. The cool blue dawn would turn the color of a bright bruise, then go deep scarlet, and the double dawn would bleed over the city. In the light of the cool dawn they would listen to the familiar wail of the muezzin and eat figs and naan and drink strong black buni and talk about the best ways to avoid a fight.

But this morning they weren't up there for a picnic. Nyx and Eshe had spent the predawn hours digging up a weapons cache Nyx had buried the year before. She had some stashes in the border towns, too, but this one had some sentimental items—stuff she didn't have room for at the storefront.

Nyx crouched in the cache hole and passed a pair of specs and a z22 carbine rifle up to Eshe.

"What do we need all these for?" Eshe asked for the third time.

Nyx waited until he reached for more, then handed him a bag of fever bursts. "Careful with those. They crack open and we'll be snorting our brains out our nose."

Eshe took the bag in both hands and made his way toward the bakkie. When he returned, the blue light of the first dawn touched his face. The call to prayer rolled out over the desert.

"I have to pray," he said.

Nyx swore.

"I'll be right back!" he insisted.

Nyx crawled out of the cache and sat at its edge. She took a long pull on a water bulb. She'd tried drinking whiskey earlier, but had retched it all up. Nothing had sat well with her since the fried plantains at lunch the day before. She'd vomited the fight night dinner she and Eshe had shared with Mercia, too.

Eshe lay prostrate on a prayer rug on the other side of the bakkie, his fingertips stretched toward the base of an old willowren tree that clawed at the sky with barren, charred branches.

She had another two hours before she was due at the gym for some conditioning. That gave her just enough time to clean up the storefront's security. She'd been expecting bel dames to come after her for a long time. Trouble was these weren't proper bel dames with notes for her head. These were rogues, and rogues were—at best—unpredictable. What protection could Fatima and her corrupt little circle give her?

Nyx walked over to the bakkie. She turned on her transceiver and punched in Suha's personal code. The bug casing used for the diplomat job belonged to the diplomat. She would miss that bit of high-end tech. It was hard to come by a secure com method that didn't require a magician to run it.

"You got me?" Nyx said.

"Yeah, I'm here. Just hitting the gym," Suha said.

"You deliver that note to the bounty office?"

"Addressed for the Queen's eyes only, yeah. I don't know how you expect to get a note to the Queen that way, but yeah, I did, right when they opened."

"She'll answer," Nyx said. The Queen would be just as interested in what the bel dames were up to as Nyx was. And the Queen might know why it was a bel dame who had tried to kill Nyx was running around the palace meeting diplomats. "Thanks."

She liked to keep transceiver conversations short. Unlike a magician-bugged communication, archaic radio signals were easy to hack. She hadn't had a com specialist on her team since the year before, when she found out the girl was selling zygotes and venom out of the storefront on fight nights. She didn't much care what her team did in their spare time, but using Nyx's hard-won resources to do it was one step to the left too many.

So until she replaced her com specialist or hired a hard up magician, her com was dodgy at best. The most secure way to get the Queen anything was through the bounty office. Best case, she'd get a list of recent bel dame visitors to the palace. She knew the Queen's head of security, Kasbah, and figured her records would be meticulous. She hadn't seen either Kasbah or the Queen in six years, not since she took their note on an alien gene pirate, but they'd remember her. Nyx was a lot of things, but forgettable wasn't one of them.

Nyx leaned against the bakkie and watched the second sun rise. Eshe straightened and rolled up his prayer rug. He walked toward her, an awkward and gangly kid. Neither of them wore their burnouses, but in another hour the sun would get too hot to stand.

"Why do we need—" Eshe began again.

He was stubborn. She'd give him that.

"Because I retired all my good gear three years ago. You think you need an acid rifle or perimeter mines to look after some drunk kid? You fight bel dames with bel dame weapons."

"You really think they're coming after us?"

"Maybe. Maybe not. Maybe we'll go after them."

"Suha says you're crazy."

"Suha's one to talk. C'mon."

They finished packing and loading the bakkie. Nyx pulled the bug door closed over the cache. They spread dirt and sand over the scar in the soil and headed to the bakkie.

As Nyx opened the driver's side door, something in the air trembled. She paused.

A boom rolled over the city. The ground beneath her shook. She ducked behind the bakkie door. The rolling wave swept over them.

The world trembled, and was still.

Eshe scrambled out from behind the bakkie. Nyx poked her head over the door.

They looked over the city.

Mushtallah was the oldest city in Nasheen, built back when the only dangers to a city in the interior were wild sand cats and virulent strains of magician-tailored bugs, usually the ones coming from the Khairian wasteland in the north. The city stretched over and among seven prominent hills. The First Families lived on five of those hills, the bel dames on another. The seventh, the one nearest the center of the city sprawl, was Palace Hill, seat of the Nasheenian monarchy for the last three hundred years and the Caliphate for a thousand years before that. The city's ancient walls had long since fallen into ruin. After the first time the city was burned out by the Chenjans, the Queen and the high council authorized the installation of an organic filter that barred all bugs and non-authorized organics from the city.

So the first thing Nyx looked for when she gazed over the city was the organic filter. Even this far out, she and Eshe were still inside the filter; it protected a refueling station just a mile west of them. Just beyond the filter was a freight rail station that unloaded the raw components of bug juice and station gear and loaded up goods destined for the front. The filter was visible as a hazy sheen along the periphery of the city.

The sun was too low and bright to make out much of anything on the other side of the city, so Nyx looked behind her for the filter. She had to rub at her eyes a couple times, but yes, there it was; the filter that kept out the worst of Chenja's munitions and mutant bug swarms. They hadn't taken that out, at least.

"That's bad, isn't it?" Eshe said, pointing.

Nyx looked.

If she squinted, a thread of smoke was just visible at the city center, a soft tail curling above Mushtallah's central hill.

The Queen's palace.

Nyx saw the tail of smoke grow wider and darken into a blue-black plume. Something was licking around the palace compound and surrounding hillside, alive.

"Hand me the specs," she said.

Eshe unpacked a pair of specs and tossed them to her.

Nyx pinched the specs to the bridge of her nose. The palace compound jumped into sharp, magnified relief. Too magnified. A blaze of white fire filled Nyx's vision. She squinted twice to zoom out. The center of the palace compound was a fiery, white-hot ruin. A black plague was crawling from the center of the wound and enveloping the palace grounds.

Nyx pulled off the specs. She knew what that was.

"What?" Eshe asked.

Nyx jumped into the bakkie and started it up. The bakkie belched and coughed. "Let's go!"

Eshe threw the rifles in front and squeezed into the jump seat.

Nyx yanked her transceiver out from under the dash. She put the bakkie in reverse and hit the quick button pattern for the hub. The connection opened.

"Checking in. We're in one piece," Nyx said.

"I'm headed to the keg now. No idea of the damage," Suha said. "I have the radio on, but I'm not getting any news. How big was the hit?"

"It's a scalper bug burst, a pretty fucking big one, on Palace Hill."

"Direct hit?"

"Dead center. It's on the move. Could contaminate the whole city in less than an hour."

"Where are you?"

"About half a kilometer from the train station. I'm getting us out before the filter freezes up. You have an out?"

"Always. I'll meet you at the safe house."

"Go," Nyx said, and tucked the transceiver into the top of her breast binding.

Nyx switched pedals and swung the wheel; the bakkie sent up a stir of dust and sand. She hit the far left pedal and they blew back down the sandy road toward the refueling station. It was going to be tight, getting through that filter, but they had less chance of survival if they were locked in the city with the burst.

"What's going on?" Eshe asked. His voice cracked. "We're not leaving Suha are we?"

"In about a quarter hour that scalper burst is going to burrow into the palace security system and release a virus that'll eat all the blood codes authorized for entry into the city," Nyx said. She had watched it happen before on a much smaller scale, when she planted a scalper burst at a Chenjan security outpost at the front, a lifetime ago. "When that happens, anybody trying to get in or out is going to get eaten alive by the filter and trapped inside with the plague. You ever seen somebody get eaten by a filter? You ever had the black plague?"

"What about the rest of the palace? What about the Queen, and the magicians?" Eshe asked.

"How the hell would I know?" Nyx said. "Maybe she got out, maybe she didn't." And if she hadn't, there was a whole bigger brew of trouble on the stove. "Let's make sure we do. I don't want to be stuck inside a filtered city with scalper bursts."

"Should we call Yahfia?" Eshe asked.

Nyx tried to concentrate on the road. Her vision was blurring again. "Yahfia left Mushtallah yesterday," she said. A magician in a plagued city had a far higher chance of survival than a teenage shape shifter and washed-up mercenary anyway.

Nyx switched pedals again as they hit the flatland and sped toward the filmy curtain of the filter. Off to her right she saw the metal tanks and steam towers of the refueling station. On the other side of the filter was the train station.

"What's your passkey say, Eshe?" Nyx asked.

Eshe stuck his arm out between the front seats, wrist bared. Beneath the tawny skin of his inner arm was a raised disk; his coded passkey into the city.

His passkey was a forgery that gave his birthplace as Heidia, but it got him in and out of the interior cities just fine. The city had switched from customs-stamped passbooks to embedded passkeys five years before. When she was a bel dame, Nyx had been inoculated against the city's filter, which meant none of her blood codes were on record in Mushtallah. By law, none of her organic material could be kept on file in a government-owned system. The bel dame council restricted access to the blood stamp information of their members; cataloguing all of that information into the imperial system would have given the Queen a logbook of bel dame blood codes, allowing her magicians to create viruses tailored to remove troublesome bel dames. In any case, it meant Nyx didn't have a key. She probably wouldn't die. But Eshe might.

"Still orange," Eshe said. "How do we know the virus hasn't spread yet?"

"You'll know," Nyx said.

"How?"

"Filter goes black," she said.

Nyx switched pedals again. The bakkie sped up. The filter loomed closer. The slow, somber howl of the city's emergency sirens filled the air.

"Don't the sirens mean we should stay in the city?" Eshe asked.

Nyx kept her eye on the filter. A dying beetle escaped through a leak in the hoses beneath her feet and flitted against her ankle.

"Sirens mean they're going to shut the filter down," Nyx said.

Shutting down the filter was an attempt to save the blood banks from contagion. They would do by default what the contagion was tailored to do: make it impossible for anyone to get in or out of the city alive until the filter's access to the blood banks was restored by a team of magicians.

They were within three hundred yards of the filter.

Nyx had seen scalper bursts at work back when they were short-range, highly temperamental bursts. Nobody would have used them on a whole city back then.

They were within a hundred yards of the filter. The curtain ahead of them wavered.

"Status, Eshe!"

"I'm orange," he said.

"We're good then," Nyx said.

Nyx pulled the clutch and shifted pedals. The bakkie leapt forward. Eshe slammed into the seat behind her.

"Hold on," Nyx said.

The bakkie hit the filter. An oily film of black spilled from the faux stone pillars along the filter perimeter.

Nyx held her breath. The filter crackled. The hairs on the back of her arms stood on end. Something inside the bakkie hissed and spat like scarabs on a griddle. The bakkie shuddered and spun. The hood flew open. A cloud of steam and the gray, wispy remains of the red roaches that had powered the bakkie burst out of the engine's cistern.

Nyx jerked in her restraints, and though she didn't smash her sternum against the steering wheel, the force that launched her against her restraints took the breath from her.

The world wavered, then slowed. When the bakkie stopped moving, Nyx raised her head and looked out at the open hood, the filmy detritus of red roaches and beetles smearing the windshield. There was sand on the hood, inside the cab.

"Eshe?" Nyx asked.

No answer.

Nyx fumbled with her restraints. She got herself loose and twisted around to peer into the jump seat. Through the back window, she saw the glistening black sheen of the filter about ten or twenty feet distant.

"Eshe?" she asked.

He lay hunkered in the back, head bowed. She smelled vomit. She touched the side of his face. When he didn't respond she grabbed him roughly by the chin.

"Answer me, you little fuck," she said.

Eshe's eyelids flickered.

"You with me?" she said.

"I threw up," he said.

Nyx saw the pool of bile at the boy's feet.

"It means you're alive," she said. "Are you hurt? You broken? Come on, the bakkie's done."

He suddenly jerked in his seat and began to thrash and claw at his arm. He started screaming; a terrible, high-pitched screeching that tore at her gut.

Nyx saw the thumbprint of the passkey on the inside of his arm glowing bright red beneath his skin. She pulled out the dagger strapped to her thigh and popped out the viral passkey.

Eshe howled and clutched at the wound. The passkey dropped into the pool of bile. Hissed.

Nyx's heart thudded loud and fast in her chest. The filter behind her began to spit and crackle. They were well clear of it, but she was worried about airborne contamination, about secondary blasts and filter breaches in addition to the weird thing with the passkeys. What if this was part of a larger assault? Was there a Chenjan ground force on the way?

Nyx struggled out of the bakkie and onto solid ground.

"We need gear," Eshe muttered, and stumbled toward the rear of the bakkie. Blood trickled down his arm.

Nyx helped him pack water and weapons. They brought it all to the train platform, and set the gear under a triangle of shade cast by the big cranes used to heft fuel cylinders onto freight cars.

"Where are we going?" he asked.

"Some conductors owe me favors."

He was already sweating heavily. His hair was plastered to his face. He hadn't covered up since prayer on the hill.

"Put your burnous on," she said. Her chest hurt, and her legs were wobbly. The sun was too high now for them to stay out very long safely. Not that that had stopped her before.

After downing some water and spending a few minutes collecting themselves, Nyx moved all their stuff further up the platform under the awning. The train wasn't due until dusk—if it came at all, now that the city had been attacked. It was a long time to go without water.

Eshe rested beside Nyx, his back against the faux stone of the station. There was an attendant shelter on the platform, but it was empty. There would be a water tap inside. Luckily, Nyx knew how to bleed a lock, even without a magician.

"That was a fucked up exit," Eshe said.

"You should see my entrances."

"Will the burst take out the whole city?"

Nyx gazed out at the black filter and ruined bakkie. She would need a good tissue mechanic to replace the entirety of the bakkie guts, and maybe the blown-out cistern . . . If somebody didn't salvage it first. The filter ate everything organic that it wasn't coded to accept—and that included the bug juice and roach colony that powered a bakkie. There were a lot of scavengers living outside Mushtallah looking for somebody desperate or stupid enough to drive through a filter.

"I don't know," Nyx said. "Magicians are coming up with weirder and weirder shit all the time."

She didn't like the idea that there were truckloads of bursts on both sides of the border that she didn't know anything about anymore. Suha might have a broader knowledge of current tech, but the best gear and munitions specialist Nyx had ever had retired to the coast six years before to raise munitions-savvy babies.

Eshe leaned against her, let his head drop onto her shoulder. Nyx stiffened, tried to relax. He scared her when he acted like a kid. She didn't like to treat him like one.

He closed his eyes.

"You need to stay awake. I don't want you slipping into any coma," Nyx said, and shrugged his head off her shoulder. She handed him a water bulb and made him drink.

"Where are we going?" he asked.

"We're going to regroup." She bunched her hands into fists, watched the muscles and tendons working beneath the skin. "Then we're going to find out who lived through that burst."

·6·

When Khos came home, he smelled of liquor and opium and
. . . the woman.

Inaya lay still in the room opposite his, listening to the sound
of his footsteps on the stairs. Even with her back turned, she
could smell the other woman. He was a shifter himself; he would
know what she could and could not see, hear, or smell. But he
padded about the house as if his other wife was a large secret,
large enough to fill the house.

He stumbled around the other room, throwing off clothes
as he went. She heard them pool onto the floor, settle over the
door of the wardrobe. He banged against something in the other
room, and swore in Mhorian.

Some days she wished the house was bigger. She wanted a
whole wing of it to herself, not just one small room. No, that
wasn't right. She wanted a house. A full house on her own salary,
a whole life to herself.

And then what would become of you? she thought. A divorced
foreign woman in Tirhan? They would deport her, and Khos
would get the children. No, marriage was about endurance.
About enduring far more than you thought you could possibly
bear.

She heard him run the water in the tub down the hall. She
finally opened her eyes and stared out the open window onto
the street. When they first moved to Tirhan, she had kept all the
upstairs windows shut. They were opaque and filtered, but still,

she closed them. She feared swarms, religious police, but mostly she feared the prying eyes of these black foreigners.

It took her months to admit that she, the tawny Ras Tiegan with the pale Mhorian shifter husband, was the foreign one.

The sound of the water stopped. Inaya closed her eyes again, kept her breathing even, and willed him to pass out. Preferably on the floor. In the other room.

But he came to her, as was also his custom on the nights he visited his other wife.

He sat next to her on the bed. The bed creaked under his weight. When he touched her, she wanted to melt into the bed, become one with the soft mattress, the bed feet, and deeper, down into the bones of the house. It was a sinful feeling, the kind that made her feel unclean, but she felt it nonetheless. In another life, perhaps, she could allow herself to do what her body desired. But not in this one.

Khos shook her gently. She turned to face him.

He was a big man, and self-conscious of it. He sat with shoulders hunched, head bowed. She had never seen him stand up straight.

"I'm sorry I'm so late," he said softly, and he placed his hand on her head and stroked her gently.

It was the gentleness that had convinced her to marry him. The gentleness and the Tirhani visa.

Inaya pulled herself out of the tub the next morning and showered with lavender soap. Lavender. It was a scent she could never get in Nasheen, but the Tirhanis loved it. They had shelves and shelves of heavily scented products. Soaps and lotions and perfumes. Smell did not trigger old memories in war veterans, was not blamed for shooting deaths in the marketplace.

Someday, she too would escape those dark triggers, the part of her that wanted to break away from the world, tug free, merge with everything else. Become someone, something, else.

Someday.

Not today.

She dressed and walked downstairs. The floor was made of soft organic matting that clung gently to the bottoms of her sandals as she walked. She stepped across the courtyard at the center of the house and through the airy archway into the amber-colored kitchen. The soft susurrus of the water moving through the walls to cool the house comforted her. There are worse fates, she thought, than being the first wife of a shifter . . . in Tirhan, at least.

The housekeeper had already taken the children to school, and left out breakfast for her and Khos at the stone table. Khos stood at the radio table at the center of the room, pulling information from the radio onto his personal slide. She watched him scroll through old recordings of council meetings and mullahs' speeches.

"Something in there you miss?" Inaya asked lightly.

"Possibly. They've started a dig on the north shore. It's looking like a Mhorian settlement that predates the one along the coast. I needed something on the geography of the region, but there's nothing here in the archives." He wiped his hand over the counter, and the bugs inside ceased their glow and transmission. The counter went blank.

"I haven't been able to find lizard eggs in a week," Inaya said, hovering over the toast and fried grub spread the housekeeper had laid out.

"I'm not hungry."

She rolled that idea around for a long moment before answering. "I'll be late tonight."

"I will too. I need to stop by the archives."

He did not, in fact, need to stop by the archives. Inaya had learned years ago what that shorthand meant. She knew he kept his other wife in the Mhorian district, a buxom woman with hair the color of dark honey. So far as Inaya knew, there was only the one Other. Tirhan permitted him four, but he had never spoken to Inaya about the other marriage. She had deduced that on her own when the local magistrate had come by for his signature. He'd signed the paperwork and said nothing to her. In fact, it was not the idea of another wife that bothered her. It was his assumption that she did not and would never know, as if she were a stupid child, a gross appendage. What bothered her was her continued complicity in pretending she did not know.

But then, there was much about her that he did not know. Perhaps there was some fairness to that. A house built on lies. It was all very Tirhani.

"You'll be at the embassy?" Khos asked.

"I'm running errands for the Minister. There's a dinner with the Mhorian ambassador and his delegation in a few days. She'd like us both to come."

Khos made a face. "I have no interest in making nice among Mhorians. You know how they are."

You can't make nice for Mhorians and the Ras Tiegan ambassador, but you have no trouble fucking your fat Mhorian wife on the other side of the district whenever it pleases you, she thought. She held her tongue. Old hurts. Dwelling on them didn't change anything.

"I will go myself then," she said, half-daring him to argue.

"It's better that way. Meet up with your friends from work. I know you always have plenty to talk about."

Inaya turned away so he could not see her anger. She packed her things and left for work without speaking another word.

The day was cool but clear, so she decided to take the long walk into town. All the houses along the street were built much like hers: two- and three-storied houses of mud-brick and bug secretions painted in brilliant colors, no windows on the first floor, surrounded by eight-foot-high polished stone fences wound in green ivy, clematis, stranglethorn, and the peculiar orange flowers they called ladylilies. Tirhanis loved their private spaces, but she knew that if she tried any of the gates along the way, they would be unlocked. No intercoms, no padlocks. It would not occur to any Tirhani to enter uninvited. Not in this neighborhood.

As she got closer to the sea, the air became cooler and wetter. The men she passed along the way often touched their fingers to their foreheads as she passed, a polite gesture of respect paid to most women—so long as they were modestly dressed.

She arrived at the gates of the Ras Tiegan embassy at the city center an hour later and checked in with the records administrator, who gave her the files for the day. In the hubbub of the embassy, she was just another records clerk. Efficient, neat, always on time. The sorting and filing did not bother her. It made her less noticeable. It was not her real work.

Inaya wound in and out of the records office, collecting sensitive files from the ambassador's offices. Top secret files weren't sent via slide or radio or any other kind of organic transmission. Information traversed through the office via clerk courier.

Her husband was a Mhorian shifter. It was why she was permitted to reside in Tirhan. He'd gotten residency as easily as breathing. Hers, as a standard Ras Tiegan refugee, had been nearly impossible. Until she married.

In Tirhan she was Inaya Khadija. She was not registered as a shifter. When she applied for the job at the embassy, it was a simple matter to alter her own blood code so it did not match that of Inaya il Parait, mutant shifter and member of the underground shifter-rights group of Ras Tieg, the Maquis, daughter to violent activists and sister to a rogue com specialist.

If Ras Tieg or Tirhan or any of the rest ever realized how easy it was for a ... thing like her to do what she did, she would spend the rest of her days having pieces cut and bottled and measured in some magician's operating theater in Ras Tieg. And it would be done with a far greater efficiency than was already being done in Ras Tieg with terror squads in their smoked-glass bakkies.

But until then, she was in the heart of the Ras Tiegan embassy, hair covered, head bowed, shuttling top secret correspondence. Her brother Taite would have appreciated the irony.

The records she was tasked with today were three months old, ready to be input into the central database for storage. That usually meant the information was old enough to pose no security risk if the database was infected.

She found a quiet corner in the transcription hall and sat down at a com unit. Com specialists were hard to come by in any country. That skill, at least, had helped her make her own way in Tirhan.

Inaya paged through the folders first. When asked why, she told her supervisors she was verifying that all of the pages listed in the index were included. In fact, it was a cursory scan to see if it was anything she could use.

She fed the pages into the com. Beetles chittered and stirred. She adjusted the chemical composition of the plate accordingly. The best types of com specialists were shifters. Magicians didn't need the inorganic components of a com to speak to one another, and regular deadtech specialists and tissue mechanics—though useful for repair work for inorganic components—often didn't have the gut feel for what the bugs needed. It was about sound, smell, impressions, just as much as intuition. You learned when and how to physically alter the environment of the bugs to get the results you desired. She did with chemical potions what magicians did with will alone.

The com spit out a transparent casing with a cocooned beetle inside, wrapped in delicate white strands of organic com code imprinted with the folder's contents.

She labeled the casing and filled out the deposit receipt. One copy for the com records here, one for her superiors, and one that would go with the casing to the archives.

The com recorded the date and time the receipt was printed in the backup module buried under the floor of the embassy, row upon row of living beetles wrapped in filament. She had glimpsed the room once from the archives. A filtered, iron-banded door had opened briefly, and inside she saw a dark room, heard the low purr of some kind of dehumidifier. Then the door closed, a second filter came down, and there was nothing.

Afternoon prayer signaled the end of her workday. Inaya packed her things and left quietly with half a dozen other clerks; a buffer of anonymity.

Most days, Inaya picked up her son Tatie from the madrassa and spent the evening helping him with his studies while the housekeeper looked after her daughter Isfahan. But today was different.

From the public call box outside the embassy, she called the housekeeper and said she would be delayed. No explanation. Most lines were bugged in Tirhan. The housekeeper agreed to pick up Tatie, and Inaya stepped onto an elevated train headed toward the Ras Tiegan district. The train smelled of peppermint and ammonia, and the floors were covered in a clear organic mesh that kept them clean.

When the train arrived, she waited half an hour more to board another train. This one smelled of smoke, cheap curry, and unwashed bodies. The men on this train did not touch their foreheads as she passed, and most of the women had their hair uncovered. The company was much more mixed. She heard

Ras Tiegan, Drucian, a few snatches of Mhorian. As the train slowed she heard a deep woman's voice speaking Nasheenian, and that made her turn.

Two women dressed in long trousers and tattered tunics sat at the back of the car, smoking. They were older women, their hair shot through with white, faces deeply lined and weathered. One of them was missing three fingers on her left hand, and she turned mid-laugh to look over at Inaya. A jagged cavern of scar tissue stared out at Inaya from the place where the woman's opposite eye should have been.

Inaya shuddered as the train slowed. She pushed the door release and stepped onto the platform—the only one to alight from the train. She hurried down the steps to the street below. Above her, the train moved on.

She waited a full five minutes more to make certain no one had followed her from the train. The train had taken her far south of Shirhazi to a little workers' settlement called Goli that circled the weapons plants. Some of the better towns were owned by the weapons manufacturers and had their own stores, churches, mosques, and entertainment halls, but not this one. Goli was just a squatter town built upon the remnants of an old Ras Tiegan city called Nouveau Nanci that the Tirhanis had obliterated during their colonization of this part of Ras Tieg more than a hundred years before.

The city had never recovered. Inaya had a special place in her heart for the crumbling buildings and empty fountains here. Nanci—the city Nouveau Nanci had been named for—was the city of her birth in Ras Tieg.

The sidewalks were clotted with filth, so she stayed to the edge of the street and picked her way to the pawn shop on the other side of the rail platform. She did not always meet her contact here, of course. They rotated locations according to their schedules. Her contact specialized in selling antiquated books and recordings, and Inaya's husband worked in archaeology and translation. Their meetings were not entirely clandestine, as their purported purpose was entirely within reason.

What they spoke of, however, was not at all reasonable.

Elodie, her contact, waited for her behind the counter. She was a short, pot-bellied Ras Tiegan woman with a pinched little face that reminded Inaya of a stag beetle. Elodie's brother owned the specialized pawn shop, but Elodie ran it.

Elodie greeted her with a warm smile. "I have some things for you in the back," Elodie said.

They walked into the cluttered back room. Her tall, fine-boned brother took her place behind the counter.

Elodie closed the door and made room for her at a battered, stone-topped table stacked with empty take-out containers and bug carapaces.

"Do you have anything for me?" Elodie asked.

Inaya passed her a transparent casing. "Has business been well?"

"Tolerable. I'm hearing some interesting buzz. I wondered what you had."

"Everything I see is three months old."

Elodie sat across from her. Above, a derelict room fan juddered irregularly, emitting a soft *whomp-whomp-whir*.

"Any odd visitors at the embassy?"

"The ambassador scheduled a dinner party with the Mhorians, but it's a public party. No one special."

"Could it be covering another meeting? Do you have the guest list?"

Inaya nodded at the recording. "It's on there. I will be at the party as well. I was worried more about what they're doing funneling money to some magistrate in Beh Ayin."

Elodie picked up the canister and slipped it into the front pocket of her vest. "Beh Ayin? I've heard of revolutionary activity there. A few isolated cases. I assumed it wasn't approved by the government."

"They'd prefer it wasn't. They'll probably blame it on us. Whatever it is, Ras Tieg is paying a magistrate in Beh Ayin a lot of money to stay quiet about it."

"Or house and supply them. I'll look into it. Have you heard anything of Nasheenians?"

"Nasheenians?" Inaya's own surprise as she said it, out loud, startled even her. "At the embassy? No. No more than usual. Nasheenians are notoriously poor negotiators. I don't see many in Tirhan."

"There have been reports from . . . others that Nasheenians have been more friendly than usual with members of the Ras Tiegan government."

"Their Queen is half Ras Tiegan. They've always been friendly."

"These aren't the Queen's people."

Inaya drew a sharp breath. "They've been approached by bel dames, then."

Elodie nodded.

"I haven't heard or seen anything of bel dames in Tirhan. Much of what I've brought is business as usual at the embassy."

"Do you think you're compromised?"

Inaya was quiet a long moment. Was she under suspicion at the embassy? No one had followed her. Her duties and hours had not changed. All the same women still spoke to her. The men remained polite but distant. There had been no changes to her station in years.

"No," she said. "Perhaps your other contact is mistaken?"

"Perhaps," Elodie said. "But it's more than one reporting on bel dames in Tirhan. We're trying to put together a full picture with only a few ragged pieces. We need more women like you at home, Inaya. I know it's safer for your children here, but a woman like you . . . should never have been able to infiltrate an embassy, let alone remain undiscovered so long. I've lost three women to that embassy. You have some gifts."

"I am merely lucky," Inaya said, and knew it was time to go. When the conversation turned to how she accomplished what she did, it was always best to end it.

Elodie passed over a large box made of pounded beetle carapaces. It was tied closed with muslin. Inside, there would be three or four ancient metal and amber casings, transmissions created hundreds of years ago. Her gift to Khos—some old work on Mhorian or Tirhani history, architecture, archaeology. Her cover story for coming out to this poor shanty town at the edge of Shirhazi.

Elodie walked her out. Inaya waited twenty minutes for the next train. By the time she arrived home, the world had gone the blue-violet wash of dusk.

The housekeeper had dinner waiting. Tatie and Isfahan were hungry and fussy. She longed for the day when she could send them out to bring home curry. Khos was not home.

Inaya ate and asked Tatie about his day at the madrassa. He stopped often to wipe at his runny nose and leaking eyes. She pretended to listen to him as he answered her questions, but in her heart, she was telling herself, it's just allergies. Just another sneezing fit, runny nose, itchy eyes. Most children had allergies. They grew out of it.

Not all of them became shifters.

After the children were in bed, she sent the housekeeper home. Inaya sat at her desk for some time, admiring the old casings. What had those people thought the world would become, so long ago? Did they foresee any of this? A world locked in perpetual strife, persecuted shifters, endless contamination, a centuries-long world war . . . .

She heard Tatie snuffling and sneezing from his room down the long hall. After a time, she went to him.

Inaya sat up with her son most of the night. She turned him onto his stomach and told him to tilt his head to keep the mucus draining from his nose instead of down his throat. She kept antibiotics on hand for his throat infections, and her own, but the more of them she could avoid, the better. Resistance to stronger strains of antibiotics happened fast. Soon, he would need a magician to treat all his ills. She'd had sinus infections all through her childhood. Allergies this severe were often the first sign of a shifter's abilities coming to the fore.

She brought him juice, and more tissues, and lay with him after he'd gone to sleep, holding him close, stroking his hair.

It was a risk. She'd always known it was a risk, to have a child with another shifter. But she had expected this from Isfahan, her legitimate child, not Tatie, not her little lizard's child. It would have been easier with Isfahan. Girls were expected to be covered and closeted. Hiding her away during the worst of it, when her shifting came into maturity, would have resulted in very little talk. But Tatie? Pulling a boy from a well-off family out of school? Unthinkable.

Unless we tell them he's sickly, she thought, the way her brother Taite was sick in Ras Tieg. Her brother had barely survived childhood. He'd been allergic to everything. He'd borne the spotty, pale face and skinny frame of a perpetually sick child his entire life.

Please, God, she thought—not my children too.

At dawn, when Inaya finally slept, Khos had still not returned.

Inaya surprised herself when she realized she missed him. When the world looked grim, she found she longed for even the most stifling routine. There was comfort in the waiting, the smoldering—being always on the edge of bursting out, bursting free.

7.

At night, when the moons were in progression, the desert did not look black but dusky violet, the color of a new bruise after a hard fight. The moons wouldn't reach their full size in the night sky for another four years; they were on a twenty-year rotation that took them so close to Umayma that they would make up a quarter of the sky at the height of their progression, and be no bigger than a thumbnail at the end of their decline.

On the night train ride across the desert, heading toward the front from Mushtallah, leaning out the window in the conductor's car, Nyx wondered if life here was better than what it had been up there. There was nothing up there on those hulking disks anymore but abandoned ore mines and shattered spires marking the pressurized gateways of subsurface cities—just ground up bone and bug secretions. The Firsts had waited it out up there for a thousand years while magicians made the world half-habitable. Now the moons were just bloody dust. Some days Nyx wasn't so sure the world down here was any better than what was up there.

The train conductor was an old acquaintance of Nyx's from her days back in primary school. Nyx hadn't gotten through school much past the threes on a schooling tier that went to five. By the time she was eleven she was already spending most of her time cleaning guns with her brothers and teaching her sister how to box.

The conductor slowed the train just before dawn so Nyx

and Eshe could get off within view of the highway. From there, they followed the ribbon of shiny organic pavement and turned off onto the Majd exit where the dunes ate at the road. As the day got hot, they walked down into the flatland sprawl of the broken little city of Basra.

Basra wasn't much of a city, more like a watering hole on the way to grander places like Mushtallah or more strategically important ones like Punjai. Most of the people living there worked at the textile and munitions plant on the southern side of the city, a government-subsidized operation that blew yellow smoke over the city all day and orange haze all night. There was a little cantina on the edge of town called the Boxing Matron. It was one of six cantinas on the main drag. Basra also had four brothels, two laundries, one grocery store, and no mosque. During most prayer times, the woman who owned the tallest building in the city—a fight club—sent a servant up to the roof to call out prayer.

Nyx pushed into the dusty interior of the Boxing Matron, and stumbled over the sandals left at the entrance by other women. She didn't take off her own. She didn't trust anybody in Basra with her sandals, not after what had happened to a pair of hers the last time she tried to act the part of a polite guest in a dried up mining town in the interior.

They were both thirsty. Eshe had the glazed look of a kid left too long in the sun. He stumbled in after her, oblivious to the shoes. Nyx went up to the sticky bar where a leathery, wind-bitten old bar matron with a right hand like a corpse tended the whiskey. She was missing her left arm. She wore a pistol on her skinny left hip.

Nyx asked the bar matron where she could find Suha, but got only a snide little leer in return. Half a buck got her to talk.

"Second floor. Third room on the left," the bar matron said.

Nyx climbed the stairs and banged on Suha's door. Suha met

them with a pistol in her hand, and lowered it when she saw who they were.

"I need you to find me a secure line," Nyx said, pushing past her into the grimy room.

Suha holstered her pistol. "In Basra? You must be joking."

"I need to make a secure call."

"To who?" Eshe asked.

"Since when do you ask questions?"

He frowned.

"You forget I used to be a bel dame."

He rolled his eyes. "Like you'd let anybody forget."

"I can still pound little boys' heads in," Nyx said, and gave Eshe's head a soft shove.

Eshe rolled his eyes.

They went out for a drink and some food, and Suha got her a mostly secure line at a laundry across the street from the Boxing Matron. Nyx punched in a call pattern she'd learned by rote nearly two decades before. She wasn't totally sure it would work, but it was worth the gamble.

The line hissed and buzzed in her ear before going flat. A familiar voice said, "Connecting to?"

"Fatima Kosan."

"One moment."

The operator on Bloodmount put her on hold. The line clicked and hissed again for a long time, then went silent.

"Identification, please," the operator said.

"Nyxnissa so Dasheem."

"One moment."

More waiting. Suha leaned against one of the warm walls of the laundry and spit sen. Nyx leaned against the call box. She wasn't sure if her voice was still on the identity reel the bel dames kept on file. She couldn't imagine they'd purge it, but you never knew.

"Connecting," the operator said.

The line clicked. Then Fatima's voice. "Better be good," Fatima said.

"Was it Chenjans or your girls?"

A long pause. Nyx heard the line hiss and pop again. Then silence. The sound of Fatima breathing, low.

Then, "What does it matter?"

"I want to bring them in. For myself. For Nasheen. Not you. I'm not yours."

Fatima laughed. It started small, like a hiccup, then became a full-throated, repeating laugh that went on for a long time.

Nyx pulled the receiver away from her ear.

Fatima's laughter abruptly stopped. "You know what's coming now, don't you?"

"What do you know about the rogues?"

"I know they're operating out of Tirhan. Little more than that. Before they wanted you dead, they asked a very good source of mine if she thought you'd join them. She didn't, but it's good to know you're worth more to all of us alive than dead. I'd use that to your advantage."

Something clicked and hissed on the line.

"You there?" Nyx asked.

"That's all I can say right now," Fatima said, quickly. "Speak to Alharazad. She can get you inside."

The line went dead.

Alharazad? The Alharazad who had cut up the council twenty years back? Where the fuck was she supposed to find Alharazad? Bel dames died on the mount or in the field.

Nyx stared at the call box for a long minute, then dialed in another pattern.

"Messages," she told the operator.

"Identify yourself, please."

"Nyxnissa so Dasheem."

The connection went dead for half a breath, then opened again.

"One moment. I'm retrieving your message."

The line spat again. Nyx took the receiver away from her ear until it quieted and the operator came back.

The voice said, "One message for Nyxnissa so Dasheem from Kasbah Parait. Message reads as follows: Meet at the Nasser Mosque in Mushirah at dawn prayer on the thirty-second. Possible job for you. Identity phrase: Nikodem. End message.

"Would you like me to repeat this message?"

"No," Nyx said, and hung up.

She stared at the call box for a full ten seconds after she hung up. Kasbah was the name of the Queen's chief security tech. Parait was the last name of one of Nyx's dead partners—Taite il Parait—who was killed during the job she ran for the Queen six years before. Nikodem was the name of the bounty she'd brought in for the Queen.

The Queen had answered the message.

"Anything good?" Suha asked.

"A job," Nyx said. "Possibly the one I'm looking for. I'm going back to the interior. You and Eshe are going to the safe house in Punjai. Three blocks from the old keg."

"You want to separate?"

"That's the job," Nyx said. "Queen's orders."

"You're joking."

"No joke."

"And you want me to babysit a boy that close to the border?"

"You put him in drag, then. I'm out of ideas," Nyx said. She stepped from the alcove and into the humid hall. Suha followed.

"I know it's not my business, but why the hell is the Queen of Nasheen answering your personal messages?" Suha asked.

Nyx walked into the deserted street. Suha trailed after her. The blast of hot, dry air was refreshing.

"The Queen only calls me when she's out of options," Nyx said. "Figured a broken council and a hit on Mushtallah would bring her out, so I checked my messages." She looked at the lavender sky and pulled up the hood of her burnous.

Suha did the same, and pulled on her goggles as well. They trudged up the street. A couple of cat-pulled carts and an empty rickshaw trundled past.

"You don't seem upset," Suha said.

"This is what I was born to do," Nyx said.

"What, get yourself killed?"

"Risk everything," Nyx said. "It's why I always make sure I have nothing to lose."

"You ask Eshe what he thinks of that?"

"Eshe is a grown kid. He can handle himself."

"You're bloody fucking crazy," Suha said.

"You wouldn't be here if I wasn't."

Nyx had grown up in Mushirah, or grown up there as much as any free Nasheenian could grow up in any city outside the coastal compounds. Back then, five was considered a small but legal family size, and after Nyx and her siblings had gone through the requisite three years of inoculations and modifications at the compounds, they were released to their mother's farm in Mushirah.

Mushirah proper was situated along both sides of the Bashinda River, but the Bashinda didn't show up on a map. At the northern border of Mushirah the river terminated in a muddy mouth at the edge of the desert, three hundred miles from the sea. Mushiran farmers used up all of the Bashinda's water before it could get out of the city.

Nyx hitched her way from Basra to the refueling station where local farmers collected bug juice for their farming equipment and personal vehicles. Eshe and Suha were headed for the safe house in Punjai. She'd meet them there in a couple days. It was safer for them if she made this particular meeting alone anyway.

Nyx alighted and started to put on her goggles as she looked out over Mushirah, then stopped. She wouldn't need her goggles here.

After the rolling desolation of the dunes and the flat white sea of the desert the last few days, the green terraced hills around Mushirah were a jarring change of scenery. She began the long walk to the river.

These were the hills of her childhood, the terraced green and amber fields that she had run into the desert to forget. Mushirah was an isolated oasis full of fat, soft, happy people. But the sand was never more than a few hours' walk away, and the trains and bakkies that ferried goods in and out of Mushirah were operated by skinny, hard-bitten desert people who knew how to use a knife for something other than carving up synthetic fuel bricks. Mushirah knew exactly what sort of world lay outside its grassy limits. And to Nyx, the world outside the grassy ring that offered all these soft people a sense of false security was the real world. Anything less than the desert was a dream.

It was the thirty-first, so Nyx had the afternoon to find herself a place, contact Eshe and Suha in Punjai, and get cleaned up before the morning meeting at the mosque. The mosque was an ancient domed relic at the center of the city, on the eastern bank of the river. Six spiraling minarets ringed the mosque. During the call to prayer, all six were staffed with muezzins, all the better to reach the ears of the farmers in the sprawling fields surrounding the city.

Nyx walked into the main square at the entrance to the grounds of the mosque and looked around for public hotels. She remembered that there was a convention complex just south of the mosque that would do fine. Long lines of children followed after their mothers, carrying baskets of starches and giant ladybug cages. The people on the street gave her looks ranging from surreptitious glances to outright stares. Most desert traders didn't come down to the square during the off-season, and bel dames and bounty hunters generally stayed out of rural areas—Nyx hadn't seen her first bel dame until she was sixteen.

If Nyx didn't want to be noticed at the mosque she'd need to buy some new clothes and swap out her sandals for work boots. She probably shouldn't be going around armed in Mushirah, either.

Not visibly, anyway.

She scouted out a hotel in the complex and walked over to the marketplace on the other side of the river and bought some new clothes. She found a public bathhouse and changed, then unbuckled her blade and scattergun and stowed them in her shopping bag. For a handful of change she got herself a bath and had a girl re-braid her hair in a style more suitable to Mushiran farm matrons. Her mother had worn her hair the same way.

When Nyx walked back onto the street she got fewer looks, but the boots hurt and she felt half-naked with her sword in a bag instead of at her back. When she found a hotel, the clerk did a double take when she walked in, but the notes Nyx handed her were mostly clean and certainly valid, and after that she got no trouble.

Nyx spent an uneasy night staring at the main square from the filtered window of her little room. The solitude was strange. She'd gotten used to Suha and Eshe's banter.

There was a balcony, so after it got dark she moved there and leaned over the railing. Nyx was tired and hungry. She ordered up enough food to feed a couple of people, ate it all, then fell into a sleep that felt like water after a day in the desert. Her dreams were cloying things; dark and tangled, full of old blood and regret.

The call to prayer woke her at midnight, and after that she couldn't get back to sleep. She went to the privy down the hall and vomited everything she'd eaten. After, she stayed curled around the hard stone basin of the privy with her cheek pressed against the rim while the roaches inside the bowl greedily devoured her vomit.

I can't fuck up now, she thought, and she tried to hold that thought in her fist like a stone. Instead, thought and reason slipped through her fingers like sand: bloody red and fine as silt.

She realized, then, how close she was to dying out here alone, hugging the stone bowl of a privy in some anonymous hotel room in the town she grew up in.

The thought terrified her enough to keep her awake all night.

✛

When dawn prayer sounded over Mushirah, Nyx waited outside the mosque in the blue light of the first dawn. Her right hand had a tremor now that she could not still, and she was having trouble keeping her eyes open. Her exhaustion was deep, like sleep was her natural state. Standing outside at dawn felt like breathing underwater.

So when a woman passed by her into the mosque and gently tugged at her burnous, Nyx actually made a half-hearted attempt to grab at the scattergun that was no longer stowed at her back.

"Hold," the woman said, and turned to look at Nyx, her fingers still clutching Nyx's burnous.

The woman wore a hood, and in the dim blue light, her face obscured, Nyx didn't know her.

"It's this way," the woman said slowly, deliberately. "I advise you to follow." Nyx remembered the voice then. Kasbah, the Queen's security tech.

"Yeah," Nyx said, and shambled in the direction Kasbah was moving.

But Kasbah stayed firm. "Are you all right? Are you drugged?"

"Of course not," Nyx said.

"You aren't well. If you weren't well why did you answer the summons?"

"I'm fine," Nyx said.

Kasbah released her elbow. Kasbah was a tall, bold-faced woman with good hands and lean shoulders. Nyx thought she would have made a good bel dame, if she hadn't been born a magician.

"I want an identity verification," Kasbah said. She held out a small red patch of paper.

"Been that long?" Nyx muttered. "I don't have any infections. My magician just checked me out."

Nyx pulled a wad of sen from her pocket, tucked it between her lip and teeth. She held out her other hand and pressed her fingers to Kasbah's coded paper. If Nyx was clean, she'd live. If she was contaminated, she'd die.

She didn't die.

Pity, she thought.

The second sun was beginning to come up over the horizon. Women streamed past them into the mosque. Kasbah had her head turned up now to peer at Nyx, and Nyx saw her frowning. Like the rest of them, Kasbah had gotten old. The braided hair that escaped from the bowl of the hood was pale. It was possible to dye one's hair, of course, but in Nasheen graying hair was a sign of strength. Not many people lived long enough to go gray.

Nyx let the sen work itself into her system. It was beginning to ease the pain in her joints.

"I told you I'll be all right. I'm just tired," Nyx said.

Kasbah spent another long moment staring into her face, then nodded. "Come with me," she said.

Nyx followed her into the throng of women heading into the mosque. Kasbah turned away from the group and took her through a low arched doorway. A woman dressed in the black robes of a mullah held the door open for them. When Nyx passed through, the mullah shut the door. Kasbah picked up a hand lantern set in a high niche in the wall. Nyx heard the chittering of scarab beetles. When she looked back, the door pulsed with their shiny, blue-black forms.

Ahead of her, Kasbah continued down the ill-lit stairway. Glow worms lined the stone, but most of them were dead or dying.

Nyx had heard about the catacombs under some of the earlier mosques, but she had never seen them. In a place so vulnerable to bugs and contagion, she couldn't imagine anyone in their right mind burying their dead instead of burning them—especially when you saw what happened to them when the heads weren't chopped off—but it had been standard practice back at the beginning of the world.

They stepped into a low chamber; the air was cool and dry. The walls were dusty red, not stone or bug secretions, but something else, and they had names and dates engraved on them in prayer script, the same written language that Nasheen shared with Chenja and Tirhan. The neat rows of names reminded Nyx of the silver memorial slabs at the coast, and the Orrizo, of course. Nyx put out her hand. The wall felt smooth, like a slab of metal. She pulled her hand away and followed after Kasbah into the semi-darkness.

Kasbah led her through a maze of chambers and then up a short stair. When they came to another door guarded by scarab beetles, Kasbah waved her hand in front of the doorway. The beetles retreated into the lintel. She pushed the door open. They came up in a round cell whose walls were decorated in gilt calligraphy. A swarm of wasps had collected around a light fixture. The swarm pulsed and droned. Three women in dark burnouses sat playing cards at the center of the room on a line of prayer rugs. They looked up when Nyx and Kasbah entered and reached for the guns at their hips.

Kasbah pushed back her hood. The three guards relaxed and went back to their game. The wasps quieted. Nyx wondered which of the guards was a magician. Maybe all of them. Behind the guards was an arched doorway into another room where two more black-clad women stood speaking. When they saw Kasbah, they moved away from the doorway.

Inside, the Queen sat at what looked like a real wooden desk. Behind her, a great metal disk with the phrase "submission to God" engraved in gold was affixed to the wall. All around the top border of the room ran red-and-gold gilt calligraphy that repeated two popular phrases from the prayer rote.

Queen Zaynab was a short, plump woman. Her hair had gone fully white now, a wispy cloud pinned at the base of her skull. Her face was soft and round, and though Nyx saw lines now at the edges of her black eyes and a sagging heaviness to her jowls that had not been there six years before, the Queen still looked far younger than her actual years. She looked the way the women from the First Family houses all looked; women who had lived out their lives for generations behind filters, shielded from the harsh light of the suns and the contagion-saturated winds from the front. The Queen had no descendants, had named no successor, had never married. It was in Nasheen's interests—and therefore, Nyx's—to keep the Queen alive. Especially now. A Nasheen engaged in civil war was a Nasheen soon overrun by Chenjans.

Kasbah gestured for the two guards inside to take up posts outside the door. When Nyx entered, Kasbah shut and secured the door behind her. A wave of scarab beetles descended from the lintel.

The Queen was dressed in a simple vest and tunic and long, too-big trousers. Her burnous was red-brown and had the soft sheen of the organic about it. Nyx had stolen a good many organic burnouses from magicians over the years. They cost a fortune in blood and body parts. It was like being clothed in the dead.

"It has been some time," the Queen said. She did not stand, but gestured for Nyx to sit. "You look terrible."

"I've been better," Nyx admitted.

The Queen exchanged a look with Kasbah. Kasbah appeared markedly older than the Queen, though Nyx suspected they were both sidling up over fifty.

"Looks like you got out of Mushtallah," Nyx said.

"Indeed. Sit," the Queen said.

Nyx eased onto one of the triangular stools facing the desk. Her head swam. She was forgetting something. As she sat, it occurred to her that Kasbah hadn't disarmed her. And no one had properly searched her for organics.

"You appear to be missing your magician," the Queen said.

"The last job you gave me was enough for him. He's retired."

"To Tirhan. Yes, I know."

Nyx wondered what they were playing at. "You called me, remember?"

"Kasbah tells me you were in Mushtallah during the bombing."

"Too big a job for me to pull off on my own."

"I'm well aware of who poisoned my filter and destroyed my city," the Queen said, "if that's what you thought to trouble me with. But I will accept your offer of bringing her to justice."

"So it *was* bel dames." Nyx's right hand began to tremble again. She stilled it with her left.

"Kasbah tells me you recently visited Bloodmount."

"Had a rogue bel dame try to kill me. Turned in her head at the mount."

The Queen and Kasbah exchanged another look.

"The bel dame council and the monarchy have a long history of . . . disagreement," the Queen said. "As is well known. Over the last decade more than half of the members of the bel dame council have been killed or retired and been replaced. These new women are young radicals fresh from the front. One of them in particular has been sowing unrest for some time.

"Now the council is turning away notes that come from the palace and forcing me to rely more heavily on bounty hunters and my own private security forces. They have been recruiting bel dames at an accelerated rate."

"You think the bel dames are putting together some kind of army?"

"Yes," the Queen said.

"With who? They're bloody women, but they can't take over a whole country on their own."

"Three members of the bel dame council are missing. They crossed the border into Tirhan six months ago. The government gave them asylum. Claimed neutrality."

So Fatima hadn't been blowing smoke. "Sorta ambitious, even for bel dames," Nyx said.

"There have been many acts of terrorism this year. Not Chenjan in origin. Bel dame," the Queen said. "Kasbah and her security team believe that some or all of the bel dame council have been conspiring to aid Chenja in overthrowing the monarchy."

"Why? If Chenja wins the war, what does that leave for the bel dames?"

Kasbah stepped away from the door and walked to Nyx's side. Nyx felt a sudden wave of dizziness. Her forehead prickled. When she wiped at it, her hand came away damp. Cold sweat.

"Simply put," Kasbah said, "we don't know."

"But you've got somebody on the inside," Nyx said. "That's the one who got you all this information, right? Why not have her chop off some heads?"

"She was killed in the attack on Mushtallah," the Queen said. "As was her sister, and two of our closest ancillary agents."

"So they weren't aiming for you. They wanted to kill their turncoats."

"I'm sure the Queen would have been a pretty bonus," Kasbah said. "Two decades ago, Alharazad cleansed the council of traitors to the monarchy. We need another Alharazad, and you all but volunteered. Why?"

"I'm no more Alharazad than the Prophet was a gene pirate," Nyx said.

"I have fond memories of you delivering a note that no one else could bring to me," the Queen said.

Nyx rubbed her eyes. "That was a long time ago. I have a price this time."

"I paid your price last time. You squandered your advance on boys and drugs."

"You say that like it's a bad thing."

"I can feed you money until you burst, Nyxnissa, but I can't invest it for you. Kasbah can give you all of the information she has."

"My price," Nyx said.

"Name it," the Queen said.

"Make me a bel dame again."

The Queen shook her head. "You know I can't do that."

"You can try."

"I submitted a petition for your reinstatement six years ago," she said. "There's been no word."

Fatima was telling the truth then, Nyx thought. That made a big difference. It had been worth the trip to Mushirah to find that out.

"So you can't do it," Nyx said.

The Queen's eyes narrowed. "I can pay you whatever—"

"I don't want money!" Nyx said. She slammed her fist on the Queen's desk.

Kasbah jumped forward and put herself between Nyx and the Queen.

Nyx stood. "That's all I needed from you," she said, and turned.

"We are not done here," the Queen said.

"Aren't we?" Nyx said. "You not done using me yet? We all have a price. This is mine."

"You bluff," Kasbah said. She was within reach now. Nyx felt dizzy again, and sat back down. She was sweating heavily, but the room was cool. "You know what will happen to Nasheen if there's civil war."

"I know . . ." Nyx started, then shook her head. She couldn't find the words. "I know everybody's asking a lot from a washed up mercenary."

"Desperate times," the Queen said grimly.

Nyx laughed. She covered her mouth. Kasbah bent over her. "Are you mad?" Kasbah asked.

Nyx started to get up again. She needed to get out of there. She couldn't breathe. She put a hand on the desk to steady herself, get some leverage. She stood, more or less. The world swayed.

"Are you all right?" Kasbah asked. She touched Nyx's arm. Nyx's skin prickled, a massive wave of pinpricks up her arm, across her chest, her neck.

"I'm fine," Nyx said. A ripple of intense heat moved through her body. A breath of fire.

"There's something wrong with her eyes," the Queen said. She took a step back.

"No, really," Nyx said. "I just need to take a piss." She let go of the desk and turned abruptly, just to prove how well she was, how capable.

She tripped over her own feet and fell hard.

Kasbah and the Queen started yelling, but their voices were muted. Nyx felt like she was at the bottom of a deep well. Her head hurt. There was something wrong with her arm. Yes. She had fallen on it.

Nyx tried to push herself up. She saw blood on the floor. She wiped at her throbbing head. Her hand came away bloody.

"I'm just a little tired," Nyx slurred.

Kasbah grabbed her by the braids and yanked her head back. Nyx was too tired to resist.

"Shit," Kasbah said.

Then everything stopped.

9.

The night train to Beh Ayin took Rhys southeast, across some of the most contaminated wilderness in the world. Unlike the interior, much of Tirhan was vividly green and verdant, so full of color it hurt Rhys's eyes. The abundance, however, was deceptive. The blue morning laid bare groves of giant, twisted mango trees draped in ropy clematis and pink-budded coral vine. Swarms of giant flying assassin bugs clotted the air above the groves, and though they were too small to see, Rhys could feel hordes of mites and scalebugs chewing at the mango grove, ladybugs and mantids eating at the pests, and more—mutant cicadas, wild locusts, giant hornets, pulsing wasp swarms with nests so big he felt their heartbeats from the train.

As the second dawn swallowed the first, the train passed through the mango groves and into the sprawl of the jungle. Rhys watched the tangle deepen, the wood darken, the light change as the train pushed on. The trees here were monstrous, three hundred feet high, and the world went dusky violet in their shadow. Giant orange fungus—bleeding yellow pus—cloaked the bases of the trees. He caught the smell of wet black soil and loam, sensed the stir of leaf beetles and mutant worms. The swarms here were vibrant, more alive than anything he'd felt outside of a magicians' gym. It was a beautiful world, and dangerous. Nothing human lived out here. Not for long.

The train went on.

They emerged from the dense jungle sometime around mid-afternoon and ascended into the more habitable part of the southeast, up into mist-clouded hills shorn of their under-growth. Rhys had never been to Beh Ayin, though he knew it was once a political and cultural center for the Ras Tiegans before the Tirhanis invaded and burned it out. The city walls were fitted stone draped in low-res filters. The flat black plain of Beh Ayin was not a plain at all but the top of a low mountain, cut smooth. The mountain was called Safid Ayin, after the Tirhani martyr who died there while trying to burn out the Ras Tiegans. In the end, the Ras Tiegans had thrown themselves from the sheer walls of the mountain rather than face death at the hands of infidels. Not so long ago, by Chenjan or Nasheenian standards—only a hundred and thirty years.

The train moved into Beh Ayin from below, curving into the dark recesses of a smooth tunnel bored into the mountainside. They ascended into the belly of the train station—an airy, amber-colored way post made of delicate arches.

At the station, a thin Tirhani woman immediately approached Rhys as he stepped off the train. She introduced herself as Tasyin Akhshan, special consulate to the Minister of Public Affairs.

"And what exactly is it that a special consulate does?" Rhys asked as they walked along the platform.

Tasyin smiled. She was, perhaps, forty, maybe fifty, difficult to say this far from the filters and opaqued windows of the cities. She could have been far closer to his age, though by the look in her eyes and the set to her shoulders, he doubted it. She dressed in simple, professional Tirhani garb; long loose tunic and loose trousers, pale gray khameez. But out here in the jungle, she wore boots instead of sandals and a deep purple wrap around her dark head. It made her eyes stand out all the more; pale whites with dark centers.

"We spend too much time on mountaintop train platforms,"

she said, "wondering why we've been sent a Chenjan for the translation of Nasheenian."

"I spent seven years in Nasheen," he said, and tried to keep his tone light. He was always a foreigner and a Chenjan, even—or perhaps especially—among the Tirhani. He'd spent his entire adult life proving that being foreign did not make him incompetent.

"Explain that to the Nasheenians," Tasyin said. "Let's get off this drafty platform. It's warmer at the hotel."

The hotel was a squat, white-washed, converted residence at the top of one of the city's artificial hills. A rolling curtain of dark clouds obscured the sky, and the wind was high and cold. They passed through an old Ras Tiegan gate and up a cobbled way that dead-ended at the hotel.

Tasyin buzzed him through the gate and into the courtyard, a tangle-filled garden with broad palms and heart-vines dressed in leaves twice the size of his head. Giant yellow lizards scampered through the undergrowth. The house staff had prepared a late breakfast for them.

Rhys sat down with Tasyin and ate a light meal of lizards' eggs, burnt toast, and cinnamon squash while she explained why she needed a Nasheenian translator at the edge of the civilized world.

"You've done work with the Minister before, so I trust you are discreet," Tasyin said. She crossed her legs at the ankle and started stuffing a pipe full of sen. "I want you to convey my words exactly, and if that means it takes you extra time, so be it. The client is sensitive, but I need to be clear about their intentions. Do you know anything about Nasheenian culture?"

Rhys considered telling her that he'd once spoken to the Queen of Nasheen, but thought better of it. "I'm familiar with several levels of Nasheenian society, yes, and the social mores of each. Are they First Families? Magicians? Or a lower sort?" He was more comfortable with the lower sort. He'd been a member of the lower sort for six years.

Tasyin cracked the carapace of a fire beetle and lit her pipe. "What do you know about bel dames?" she said.

Rhys had trouble swallowing his toast. He covered his discomfort with a mouthful of juice, and took his time recovering. He thought he'd left all of those bloodletting lunatics back in Nasheen.

"You know something of bel dames, then?" she asked, amused.

"I've known a few, yes," he said, and drank again. More than a few. What business did the Tirhani government have with bel dames?

"Excellent."

"You do realize bel dames are not representative of the monarchy? Your negotiation with a bel dame won't be honored by the Nasheenian government."

"We're well aware of how the Nasheenian government operates," Tasyin said. "This is a personal negotiation of goods and services."

"Of course," Rhys said. "I meant no disrespect." A personal transaction officiated by the Tirhani Minister of Public Affairs? Remember that you're an employee, he thought. You're not a consultant.

But there it was, tickling his mind, nonetheless: Tirhanis doing business with bel dames.

"They'll meet with us here for high tea," Tasyin said. High tea was a Ras Tiegan custom, taken up by Tirhanis after the colonization of this part of Ras Tieg. "If all goes well you should make the evening train back to Shirhazi. I'll ask that you don't make any calls or outgoing transmissions while you're here. We'll be filtering the hotel in an hour."

They sat for a few minutes more while Tasyin finished her pipe and Rhys finished breakfast. Tasyin had one of the house staff, a veiled Ras Tiegan girl, show him to his room. He had at least four hours until high tea. If he could not contact Elahyiah and the children, his time would be best spent working on some of his side translations for local merchants and friends of Elahyiah's family. But Tasyin's invocation of Nasheenian bel dames had put him on edge, and there was an old Tirhani city to explore. He wanted a mosque. A cool, quiet mosque.

Rhys exchanged his sandals for sturdier shoes and asked to borrow a coat from one of the house staff. He pulled it on under his khameez and walked back through the old Ras Tiegan gate and into the city center. The red sandstone Ras Tiegan cathedral had been converted to a mosque, and much of its somber, image-heavy exterior had been defaced and resculpted into images of magicians and half-human shifters. There was talk that the Tirhani martyr had been a magician-shifter, an impossible combination that no one had heard of before or since, but that combined with the country's lack of native shifters and magicians meant he saw their images far more often than he was comfortable with.

It was still some time before the next prayer—they only announced four here, not the six he was used to in Chenja and Nasheen—so he simply walked alone into the mosaic-tiled courtyard, across brilliant crimson and green figures of thorn bugs and fire beetles and glittering yellow farseblooms. He stepped into the covered promenade and then under the archway that led into the deep mouth of the mosque. Inside, the air was cool and dim. He waited just inside for his eyes to adjust. Before him stretched colonnade after colonnade, staggered like pawns across the sandy red floor. They supported a peaked ceiling so high and shadowed he could not see its end.

As his eyes adjusted, he walked further into the mosque. He saw light there, at the center of the forest of columns just ahead of him. He followed the column of light, drawn to it like a locust to a body. The light fell into a small round courtyard, by accident or design, he wasn't certain. As he approached, he saw water bubbling up from the center of a smooth layer of red pebbles. A single thorn tree grew there, scraggly and thin, clawing toward the bruised sky.

He heard the far-off scrape of footsteps on sandstone, the low whisper of the wind outside. But as he stepped into the light he heard another sound: the rustle of wings; a bird taking flight. He raised his head, too late. He saw no bird. Instead, a feather floated down from the top of the tree, at the edge of the open roof.

Rhys watched the feather settle onto the crimson stones at his feet. A single white feather.

Something inside of him stirred. Old memories. And there, somewhere deep—an aching, missing piece.

He reached for a pistol at his hip that he no longer carried.

"Rasheeda," he said aloud.

And suddenly the mosque was dead stone, cold and dark. No sanctuary.

God had warned him of what waited back at the hotel.

What he didn't know was why it had taken them so long to find him.

Heavy rain burst from the darkening sky just in time for high tea. Rhys stood on the veranda with Tasyin as the three bel dames walked across the sodden courtyard and under the veranda awning. He noted as they crossed the yard that none of them were shifters. The air did not bend and move around them as it did shifters. That meant none of these three was Rasheeda, the white raven. But that knowledge did not put him at ease. He touched the feather deep in his pocket, and did not take his eyes from the women.

As the bel dames raised their hoods, he peered into each face in turn, looking for some resemblance to women he once knew—heads he had seen beaten, bashed, broken in. Women he had shot or maimed or attacked with some swarm of hornets.

But none of the faces looked familiar. The lifespan of bel dames was notoriously short. He pulled his fingers away from the feather. He needed to step lightly, here. Bel dames were often solitary hunters. These were a pack. It made him uneasy.

When the women stepped onto the veranda, Rhys took an involuntary step back. They were big women—most bel dames were—and the one to his left was a hand taller and thirty kilos heavier than he was. The other two were about Rhys's height, broad in the shoulders. Though they were all dark and wind-bitten, he knew right away who was in charge. She stood a step ahead of the other two, and when she pulled the hood from her mane of tangled dark hair, she assessed Rhys with the same steely gaze he gave her. An ingrained sense of politeness urged him to look away, but this was Tirhan, and in Tirhan, men still had some measure of power and influence. It was all very well to send women from good families into government work, but if their husbands or fathers or sons wished to keep them home, it was their right—a right not often exercised in Tirhan anymore, and seen as rather backward and gauche—but a right nonetheless. Men were still tasked with the care of women. Some days, he found that very comforting.

"Praise be to God," the tallest of the women said, in the prayer language; the only tongue shared by Tirhan, Chenja, and Nasheen.

Rhys said, in Nasheenian, "Praise be to God. Please accept the welcome and hospitality of Tirhan. This is Tasyin Akhshan, special consulate to the Tirhani Minister of Public Affairs, and I am Rhys Shahkam, your translator."

"You learned Nasheenian at the front," the tall woman said. Not a question. She had a thick, burn-scarred neck. Her features were sharp, petite, and the way she pursed her mouth reminded Rhys of a smudged thumbprint.

"I learned Nasheenian in Nasheen," Rhys said. He had hoped they'd mistake him for Tirhani, but his accent was still too noticeable. "Please, be comfortable. The consulate has had tea prepared."

"You have any whiskey?" this was their tangle-haired leader again. Her voice was smoky, with a hard edge, like burnt pepper. She suddenly reminded him of Nyx, his former employer, and he felt a dull ache in his chest, like the throbbing of an old wound. Why had these women come here?

"Beh Ayin is a dry town," Rhys said.

"Ah," she said. She made a gesture to the third one, youngest of them, and slimmer, though still heavier than Rhys. At the gesture, the younger one walked back out into the rainy courtyard and posted herself at the gate.

Tasyin asked for a translation.

"They wanted liquor," Rhys said.

Tasyin showed her teeth. "Liquor before names?"

"Would you like to introduce yourselves?" Rhys asked the bel dames.

"Ah, yes," the tangle-haired woman said. "I am Shadha so Murshida, lead councilwoman of the Muhajhadyn. This is Dhiya, my blooded right hand."

"Dhiya," the tall one said.

Rhys wasn't sure how to translate "Muhajhadyn." It wasn't a term he was familiar with, so he left it out. In Tirhan, they used the term Muhajhadeen as the title of their Minister of War. This sounded similar, but that didn't mean it was anything like its homonym. He'd learned that the hard way with many Chenjan and Nasheenian words.

Shadha paced around her chair, like a cat. It was a full minute before she sat.

Tasyin waited for her to sit, then followed suit.

Rhys and Dhiya remained standing.

Tasyin exchanged some pleasantries, through Rhys, to Shadha. They drank tea. Or, rather, Tasyin drank tea. Shadha fidgeted. She kept her hands on the table, as was polite among Nasheenians doing business—especially bel dames—but she was obviously uncomfortable with it. Keeping your hands on the table proved you weren't holding a weapon. Holding a weapon while in negotiations was a foreign concept in Tirhan. Tasyin wouldn't appreciate the gesture, but Rhys did. He didn't like it when he couldn't see a bel dame's hands.

Shadha tired quickly of Tirhani politeness and said, "Are we going to talk about the shit I humped across the mountain, or fuck over tea for another hour?"

Rhys translated, "She'd like to know if you're interested in beginning negotiations."

"Of course," Tasyin said, "if she's brought me the item she promised."

"She wants to see the goods," Rhys said to Shadha.

Shadha gestured to Dhiya.

The tall bel dame shrugged out of a small pack set low on her back, hidden beneath her burnous.

Rhys watched her carefully untie the leather pack. She reached inside and unwrapped a clear cylinder half-filled with what looked like gray sand. She set the cylinder at the center of the table, next to the tea biscuits.

Tasyin peered through the opaque cylinder. Rhys knew it wasn't glass; the composition of the material was all wrong for glass. Rhys guessed it was organic. His fingers tingled. Something whispered at the edge of his mind. If there was some kind of bug in the jar, or the sand was laced with something organic, it was nothing that would speak to him, nothing he could identify, not that that meant anything—he was a notoriously poor magician, which is why he'd never actually earned the title in Nasheen.

"I want a demonstration," Tasyin said. "This is nothing but desert silt." She reached out and tapped the container.

Rhys translated.

Shadha snorted. "Tell that soft bitch to get it to a magician and lock it down. She wants a demonstration? You tap that thing yourself. You watch."

Tasyin waited.

Rhys translated.

"Well?" Tasyin said.

Rhys shook his head. "Special consulate, if this is an organic contagion that—"

"Do as she says," Tasyin said, hard.

"Pardon, mother," Rhys said, using the honorific given a Tirhani crone, one whose only children were those orphaned in the conflict between Tirhan and Ras Tieg. It had once been a polite term, he knew, but had since fallen into slang as a derogatory name for a bitter old woman who had given up prayer and never married. "I was hired as a translator, not a beast."

Shadha, following their interaction with her eyes, said, "It won't kill you. It's sealed. Only a magician can open it."

Rhys looked again at the cylinder. He did not volunteer his paltry magician's skill.

"What does she say?" Tasyin asked.

"She says only a magician can open it."

Rhys hesitated a moment more. Tirhanis bought, sold, and manufactured weapons. He was under no illusion that the contents of the cylinder were innocuous. But he still felt that itch in his mind, that desire to know, to understand, the presence he felt locked inside the container.

He reached toward the cylinder.

As he did, the whisper at the back of his mind intensified. Something hissed and spat. His fingers touched the container. The dead sand leapt toward him like something alive. He jerked his hand away. The container toppled onto its side.

Tasyin was stone-faced in her seat. Shadha's smile was grim.

"It's hungry," Shadha said. "That's why it's gray. Up north, that stuff is red as fresh blood. I don't know how long it lasts before it needs to eat. You'll want to get it to your magicians soon. Get it fed."

Rhys translated for Tasyin.

"What does it eat?" Tasyin asked.

"What do you think, woman?" Shadha said. "It eats blood."

Rhys translated, and Tasyin asked, "Whose blood? Not yours or mine? Just his?"

"Oh, it would eat ours too," Shadha said, "but Dhiya's bleeding out, you know. The sand has rules. Fucked up rules, but rules nonetheless. It doesn't kill bleeding women. This stuff is wild up north, but the nomads worked out ways to live on it."

Rhys tried to muddle out a polite way to use the word "menstruation." In Tirhani, it was a mildly dirty word, and "bleeding" generally referred to something that only pertained to martyrs.

"It does not attack women who . . . are at the end of their cycle," he said.

Tasyin's eyes widened. He was doubly glad he hadn't used the dirtier term.

"How did you bring it down here?" Tasyin asked. "Something this volatile . . . if it got out . . ."

Rhys muddled through a translation of that. "How did you get it out of the desert without contaminating everything you contacted?"

"I told you—it has rules," Shadha said. "Draw a circle around it, you can contain it. Break the circle, you die. It's less likely to eat up women, and it won't eat a woman who's bleeding out. But boys, men, dogs . . . shifters. Yes, it will eat them just like you and me eat scaled chickens and cheese."

Rhys translated. They didn't have scaled chickens in Tirhan. He said "lizards" instead.

"All right," Tasyin said. "I do have magicians on call, should we reach an agreement. But I still have no guarantee that what you're here to sell me will do what you propose. You could have miniature flesh beetles in there tailored to male blood codes. Useful in itself, certainly, but not what I'm here to bargain for. I need to know where this contagion came from, and who my contact is on how to use it."

Shadha listened to the translation with head cocked, fingers splayed on the table.

"It's wild, not grown in a magicians' gym or organic tech lab. That's all we know. If you want more, we can get you more. But I don't think you have a chance in hell of replicating it. I know a team that's been trying for fifty years. But I can tap the source. If Tirhan wants it, I can get you access to it."

"You do know my next question, of course," Tasyin said when Rhys had finished translating. "Why bring this to us? Why not Nasheen? If it does as you say, your magicians could tailor it to win your war for you."

Shadha shook her shaggy head. "Nasheen does not possess this weapon. The bel dames do. Smart bel dames aren't looking for an end to the war, just an end to the monarchy. We know Tirhan isn't looking for an end, either. What happens to your war economy then? All we ask is your support of the bel dames in Nasheen when the time comes."

"Oh, is that all?" Tasyin said lightly. She perched at the edge of her chair now. "I'll speak with my superiors. We'll need to test this . . . gift of yours before we make a formal agreement."

Rhys translated "formal agreement" as "blood oath," in

Nasheenian. Bel dames understood and respected blood oaths. "Formal agreements" were just words.

Shadha frowned. She sat back in her chair and glanced up at Dhiya. The corners of Dhiya's mouth turned down, and she turned her palms up flat, as if saying, "What more can you do?"

"We'll end here then," Shadha said. "It's a long way to come for half-assed promises. I could make the same offer to Mhoria and get a blood oath here at the table."

"And who's to say you have not or will not?" Tasyin said after Rhys translated. "You say you give us a weapon your bel dames already possess. A weapon shared by the whole world is a useless weapon, no matter how powerful."

"I offer you an edge," Shadha said. "Tirhan alone. Swear the bel dames a blood oath and it's yours. Tirhan and Nasheen will control the world. Provided, of course, you do not sell it. To Chenja, the Nasheenian monarchy, Mhoria, and of course, not to Ras Tieg. But you wouldn't do that, would you? No, you'd use it to burn what's left of Ras Tieg to the ground. And that would be fine with us, you understand? We'll expect a deal soon. I want this done before the season turns.

"There is a great shift coming, woman," Shadha continued, pushing back from her seat. Dhiya moved away from the table. "You can play partner to all sides or none. It doesn't concern me. What should concern you is whose side you're on when the bel dames take power in Nasheen. Will you be able to match us? Or will we take you by force? That is up to you and your mullahs and ministers."

Shadha joined Dhiya at the edge of the yard. Tasyin stood. Rhys rapidly translated.

Rhys asked Tasyin, "Do you want to respond?"

Tasyin's mouth was hard. She gave a small shake of her head. "Let them go."

They watched the bel dames exit the yard. The women joined

their companion at the gate and walked off quietly down the wet street.

Rhys turned his attention to the cylinder on the table.

"You can still make the evening train to Shirhazi," Tasyin said.

"Special consulate—" he began.

"The Tirhani Minister will handle the deposit to your account. You're no longer needed."

"Yes, special consulate," he said, and bowed his head.

Tasyin reached forward and carefully wrapped her napkin around the cylinder. The sand hissed softly. She kept it tucked against her body, braced with both hands. She walked inside.

Rhys remained on the veranda, watching the rain flood the courtyard. His job was done. He needed to get on a train. What happened between Tirhan and Nasheen was none of his concern. Coups in Nasheen were none of his concern, either, not anymore. But Tirhan at war with Ras Tieg...? Chenja at war with Nasheen? Bel dames at war with the monarchy?

Rhys turned his gaze to the metallic sky. He pulled the white feather out of his pocket, remembered bloody days in Nasheen.

"Wars don't end," Nyx once told him. "They just get bigger."

10.

"There's nobody going to save you but yourself," Nyx said. The cantina was crowded and the crowd was boozy. Everything smelled of sen and opium. She knew then that something wasn't right because the smell of opium made her sick—too sweet—and for some reason she felt good.

"What about you, at the front? After you got all burned up somebody had to save you," Eshe said. He was eight years old again, a pouty-mouthed street maggot with hooked fingers and a curve in his spine from too many shiftings. Most kids weren't able to shift before puberty, but Eshe had taken to shifting like a bel dame to bloodletting.

Nyx opened her mouth to say, "I didn't want to be saved," and took another drink instead. Whether she wanted it or not, she had been, and she was sitting here because of the quick work of others. And that knowledge of her dependence, her reliance on something besides herself, always pissed her off.

Too bad no one had figured out how to kill her yet.

It was the same thing she thought every time they brought her back.

✛

"Do you know where you are?"

Nyx opened her eyes. Her head hurt, but the rest of her was dead weight. She was in some kind of tub. Reddish water bubbled

115

around her. The light in the room was bad, or maybe that was her eyes. There was a woman crouched next to the tub, peering at her intently. The woman wore clothes in somber men's colors, and there was something very angular about her face, something very off.

"Nyx?"

"Yahfia," Nyx said.

"I'm pinching your foot. Can you feel it?"

Yahfia had her hand in the water at the base of the tub. The water was so red that Nyx could see nothing of what she touched.

If I'm in the water, why don't I feel wet? she thought. Her face was damp, but the rest of her only felt warm.

Then, suddenly, she felt pressure on her right foot. The pressure became shooting needles of pain.

"Yeah, yeah, stop!" she said, and squirmed in the water. Something moved beneath the bubbling water, something ropy and red-violet, like raw meat.

"Good," Yahfia said.

Her body was starting to hurt—a dull, all-over throbbing. She tried to lift her arms.

"Not yet," Yahfia said. She dipped her hand into the muddied water again and pressed gently on her sternum. Nyx felt more pressure, the promise of pain.

Nyx closed her eyes. "What the hell happened?"

"You made a mess of a mosque in downtown Mushirah," Yahfia said. She reached into the water again, pinched at Nyx's arm.

"Feel that?" Yahfia asked.

"Yeah. Pressure."

"No pain?"

"No."

"Give it a while yet. Can you make a fist?"

She could, but it was like her veins were full of lead, and her palms hurt. There was something wrong with her hand. What she could feel of it, the texture, was all wrong.

"Where is everyone? Where's Eshe and Suha?"

"They're here, in Faleen."

"Faleen? What the fuck am I doing in Faleen?" She tried to get up. Yahfia pressed her hand to Nyx's sternum again. Her firm touch was enough to keep Nyx down. That alone was remarkable.

"You'll be here awhile yet," Yahfia said.

"What happened?"

Yahfia did not look at her. "You were infected," she said.

"What? In Mushtallah?"

"We're not certain when. What was left of you was sent here to Faleen because it has the highest concentration of magicians outside of Mushtallah. Yah Reza called me in because I had your case history. You're lucky I was in Amtullah when the burst hit. Mushtallah is still closed, even the magicians' gateways between the cities."

"How long has it been? How bad was it?"

"A few days. Don't worry about Suha and Eshe. I put them up at the magicians' gym. Eshe wasn't terribly happy about it, but with your status uncertain, neither of them had access to your accounts, and with their relationship to you . . ." Yahfia trailed off, looked away.

"What does that have to do with anything?"

Yahfia moistened her lips. "It's not common knowledge that you're alive. We'd like to keep it that way."

"Who's we?"

"Yah Reza has requested—"

"Is the Queen still alive?"

Yahfia paused a long moment. Too long. Then, "Yes."

"But? There's a but in there, isn't there?"

"Kasbah, her head of security, is dead."

Fuck. Fuck. Fuck.

No wonder Yah Reza wanted to keep her dead awhile longer. Dead women didn't get hunted down by rightfully pissed-off monarchs.

"Yah Reza called you," Nyx said, "but who called Yah Reza?"

"The Queen. She wanted you brought to the Plague Sisters for reanimation. Yah Reza called me in to see if we could do it without them."

So Nyx had been contaminated, like a boy at the front or a body carted home from the field. The probability of Nyx picking up a random infection at the front or in a morgue and harboring it until now were pretty slim. But when? An infection tailored to go off in the presence of a particular individual—like the Queen of Nasheen—could have been planted on her at any time. But that infection should have chemically altered Nyx's blood code. Yahfia should have caught an infection during her last exam; it was why she'd been so confident when Kasbah tested her in the mosque.

"Why didn't you find it?" Nyx asked.

"It's a subtle contagion," Yahfia said. "Instead of propagating itself outside of the cells it replicates itself within a cell and effectively becomes a part of the body. Once the conditions it's been programmed with are present, it mutates and fires from within the cells where it's incubated. This is something I've never seen before—probably not Nasheenian."

Nyx struggled in the tub. Water splashed over the lip. The body moving under the water was hers, but the meaty color was not.

Yahfia pressed her palm to Nyx's sternum again. "Don't. You're not ready," she said.

"What did I lose?" She wasn't sure how much of her actual body was in the water.

"To hear Yah Reza tell it, your skin bubbled and burst. You lost most of the tissue on your arms, neck, and chest.

It meant you had no protection for your organs on the ride here. We wanted to take you via the magicians' gateways, but Yah Reza didn't want to risk infection of the system until we knew what you had. The suns did a lot of damage. I had to give you something for radiation poisoning. I cut out some cancerous tissue."

"But the Queen's alive?"

"It wasn't meant for the Queen. Yah Reza says you never touched her. The infection was tailored to trigger only when you came into physical contact with the intended victim."

"Hold on." Nyx closed her eyes so she didn't have to see any more of her own blood bubbling around her in the tub. "You're telling me I got a virus meant for the Queen's head of security, not the Queen?"

"Yes."

"That's disappointing."

"We can't all be hill assassins."

She opened her eyes again, and saw Yahfia smiling. Yahfia reached out and touched Nyx's forehead. "It's good to see you cognizant."

"I'm too stubborn to die."

"So you keep telling me."

"You going to graft some new skin, or what?"

"I have a flesh beetle skein that I put over you each evening after this water treatment. It should take, but it will be some time." Yahfia stood and washed her hands in the big stone basin at the center of the room.

"How long?"

"Another three, four days." Yahfia wiped her hands on her apron and approached the tub.

"That's too long."

"There's more to it, Nyxnissa." She resumed her seat and neatly folded her hands in her lap.

"What do you mean?"

"Yah Reza wants to speak with you. Kasbah is dead, and the Queen isn't too keen on that. She has some questions for you."

"And if I don't answer right, Yah Reza kills me or turns me over to the Queen, is that it?"

"This is a delicate time, Nyxnissa."

"No shit. How much is that going to cost? For the rebuilding?"

"There'll be some state support, if . . ." Yahfia made a vague gesture.

"If I live."

"If you live."

"Fuck," Nyx said. "Why does everyone want to kill me *now?*"

"Perhaps you've been snooping where you're not wanted, Nyxnissa."

"You heard something about that?" Nyx looked at her sidelong. Information was at a premium right now, and Yahfia was a more or less respected magician. They trusted her with things Nyx couldn't buy with twenty kilos in notes.

"I know you, Nyx," Yahfia said. She sighed. "And I know the Queen wouldn't call you in for a Chenjan dispute. She has bel dames for that."

"Then you know why I need to get out of here alive."

"That is for Yah Reza to decide."

Nyx studied her. "I might need to call in that favor, Yahfia."

Yahfia frowned, averted her gaze. "That is a very large favor. I've mended you half a dozen times, and now I've rebuilt you once. We are even, you and I."

"The bel dames are going rogue," Nyx said. "Without me, you'll see another city go just like Mushtallah."

"There are other agents."

"Nobody like me."

"We are even, Nyxnissa."

"It's not rebuilding if Yah Reza guts me tonight. We're not even if I don't get a chance to live. One last time, Yahfia."

Yahfia pursed her lips. She looked across the tub at the far wall. Nyx tried to turn to see what she was looking at. Pain webbed across the back of her neck, through her left shoulder. She winced. But the struggle had afforded her a glimpse of a giant dragonfly as big as her palm, its blue iridescent wings perfectly still.

"We will see what Yah Reza says," Yahfia said.

"And if she says I die?"

Yahfia still did not look at her. She moved her hand, and Nyx heard something fall softly to the floor. The dragonfly was dead. Yah Reza's little spy.

"Then I need you to bring me a body," Yahfia said. "As fresh as you can make it."

11.

The magicians' gym in Faleen was probably one of the most secure places in the country, but for Nyx that safety was based on the assumption that the magicians inside its ever-shifting walls were on her side—the side of God, Queen, and country. Right?

Most bel dames had trained with the magicians at one time or another, including Nyx, and loyalty was a tricky thing. When she had come back from the front, the magicians handled her reconstitution in Faleen. After a stint working at the morgues to pay off her debts, they had even taught her how to box professionally. Nyx's memories of Faleen were of pain and blood and body parts.

Yes, loyalty was a tricky thing.

There was a new crop of apprentices at the magicians' quarters. The girls and boys—boys too young for the front but soon to enter government training—helped Yahfia with the restoration of Nyx's skin. A couple other magicians checked in on her that day, women she'd known back when she used to box.

It was full evening, best Nyx could guess by the water clock, when Yah Reza, lean and neat, showed up at the entrance to Nyx's little cell-like room. She gazed at Nyx with her illusionary sapphire-fly eyes. She didn't squint, but her magician-tinted eyes looked too small, nearly lost in the loose, leathery folds of her face. Yah Reza grinned at her while chomping sen, showing red-stained teeth. She was sixty or seventy now, and her matted nest of hair had gone completely white a long time before. She wore it proudly, like a crown.

"You're looking a lot better, baby doll," Yah Reza said.

Nyx lay on a padded slab atop a couple layers of white muslin. The flesh beetle grafts on her back and ass and thighs had already taken. Yahfia had her lying on her back. The apprentices were busy slathering the grafts on her front with organic paste to keep her damp and the bugs fed.

Nyx looked over her body. The papery, foreign-looking skin was oily and wet. Beneath the oil, the skin seemed to pulse faintly as the bugs worked their way into her flesh and fused with it. They hadn't had to cut off her nipples, but she'd lost some breast tissue, and when Yahfia had asked her if she wanted to have fat from her ass taken out to restore her profile, she'd declined. Her tits had always been too big anyway. And she liked her ass just the way it was.

Even so, it was hard to wrap her head around the idea that this too-skinny, small-breasted woman with the oily skin two shades darker than the hue she'd been born with was actually, well . . . Nyx. She wondered how much of her had to get replaced before she became a new person entirely.

"I feel like shit," Nyx said.

"I know that's a feeling you're intimately familiar with," Yah Reza said, "so I'll take your word for it."

"You here to kill me?"

"Are you here to die?"

"Not my intention, no."

Yah Reza snorted. She wore a saffron robe with red bands at the hem and crimson trousers. Cicadas clung to the hem of her robe. A couple of dragonflies circled her head.

"I'm glad you procured yourself a magician to replace Yah Tayyib," Yah Reza said. "I have always been fond of Yah Yahfia. I do have to wonder why one of her standing took on a bit of gutter trash like you. No doubt she favors you."

Nyx grimaced. "Is my magician around?"

"Yah Yahfia, or Yah Tayyib?"

"I'd take either right now."

Even bloody traitor Yah Tayyib. Where had Nyx left him last? Ah, yes—stumbling out the door of an abandoned waterworks in Chenja with a knife in his chest. Her magicians never made out well.

"None of us have seen Yah Tayyib since the incident in Chenja. I have heard rumors, of course. Tirhan is notoriously short on magicians, and welcoming of foreigners like Yah Tayyib. Heidia and Ras Tieg are less accommodating."

The apprentices finished slathering and wiped their hands on the organic aprons they wore. The aprons ate the paste. The apprentices bid Nyx and Yah Reza good day and said they would return in an hour to wipe Nyx down again.

"Do you know who contaminated you?" Yah Reza asked.

"If I knew that I wouldn't be here. What kind of idiot gives you a contagion for the Queen's head of security and not the Queen?"

"Oh come now, has the disease rattled your brain that badly? You weren't the assassin, just the pawn. They moved you to take out the Queen's primary piece."

"She's just a security tech."

"Kasbah is more than her security detail. She's the Queen's primary advisor . . . and her lover. It's like taking away the King on the chessboard, isn't it, baby doll? The game isn't over, but the Queen is left with shockingly little maneuverability."

I'm pretty fucked then, Nyx thought.

Nyx shook her head. "You know I wasn't in on it."

"You're not the self-sacrificing type, baby doll. If I'd thought you purposely contaminated our Queen's little security piece, I'd have cut your throat myself."

Nyx grunted. "Yeah, I grew out of that."

"Most of us have. That leaves us with few options. The Queen may know you weren't aware of the contagion, but I can't believe she'd let you walk away after Kasbah's death. If we feign your death, well . . . I'll have half a hundred of the Queen's magicians nosing around my gym . . . and next thing you know, six of my best apprentices get purged for minor paperwork discrepancies and perhaps an unreported cock or two."

"Don't tell me you harbor boys here."

"I harbor a good many undesirables here."

"Tell her I'm dead. What difference does it make to you?"

"I believe I explained the difference."

"So sacrifice a few boys on my behalf."

"Spoken like a bel dame."

"I need to find out who put out the hit on Mushtallah," Nyx said. "Best guess is there are rogue bel dames involved."

Yah Reza showed her crimson-stained teeth. "Oh, baby doll, it's always interesting when you show up in my gym."

"You do what you got to do, Yah Reza."

Yah Reza flicked back her sleeves, revealing three large locusts clinging to her wrists. The bugs crawled back up into the darkness of the sleeves. Yah Reza settled neatly on the hard stool at Nyx's bedside.

She leaned in close. Nyx could smell the tangy sen on her breath. "Here's what we'll do, doll," Yah Reza said. "I'll wait on what the Queen says she wants to do with you. You sit it out here like a pretty little boy. We understand each other?"

"Perfectly," Nyx said. She wondered what the hell else she was supposed to say.

✦

It was another two days before Yah Reza let her see Suha and Eshe. By then, Nyx was bored and increasingly uncomfortable.

Her new skin itched, and Yah Reza's kid techs weren't very sympathetic. She hadn't seen Yahfia. Whether there was still the promise of help if she could procure a body, Nyx didn't know. But it was what she had.

Suha walked right in, but Eshe lingered at the door. He looked skinny and worn out. Suha, for her part, had dark circles under her eyes. She walked like somebody who'd been walking for days.

Suha dropped onto the stool next to Nyx and said, "I heard you killed the Queen's head security tech."

"Shit happens."

"How you feeling?"

"Fit as a harem girl."

"You're as much a harem girl as I am a mullah," Suha said.

"I need you to make a delivery to Yahfia."

Suha nodded slowly. She spit a wad of sen on the floor, gestured for Eshe to come close. "We figured things might be bad. She got bugs in here?"

Nyx nodded. She only trusted a conversation in a magicians' gym when she had another magician with her to block communication. Two standards and a shifter didn't have a chance. You had a team long enough, you got used to talking around what needed saying.

"What's the delivery?" Suha said.

"That second package in our freezer."

Suha raised her brows. "You kidding? Mushtallah is still closed."

"To civilians. Not magicians. Rumor around here has it they opened up the magicians' tunnels into Mushtallah this morning. Go ask around for Yahfia. Have her escort you to Mushtallah through the magicians' tunnels. Go through here and it won't take you an hour. It's something I owe her."

Suha grunted and stood. Her movement startled a locust on the far wall. It fluttered madly for a long moment, then landed on Nyx's elbow. Her fragile skin tingled. She flinched and sucked her teeth.

Suha waved away the insect.

Nyx heard footsteps outside.

Yah Reza walked into the room. Suha looked the magician over with a surly frown, uglier than usual.

"There's a Queen's messenger here for you," Yah Reza said.

Suha exchanged a look with Nyx. Nyx shook her head. Fucked so soon? she thought.

Nyx closed her eyes. She flexed her fingers. The skin still felt tight. She opened her eyes, turned to look at Yah Reza's leathery face. Yah Reza had put off giving her access to Suha and Eshe until it was too late.

"You can let her in. But I'm not covering up, so she better not be a conservative with a weak stomach."

"Of course, baby doll," Yah Reza said. She walked back out.

"How we running this?" Suha asked.

"My plan just fucked out the window," Nyx said. "Without Yahfia, I got nothing."

"She'd have told you if it was a bel dame," Suha said.

"I wouldn't count on that. Yah Reza plays by her own rules."

The door opened. Yah Reza escorted in a small, cloaked figure wearing trousers and sandals. The little messenger pulled back her hood; Nyx had expected someone young, to match the petite figure, but this woman was middle-aged, her hair cropped short. She had a narrow, severe little face like a stone crag.

"Thank you, Yah Reza," the messenger said.

Yah Reza nodded. She shut the door behind her, leaving the three of them with the messenger. Nyx had a moment of fear. She was broken and weaponless, and the magician least likely to stab her in the back hadn't been around for two days.

The messenger raised a hand. She held out a red letter. "Queen Zaynab sends her regards," the messenger said.

"Excuse me if I don't take that up," Nyx said. She used to poison correspondence for jilted lovers, back in the day. All you needed was a half-assed magician and somebody hard up enough to put on some gloves and deliver it. "You killing me now or later?"

"That depends fully on your answers."

Suha sat back down. Eshe hunched his shoulders and peered at the messenger.

Three roaches skittered in from under the door. Nyx grunted. What was the best way to assassinate her in a magicians' gym? With a magician, of course. The messenger hadn't played her hand yet, but Nyx suspected she'd at least have a low level of talent.

"I'm fit for answering," Nyx said.

"Who approached you about this assassination?"

"I didn't know I was infected any more than they did. My magician said I was clean not a week before. She'll tell you that herself."

"She has. We went over your case before I arrived. Do you know who targeted you?"

"No."

"These are not satisfactory answers."

"You could try torture," Nyx said, "but I don't know that there's much left of me to torture." She paused, eyed the little woman over again. "And you don't look like the torturing type."

Suha spit sen. Eshe shifted his weight from foot to foot. Nyx knew why they hesitated. Kasbah was an accident. This would be on purpose.

"You're entirely right." The magician walked to the edge of the slab and looked over Nyx's ruined body.

"I've bled and fucked and died for this country," Nyx said. It came out whiny, broken, not at all how it had sounded in her head. "Now you want to kill me? I'm out to protect Nasheen. After so much fucking and dying for one country, we're practically the same thing."

The corners of the messenger's mouth turned up, though it looked more like a grimace than a smile. "There are few bel dames still loyal to the Queen. Few who uphold their blood oath. I am sorry we could not add your name to Alharazad's as a true patriot of Nasheen."

Alharazad again. Nyx's stomach knotted.

"So, you going to kill her?" Suha asked in her slow drawl. She spit on the floor again.

"We'll bring her to trial," the messenger said. "There has been no decision."

"No trial, no decision," Eshe said softly. He sidled up behind the messenger.

The messenger eyed him sharply. "I've been tasked by the Queen to bring her in for the trial. It won't take long for a decision."

"Only if she gets there," Suha said.

The messenger knit her brows. The locust on Nyx's arm took flight—straight into the messenger's face. She started, raised her hand to call it away—

Eshe moved so fast that all Nyx saw was his arm whipping into the messenger's kidney. Heard the soft hiss of a short blade. The messenger fell. Suha locked both hands together and delivered a devastating hammer blow to the side of the messenger's head.

The door opened.

Suha jerked back, raised her hands again.

But it was Yahfia. Fast as a shadow, she slipped into the room and shut the door. Almost immediately, a shimmery haze of red beetles bloomed up from the edges of the room and covered the surrounding walls. A perfect sound barrier.

"God be merciful, what have you done?" she said. "Couldn't you wait?"

Nyx grit her teeth. She tried to sit up. With tingling, half-numb fingers, she pulled her legs from the bench and gingerly rested her feet on the floor. Her whole body burned.

"Don't!" Yahfia chided.

"You getting me out some other way?" Nyx hissed.

"The messenger . . ." Yahfia said.

"She's not dead yet," Nyx said. "Eshe, strip the messenger and put her clothes on. Yahfia can escort you out. That buys us time."

"They'll know I'm not a magician," Eshe said. "They can feel it."

"Just keep your hood down. You think Yah Reza's eyes are really that color? Magicians are just as good at making shit up as mending it. Yahfia, you can do a glamour?"

"I . . . you want me to fool half a hundred magicians that he's a messenger? You overestimate my abilities."

"The best way is back up through the magicians' gateway in Punjai. You know it?"

"Yes," Yahfia said. Her voice was rough.

"It's not staffed heavy. By my reckoning, it's not a fight night. Take him up through there and you might pass a couple of rookie fighters and a bored ring matron. Not a madhouse of magicians."

Yahfia shook her head. "Nyx, I don't—"

"What was *your* plan, exactly?"

"I—" Yahfia began. She stared down at the unconscious messenger. "I hoped to reason with her."

"I like Nyx's plan better," Suha said. She started unpacking her pack.

"I liked my first plan better," Nyx said. She stared at the messenger's body. "What can you do with that body, Yahfia? Can you still do what I asked?"

Yahfia's face was stricken. "They won't swallow this deception. They'll blame you for the death. I wanted the body of some unfortunate, not a messenger of the Queen of Nasheen. A dead messenger . . . This is worse than Kasbah. At least you could claim ignorance of Kasbah."

"Like anyone is going to believe that? Listen, you don't have to kill her. She just needs to wake up somewhere else. I need you to think fast on this one, Yahfia. I don't have a lot of cards."

Yahfia firmed her mouth. "I do this, and I never see you again."

"Never again."

Suha handed Nyx a loose tunic from her pack. Nyx tried to pull her arm through a sleeve, cringed.

Eshe helped her put it on. Did he look more grim? Or less? She couldn't tell.

"The body's as fresh as I could make it," Nyx said. "Now I need you. I gave you your life back. You know that? If you lose it again, think of all the extra years you got."

"Hardly a fair trade."

"No? I've been to the front, Yahfia. You know how many boys actually make it back at forty? How many have you seen around? Figure out a way to do what you need to do while keeping the messenger alive and you'll be doing Yah Reza a favor. Tell her if she doesn't you'll turn in her boys."

"She's harboring boys here?"

"Don't say I never gave you anything."

"We should go," Suha said. "I can't get any com out from a magicians' gym."

"Where are we going?" Eshe asked. He began to strip the messenger.

Nyx looked over at Yahfia. "Well?"

"All right. Punjai. As you said." She began to wring her hands. The bugs along the walls shivered.

Nyx shuffled over to Yahfia. Nyx's body seemed to writhe and ripple just beneath her new skin, as if her body wanted to slough the whole skin off. She put a freshly skinned hand on Yahfia's shoulder, met her look. The magician's eyes were wide, terrified.

"I'm going to need a drink," Nyx said. "And a stretcher."

12.

Inaya arrived at the embassy alone, dressed in a tasteful abaya and proper Ras Tiegan headscarf, a wimple. She found the attire often attracted more attention than it dissuaded in Tirhan, but this was a Ras Tiegan party, not a Tirhani one, and she needed to look properly Ras Tiegan, even if it made her face look like it had wings.

The party at the embassy was not one she had particularly looked forward to, but her work demanded she at least make a showing. Relations between Mhorians and Ras Tiegans were not traditionally easy, which was why her marriage was so often commented upon. Part of her was disappointed it did not represent the possibility of peace that people imbued it with.

She met several other women she worked with just inside the embassy gates, and they immediately made their way out of the warm night and into the cooler inner courtyard where the food was set out. It wasn't often Inaya ate authentic Ras Tiegan food she wasn't cooking herself. The smell of curry and fried bread was a delight.

The Mhorians had brought their own spread, kosher meats and cheeses, bland breads and crackers, and a peculiar dish that Inaya had heard was actually a blood soup cooked inside of a cat's stomach.

After a time, she wandered away from her gaggle of coworkers and walked away from the din of talk and whirl of bishts and habits and abayas down to the fountain at the other side of the courtyard. A Ras Tiegan man waited there, tall and lean, with a balding pate and a slight paunch. He had a kind face set with blue eyes, like a Mhorian.

"I see you are partnerless as well this evening, Philie," Inaya said.

"God bless, Inaya. It is ever a pleasure to hear someone pronounce my name correctly."

"How long have you been in country this time?"

He dabbed at his sweaty face with a kerchief. Inaya had met Philie through Elodie two years before. He was special assistant to the deputy ambassador, and spent much of his time traveling between Ras Tieg and Tirhan. She did not envy him his job, though it gave him access to a wealth of information she could only dream of.

"Six weeks in Ras Tieg. Gisele stayed behind this time. She insists that the heat disagrees with her."

"The heat is much better than Nasheen," Inaya said.

Philie shook his head. "How a woman as delicate and refined as yourself endured such a place, I have little idea. You know, I finally met some of those women your husband always goes on about."

"Nasheenian women? They are a varied lot."

"No, no, the assassins. Those women assassins."

"Bel dames?"

"Yes. Inaccurately named." In Ras Tiegan, "bel dame" was a homonym of the Ras Tiegan term for "beautiful woman."

"Oh? I didn't expect Ras Tiegans were interested in them. They don't speak for the government," Inaya said carefully. Was Philie one of the people who'd told Elodie the Ras Tiegans were meeting with bel dames? Or was it some other agent? Inaya couldn't hope to know them all. Her assumption that Philie worked for the underground was a dangerous one at best. Elodie had never come out and said it, merely noted that he was a shifter sympathizer. Feeling sympathy for a cause and risking one's life for a cause were entirely different things.

"There are—" Philie began.

He was interrupted by the arrival of two more Ras Tiegan men, whom Inaya did not recognize: a slight, blunt-nosed man and a beefier young man, both well-dressed.

"Philie, a pleasure to see you here," the slight one said.

"Jaque, wonderful. God bless you. And who is this?"

"I have meant to introduce you for some time. Deni is our deputy ambassador's special assistant to the Mhorian ambassador. Deni, this is Philie, your counterpart to Deputy Ambassador Leone in Ras Tieg."

"A pleasure," Philie said, and they bowed slightly to one another. Philie gestured to Inaya. "Allow me to introduce Inaya Khadija, wife of Khos Khadija of Mhoria."

Deni's eyes widened. "Khos Khadija?"

Inaya mustered up a smile. Shirhazi was a small place for refugees, especially Mhorian and Ras Tiegan ones. Few managed to leave their home countries, and those that did were often not wanted. She and Khos were considered a strange pair because of their backgrounds, and commented on more than Inaya felt comfortable with. This gathering of Mhorians was loosely mixed, but only loosely. Mhorian men and women did not live together. They had constructed entirely different societies on either side of the country's Great Divide. Even here, Inaya watched women with their ornate hair and intricate robes cluster on one side of the yard, and their male Mhorian counterparts, in equally stunning robes and elaborate dreadlocks, milled about the other.

"Your husband is a . . . shifter?" Deni said, as if it were a bad word. Of course, in Ras Tieg, it was.

"Yes. And Mhorian. Among Mhorians it is not sinful."

Jaque kept his tone light. "Yet he is not here tonight watching over his wife?"

"He did not wish to upset our Ras Tiegan partners," Inaya said, still smiling at Deni.

"Excuse my bold words," Deni said, "but how is it a Ras Tiegan such as yourself could possibly——"

"She is a half-breed," Jaque said. "Pardon, from your features and complexion I assumed——"

"A quarter, to be precise," Inaya said. Leave it to a Ras Tiegan to argue blood. Impurities. "My father was half-Nasheenian. My grandfather converted when he fled the war. In Ras Tieg, we have full citizenship."

"Yet you stay here because of your shifter husband?" Deni said. "I'm sorry if my words are forward, but these things concern me, as someone striving to understand Mhorians. I will not ask if you share rooms——I would not be so bold——but what of your children? Do you not fear that they, too, may become abominations? And how is it a Mhorian man knows anything about raising children? Only women raise children in Mhoria. They have a whole cast one belongs to when——"

"I think you are being a little forward, Deni," Philie said softly.

"I'm sorry. I understand Mhorians think differently. I do respect those differences. But you are Ras Tiegan. Are you not worried that your children may become as he is?"

"Perhaps I hope my blood is stronger than his." Wouldn't that be just the thing? Inaya thought grimly.

"Ah, of course. It is women's wombs that determine whether a child is carried to term, but——"

She felt her face redden. If she had a drink, she may have dumped it on him. It was a popular, poisonous lie in Ras Tieg propagated by priests, that women chose to miscarry their non-shifter children, ensuring that only shifters were born. Why women would endure five miscarriages the way her mother had at a whim was anyone's guess. The priests nattered on about women being unknowable. Inaya had a great respect and reverence for God, but it had been some time since she could stomach the words of His priests.

"Deni, I do think that is enough talk of wombs and shifters to an unescorted young woman," Philie said. "Come, join me for some curried rice and we will speak of all things Mhorian." Philie extended his hand.

Deni bowed his head slightly to Inaya. "Of course. My apologies. I am often too forthright, even among our own people."

And I am unescorted, Inaya thought. What concern should one give to a woman whose husband did not see fit to protect her? It was an old Ras Tiegan assumption, but one that was dying only slowly. Unescorted women were still talked to and about as if they were loose women, whores. If her husband had been at her side, no one would have dared speak to her of wombs and bedrooms.

Jaque bowed to her as well and went off with the others, leaving her alone at the edge of the courtyard.

Inaya had left Ras Tieg without much care for where she was headed. She had simply stolen her first husband's bakkie and started driving . . . and didn't stop. She may not have gone as far as she did in a regular bakkie, but it was a prototype sun-powered hybrid from Tirhan, which meant she went twice as far on the full tank of bug juice. When the bakkie finally gave out, it had been full dark for three hours, and she was lost somewhere in northern Ras Tieg, near the Nasheenian border.

The land out there was rocky, barren, full of twisted, sappy evergreens with thorny crowns and bulbous roots. The bugs in the scrub-land weren't as large or as plentiful as they were further south, but she didn't know that then. She had never been that far north. The whole world was a void. A nothing. Just like she felt.

She had wandered most the night before she came upon the border station. It was minimally staffed, just three men. Men like these ones. Privileged, well-meaning, with old ideas about what could and should be done to women out wandering the desert alone. She had spent endless years wondering if she could have done or said something differently that night to make it end some other way.

It had taken her a long time to realize that it was not her and her behavior that was at issue, though she had often thought God had simply punished her for stealing her dead husband's bakkie. But no, it was not God that had caused the events of that night, just as it was not God who beat her mother in the street for being a shifter. It was men, not God, who had done those things, and it was she herself who had retaliated.

And it will always be like that, Inaya thought, watching them walk back to the food tables, chatting and laughing as if nothing ill was said while she stood alone, feeling oily and vaguely dirty for the implication that she would abort her own wanted babies. It will be like that until someone decides to change it. All of it. But how did you change an entire culture? Revolutions were about politics, not perceptions, weren't they?

Not in Nasheen, she thought, and pondered that. In Nasheen, women decided how they would be treated. They policed it. Enforced it. Was there a way to do that without becoming monstrous like them or building a whole new martyr the way the Tirhanis had? Inaya had no wish to be a martyr. But she wondered how she could continue to tolerate a world where men's actions would confront her daughter with the same impossible choice she was forced to make that night on the border.

"Excuse me?"

A young man had approached from the rooms behind her. He was dressed in yellow livery, like a servant, and as she turned she saw he had a clubbed foot. It was an odd affliction, something that should have been easily fixed by a magician. She caught herself staring at it and had to make herself look up, into his face. There was something sly and moppish there, something she did not like.

"And what is it you'd like to ridicule me about?" Inaya snapped.

The man's eyes widened, and he grinned. She decided she liked the grin even less.

"Me? Madame, I was merely looking for the privy. Point the way?"

She pointed.

He bowed, absurdly, and trundled off across the courtyard.

Inaya firmed her mouth. She stared off toward the entrance. Her husband was not coming. He had thought she could handle herself at an embassy dinner, and perhaps that was true. But her whole life, she had expected to marry a man who would escort her. Protect her. Look after her. For a time, she thought she had found that in Ras Tieg as the lesser wife—well, not really a wife, but it suited the same purpose—to an old man associated with the persecution of shifters. He had never known what she was, and while he lived, she was safe. But her husband died, just like everyone else, and then she was alone again. Wandering along a stricken border. Fleeing a household in chaos.

Even after all this time, she still hoped Khos would appear now, looking proud and tall and intimidating, and push all these other men from her path. She wanted protection. She wanted autonomy. But she could not have both.

It is time you learned that no one is coming, she thought, and began walking back into the stir of strained contentment.

13.

Nyx steadied herself with her cane and listened to the radio in the tea shop window. She had her hood up. Suha had nicked an extra long organic burnous with wide sleeves. It kept her a lot cooler, a good thing considering how much she had to cover herself up now that she had baby-soft skin. She was chewing sen, but the pain was still bad, and her new skin itched like she'd ingested six jars of spider mites. Eshe stood next to her, looking anxious and girlish with his long hair and belled trousers. Suha sat on the lip of the fountain behind them, hood up, pistols visible.

The news was all about Mushtallah. Nothing about a rogue bounty hunter. Or a dead Queen's messenger. No news of another slick magician hauled into Amtullah for interrogation.

"You think they think you're dead?" Eshe said, passing Nyx a water bulb.

"Unlikely," Nyx said. She shifted her weight to her right foot and leaned a little more on the cane. She hated the cane, but figured she could use it to bash somebody's head in if the situation called for it. "Even if she killed and skinned the messenger, the glamour would wear off after a while. They'd know it wasn't my body."

"So we got borrowed time?" Suha said.

"Yeah," Nyx said.

"You think they'll send the bel dames after you?" Eshe asked.

"Likely."

"When?"

"I don't know. We don't have much time."

Nyx started toward the bakkie. Suha carried the supplies they'd bought. They were twenty kilometers outside Punjai, on the outskirts of the boxing town of Aludra. Border towns were still the best towns to get lost in. Nobody asked your business.

"You still haven't said where we're going," Suha said.

"I haven't been so sure we'd be alive to get there," Nyx said. Yahfia had escorted Eshe up through the magicians' twisting corridors and into the boxing gym in Punjai to change and wait. They got Nyx out on a stretcher, with a fine cicada glamour that left her skin still slightly ruddy. But no one had died. And Yahfia hadn't broken their cover. Not yet.

"So, where?" Eshe asked.

Nyx spit sen. "We're going to meet the only bel dame who doesn't die," Nyx said.

Suha grunted. "You two should have a lot in common, then."

"You wouldn't believe," Nyx said.

✛

Nyx had Suha look up Alharazad's address with her bounty collector contact at the reclamation office in Aludra. The former bel dame was supposed to be living northeast of Faouda along the border, at the edge of the Khairi wasteland.

Nyx paid for a night at a roadhouse on the way north to Faouda, and slept late. Suha and Eshe were quiet. Nyx let the silence stretch. When Eshe went out to get them breakfast from the restaurant downstairs after midday prayer, Suha sat on the end of Nyx's bed and started taking apart her pistols.

"You really think there's been a coup?" Suha asked.

"I wouldn't be out here if I didn't."

Suha looked up at her, frowned. "You sure about that?"

Nyx watched her. "What do you think?"

"I don't want to run a revenge note, you know? We're in a kettle now if the Queen puts out a note on you. Why not get out of the country, go set up in Ras Tieg? I got no problem with working out of Ras Tieg."

"I couldn't take Eshe with us."

Suha sucked her lip. "Yeah. Fuck, Nyx. I did my time at the front, all right? I've done my time for God."

"You don't have to come. You signed an employment contract. You can break it any time you want."

Suha gave a surprisingly savage shake of her head. "No. Don't do that."

"What?"

"You know I ain't employable."

"I employed you, didn't I?"

"You take risks," Suha said. She raised her head, met Nyx's look. "Other folks don't. I was an addict, Nyx. They can still count the worm scars on my arms. You think I could make money with anybody else?"

Nyx palmed some sen. "Go home, then," Nyx said. "Your mother and sisters can get fucking jobs."

Suha snorted. "You don't know my family."

"They're all alike," Nyx said. "They'll take you for what they can and dump you."

"Not every family's like yours."

"Never said that's what mine did," Nyx said. She tried rolling over onto her side so she could reach the ointment next to the bed. Her new skin protested. She cringed. Suha leaned over and handed her the ointment. Yahfia had stuffed it into her hand before ducking back into the twisting corridors of the magicians' underground quarters. Nyx would remember her look. Furtive, intense—a woman who had just risked everything for a lost cause. Nyx wondered if she'd ever looked like that. Had Nyx ever really risked anything for anybody else?

You've never cared about anybody that much, she thought. Not anybody she'd admit to, anyway.

"First Families as fucked up as ours rule the world," Suha said. "Who says bel dames running things would be any worse?"

Nyx rubbed the ointment onto her new, darker skin. She was nearly as dark as Suha now. She supposed it would protect her from more cancers, but it was funny-looking. At least her face was the same. At least her face didn't look Chenjan.

I'm never going to get laid again, Nyx thought.

"You heard the old stories about the bel dames?" Nyx asked.

"I know all the stories. That was a long time ago."

"You ever think the bel dames want to get back to a time when they were the only ones policing the world? You know what they got away with back then?"

"That's ancient times."

"Not to them," Nyx said. "All we need to do is bring in a body. The Queen does the rest."

"You trust she can do that?"

Nyx rubbed at her other elbow. No, she didn't trust the Queen to fix this bloody mess, but she wouldn't say that out loud. She had an idea of where this was all going, and she didn't like it. She could see the corpses already, the long line of bodies between her and the last rogue bel dame to fall. But she could also see the alternative, and she didn't like that either.

"You really think she'll forgive you for Kasbah? And the messenger?" Suha persisted.

Nyx set the ointment back on the counter. Suha had not raised her head again from her cleaning. Nyx listened to the whisper of oil on metal.

"No," Nyx said.

Eshe returned with breakfast. Suha put her gun back together without looking at Nyx. The silence stretched. Nyx wondered sometimes why people stayed on her team. Eshe, she understood.

He'd stay until he got caught up with some girl, or until the war took him. Suha would stay until she found another job. Or pissed on her family. Nyx didn't know why she wasn't on her way to doing one or the other. Or both.

They ate. Eshe helped Nyx get dressed. Covering up her new skin was agony.

Suha drove, and kept the silence. Nyx liked it that way. Talking about things just made everything messy. She needed silence now. She had a lot to work out.

They turned off the Queen Mushana Way, the highway that would have taken them northeast, toward the far coastal cities. Instead, they followed the pitted track of Road 10, which was the only route in Nasheen that went more or less directly north. The color of the desert changed as they moved north, from pale dunes and blinding white flatlands to crumbling red-brown rock and pitted amber gullies, their bottoms muddy with the memory of water. The rocky gulches became reddish scrubland of stunted everpine trees with enormous, sap-laden cones the size of a child's head. Twisted bulb trees cast red-hued leaves across the sandy soil, their bloated, water-laden roots bulging aboveground where they provided water and shelter from the wind for a dozen kinds of flowering sage and desert grasses. All along the roadway were the broken, twisted remains of abandoned waterworks and irrigation pipelines leftover from the days before they'd drained the aquifers. In the distance, Nyx sometimes saw the outline of a farmstead or a telltale ladybug swarm marking a plot of cultivated land otherwise hidden from view by the rocky landscape.

Most of Nasheen's proper farming went on at the coast or in oases like Mushirah. People who set up out north were small-time homesteaders, most of them fleeing the constant warring along the border and high cost of the coast. The problem with the north was that the bulk of the water reserves had been piped out centuries ago, and what was left was still wild with contagion. The air and soil in the north were just as contaminated; mutant bug swarms ruled the wasteland.

The magicians that had reworked Umayma into a habitable world had been good, but they weren't gods. The bugs they tailored to remake the world had gone rogue and viral half the time. They'd lost control of most of their concoctions. They were still wreaking havoc. The magicians had cleaned up the worst of the problems in the interior over the centuries, but the north was still wild. Only law breakers, rogue magicians, and crazy people settled in the north.

Nyx supposed it was a fitting place for Alharazad.

She knew Alharazad by reputation; most people did. Alharazad had been clearing blood debt for fifty years. Nyx had heard a hundred harrowing stories about bug-addled magicians, cross-dressing Chenjan mullahs, and rogue Nasheenian princesses the old woman had brought in over the years. Bel dames spent most of their time running after criminals in dingy, unfiltered cities, making enemies with other bel dames whose notes they stole, girlfriends they fucked, and sons they killed. Among bel dames, staying alive was an endurance sport, and Alharazad had been the best at it.

They followed the signs for Faouda, but got lost on bug-grazed tracks and back roads. They stopped and asked for directions from a blind creeper with a net full of sand roaches camping out on a lice-ridden sand cat pelt.

Suha followed a sandy paved road around a low, rocky plateau. As the bakkie pulled around the curve, Nyx saw what passed for the town of Faouda in the shallow valley below. Two tall, rusted towers to the north and east were contagion sensors; Nyx had seen a few like them at the front. When mutant bugs or miasmas came in from the wasteland, the towers let out a high, keening cry and saturated the air with a neutralizing agent. Sometimes the bugs got through; sometimes they didn't. When the sirens went off, it was best to turn on your filters and cover up.

They stopped for bug juice outside a rusty little diner. Suha filled the cistern with bug juice at an overpriced pump. Nyx sprayed the bakkie with repellent. Finger-length fire ants crawled up from the seams between the stones at the fuel station.

"I wish we had a magician," Eshe said, grinding one of the giant ants under his sandal.

"Yeah," Nyx said, "but I'm not exactly in favor with any magician on the dole right now." It would take a long time for Yah Reza to forgive her about the messenger. If ever.

"Tell me about this Alharazad," Suha said, capping off the tank. "If her sort are gonna rule the world, I should know something about them."

Nyx peeled off a buck and gave it to Eshe to feed into the big central money repository. "She retired when I was still a bel dame, back before Queen Ayyad abdicated," Nyx said. "There was a big shift in the bel dame council after Ayyad restricted notes to terrorists and draft dodgers. Made the bel dames more an arm of the monarchy than an independent force, you know?"

"And she didn't take to that?" Suha said.

"Alharazad goes by the old code. Nobody liked it, but bel dames take a blood oath to the Queen. That's new since the monarchy, sure . . . we didn't swear to shit before that. But we all swear that her word's God's law. You break a blood oath, you know what happens?"

"Bel dames kill you," Eshe said. He gave her the change. Nyx took it and nodded.

"Yeah, bel dames kill you. Alharazad reminded the council of that after she watched them vote on whether or not to split from the Queen. The ones who voted yes? She chopped their heads off."

"Must have made her real popular," Suha said, spitting sen.

"To some people, sure. Can't pick and choose with the law. You break your blood oath in favor of some old Caliphate law that says bel dames rule the world, and you get taken out for breaking the first blood oath. Not the Caliphate law."

"Is that why you keep taking the Queen's notes?" Eshe asked.

Nyx peered at him. He was running around uncovered, as usual, burnous flapping loosely behind him, no hood, shoulders bare.

"Cover up, would you?" she said. "You're going to get cancer."

He rolled his eyes, pulled the burnous back over his shoulders. "Is it? Is that why you took the note?"

"I took the note because it's what I do," Nyx said. She shuffled back toward the bakkie. She hadn't told them this wasn't an official note.

Suha opened the door for her. "I bet Alharazad thought it was her job to kill half the council, too," Suha said.

"No shit," Nyx said.

Suha shut the door.

Nyx leaned out the window. "Let's have you drive, Eshe."

"Why?" he said.

"Cause Alharazad won't shoot a boy unless she's provoked." She saw Eshe lose some color. "This is why I taught you how to use a pistol," she said.

"And we're lucky he's a better shot than you are," Suha said.

She switched places with Eshe. He started the bakkie and got them back on the road.

Nyx sat up front and watched the pitted landscape roll by.

"She have any kids, Alharazad?" Suha asked.

"Why, you planning on pissing her off?"

"Just wondering if she lives alone," Suha said. "I need to know if I'm facing some old bel dame or a bel dame army."

Nyx grunted. "Her twenty kids all went to the front. Three came back. Crazy girl got killed in a locust storm out along the badlands border. Another girl went so bug-crazy after her year in the trenches she got locked up in a ward in Mushtallah."

"What about the other one?" Eshe said.

"Did you get any rotis or fried grasshoppers when we were back there?" Nyx said.

"Nobody asked me to," Eshe said.

"What, no food?" Suha said. "Shit."

Nyx let them bicker. She thought about Raine al Alharazad, the only one of Alharazad's boys to come back from the front. A boy actually coming back from the front—living all the way to retirement age—was odd enough. But he had come back with strange ideas, too, about how Nasheen should be run. He became a bounty hunter, started hanging around the magicians' gyms in Faleen, recruiting boxers and girls fresh off their own mandatory two years at the front. He was known for his strong moral and religious arguments against the drafting of men, his passionate desire to disband the bel dame council, and his uncanny ability to hunt down terrorists. He believed bel dames were an unregulated army of bloodletters. They answered to no Queen, no Imam, not even God.

He'd recruited Nyx at the magicians' gym when she was twenty and taught her how to bring in a bloodless bounty, kill with her bare hands, and how to drive a bakkie like a bel dame on a blood note.

Ten years after leaving his crew, she put a sword through his gut and left him to die in a gully in Chenja.

So she was really looking forward to meeting his mother.

Eshe drove them deeper into the wasteland. They got lost three or four more times, and finally pulled down a winding dirt drive. Pits of yellowish runoff lined the road. Twisted, cancerous pine trees clawed at the pale violet sky. There wasn't a lot of shade; all the trees were stunted, and the low hills of rubble and stone and battered metal-and-mesh didn't cast much shadow.

The house was built into the side of a derelict that had taken on the form of a corroded hill; bloody amber rivulets were carved into the face of it—traces of the minerals left behind by wind and rain or the interior of the metals revealed after thousands of years of exposure. Alharazad had converted the shell of some old ruin; there were a lot of them out in the wasteland, sky pods and flying machines, abandoned subsurface dwellings and bunkers and sealed, self-sufficient agricultural gardens whose contents withered and died after exposure to the contaminated air. Most of them had been hacked up and broken down for parts, their guts hauled into the interior, but the organic mesh shells remained.

There was a stone porch at the front. The door was round and filtered, not an original entrance. Somebody had blasted or eaten their way in and looted whatever was inside a long time before, but the edges of the entryway had been smoothed, and the hull of most derelicts acted like a smart door most days—letting you see out, but nobody see in. There was laundry hanging on a line at the far end of the porch. The dark, shiny material of the tunics and trousers stirring in the wind was just starting to turn green. When you hung out your laundry in the sun it was to feed the bugs that made up the weave. Expensive stuff.

At the top of the artificial hill, scrub pine trees grew. There was an old-fashioned transmissions antenna up there next to a metal contagion sensor.

Eshe parked the bakkie and turned off the supply of bug juice to the cistern. Nyx picked up her cane and spent a long minute staring at the filtered doorway. There were some chairs on the porch, and a workbench covered in tools and kill jars.

Nyx opened the bakkie door and used her cane to help herself out. The sun was merciless. She felt the heat of it even through her organic burnous. Her skin crawled as the bugs in the weave shuddered and dropped their body temperature.

"Put up your damn hood, Eshe," Nyx said as he got out the other side. Suha muttered something.

Nyx walked across the dusty road. The air was filled with a pervasive whirring sound, like cicadas, only higher in pitch. She saw a lot of dead, winged insects scattered across the road, large as her palm. They looked like mutated black cicadas, the sort magicians used at the coast for minor repairs to filters.

"I hate this crap," Suha said.

Nyx shuffled onto the porch. She looked for a bell pull or a buzzer or a faceplate.

"Suha, go check around back," Nyx said. "Take Eshe with you, and watch out for traps and scorpions."

Suha mumbled something in Chenjan again, too low for Nyx to make out. She and Eshe started to trek around the derelict.

Nyx looked back down the road they'd come. This time of day, Alharazad should have been inside. They all should have been inside. Nyx found a single round window—a new addition, like the door. It was opaque, like the hull. She saw only her own reflection; a broad-shouldered, hollow-eyed woman in a burnous. It was the first time she'd clearly seen her reflection since Mushirah, and it was like looking into the face of a stranger, sick and starving: soft face gone gaunt, eyes too big. It wasn't the sort of face she wanted to present to the world. She pulled away from the window, and heard the scuff of feet on stones behind her. It took a great deal of effort not to reach for a weapon. She turned—

—and stared down the wide double barrel of a shotgun.

"Get the fuck off my porch," Alharazad said.

14.

Rhys arrived home with the evening train. As a general rule, he could keep time by Tirhani trains, but a section of track had been swallowed twelve kilometers out of Beh Ayin by a swarm of giant acid-spitting locusts, and it cost him hours in the hot, moist air while the jungle around him pulsed and stirred like a living thing.

The children were out with the housekeeper. Elahyiah met him at the door. Her hair was tucked under her headscarf. A springy black tendril had pulled free. In the moment she greeted him at the door, he thought that loose curl the most beautiful thing in the world.

"You look like death," Elahyiah said, and laughed.

He cupped the back of her head and pulled her to him. He kissed her full on the mouth. Her surprise faded quickly. There was no resistance, no shock, no displeasure. She weakened under him like ripe fruit, a mango left too long on the tree. It was a heady sensation, sweet, like a drug. A kiss. She responded, nearly always, with just a kiss.

Memory flushed through him. The bel dames in the rain. The sand churning in the glass, and old horrors. Things better left unseen. Things best forgotten. Another life.

Elahyiah and I built this.

God, Elahyiah.

He pulled off her headscarf and pushed her further inside, away from the peering eyes of the street. He kicked the door closed. He pulled his fingers through her loose hair. She gripped him like a spent swimmer. They tumbled together onto the cool tile floor.

He started to pull away her robe, and she stopped him, cupped his face in her hands.

"I think of this," she said softly.

His hands moved up her thigh. "I do too."

"No, I . . ." she looked almost hurt. She bit her lip. "I . . . think of you. I do all that's expected of me. I clean up the children and mind the housekeeper. I pray. And I sit here and wait for you. For this. I think of this all day. You. Here. Us. It feels . . ."

He kissed her. "Hush. I know, I . . ."

"You don't," she whispered fiercely. "You're everything. My whole life. Did you know that? I never thought I could desire a man so much, not even my husband. Is that blasphemous?"

The evening was not long enough.

Later that night, long after the children had been put to bed, Rhys sat at his desk and looked out into the garden. His garden. His house. His wife. His daughters. His father had wanted to sacrifice him to the front. Instead, Rhys had fled into the desert, and built this from nothing.

In Tirhan, the God they prayed to was not that vengeful desert God, it was the God that gave them this beautiful, clean world. A world without locked gates or security fences or filth or blood. Let Nasheen and Chenja fight their wars and destroy each other. He wanted no part in it.

His father, he knew, would call him coward. His father would call him infidel.

Rhys put his books and papers away. He locked up some notes about his translation in Beh Ayin. Whatever bel dames wanted with Tirhan in the wilderness was something he wanted no part of. It meant a loss of face, and the potential loss of a good deal more, to request that the Minister pull him from such assignments. But it protected Elahyiah. It protected Laleh. It protected Souri. Everything he had built. What if those bel dames had known him? What door could have opened there on that blasted mountaintop?

Rhys went upstairs and into the dim of his room. He saw Elahyiah asleep, wrapped in nothing but a silk sheet, the latticed doors open to the ruddy light of the big, round-faced moons, her bare feet exposed. He pulled the gauzy curtain above the bed over another few inches to cover her exposed foot. She would lie like that the same way at midday, heedless of the unfiltered sun.

Elahyiah stirred in her sleep and turned onto her side. He saw the fullness of one bare breast in the red moonlight. Her eyelids flickered, and she smiled at him, still sleepy. He palmed her breast, teased the nipple with his thumb, and leaned in to kiss her.

"I love you," he said.

She pulled him down next to her. "You say it as if I don't know."

"I love you," he said again, whispered into her ear, against her neck, again and again until she laughed and he had to laugh, too, at the absurdity of it. As if she did not know.

"Marry me," she said.

"Yes," he said. Yes and yes, a thousand times yes. He would choose this again and again, until the end of the world.

Now keep it safe, he thought, and moved with her in the darkness.

✝

Rhys woke from a dream of drowning. Not in water, no, but sand. His mouth was full of it, sharp and chalky dry, ground glass. He tasted blood.

He thrashed in his bed and sat up, disoriented, listening to the persistent buzzing from something … somewhere … downstairs.

The call box. He wiped at his eyes and looked first for Elahyiah. She lay curled on her side, fingers hooked into a pillow, her face slack and soft. She could sleep through a sandstorm, that woman.

Rhys pushed out of bed and slipped on his khameez. The dim blue-gray along the horizon told him it was another hour or so before the first dawn, maybe seven in the morning—they kept time by the twenty-seven-hour clock in Tirhan. Trust the government to wake him a full hour before dawn prayer. He had already sent his brief of the meeting with the bel dames to the Tirhani Minister. He could think of no one else who would call at this hour. Another assignment so soon?

The call box was still buzzing as he passed his girls' room. Souri peered at him from the open doorway.

"Da? I dreamed locusts in the hall," she said.

"Hush. It's just the call box." He picked her up. Souri was wide-eyed and covered in a thin film of sweat. He was not the only one with nightmares. He brought her back into the room, across the soft organic flooring. Laleh, like her mother, slept soundly in her bed.

"Stay here. I'll stop the buzzing," Rhys said. "I'll get you something to drink. I need you to be brave, though. Can you be brave while I get the call?"

"I'm scared, Da," she whispered, and curled her little fingers into his khameez.

"All right, hush," he said.

He brought her downstairs with him, heedless of the creaking steps. The only ones in the house who would wake were already awake.

He picked up the call box receiver with his free hand.

"Yes?" he said.

"Rhys Dashasa?" the voice on the other end said.

A cold knife cut through his gut. Rhys hung up.

That hadn't been his name in six years.

He stared at the call box a good half minute. Souri began tugging at his khameez.

"Da, I'm thirsty. Da?"

Rhys set his daughter down and walked with her into the kitchen. His mind had gone coolly blank. He poured her a glass of lime-flavored water and helped her with the cup. He watched her drink.

Dreaming. Nightmares. Too many nightmares.

The call box buzzed again.

"Da?" Souri said.

"Stay here, love," he said. He crossed to the call box again. He took a deep breath, squeezed his eyes shut, opened them. He was awake. He took up the receiver, pressed it against his ear. Said nothing.

He heard the soft, chittering mumble of an open line. Then, "Peace be upon you? Rhys? Is Rhys there? This is the Minister of Public Affairs. I need to speak to Rhys Shahkam please."

Rhys let out his breath. He rested his forehead against the wall. "Yes, Minister?" he said.

"I need to speak with you about your report. Were you coming in today? You know I start my day at nine."

"Of course. Yes. When would you like to meet?"

"If it's not troubling to your affairs—"

"It is never troubling to my affairs to meet with you," he said, and felt a sudden vague tiredness at the expectation of the dance. They circled a few more times, exchanging pleasantries. He agreed to meet her in an hour, downtown—after prayer of course.

Rhys put Souri back to bed.

He dithered in the kitchen for some time, cleaning up ahead of the housekeeper. He kissed Elahyiah and the girls. Then he washed and dressed and walked outside to catch a taxi. The way to the taxi ranks was through the park, so he stepped across the street and onto the gravel path. The blue-gray haze on the horizon was beginning to blossom. He sensed a wasp swarm off to his left, patrolling.

The morning was surprisingly quiet. He slowed his walk, listening. A rickshaw passed down a narrow road on the other side of the park, just visible through the trees. Bugs still infested the park; he could feel them vibrating, humming, pliant and prepared to receive direction . . . but the cicadas were quiet.

Cicadas did not quiet for magicians.

Rhys paused. He could see the other side of the park from where he stood. Unease filled him. The phone call came back to him . . . and the white raven in Beh Ayin.

Rhys held out his left hand at his side, palm splayed, and called for a wasp swarm. The swarm patrolling the street at his left paused, buzzed, waited. He put out a second thread to the cicadas, but could not contact them. Not for the first time, he wished he were a more skilled magician.

Rhys continued walking down the soft path, every part of him humming. His right hand flexed, itching to take the hilt of a pistol he no longer carried. What use was there for a pistol, in Tirhan?

My safe country, he thought. My safe little country. What a bloody fool I am.

He crossed the park. The sidewalk on the other side was empty. Two belching taxis and a rickshaw waited just up the street. He took a deep breath.

Bloody fool, indeed.

Elahyiah would laugh at him. Rhys Dashasa. No one knew him here. Bad dreams and call boxes. Too many bel dames and nervous ministers.

He tried to smile as he got into the taxi.

16.

Alharazad was a head and shoulders shorter than Nyx, heavy in the hips and jowls. The weathered hands that held the gun were sure and steady. The hood of her shiny green burnous was pulled back, and she wore a white turban and a pair of dark goggles. The hilt of a sword stuck up from a slit in the back of her burnous. Nyx wondered if it was the same one she'd used to behead half the bel dame council. Her gloves covered her from fingertips to elbows, and matched the burnous. Nyx saw something of her son Raine in her aged, sun-sore face: the full mouth and square jaw.

"Thought you'd be bigger," Nyx said.

"Off," Alharazad said.

Nyx clattered off the porch and faced the gun again.

"I was told you could help me with a note," Nyx said.

"I don't run notes anymore." Alharazad didn't lower the gun.

Nyx saw movement at the corner of her eye—Suha and Eshe coming around from the back of the house.

Stay fucking still, she thought. Nyx couldn't see Alharazad's eyes behind the goggles.

"The bel dame council is staging a coup," Nyx said. "I need somebody to help me figure who's leading it so I can take her out."

The line between Alharazad's pale brows deepened. She spit a wad of sen onto the porch.

"That so?"

"They set off a scalper burst on Palace Hill a week and a half ago. Lost ten or twenty thousand people, best guess."

Alharazad lowered the gun. "The Queen get out, then?"

"That's why I'm here."

"Tell your friends to stand down."

Nyx raised her hand.

Suha and Eshe came to a standstill at the other end of the porch. Suha's hands twitched at her hips where her pistols were holstered.

Alharazad turned now to look over at Suha and Eshe.

"That a boy you have with you?" Alharazad asked.

"Yeah."

"Mighty strange team for a bounty hunter."

"I've been more than a bounty hunter."

Alharazad lowered her gun. She spent a long moment working her jaw. "I've heard of you," she said.

"I've heard of you too," Nyx said.

Nyx waited for Alharazad to bring up the gun again and blow her head off. They stood in the sun and waited for a good long minute while the mutant cicadas buzzed.

Alharazad spit on the porch again. "Get inside," she said.

"Somebody told me there was a traitor by your name working for gene pirates," Alharazad said.

Alharazad sat across from Nyx at a battered table made from a slab of molded bug secretions. The secreted slab was the slick, too-shiny type that made up the façades of some of the older ruins in the north. Alharazad had her feet up, and smoked a long pipe full of hashish. The whole place smelled like marijuana, and it made Nyx queasy. In the loft above them, Nyx saw the tall, brilliant green fronds of marijuana plants reaching toward the ceiling. Every few minutes, some kind of mechanical device sprayed a mist of water over the plants; the water evaporated in the dry air before any of it reached the cramped living space below.

"I'm a mercenary," Nyx said. "Bounty hunter, mostly. Sometime security guard."

"Yeah. Like I said."

Alharazad barked at Eshe to serve them up a pot of grubs and dandelion heads from a pot that simmered over her battered fire-beetle stove, like he was some kind of house boy. As he sat down, Alharazad patted his head in the absent way old women who were used to having boys around the house did. Eshe flinched, but didn't say anything.

Nyx stared into the heap of boiled grubs and felt her stomach roil. She picked up one of the communal spoons and resolved to get all the food down regardless of how her stomach felt. Her reflection in the derelict's windows had unsettled her. She needed to put on weight.

Suha dug in.

"Fatima sent me," Nyx said. "She thinks you might know something about the bel dames who took out Mushtallah."

"Oh, I have a lot of ideas," Alharazad said. She had taken off her goggles, and her dark eyes were bloodshot. "There were days when I wanted to take out Mushtallah myself."

"Fatima seemed to think you could give me a lead on who they are," Nyx said.

Alharazad's mouth softened, like she wanted to smile. "That so?" she said.

"Why'd you want to bomb out Mushtallah?" Eshe said.

Nyx shot him a look.

"Why not?" Alharazad said. "It's a wasteland of corruption. You think the bel dame council is power hungry, you should spend some time with the First Families. Soft, fat, rich—can't wipe their asses without somebody around to tell them what hand to use."

"Firsts don't bomb cities. Bel dames do," Nyx said. "You've taken rogues before."

Alharazad puffed away. "You making up your own notes now?"

"I'm working for Nasheen," Nyx snapped.

"You need to kill ideas, girl, not people," Alharazad said. "The council's been hooked on the idea of running the country for a good long while. We used to do it, back in the wild days. Back when the whole world was like this." She waved her hand at the dusty landscape beyond the windows.

"I'm a bloodletter, not a politician," Nyx said. "I just take off heads."

"Do you now?" Alharazad snorted. "If that was so, the Queen would have told me you were coming. No, this isn't about a head, is it, girl?" She put down her pipe and fished around in her vest. She pulled out a marijuana cigarette. "You follow an idea, too. You believe the Queen is the rightful ruler of Nasheen. You don't believe as the Tirhanis believe, that the absolving of the Caliphate was an affront against God."

"I don't believe in God," Nyx said.

Alharazad pounded a fist on the table. The flatware shuddered. Soup slopped over the side of Nyx's bowl. The bel dame's face twisted into an angry grimace. "Don't say that shit in my house. You want a bug swarm to pick you clean? This isn't the place to go cursing God."

"Damn," Eshe muttered.

"Save the cursing for shit that's actually happening," Nyx said. She turned to Alharazad. "Rumor has it that half the council may be rogue. I need to know what you've heard."

"I don't hear much out here," Alharazad said. "But anyone with a head can tell you where those bel dames are."

"I know they're in Tirhan, but it's a big country. I need more than that."

"Try Shirhazi, political center."

"You have a contact there?"

"Might be. Old magician named Behdis ma Yasrah. Hard on her luck. You know the type. She's a magician of mine. Smuggled a lot of stuff out before the council broke down. She had some trouble with venom, got herself kicked out of the magicians' circle."

"You think this magician knows something about the bel dames in Tirhan, then? She helping them?"

Alharazad shrugged. "Couldn't say. But if there are bel dames in Tirhan, she'll have heard where. Give her my name and a handful of notes and she'll squeal. She was always good like that. Get you what you need, for a price. Too bad nobody uses voice reels anymore. Might give you somewhere to start."

"I don't—" an old memory tugged at Nyx—a headless body in a trunk, a recording in his pocket. Six years ago Rhys had opened up the recording and found that it contained orders from a bel dame asking a mercenary to drop a note against the same gene pirate Nyx and her crew were pursuing ... Nyx had run the transmission through her voice recognition reel back then, but her reel was out of date. At the time, she hadn't had any way of matching the voice to a name. But if Alharazad had an up-to-date reel ... She could figure out just how long these rogue bel dames had been stirring up shit.

"You have an updated reel?" Nyx asked.

"What, this woman been talking to you?" Alharazad said sharply.

"I might have use for a reel," Nyx said. "Be nice to have an updated one with all bel dame voices and blood codes."

"Huh," Alharazad said. She eyed Nyx over, one long look, then barked, "Boy!" at Eshe. "Go unroll the top of that desk and bring me that amber box."

Eshe pushed his stool back and walked across the spongy floor. He rolled open the desk. Three giant moths flapped out into the hot air. Alharazad caught one in her hands and trapped it under her empty wine glass.

"They're tastier fresh-killed," she explained.

Eshe brought over a roughly rectangular box covered in hard, shiny resin and set it in front of Alharazad.

Alharazad opened the box. Inside was a battered collection of small, thumb-sized canisters. Some were transparent. Nyx could see the lethargic bugs within them stir at the sudden movement. Alharazad picked out a rust-colored canister and handed it to Nyx.

"You'll need a magician to decode that," Alharazad said.

"Yeah," Nyx said. She tucked the canister into her breast binding beneath her tunic.

"Look for Behdis around the boxing gyms in the Ras Tiegan district in Shirhazi. You'll find her. She doesn't keep a regular call pattern I could point you at, but if you tell her I sent you, might be she can help." She closed the box. "The rest I can't help you with. I'm retired."

"Eshe, Suha, I'll meet you outside," Nyx said. "I want to talk to Alharazad a minute more."

Alharazad raised a brow.

Suha jammed in one more mouthful of stew and grabbed Eshe by the elbow. He shook her off and looked back over his shoulder, once, at Nyx. Then they were both out the door. Suha pulled it closed behind them.

Alharazad spit on the floor again.

"You have some love for the Queen," Nyx said, "so why didn't she ever come to you about this?"

"If you'd gotten a real red letter, you'd be waving it in my face.

This isn't official business. This is personal business. I know the difference, myself. What did Fatima promise you?"

"Why wouldn't you help Fatima? Why did she send me here?"

"I told you. Retired."

"I know what you told me. I also know catshit when I smell it."

A slow smile broke across Alharazad's haggard face. "Cheeky woman, aren't you?"

"I'm tired of getting blown up for no good reason."

"A country at war with itself will lose a war with outsiders. That's a rule," Alharazad said. "Nasheen has to be united to win a war against Chenja. The Chenjan civil war that gave them Tirhan extended the war another century. By all accounts, they had us on our knees before that war. Civil war in Chenja gave us a chance to recover."

"We don't exactly have Chenja by the throat right now. We go to war, they take everything. You'd rather the bel dames laid out the Queen?"

Alharazad reached into her pocket and rolled a ball of sen between her crimson-stained fingers. She tucked it into her mouth. "You won't stop the bel dames by killing one of them. And whatever Fatima promised is hollow. She's fighting on the losing side. You ever asked the Queen about who she's lined up next for the throne?"

"She doesn't have an heir."

"Ha!" Alharazad spit on the floor again. Nyx realized the rust-red color had accreted over time; ten years of spent sen and red dirt tracked in over the ancient floor of the derelict.

"The Queen won't give us a real successor," Alharazad said. "She's going to name her body guard."

Nyx started. "Kasbah?"

"They've been lovers for years. Kasbah has daughters. Zaynab's got none. That's a regime change, right there. Three hundred years of royal blood, erased in a single lifetime. Might as well go back to the Caliphate days. Or further, to the bel dame days. Ask me who I side with—a washed up magician who can't do her job keeping rogue magicians out of her Queen's palace, or a council full of bloody bel dames who want to rule the world again. Either way you hack it, it turns out rotten."

"You think the bel dames could end the war if they dethroned the Queen? No. That's like asking Chenja to set up camp in Mushtallah."

"I think the war's going to end, one way or another."

"People have been saying that for three hundred years."

"Chances are, someday they'll be right."

Nyx pushed back from the table, groped for her cane. Bloody fucking cane. "If that was true, then someday the Mhorians would get their prophet reborn and temple built." A fine day it would be, if every Book got its End Days. "Thanks for the recording."

Alharazad spit and stood. The water sprayer above them went off again, dousing the marijuana plants. Little rainbows colored the wall above the door.

"You be careful coming out here again," Alharazad said. "We've got a lot of miasmas coming in from the north, shit I haven't seen in fifty years."

"I'm hoping I won't have to come out again."

"That's what I keep saying, but here I am."

Nyx pulled up the hood of her burnous, turned to go.

"Nyx," Alharazad said.

Nyx paused, glanced over her shoulder.

Alharazad was pulling back on her goggles. "You think long and hard about why you're doing this. Who you're doing it for. You decide you want answers instead of playing fetch, you come back to me."

"There something you want to tell me?" Nyx said.

Alharazad showed her teeth. "I been a bel dame long enough

to see when somebody's on a death march. You got that look. Nothing I can say'll stop you from taking in your note. But if you decide different . . . Well, I got lots to do out here."

"Sure," Nyx said. She walked back onto the porch, shut the door behind her.

Suha and Eshe were standing under the scant shade beneath the twisted skeleton of a bulb tree, hoods up. Suha leaned against the tree. Eshe threw stones at the contagion sensor at the top of the house.

"Cut that out," Nyx yelled. "Let's go."

Suha started the bakkie and Nyx and Eshe piled in.

"She tell you anything useful?" Suha asked.

"Nothing I wanted to hear," Nyx said.

"Where we headed?" Suha asked as she turned back down the sandy drive.

"I don't want to spend the night here at the edge. Head east. Get us back to civilization. I need to call an old friend. And you and Eshe need to do some research."

"Anything good?" Eshe asked.

"Poke around the bounty boards again. Make sure we're not on them. Keep an ear out for Yahfia, too."

"Magicians are like bel dames. They clean up everything among themselves. Ain't none of it going to be public," Suha said.

"What's on the recording?" Eshe asked.

Nyx pressed her fingers to the canister tucked into her binding. "I know somebody who can tell us something about it. Somebody who's got something that might be useful to pair up with it."

She thought about Alharazad's offer. Wondered if it meant things were as bad as they looked. Decided they were probably worse.

16:

Nyx opened the parcel with stiff fingers. She peered inside. She had called up her old mercenary buddy, Anneke, and asked her for an address, not a novel. Yet here it was: a stack of letters from Rhys Dashasa, some of them dating back over five years. All addressed to Anneke. Not to Nyx. Not that she'd expected him to write, even if it was a far more secure way of transmitting messages across borders than calling. But why had he written to Anneke?

She and Eshe and Suha were in Punjai, holed up in a little hotel room with a terrace at the edge of the Chenjan district. The call to evening prayer rolled over the city. It was taken up by half a hundred muezzins out on their mud-brick rooftops. The air vibrated with the sound of it; just another warm, close night in the desert.

She sat on a rickety wicker chair on the terrace with a cup of buni in one hand and the letters in the other. There was a bottle of whiskey and a glass on the table, too, but she hadn't had the strength to open the bottle, and every magician had warned her off the bottle after a stint in the recovery room. Bloody fucking bottle.

Her burnous was wrapped snugly around her. Winter warmth was a different sort of warmth than the summer kind that drove rich First Families out into the surrounding hills and the poorer sort up onto their rooftops. Winter meant sleeping with your clothes on.

She tugged a letter out of the bunch at random. Rhys's neat, familiar script curled across the front of the pale beige paper. She flicked the letter open and found the return address there at the bottom, next to his signature. Rhys Dashasa, his old *nom de guerre*.

Nyx didn't know Tirhan very well, but she knew the city he'd listed: Shirhazi. The same one Alharazad pointed her to. Shirhazi was an inland city. That meant she needed to find some way to get across the border through one of the mountain passes. During winter. She'd heard about snow up in the mountains, and seen some images on the radio, but never experienced it. Frozen water, all around. It sounded bloody awful.

"Bloody hell," she muttered, and put the letter back with the rest on the stool next to her. She sipped at the buni. She didn't like anything about this note.

Suha came out onto the terrace. "You hear what's on the radio?" she asked.

Nyx shook her head. A few muezzin calls still sounded at the outer edges of the city, moving into the desert. Now, though, she could hear the low, tinny murmur of the radio inside.

"They're opening up Mushtallah tomorrow," Suha said.

"What's the final count?"

"Eighty-four thousand dead. Already burned to stop the contagion spreading."

"Any First Families?"

"Huh. Don't know. I'll look into it."

"Do that. I want to know who lost a first born and who didn't."

"Sure." Suha leaned against the railing, looked out over the narrow street below, the flat rooftops. The dark sky had a hazy orange glow, a perpetual haze created by dead and dying bugs of a hundred thousand kinds reflecting the ruddy light from glow globes and other forms of bug light. There were no gas lamps this far from the interior, just the constant piss and reek of the bugs.

"Quiet," Suha said.

"Usually is, after the muezzin."

"Eshe's asleep. Been throwing up since we got in," Suha said. "Tried to wake him up for prayer."

"Fuck's sake, don't bother him with that catshit."

Suha's mouth bunched up. "Don't go mixing his head up with your ideas about God. Let him make up his own mind."

"Because those lies worked out so well for us?"

"Not all of us left God, Nyx," Suha said. She leaned over and neatly uncapped the whiskey bottle next to Nyx and poured herself a drink.

Nyx gazed back out over the balcony rail. Suha's maudlin moods always annoyed her.

"You know I need to look up a guy in Tirhan?" Nyx said.

"The magician? Yeah, I heard about him. You need me to look up a boat?"

"Rather go overland."

Suha gave a slow nod. "At least we're not on the bounty boards yet." She leaned against the rail and gazed over the rooftops, eyes glassy, big mouth set. She worked her jaw for a while. "One of my sisters is a gun-runner," she said.

"I remember," Nyx said.

Suha sighed. "They do a lot of work during the spring and summer running shit up through the mountains and into Tirhan, but I don't know what they're running this time of year. She can probably get us overland. Don't know how long, though."

"I've heard it's a six- or eight-day trip."

"I mean, how long till she can set us up."

"Tell her there's money in it if she wants to play guide."

Suha clasped her hands. They were big hands, too, like her mouth—dark and bruised as wine-stained leather. "You want to take Eshe with us?"

"Where else he going to go?"

"Dangerous crossing for a boy."

"He can shift it."

"Long way to go and stay in that form."

"Since when are you his mother?" Nyx said. "I'm not a fool."

"Just wanted to say it out loud."

"You think he'd stay behind if I asked?"

"No."

"Then don't nag at me. What the fuck do you think he's going to be, Suha? A farmer? I'm teaching him how to survive the front. Boys don't come home. Why don't they come home? Because they learn shit ideas about honor and sacrifice."

"Just saying . . . I don't know."

"He's a Nasheenian boy. I'm not going to raise him like some useless Ras Tiegan noble. Whose fault is it then when he lasts half a day at the front before some Chenjan mashes his face in?"

Suha shook her head. "It's always one shitty thing or the other with you. Ain't there ever a middle ground?"

"No. It's easier to make decisions that way."

Suha snorted.

Nyx gazed at the street again. A group of women passed below, talking in loud, drunken voices. They wore crimson burnouses and had the confident swagger of university students. Smart, rich girls—the sort who would never know death or disfigurement at the front. If they had brothers, they had never met them, or they took the Kitab at its word and relinquished their boys to the front with a final thought: thank God I wasn't born a man.

Nyx let herself wish for a life like theirs; a young body, a future. Why not? She needed a drink.

As the girls passed by the dark recesses of an arched doorway mounted with metal studs, Nyx saw a shadow there at the mouth of it, something more substantial than gaping blackness. The door was already cast half in shadow, lingering at the edge of the halo of light cast across the street from the bug lamps at the front of the hotel.

Nyx turned her head away, but watched the doorway from the corner of her eye. The shadow moved; a figure pulled in the edge of a dark burnous that had a sheen of the organic about it—far too new and expensive for this part of town.

Nyx set her empty cup on the stool.

"We have spiders," Nyx said.

"I saw her," Suha said. "The door? I wasn't sure."

"Yeah, that's the one."

"I have us set up with a back exit."

"If they wanted us, they would have moved already." Why hadn't they moved, then? It was a busy street this time of night, sure, but her place didn't have great security; no filters and one lonely house guard who spent most of her time snickering in the kitchen with the cooks and some spindly Drucian runner.

"We'll need to get out discreet in the morning," Nyx said. "They may be hanging out to see where we're going." Or to see how much we know, she amended. But know from who? Alharazad? Alharazad had told them next to nothing.

"You think they'll follow us into Tirhan?"

"I'm not looking to find out."

Suha cocked her head. "You hear that?"

"What?" Nyx twisted to look into the room behind them.

Suha pulled one of her pistols. "Eshe?" She left her drink on the rail and moved into the room.

Nyx heard a thump, then a bang. She pulled her scattergun and tried to get up, too fast. She stumbled as she came out of the chair. A gun went off. A blast of yellow smoke filled her vision. Chunks of the railing behind her pelted the floor.

She ducked behind the door and brought up her gun. Blood ran freely down her palm and elbow where she'd caught her tender skin on the door. Her skin throbbed.

Nyx chanced a look into the hotel room. The door was busted open. A woman crouched in the hall. Nyx fired. The woman fell back. Nyx twisted into the room. Suha grappled with a second woman near the double beds.

A third came at Nyx from the left, hefting a skinny sniper rifle. Very bad for close combat, Nyx thought as she brought up the barrel of her scattergun and caught the woman in the gut. The woman screeched and fell back. Just a kid, really, soft-faced and clear-eyed and dangerous as fuck. Somebody fired another shot from the door. Nyx ducked and rolled behind the tatty divan at the far end of the room.

Eshe leapt up from behind one of the beds and darted into the hall, knife out. It was already bloody.

"Eshe!" Nyx yelled.

The woman on the floor shot at her again. Nyx swore and aimed the scattergun at the woman's face this time. The soft features shattered. Blood splattered across Nyx's face. She heard more shots outside.

Nyx ran into the hall. Her legs gave out halfway there, and she stumbled, skinned her hands again. She struggled up and burst into the hall, gun first.

Eshe lay on the floor clutching at his gut. Dark blood drooled from a deep open wound. Nyx saw the tail end of a burnous disappearing down the steps. She leapt over Eshe and pulled one of the poisoned needles from her hair.

She hurled herself at the fleeing figure. Her body connected. The assassin collapsed under Nyx's weight and took the full force of the impact. Nyx jabbed her with the needle as they tumbled down the stairs. They came to a halt on the next landing, with Nyx squarely on top of the assassin.

Nyx bunched up her other fist and pummeled the woman in the face. She went limp. Nyx hauled herself up. She saw raw, peeling skin on her forearms; felt blood dripping down her face.

The woman she'd tackled lay still. Nyx pulled back the hood of the woman's burnous. Another kid. Not much older than Eshe. Nyx hit her in the face again with the gun, for good measure, then hauled herself upstairs.

"Eshe!" she called. Her knees trembled. Too much, too soon. Her skin felt like burnt paper.

She crawled up the last couple of steps and dragged herself next to Eshe. She knelt in a pool of his blood and pressed her hands to his wound to stop the rising tide.

"Eshe, c'mon," she said. His face was alarmingly pale. He was conscious, though—glassy-eyed and squirming.

"Fuck," he murmured. "Fuck, fuck . . ."

"Suha!" Nyx yelled. "Suha!"

Suha stumbled into the hall. She was clutching at her hip. Nyx saw more blood.

"They down?" Nyx said.

Suha nodded.

"Help me get him up," Nyx said. "There's a hedge witch across the way."

Suha tore off the end of her own burnous and knotted it around her waist.

"Don't let me die," Eshe whispered. His voice broke.

Nyx felt his warm blood pumping up through her fingers. She clenched her jaw, and refused to look at his twisted face. She stared at her bloody hands instead, trying to keep all that life inside such a little body.

"Please don't let me die." He clawed at her burnous, left streaks of blood. "Please, please."

How many boys had she watched die like this? Please, please . . . Clawing at her, begging for life.

"Get him up," Nyx said. "Get moving."

Eshe started crying. "Don't let me die . . ."

"You're fine," Nyx said. "Everything's fine."

✦

"We need to get out of Nasheen," Suha said.

They stood outside the hedge witch's tin-roofed hovel three streets over, smoking clove cigarettes. Nyx had pulled out one of their organic carbine rifles. Suha kept her pistol out. They stayed in the shadows under the tin roof. The street smelled of dog shit and human piss and some rotting thing at least three days dead left among the heaps of refuse in the alley behind them.

"You think your sister will take us into Shirhazi?"

"You still want to run after those bel dames?"

"Those weren't bel dames back there. I searched them after you got Eshe inside. Forty notes each in their pockets, and one of them had an unlocked slide with her bel dame class schedule on it. They were apprentices. Not the real thing."

"Young and fast is what they were," Suha said. "I put a trap on that door. That one Eshe killed took it out without a hitch. We're lucky we got out alive."

Nyx heard the battered door behind her scrape open, and turned. The witch joined them outside. She was an impossibly tiny, stooped, scraggly-haired woman—not old, just filthy. Her pale arms bore the flowery scars of long years of venom use—one of the reasons she was out here and not treating wealthy patrons at some high-end hotel. Unlicensed hedge witches were a lot cheaper than magicians. Less skilled, sure, but easier to get to and easier to shut up. They couldn't bring you back from the dead, but they could patch up most complaints.

"He gonna live?" Nyx asked. Her voice was gruff. She cleared her throat and spit.

"Looks like," the witch said. She looked at Nyx's scabby arms. "You need to wet that down."

"It's fine," Nyx said.

"That's a new skein," the witch said. Her eyes were better than they looked, then, Nyx thought.

"Yeah?"

"Good chance of infection, you scrape up a new skein like this. Your friend got cleaned up," she said, nodding at Suha. She'd taken a bullet to the hip that the witch had dug out. "Your turn now."

"Yeah, all right. You got something for that doesn't cost a cat's ass?"

"When can we move him?" Suha asked.

"Not tonight," the witch said, and mumbled something in . . . Drucian? Nyx didn't hear that language a lot, and couldn't be sure. "Foolish question. Come inside. There are more women in the street."

Nyx looked into the street again, but didn't see anything.

The hedge witch nodded. "There will be," she said. "Come inside."

"We've gotta keep watch," Suha said.

"Only need one for that," the witch said. "Come," she said, motioning for Nyx. "Someone the boy knows must sit with him. Come."

Nyx grit her teeth. "I should—"

"I got it," Suha said. "Go sit with him."

Nyx sighed.

The hedge witch ushered her into the cramped hovel. A stir of fire beetles chattered in an open brick stove at the center of the room. Jars of beetles and moths and cicadas were stacked all along one wall, so many that they'd collapsed under their own weight. Broken jars littered the hearth. The air carried the tangy stink of fire beetle offal, preservation alcohol, and unwashed hedge witch.

The witch had hung a curtain between the main room and

her sleeping area, where Eshe was. She pulled the curtain back and motioned Nyx inside.

Nyx looked down at him. Pale, skinny little kid. He was naked save for his dhoti, and covered in a thin film of sweat. The witch had packed his wound full of flesh beetles, sewed it closed, and put layers of filmy gauze over the top to absorb the blood and bug excrement. Something in Nyx hurt so bad at the sight of him that she wanted to run back into the street.

Your fault, she thought. Just like all the others.

She knelt next to him, not sure what to do next. Just sit, the hedge witch had said.

So she sat.

The hedge witch brought some kind of foul-smelling tea and slathered Nyx's bloody arms in a stinking unguent even ranker than the tea.

"Sit, that's good," the hedge witch said, and left her again— plastered in sticky unguent and reeking of the dead. She poured the tea out on the bare dirt floor and wiped dust over it.

Eshe stirred. "Nyx?" he murmured.

"Things got dicey back there," Nyx said.

He gingerly touched his dressing and winced.

"You panicked a little," she said.

"I thought I was going to die."

"It's a scary thing, sometimes," Nyx said.

"Only sometimes?"

Nyx patted his thigh. "Someday you might not be so scared." Someday you might even be happy about it, Nyx thought. Then everything would stop—pain, guilt, sorrow.

"I've never seen so much blood come out of me."

"It was a lot," Nyx agreed. She touched his face, then, hesitant. He'd come back in one piece.

And in two years you'll feed him to the front, she thought,

bitterly. You've saved a piece of meat for the grinder. She squeezed her eyes shut.

"What is it?" he asked. "You all right?" He took her fingers in his hand.

She pulled her hand away. "I'll be outside. You sleep this off, you hear? I need you strong for what's coming."

She stood.

"I will," he said.

She turned.

"Nyx?"

Looked back. He was still a little feverish. His face looked terribly plain, and terribly earnest. "I won't panic like that again," he said. "I promise."

"I know," she said, and ducked under the curtain into the main room. Her vision swam, and she wiped away the wet gathering in her eyes. Nothing to cry over, she thought. He's just another body. Just another boy. Something caught in her throat.

She stood in the warm room as the hedge witch stirred her fire beetle stove. The witch clucked at her.

"It is difficult to have boys," the witch said.

Nyx let herself sag onto the dirt floor across from the witch. Her eyes were still leaking. Wasn't a good idea to go out and talk to Suha like that. She wiped her face with her burnous. Her skin throbbed.

"You ever raised any kids?" Nyx asked.

"Everyone in Nasheen has babies. Didn't you?" The witch peered up at her. "Ah, but no, you did not, of course. You became a bel dame instead, yes?"

Nyx felt a moment of unease. Did she just look like a bel dame to everybody? "You can choose how you give yours up. I chose chopping off heads. Sounded a lot better than being a breeder."

"I have seen how bel dames must twist themselves, to be with people. In a bel dame's world, people are things. Meat."

She pointed at the stove. "It is not the perils that kill bel dames before their time. It is the despair."

"Despair over what?"

"They have no one to live for," the hedge witch said, and shrugged. "When they have nothing to live for, they let others kill them. I have seen it many times."

Nyx frowned. "Some career breeder popped out kids from my stuff, probably. They're around. Getting ground up somewhere. Like everybody else's. Why get attached to somebody who'll be dead tomorrow? That's weakness."

"Perhaps those babies are among the women you kill, yes?"

Nyx chewed on that for a while. She'd turned over her genetic stuff when she was seventeen or eighteen, when she went to the front. Those kids would be Mercia's age by now, maybe older. Like the bel dame apprentices.

The witch looked on her with something like pity. It made her angry.

"What?" Nyx said.

"I patch up boys like yours all the time," the hedge witch said. "We save moments. Not decades."

"No use getting worked up over somebody that's already dead."

The witch shook her head. "No, no. When you dare to love, you dare to be free."

"You really are Drucian, aren't you? Syrupy loving-kindness, God-loves-everybody stuff. Catshit."

The hedge witch smiled. It was like watching old leather wrinkle. "I am human. As are you. Though you may not like it."

Nyx stood. "Thanks for looking after him," she said.

She met Suha out front. Suha was tossing stones at a mutant carrion beetle—tall as Nyx's knee—scavenging in the alley behind them.

"He all right?" Suha asked.

"You think there's a hell?" Nyx asked.

"Yeah," Suha said. "Why make up something so bad if life is already like this?"

Nyx grunted.

"Why?" Suha said.

"Because if there is, I'm going there," Nyx said.

One of Suha's stones connected with the carrion beetle. It screeched and skittered off into a nearby pile of refuse. Suha straightened and dusted her hands on her trousers. "Good thing," she said. "There'll be a lot of interesting folks there."

17.

Rhys waited for the Tirhani Minister for over an hour. Some of that he spent washing up in the floor washroom, trying to sort out his muddled thoughts.

"Well," the Tirhani Minister said, when he was finally summoned into her office. "Can I offer you some tea?"

"Certainly, yes," Rhys said. She seemed a bit taken aback at his acceptance, but acquiesced.

"Are you well?" the Minister asked as he took his seat.

"Yes. The weather in Beh Ayin does not agree with me."

"It is a cool . . . complex, place," the Minister said.

"It is," Rhys said.

Her assistant brought them tea. When she was gone again, the Minister said, "Your services were well thought of in Beh Ayin. I do thank you for your willingness to travel on such short notice, and for your discretion."

Rhys sipped his tea. "May I ask, Minister, what happened to the other translator you chose for this job?"

The Minister's face softened. "Is that all? It was thought his presence would be offensive to our proposed business partners. There was some concern over you, as well, though we hoped they would mistake you for a Tirhani."

"Pardon, Minister, but just because they are coarse does not mean that they are fools."

"I understand that. But it was also my understanding that these female assassins of Nasheen's spend most of their time cutting off the heads of their own people, not the heads of Chenjans."

"That is true," Rhys said. "It's also true that they are all war veterans."

"Ah, of course. Well. Can I offer you something to eat?"

"No," Rhys said, suddenly weary. "I would request a favor, however."

The Minister raised her brows.

"I have no further interest in negotiating contracts with Nasheenians. I am happy to serve you in the translation of Chenjan, Mhorian, even Ras Tiegan—but no more Nasheenian."

"Of course," the Minister said. "It was . . . imprudent of me. However, you must understand that time was short. And you did agree to the work. For a fairly sizable sum."

She tapped her desk and pulled out her pay book. Rhys opened his mouth to begin negotiations, but she simply wrote out the amount he had requested in his formal acceptance and passed it to him.

As Rhys took the pay slip, he said, "You do understand that I appreciate the work I do here."

"And I do appreciate having you," the Minister said. She met his look.

"Thank you," he said. He stood. "Peace be upon you."

"And to you," the Minister said. "That is all we seek, isn't it? Peace. The work that we do ensures God's peace in Tirhan. Do not forget that."

"I don't," Rhys said.

He took the receipt down to the clerk and collected his pay. He stopped at the national bank to square a few accounts. On the way back, he paused outside the big central magicians' boxing gym. Only the best practiced there—exiles from every country on the map. He had been inside a handful of times, but his magician's skill was not up to the gym's standards. They were nice enough to him there, of course—magicians in Tirhan were nothing if not courteous—and his acquaintance with some of the more notorious of the exiled magicians made him welcome, if not respected, among them.

When he wanted to practice his right hook, he had to travel further afield.

But instead of heading to the boxing gym or back to his translation office, he got into a taxi and went home.

It was still early morning, and traffic was light. He strolled through the park and went inside.

The housekeeper had arrived, and was dutifully cleaning up the kitchen. He walked upstairs to find both girls playing in their room.

Inaya was still lying in bed, tangled in the sheets. He undressed and crawled into bed with her. She reached out and ran her hands over his shaved head.

"No work today?"

"Not today," he said.

"I'd love to spend the day abed, but I have lunch with my mother and sisters. Then my reading group. You don't want me to sound like a refugee forever, do you?"

"I love the way you speak," he said, and pressed his finger to her lips.

She laughed and pulled her lean, delicate body out of bed. He admired her as she dressed, carefully and fully concealing the body that belonged only to him and God. He watched as she finished covering her hair, sighed as she kissed him and went downstairs.

He rose and walked to the filtered window and gazed onto the quiet street. The sun was rising high and hot now, and he heard the call to mid-morning prayer. For a time, he watched those on the street below move toward the local mosque. He heard the housekeeper below, instructing the girls on the proper prayer form. They were too young to observe even the four daily prayers called out in Tirhan, let alone the six that Rhys had once followed. As the years passed, he found it was easier to adjust to the Tirhani prayer schedule, though there were still nights when he rose for midnight prayer. They were still some of the most peaceful hours of the night.

Though he had submitted to God from the time he was small, he had never thought that peace and God were synonymous until he came to this country. Until he saw how prosperous a country could be. Yes, his family did well in Chenja. His father was a powerful man, and his mothers came from good families—he had wanted for nothing. But the war had touched him, as it had touched all of them. It had eaten most of his uncles, and he had seen castrated Nasheenian men working in the fields his father owned on more than one occasion.

The war was everything even on the Chenjan interior, among the close-knit families of the mullahs who ruled the country. The war made a few men rich there, yes, but not the way it did in Tirhan. He wasn't sure how he felt about that, some days.

But he was done with Chenja and Nasheen and their wars forever, now.

After a time, he realized that the call to prayer had died off, and he still had not prayed. He stood at the window a good while longer before finally pulling down his prayer rug and submitting his will to the one peaceful God he had found on this ravaged world.

✛

When the housekeeper knocked at his door, Rhys was awake and freshly bathed. She handed him an organic paper note with the seal of the Tirhani Minister of Public Affairs. His stomach clenched.

He dismissed her and quickly tore open the note.

It was flowery, polite, and took nearly a full page to tell him that she would no longer be requiring his services.

Rhys sat down on the bed, stricken.

It was not the end of the world, but it was a lucrative contract. It meant spending more time at his storefront instead of lying around in bed with Elahyiah. He remembered the long hours he used to spend at his storefront, from before dawn to after dusk, sixteen or eighteen hours a day, just scraping along. It was the Minister's regular use of his services that had made him financially solvent enough to marry.

When Elahyiah returned, he was sitting downstairs at his desk, staring into the living room as the housekeeper picked lemons with the girls in the yard.

"What is it, love?" Elahyiah asked. She sat next to his chair, placed one hand on his knee.

"The Minister told me that my services . . . are no longer required."

"Forever? What happened?"

"I . . . don't know. I'll work on getting more contracts. I—"

"We have some savings, don't we? It will be all right."

"I'm afraid I've angered her."

Elahyiah laughed. "Impossible. You could never anger anyone, Rhys. Not like that." She touched his hand. "We'll make our way. I can go back to working if you need me to—"

"No. I'm sure it will be fine. It's just a shock," he said.

Elahyiah slowly pulled the scarf from her hair and knotted it in her hands. "I'm sorry," she said.

"We'll be all right."

She took his hand. He squeezed back. They sat together like that in silence for some time as the night deepened and the crickets began their slow song.

"Well," Elahyiah said finally, standing. "If this is the worst that happens to us, we must consider ourselves lucky. Come, I told Ella to make that Ras Tiegan dish you like. The ratatouille." She walked toward the kitchen.

But Rhys did not go after her. He continued to stare at his girls in the courtyard as they counted out lemons on the porch, laughing. He tried to remember a happy time like that from his own childhood. Something warm and tangible. He found very little. He had wanted peace. Just peace. And perhaps happy children. A good wife.

You still have all that, he thought, but there was something nagging at him now, some dull, but insistent urging.

Peace came with a price. Especially for men who had sinned as deeply as he had. He knew, in his bones, that this was not the price. And he lived in terror of what the final price would actually be.

18.

In Tirhan, Nyx could not smell the war. On the other side of the pass, the first thing she noticed was the absence of the tangy reek of bug haze and burst residue. Tirhan was big and green and rolling, and as they descended into the grasses of the valley below, Nyx found herself suddenly claustrophobic, though the stands of twisty amber trees that clotted the landscape were huddled far off the roadway.

Eshe rode on her shoulder in raven form. He slept most of the way, so she kept her burnous up to protect him from the worst of the cold. The air was different here. Cleaner. Colder. Drier than she expected, too, for such a green country.

Suha's gun-running sister, Azizah, had agreed to let them join her caravan. They stopped at a bustling road house at noon and waited out the heat. It wasn't like the dry heat of the desert, but something mild and salty and altogether . . . different. Eshe and Suha prayed with the rest when the call came out from the muezzin on top of the flat tiled blue roof of the road house.

Inside, Nyx found that they didn't serve anything harder than red wine. She bought a couple bottles for the road and pushed on.

"You'll be on your own up here," Azizah said as the hills turned to plots of square, flat-roofed houses set at the center of dirt lots, their gardens and vegetation carefully walled off or walled in.

"We'll set you at the main way, but we head south after this. I don't go through the city center if I can help it."

And as they rounded the next hill, there it was. Nyx had heard all about Tirhan, all about rich, pretty cities. But she still caught her breath. Like choking.

Shirhazi rose from the spiraling plain of blue-tiled houses and outbuildings and warehouses and road houses. A dozen——maybe more——twisted buildings of glass and metal and bug secretions clawed up toward the sky at the edge of a flat, glassy inland sea. The reach of it touched the horizon. Nyx couldn't see the other side. A lake? A sea. Vast, milky blue now in the pale violet sky of late afternoon. She had almost gotten used to the stink of it by then, but the wind hit her hard and hot. She got a choking slap of it. Death——rot from within. A beautiful city, growing fat on death.

Quiet as death, too. No bursts. No street music. No yammering vendors or crazy street trash. Just a low city hum, static.

Azizah dropped them at the crook in the road. Nyx stepped carefully onto the tiled street and pulled on a hat. She wanted back her burnous. It was easier to hide weapons. The long coat and hat she'd gotten from a Tirhani trading post were awkward. She was just starting to get used to the boots. She pulled out the cane and leaned on it a long moment. It was a long walk to the city center.

Suha bid her sister goodbye. Eshe stepped next to Nyx and folded his thin arms against his chest. He stooped a little now after a week in raven form, and his face still had a pinched, angular look to it. "Pretty," he said.

"Alharazad used to be pretty too," Nyx said. "Remember that."

Nyx didn't know Shirhazi, but she and Suha had asked around at the border and again at the road house. The address on Rhys's letters was in a part of town that would have been on a hill back in Mushtallah. Suha spoke fluent Chenjan, and Tirhani was enough like Chenjan that they could all order food and ask for directions without much trouble. Even Nyx knew a little Chenjan, but deciphering some of the more rapid speech in the dialect and making sense of the slang on the street made Nyx's head hurt. Not that Shirhazi seemed to have much in the way of a raucous crowd. The tall, neat figures of the Tirhanis downtown were as clean and unsullied as their streets.

Even the taxi ranks were clean, free of trash and clutter. Folks waited their turn. When Nyx stepped into a taxi downtown, a waft of lavender hit her in the face. She gagged. Only a Tirhani would scent a taxi in lavender, the taste of one of the deadliest bursts at the front.

They chose another taxi and piled in. The driver's beard was neatly trimmed. He had all his limbs and facial bits; his eyes, too, were clear, as if both were originally his own. It took Nyx nearly a quarter hour to realize that what bugged her about their somber taxi ride was the eerie silence. None of them were hacking up bug contagions. She heard no bursts overhead. No burst sirens. She wondered how far she could see in the clear air from the top of one of the huge pillars of glass and metal and bug secretions that dwarfed the skyline. She wondered how anybody got up that many stairs in the first place.

The driver let them out next to a small green park.

When Nyx stepped out of the smoked-glass of the taxi, she was dazzled by the light. She tugged at the brim of her hat, and wished she'd brought her goggles.

She heard Suha get out behind her, ask the cabbie how much.

"Oh, it was my pleasure," the cabbie said.

"Seriously," Suha said.

"I could not accept coin from visitors to this district."

Suha shrugged and stepped onto the smooth, tiled sidewalk with Nyx.

"Hey now!" The cabbie yelled, his formerly neat, placid face suddenly erupting in a snarl. He held out a big fist. "You want me to call the order guard, eh? You thief! Thieves!"

At least, Nyx assumed the term was something a lot like "order guard." Whatever word it actually was carried the same kind of righteous threat behind it.

"What?" Suha said, and her face got bunched up and ugly to match. Nyx smirked.

"You fat woman, you think this world is free?"

Suha cut a look at Nyx. Nyx shrugged. "Maybe he'll learn how to ask for what he wants next time."

"How much then, old man?" Suha said. There were no old men in Nasheen, not really. Good men died at the front. Old men were cowards. Nyx supposed the cab driver wouldn't understand the insult.

"You are impolite whores of roaches," the cabbie spat.

"Did he just call you whores of roaches?" Eshe said.

Nyx was sure that that particular insult would see some heat on the streets of Mushtallah when Eshe got back.

"Seems so," Nyx said. She put a pinch of sen between her lip and teeth and surveyed the green, humming park at her left. Something moved and shimmered in the trees. "But he's the one asking for money. Not so sure that makes us the whores. Maybe they do things different in Tirhan."

Eshe snickered.

Suha and the cabbie haggled and insulted one another a good while longer.

Nyx holstered her cane at her back and started up the street, keeping the broad, leafy park at her left. Eshe had drawn up a map with Azizah. He held it out before him now as they walked.

Her body ached, but the pinching, painful protest was gone. She could go a couple hours more, she figured, before she needed to bring out the cane and look like a fucking invalid. That would be enough time to present herself at Rhys's door like she was still a whole person.

"Here," Eshe said at the next intersection. The streets were clean and sterile, cleaner than downtown, like a filtered laundry deep in the interior. Nyx had never seen streets so clean in Nasheen, not even around the Orrizo.

Eshe pointed across the street from the park at a big two-storied house. All the houses here had the same blue tile and scabby-looking exteriors.

Nyx looked for laundry on a line, maybe kids playing with dead bugs in the street, but there was none of that—just the low, lazy whir of hoppers and thorn roaches, the occasional wail of a palm bug, muted, from the park behind them. The whole row of houses was surrounded only by tall privacy fencing: flimsy, filled in with decorative, non-lethal vegetation. No filters. No buzzers or faceplates she could see. No fear.

Fuck me, Nyx thought.

It was clean and quiet as the Queen's palace, but not a whiff of security beyond the occasional hum of some wasp swarm a couple streets over.

It was suicidal.

Nyx heard Suha catch up with them, and noted the *clunk-clunk-belch* of the taxi as it turned around in the dead-end roundabout and belched again.

"Sure this is it?" Nyx asked. She slid her wad of sen to the other side of her mouth.

"Think they'll feed us?" Eshe asked

"Feed us or shoot us," Nyx said.

She stepped across the street and walked to the gate of the house with Rhys's return address. Her first impression had been right: no buzzers, no faceplates. How did you get in, then?

Nyx put a hand on the gate to move away some of the vegetation. Was it underneath something?

The gate swung open.

The gates weren't locked!

"Fuck me," she said aloud.

She walked across the front yard and onto the porch. She still expected a filter, maybe a bug swarm, somewhere between the gate and door, but she got there unchallenged.

The door was prism glass, smoked, and she finally saw the familiar soft haze of a filter. That was something, at least. She looked for a faceplate, but found a simple bell pull instead. She looked at it a long moment, then turned to Eshe beside her.

"You sure this is the right place?"

He knit his dark brows and peered again at the page in his hands. He kept his shoulders hunched.

"Mehr-Az," he said, "Number 104."

Nyx looked at the number engraved on the bug collection pillar adjacent to the door. All the numbers and street names were in the prayer script; 104 was embossed in neat silver, vertically, down the pillar.

Well.

She didn't realize how long she'd been staring at the hazy door until Suha said, "You reach the bell pull?"

"I can reach it just fine," Nyx said. She snapped her arm out and jerked the bell pull.

She waited. Wrong house, maybe. It'd be the wrong house.

She pulled at her hat again and took a deep breath to ease the constriction in her chest. The air here just didn't agree with her. Nothing about this place agreed with her.

She heard something inside the house. Voices, the low thump of movement.

The door pulled open.

Nyx opened her mouth.

A kid stood in the door, head at about the same height as the door knob.

The kid looked up at Nyx with big dark eyes and a serious mouth that put Nyx in mind of somebody, some other time.

"Hello," Nyx said, in what she hoped sounded like Tirhani.

"Hello," the kid said.

The kid didn't seem all that startled to see them, which Nyx had to respect. They were kind of a fucked up bunch of people to find standing on your front porch.

"Mam!" the kid yelled over her shoulder, without taking her eyes off Nyx.

And as she did, Nyx thought, it's all right—she's the wrong color.

This big-eyed, tawny-skinned kid looked nothing like Rhys.

Wrong fucking house.

And then a large man came up behind the kid, and the bulk of him blocked the entryway. Nyx lifted her attention from the kid and looked the blue-eyed man in the face.

There was a staggering moment of dissonance.

She recovered first.

"Hello, Khos," Nyx said.

19.

For a long minute, Nyx didn't think he recognized her. His large, square face was hard and blank, like the face of the mountain pass they'd just trudged through. He went very still. Then something in him seemed to catch, and his gaze darted to Eshe and Suha beside her, and out again into the street, as if they brought a plague of locusts with them.

"Get in," he said, and pressed his hand to the filter release inside the doorway. The haze of the filter popped.

Nyx took off her hat as she stepped inside. Her boots squelched on the organic flooring. Khos was a big man. She had to turn sideways to move past him into the foyer. She was oddly aware of the heat of him behind her. As a general rule, she didn't fuck people on her team anymore. He'd been a fun but brief exception.

"I'm not looking for you," Nyx said. "Came looking for someone else."

Khos shut the door behind Eshe and Suha. The foyer was suddenly dim. Nyx blinked and looked into the courtyard at the center of the house. To her left, the kitchen was brighter. The house had a funny smell, like old books and leather fermented in wine.

"This is Eshe and Suha," Nyx said, without looking back at them. She stepped into the kitchen. The floor sucked the dust and grit on the soles of her boots. A thin shouldered but broad-hipped woman stood at a massive butcher block, hands elbow-deep in pastry dough. A smear of flour powdered her already pale face. Her hair was covered, tightly bound in a blue scarf. She raised her head and met Nyx's look. Her battle with the pastry ceased.

A boy stood next to her, one chubby hand clutching at her apron string. It was all very domestic, all very Tirhani. If they had a couple more wives bickering upstairs with the nanny and a Ras Tiegan servant out back finishing up the laundry, Nyx would have called them native.

"You breeding an army?" Nyx asked.

"Women have babies," Inaya said, pulling her hands from the dough as nonchalantly as if Nyx showed up at her house every ninth day for fried grasshoppers and tea. "Some of us even enjoy them."

The kid turned his attention to Nyx. He was, what, five? Six? Had to be about right. Nyx was bad at guessing how old kids were. She didn't see a lot of them, and certainly not all sorts of ages of them together.

"This is Taite," Inaya said. "Taite, this is a bad woman."

Well, Nyx thought. At least nothing's changed.

The kid turned his eyes toward Nyx, and sized her up with the dead reckoning of a six-year-old from the desert. "What did she do?"

"Question is, what haven't I done?" Nyx said. "Taite, huh?" She grimaced. "Tell your mother she's morbid."

Taite. Walking and talking. She remembered the squalling brat Anneke had carried around the garret back in Chenja, the wailing little feeder always at Inaya's breast. And here he was, a real person. It always startled her, how that happened. She had seen magicians do some pretty fantastic, impossible things, but turning a squalling, half-formed brat into a person, well, that sort of happened all on its own, but it was no less fantastic for all that.

"I have a baby sister," the kid said. "She's three." He held up the appropriate number of fingers.

"Yeah, I saw her," Nyx said. "I used to have a sister."

"Where is she?" the kid asked.

"Dead," Nyx said.

"Like Uncle Taite," the kid said.

"Yes," Inaya said, placing a floury hand on the boy's head. Nyx wondered if it was Nasheenian flour. Nasheen traded bugs and magicians for guns most often, but she'd heard they lost a lot of homegrown food that way, too. Good old Mushiran rye.

"Why don't you take your sister and go play? Papa and I need to talk to this bad woman."

The kid clung a moment longer to her apron string. But when Khos and the other kid came in, he ran past Nyx to Khos and caught at Khos's sleeve instead, cut another look at Nyx.

"Go on," Khos told the boy.

Taite took his sister's hand. The two of them wandered toward the dim front room.

Nyx raised a brow at Khos. "Papa?"

Khos blushed. She'd forgotten how easy it was to make him blush.

"I've been known to answer to it," he said.

"Can I get you tea?" Inaya asked. "Sugar soda?"

"What, you don't have servants for that?" Nyx said, and it came out slyer than she meant it to. A chaff-scrubbed little Tirhani family in this big, neat house, they were, getting fat on dead Nasheenian boys, just like the rest of Tirhan. The whole country was soft as old cheese.

"Our girl's off today," Inaya said.

Nyx remembered that she'd once watched this woman shoot a hole through a terrorist. Step light, she reminded herself. It's their house. You're the one who needs a favor, not them. She hadn't had enough whiskey this morning to be that bold.

Nyx helped herself to a seat at the table in the dining room. The ceiling was high and bright. She saw the large, silky webs of house spiders crisscrossing the eaves, tangling the chandelier. Nyx ran her hand over the tabletop. "Real wood?" she asked.

"I'll have sugar soda," Eshe said, still hovering on the other side of the kitchen, expecting Inaya to ask him to dole it out like he was a house boy.

"We have fizzy lemon soda," Inaya said. She pumped water into the sink and washed her hands, then moved to the ice box.

Suha wandered over to the filtered picture window on the other side of the dining room and peered into the back garden. Nyx had wanted to leave her as lookout on the porch, but in this neighborhood, bashed-up Suha spitting sen on the porch would just attract attention. The last thing Nyx needed was to answer questions from Tirhani order keepers. Order guards. Whatever they called them here.

Nyx sat on the edge of the table. Her cane bumped the tabletop. She shifted it under her coat.

"Anyway, I'm not here for you," Nyx said. "This'll be quick."

Khos kept his distance. He stood by the butcher block while Inaya poured the soda. Eshe, realizing he wasn't going to be asked to play house boy, sat gingerly next to Nyx. He didn't relax, but sat as straight as he could make himself, jaw clenched.

"I know you're not," Khos said, and his voice was, what—hard? Something else was there, something that wasn't anger. Disappointment, maybe? "You wouldn't come all this way for either of us. You're here for Rhys."

"Yes," Nyx said. She met his look. Hard blue eyes, milky blue like that inland sea. Yeah, he'd been a good fuck, once upon a time. How long had it been since she took somebody to bed? "I'm here for Rhys."

"He's not here," Inaya said. She brought the soda to Eshe and Suha and Nyx, like a good Ras Tiegan wife. Nyx let hers sit on the table. Suha took her glass over to the window. Keeping watch, whether asked to or not, got to be a habit after a while. Eshe drained his glass and grabbed Nyx's.

"You still know how to shoot?" Nyx asked Inaya.

"I don't have a reason for it here."

"Yeah? Peaceful little country, I guess."

"It was," Inaya said, and looked pointedly at her.

Half a decade before, Khos and his freakish shifter wife wouldn't have compelled her to move before she was ready. But Nyx had made this trip with a cane, a team of two, and a lot of luck. Her muzzy brain and fucked up body were getting better, sure, but she didn't expect miracles from magicians. Old bitches learned new tricks or died in the desert.

"I didn't want to hit up your house." Nyx pushed off the table. "This was the address Rhys gave Anneke. Thought we'd find him here, bumped into you instead. You know where he is?"

Khos opened his mouth.

"No," Inaya said.

Nyx waited for Khos. He shut his mouth. She looked over at Inaya again. "No? But he was here, right? All three of you together, before the family got too big? Before he got his own, maybe?" She looked right at Khos as she said it. He was the one she'd been able to read, when? An age ago. A bloody fucking age ago. He was a little heavier now and it showed—especially in the face. He'd cropped his hair, too. No more dreads. The blue tattoos were unmistakable though, as were the eyes, but his face was carved deep like the desert now.

"You should go," Inaya said. "We have another life now."

"Yeah, I see that," Nyx said, taking in the clean, bright interior of the house again. "What secrets you sell to the Tirhanis for this? How much did you whore out?" She felt the heat in her voice as she prepared to rattle off the next bit, wanted to call out Khos for pimping his bony little wife.

"Nyx, can we go?" Eshe said from behind her.

She turned. He had finished her soda and was standing now, still slightly hunched over, skinny arms hugging his chest. He had a pale, sick look about him. Sugar-sick, likely. They hadn't been eating well.

"Yeah, we'll go," she said. Fuck this fucking country, she thought.

She grabbed her hat off the table.

"I'll walk you out," Khos said.

"I know my way," Nyx said. She herded Eshe ahead of her, and waited for Suha on the porch. The day was still too bright, so much brighter than the house. Bloody fucking fools, to make all their streets and sidewalks some pale fucking color. She wondered how many Tirhanis it blinded every year.

Suha walked out. Khos was right on her heels. He breached the foyer just as Nyx was putting her hat back on.

"What are you doing here?" he said, voice low. He stood half inside the doorway. "What happened? You look horrible. Are you sick?"

"You get news from Nasheen?"

"Sometimes."

"What have you heard?"

"I don't listen much, Nyx."

"My fuckups are so big now that I make all the swarms."

"Are they back?"

"Who?"

"The aliens."

Nyx shrugged. "Not that I heard. You'd have heard that, even you, if somebody had docked in Nasheen. No, this is old catshit. Bloody bel dames and arms deals."

"You don't have bel dames after you, do you?"

"Maybe," she said.

He pulled back into the doorway. He'd always been a bloody coward, when it suited him. "You should go."

"Yeah, I know. Don't bust your big head. You're not the one I'm here for." She turned to start down the porch.

"Nyx?"

When she looked back, she saw that he was standing on the porch again, hand almost outstretched, as if he were thinking better of it.

"I'm sorry," he said.

"What for?"

"The bakkie. When I left you in the desert. In Chenja."

Nyx grinned, shook her head. "There's always somebody on my team that betrays me. At least you came back when it counted. Even if it took Inaya to get you there."

She patted Eshe on the shoulder and descended the porch with her team. She remembered that blue-dawn morning back in Chenja when her team drove off and left her. Not one of them had looked back. Not one. Not even Rhys. She knew. She had watched them until their bakkie was swallowed by the dawn.

And now, in Tirhan, she did not look back. She didn't need them.

This wasn't their fight.

20.

"She's got a face like a battlefield," Suha said.

The magician fighting in the ring was in fine form; her left hook was good, and the wasp swarm that shut up the shifter dog on the other side of the ring wasn't half bad either.

Problem was, that wasn't the magician they'd come in here looking for. The one they wanted was emptying the spit buckets into a drain on the far side of the gym. Her eyes were gray and bloodshot. As she shuffled across the floor, Nyx noted the trembling in her right hand, the slack-eyed, slack-jawed look of her—clear signs of old and established venom addiction.

And, like Suha said, she wasn't much to look at.

"Let's talk with her, at least," Nyx said. "Alharazad isn't much to look at either, but she recommended her." Nyx watched the puttering old woman, noted, again, the trembling hand. "I don't like working with addicts."

"Might sell us out, sure," Suha said. "But knowing we're a sure source of a drip might keep her close. I ain't got no advice on that."

"No advice for somebody on a drip? Really?"

Suha pushed out her mouth into that trout-look that Eshe so loved to tease her about. Eshe looked up from halfway across the gym where he was practicing with some other kids on a speed bag, and snickered.

"Giving up the drip is up to God and chance," Suha said. "There's no advice to run on about. You do or you don't."

"I never did like the idea of luck," Nyx said. Probably because it never favored her any.

She crossed the dim floor and approached the stooped old woman. Not so old, she realized as they met under the cupped, hooded glow of a bug light. The magician's hair was a ratty gray nest twisted back from her skinny little head. Her face was haggard, yes, but the hands that gripped the bucket were strong and smooth. Magicians' hands. The flesh of her neck was loose, but not fleshy folded like an old woman's. What was she, then, forty? Forty-five? Old for a bel dame, maybe, but not for a magician.

"I'm looking for a half-gifted magician," Nyx said.

The woman peered up at her. "That so, eh? I want a good fuck. Get outta the way." She pushed out her elbow and caught Nyx in the gut. The blow was enough to make Nyx unsteady on her feet. Damn, I've gotten soft, Nyx thought.

"You Behdis ma Yasrah?" Suha asked.

"Lot of old women's names out here. I ain't heard that one. Ain't heard that one even longer without a yah-yah at the front of it."

She kept walking.

"Alharazad said it's been a long time since you heard anybody yah-yahing at you. Thought you'd be used to it," Nyx said, watching her.

Behdis paused. She turned, squinted at the two of them.

"Who said that?"

"You heard," Nyx said. "I buy you a drink?"

"Gotta warn you, woman. They don't serve hard shit here."

"Yeah, I figured. I pay for drinks . . . and drips if the information's right."

"I ain't that hard up."

"Sure you ain't."

Nyx told Eshe they'd be across the street and left him to flirt with the girls. At least they let the girls box here. Nyx had never seen so many Ras Tiegan half-breeds. Eshe fit right in. The three women walked over to a Ras Tiegan tea house on the other side of the bright, cracked surface of the road running along the ass-end of the gym. Turned out not every district in Tirhan was cleaner than a breeding compound, but it had taken them three magicians' gyms to find one this shoddy. Magicians in Tirhan were a publicly groomed and traded lot, and the big magicians' gyms downtown catered to an elite clientele. Finding the outcasts' gym was a matter of smell and feel. Nyx had a way of finding herself in the worst parts of town with the least amount of effort.

A couple of Ras Tiegan girls brought them tea, and hot buni for Nyx, who still couldn't stomach the idea of drinking something that didn't alter her blood chemistry.

"I'm looking for a new magician for my team," Nyx said right off. "Somebody with ties to Tirhan, maybe access to some back channels. I watched you around the gym, heard you speaking Tirhani. It's not bad. You ain't respected around there, but that suits me fine. You're the sort nobody notices. I need somebody who doesn't warrant notice."

Behdis snarled into her tea. "There was a time I danced that ring like a Chenjan harem girl at dusk during the fasting month. I'd have pounded those girls silly." She reached for her tea with her left hand, but she wasn't a south paw. The right hand stayed clutched in her lap, to hide the trembling.

"How long you been on the drip?" Suha asked.

Behdis cut a look at her, peered for a long moment. "How long you been off?"

"Five years," Suha said.

"Eh, big girl then, aren't you? Went to the front and they hooked you up."

Suha leaned back in her chair, frowned.

The buni arrived in a clay jar. The Ras Tiegan girl holstered it on a rattan-wrapped ring at the center of the table and placed a tiny clay cup in front of Nyx. They never did anything to excess in Ras Tieg, not even sex, which probably explained something about Khos and Inaya's uptight attitude.

Nyx poured herself a drink.

"I quit a couple times," Behdis said, hedging. She sipped at her tea and scanned the empty tables, as if expecting one of the wanna-be magicians across the way would appear and recognize her. Recognize her as what? The janitor? Who noticed one more washed-up, underemployed foreign woman slumming around the seediest part of Shirhazi? Nyx had asked six people at the gym for Behdis by name, and not one of them knew who the hell she was talking about. It was the seventh—the delivery boy they bumped into out back—who knew that Behdis was "that old lady who mops up the blood and vomit."

"I don't mind keeping an ear out. I gotta know payment, though. Know what I'm digging for."

"What's your drip go for these days?" Nyx asked.

"Depends on the day," Behdis said.

Nyx exchanged a look with Suha.

Suha shrugged.

"I'll pay you based on what you dig up. You bring me something solid, I give you ten notes."

"Nasheenian or Tirhani?"

"Nasheenian."

"Your currency ain't worth enough to wipe my ass," Behdis said.

"Unless you're looking for venom," Nyx said. "Last I checked, Nasheen supplied the cheapest. Where you going to find good venom in Tirhan that isn't priced for those magicians at the city center?"

"What you think I can get you, woman?"

"Bel dames," Nyx said. She watched the old woman's face as she said it.

Behdis sneered. "Alharazad sent you, you say?"

"You check with her if you want. She said if anybody'd know anything about bel dames in Tirhan, it'd be you."

"You a little sticky about what your own government's doing?"

Nyx smiled thinly. She knocked back a cup of buni and pulled her hat on, then stood. "Who ever wanted to know what their government's doing? You know that, and you have to take responsibility for it. I have a good idea you know where I can find some bel dames in Shirhazi. All I need is an address and names."

"I'll . . . see what I can do. Where do I find you?"

Nyx considered that for a minute. Then she pulled out Khos and Inaya's address from her coat and slid it across the table. Suha eyed the map with some interest.

"You have information, you tie a black string on the door of the gate here. I'll come find you."

Behdis curled her lip. "A little out of my way. They'll stop me, coming into that part of town. They got wasp swarms to keep folks like me out."

"Thought you were a magician?"

"Better than a lot you'd know."

"Then I think you can handle a couple wasp swarms." Nyx put a note down on the table, which covered the tea and buni four times over. "You let us know."

Nyx left the table, and Suha followed. Behdis immediately snatched up the note.

"What's that about?" Suha asked as they stepped onto the street. "You don't want her knowing where we are?"

"I like keeping folks guessing."

"And it gives you an excuse to stake out that shifter's house?"

Nyx snorted. "I just don't trust addicts. No offense."

"We'd know more sooner if she could come to us."

"Would we?" Nyx stepped onto the sidewalk outside the gym. Two kids with a mangy sand cat on a chain ran past them. Both boys. She didn't see many women on the street in the Ras Tiegan district. Nyx heard the sound of noon prayer start at the big central city mosque, heard it roll over the city. They had passed a row of Chenjan prayer wheels at the edge of the district, but Tirhanis had their own martyr and their own additions to the Kitab. Their prayer times were off, too.

"I didn't like what I saw of her," Nyx said.

"What? So, she's an addict. You knew she was an addict."

"It's not that," Nyx said. "Alharazad recommends her, sure, so I'm supposed to swallow that she'll give us anything?"

"What the hell are you talking about?"

Nyx stared into the street, tried to work it out for Suha in words. "We all got morals, honor. Fucked up sorts, maybe, but we got them, even crazies. I don't know hers."

"Addicts don't have morals."

"Didn't you? When you fucked up you still felt real bad, didn't you?"

"Sometimes," Suha said. "When I could remember." She folded her arms and rocked back on her heels. "Don't know how much you care when you're in it. You're just hungry. You don't think about much else."

"Cleaned up or not, I'd have taken you on."

"Catshit."

"Truth. Know why?"

"Why?" Suha spit sen.

"Cause some women you watch closer than others. And some you put on your team. I know the difference."

"That always worked out for you?"

"No." She thought of Khos.

"No doubt."

"Come on," Nyx said. She had a sudden, powerful need to get in a fight. "Let's see who we're pulling Eshe off tonight."

"Kid's got more kick than a cat in heat," Suha muttered as they pushed inside.

"I was young once," Nyx said.

"I wasn't," Suha said.

21.

Rhys spent all day at his storefront, cleaning the windows and organizing the translation desks. He had spent several days open for business during regular hours instead of by appointment, and had been rewarded with a note fifty from a poor widow who wanted to send a non-bugged letter to her son in the south.

Three days of work for a note fifty.

He stopped for something to eat at a cheap food stall, made midday prayer at the mosque, and took the elevated train out to the eastern edge of the city. The color of the city changed from pale and sterile to muted, hazy hues of maroon and turquoise, and the landscape drew closer to the ground, hunkered. The smell, too, changed. When he stepped off the train platform the world smelled of fried dough and curry. Ras Tiegans fried everything, from grasshoppers to pickles to hunks of curried dog.

Rhys had lived in the Ras Tiegan district when he first came to Tirhan, before he and Inaya and Khos moved into the suburbs. From the street outside the gym, he could see the roof of their old tenement building. Four blocks down, he and Khos used to drink honeyed tea and eat samosas by the handful while working on translations. Six streets over was the brothel where Khos's contacts had gotten them all rooms for the first three weeks in Tirhan.

Six years. It felt longer, Rhys thought as he stood outside the gym. Some Ras Tiegan kids passed him and pushed inside. He followed.

The plump Ras Tiegan gym owner, Lisbel, waved at him from behind the lattice of her office window. She kept her hair covered. In all his years using this gym, he had never seen the flesh above her wrists or ankles, even when she boxed.

"Been a while, Yah Rhys," she said, with a wink and a smile.

He walked across the gym floor, pulling off his bisht as he went. There was a small crowd around one of the rings at the back of the gym. Two brown Nasheenian fighters circled one another. He paused, and watched. One was nearly dark as a Tirhani, undeniably ugly, with a mashed in nose and protruding jaw. She had a stocky, powerful little body though. A woman who could square her body like that would keep her feet in the ring a lot longer than most.

Rhys walked toward the ring to get a better look. The other fighter had her back to him. She was tall and dark, big in the hips and shoulders, but too skinny for her frame. As she turned under the ring lights Rhys saw that there was something familiar about her. Something in the way she stood, the set of her shoulders.

They danced around a few minutes more until the ugly one knocked the other woman to the mat with a hard left uppercut. Her opponent didn't have a chance, thumped onto the mat, sprawled back.

And laughed.

Recognition cut through Rhys like a knife; a sudden burst of knowing.

The ugly one helped up the one on the floor. As the loser stood and turned to the crowd, Rhys knew her.

She saw him looking. Her jaw worked.

Rhys walked forward.

Nyx jumped out of the ring.

They stopped a pace from one another.

She was older, thinner, and there was something wrong with her skin. It looked oddly mismatched, and darker than he remembered. Had he aged as much as she had? He saw it in her face the most, but also in the way she moved. A little slower, less swagger.

Nyx put her hands on her wide hips. They'd been bigger hips, he remembered. She'd lost a staggering amount of weight. Loss of mass meant loss of leverage, loss of strength. Women like Nyx didn't drop weight like that on purpose.

Rhys wanted to say something smart and dry. He wanted something to cover that cold terror and burst of recognition. He wanted to say something about his life, about Tirhan, about how happy he was. He wanted to tell her she looked like death.

But in the face of Nyxnissa so Dasheem, the words all left him in a rush.

"I—" he started, and stopped.

"We've been hanging around here a couple days," she said. "Magicians in this quarter remember you and the Mhorian. Figured you'd show up eventually. I need a favor."

Of course she wanted something. Why else cross half a continent? Certainly not for high tea.

He'd spent years imagining what he would say to her in this moment—how he would rebuke her, belittle her, revile her. Two years he had waited, expecting her to knock on his door.

Two years. Then he rebuilt his life.

And now she was here.

Of course she was here.

"I see you still frequent the same high-quality establishments," he said. Getting that out made him feel better.

"I knew better than to look downtown. They only let real magicians in there."

"And real women."

"Which is why there were no Chenjan women there."

"Still Godless?"

"Still Godful?"

"You're not drunk. I expected that."

"I'm a better shot when I'm sober."

"No you're not."

"No, I'm not."

She grinned.

He felt his resolve soften. This is the woman who'd sell you out as soon as look at you, he reminded himself.

But she hadn't, had she?

And now she was here.

Because she wanted something.

"What are you looking for?" he asked.

"Best we talk about that in private. You eat? I'm starving. Let me get my team and we'll get out of here." She turned away and called back at the ugly woman in the ring. "Suha! Clean up and get Eshe. We're moving."

Another team? Of course. Only the most foolish hunters ran alone.

"Come on," Nyx said. She leaned toward him and put her hand on his shoulder. "I missed your catshit," she said.

He felt something then, when she touched him. Something missing was suddenly full to bursting. *I'll take care of you. I'll protect you. I'll always come for you.*

Six years missing—that feeling of absolute strength, safety, gone so long he'd forgotten to miss it at all. He had replaced it with something else, in Tirhan. His own strength, his own resolve. In a peaceful country, he did not need a woman like Nyx to protect him.

He knew then that everything was falling apart.

22.

Rhys stood on the veranda with a cup of mint tea in one hand and a fruit knife in the other, looking like he wanted to cut something out or cut something up. The fruit tray itself was on the tea table between them. Nyx had her feet on the table. She'd left her cane back at the dive they were staying in in the Ras Tiegan quarter. Rhys had insisted on something more upscale for lunch, something a little more upscale than Suha and Eshe could stomach. She watched them standing out in the garden beyond the veranda, talking about something that had Suha making sweeping motions with her hands. How to blow shit up, likely.

Rhys looked good, Nyx conceded as she watched him standing at the railing. He stood with a straight spine now, like a full citizen, not a Chenjan exile. He dressed in a loose-fitting robe too, and a silly, gauzy bisht. No belted trousers, no pistols at his hips. She had a sudden, passionate desire to see the outline of his legs. God, how she missed Rhys in trousers.

"I'm married," Rhys said.

Nyx moved her gaze up from his covered legs to his face. He still looked out across the garden. Two women wearing immaculate azure robes and scarves moved passed them across the stones of the garden path.

"I figured," Nyx said. She had a memory of Yah Tayyib, then, who'd been at her side the first time she saw Rhys. He'd told her Rhys was worth two of her. Nyx couldn't debate that.

"She virtuous?" Nyx asked.

"Yes, she's virtuous," Rhys said.

A serving boy in a neat white tunic came by to refill their drinks. Nyx waved him away from the half-empty bottle of red wine she kept next to her chair. She picked it up, took a long swig. The serving boy eyed her askance and then danced away. Inside the restaurant behind them, someone played a stringed instrument, one she had no name for. Some kind of harp, maybe?

"You're scaring the help," Rhys said. He watched her now with his dark eyes.

"I scare a lot of people," Nyx said.

"I'm not joining your team again."

"I'm not here for that."

"No?"

"No."

"But there's no magician on your team."

"I'm hiring one out of Tirhan, for as long as we're here. Won't be too long. Six weeks, maybe." Much longer than that, and whatever she came here to stop would be over already.

"Then what?"

"Bugs," she said.

"Ah," he said, and moved away from the railing. He sat across from her, set the fruit knife back on the table. She wondered if he'd held it that long thinking to use it against her if she asked him to come back to Nasheen.

Silly magician.

"I need the transmissions Taite packed over the border. The one from the mercenary Khos killed and put in our trunk. When I got back to the garret, I saw you'd all stopped by and picked up your shit. I figured you took that transmission with you."

"I did, I suppose. I picked up everything at the garret on the way out. I've got it in storage somewhere, at the house or at my translation office. How does that help you? I thought you'd want to know more about Kine's research."

"I have an interest in seeing how deep this goes. Wondering if our current roach is the same one looking to get me dead six years ago."

"You'll need an updated reel."

"Alharazad gave me an updated reel."

Rhys sat back in the chair. "Alharazad?" he breathed.

"There's only one, so far as I know."

"Nyx, what have you gotten yourself into?"

"Same shit, different day."

He looked out into the garden. She watched him work it over.

"I'm not here to mess with your life," she said. "I just need the reel. I got a team to take care of, rent to pay, my ass to save."

"And you intend to save your own ass all by yourself?"

She shrugged. "I got a team."

"You have a surly weapons tech and a pock-marked shifter who won't be good at what he does much longer, from the look of his spine."

"Hate to say it, but a pretty face isn't required in my line of work."

"You're not half as ugly as that blocky woman."

Nyx rolled her eyes. "You say that to her face and she'll cleave you in two. You forget how Nasheen works, all cozied up at the tit of your milk and honey country. We measure worth differently in Nasheen."

"And then you destroy it."

"Don't talk morals at me, gravy-eater."

"Call me infidel. It has more weight in Tirhan."

"I'm not a Tirhani."

"Isn't that bloody obvious . . ."

"You speak to your wife that way?" Nyx took another pull on the wine bottle.

Rhys shook his head. He reached for the knife and a mango,

started cutting a portion. "God has blessed me, Nyx. He doesn't forsake all of us."

"Don't preach at me. You let this soft country fool you into thinking you're clean? Ain't nobody in this world who's clean, Rhys. Tirhan's got the bloodiest hands of all, and you and Khos and Inaya are part of it."

He paused, fruit in hand, and met her look. "You saw Inaya and Khos? You've been to the house?"

Nyx snorted. "They invited me in for soda."

Rhys's face twisted, as if he were suddenly sick. "What did you say?"

"I don't drink it, myself. Too sweet. But Eshe——"

"No. To my wife. What did you say to Elahyiah?"

So that was her name.

"What the hell are you talking about? I didn't see your wife at Khos's."

"You were at Khos's?"

"Yeah."

"But not my house?"

"How the hell would I know your place? They lied like kids. They said they had no idea where you were."

Rhys grinned, then laughed.

"What? What the hell's so funny?"

Rhys's shoulders shook. He put down the knife and fruit all together and laughed out loud. "We're neighbors," Rhys said. "They live just across the park. You were practically at my doorstep. God, they must have laughed after you were gone."

"It's not funny," Nyx said. "Walking around half of Tirhan knocking on doors ain't exactly my idea of a good time. I kept waiting for one of your neighbors to shoot me."

"Then how did you find me? Who told you about the gym?"

"Found out about it at another gym down the street. Asked

around. Folks remember you. Pretty Chenjan magician with the funny name."

"I can't believe Inaya let you inside the house."

"Khos answered."

"Ah."

"Ah?"

"He's always been keen on you."

"Has he? Never noticed."

"You never notice anything that might inconvenience you," he said. "Knowing he's keen on you, I'm doubly surprised Inaya let you in."

"I do recall she's good with a shotgun."

"She's good with far more than that. She's a mutant shifter."

"A what?"

Rhys hesitated, as if he'd said something he wasn't supposed to.

"What?" Nyx repeated.

Rhys cleared his throat. "Did you ever wonder how she got that bakkie over the border back in Chenja?"

"Yeah, I guess. Not exactly easy to drive a bakkie over a war front, especially for somebody pale as piss like her."

"She . . . became the bakkie. Displaced the matter. Turned it into something else."

"She tell you that?"

"Not in so many words. I became curious after Chenja. I did some reading on Ras Tiegan politics and Inaya's family in particular. Let's just say she's far more dangerous without the shotgun than you might think."

"I'll keep that in mind. There many shifters like that?"

"I don't know. Your sister, Kine, knew more about that."

"Her bloody fucking experiments. Wish the whole program burned with her."

"It didn't."

Nyx frowned. "I only got so many fights I can manage today,

Rhys." She couldn't fight everybody's wars and Nasheen's too.

"I'm not sure where the transcription is," he said, and shrugged. "I'll go through my records at the house first, then the transcription office. I'll get you the recording tomorrow."

She looked over the veranda. "Let's not wait. I'll drop off Suha and Eshe at the hotel." She thought about that a minute. "Mutant shifting, that's something you're born with, right? Not something they can turn into?"

"I assume it's from the start, yes. Why?"

"No reason," Nyx said. "Inaya's government must be itching to have her back, is all."

"Don't tell her I said anything. It's a suspicion, nothing more. I was as curious about how she followed us back then as you were."

"I don't plan on seeing her again, anyway. Let's get going."

"I'd rather bring it to you tomorrow. There's a festival tonight."

"Festival?"

"The Martyr's festival. I promised my family I would take them."

"This a big deal?"

"The whole city goes."

"So it'll be quiet. Good. Let me get it and get out of your hair, Rhys. The more I hear about how deep this goes, the more I don't like it."

"Nyx . . ."

"You don't have to bring me inside," Nyx said. She didn't want to see his pious little wife either. And him talking about having children was enough to turn her stomach. Children. Children just reminded her that he was fucking his wife. And the idea of pretty, leggy Rhys having sex was more than she cared to dwell on.

"All right," he said. He called over the waiter. Nyx was going to insist they split the tab, then remembered Khos and Inaya's house, and remembered Rhys lived across the park. He could cover it. She was going to have to stretch her notes a good deal further before this was over.

23.

"I don't like him," Eshe said.

Nyx grinned. "Is that so?"

Rhys had stopped at a call box outside the café to call his wife. Nyx stayed out of earshot, tucked into a nearby doorway while she caught up Eshe and Suha on events.

Eshe's face remained serious. "It's not a joke. He's a magician, ain't he? You always said not to trust them. Why don't I stay on point?"

"And you've always trusted them, even when I said not to," Nyx said. "What's the change?"

Eshe folded his arms. "I just don't like him."

"Suha, I need you to poke around the dives near Behdis's place. If she's seeing bel dames and not squealing, I want to know about it. Eshe, I want you watching after Suha."

Eshe shook his head. "Let me fly point for you. I can do it."

"I'm well aware you can do it. But Suha needs you more than me. You think there's going to be trouble in that slick little neighborhood of his? Suha needs you to watch her back."

Eshe shook his head and marched off toward the train.

"And put on your damn hat!" Nyx yelled after him.

Suha spit sen into a takeaway cup. They'd been fined by two Tirhani "public order police" for spitting on the sidewalks. Nyx wondered how the fuck keepers had time to police something so ridiculous. She supposed that without a bunch of deserters, mercenaries, and gene pirates running around, you had a lot less to do.

"I'll ask around, but I don't expect to start earning some trust for a couple weeks," Suha said.

"We should have the time. Just stay low. I'd rather we hear about them before they hear about us."

"Unless Behdis told them about us."

"Possible. But that'll make them easier to find."

Suha grunted.

"I'm an optimist," Nyx said.

"You're something all right," Suha said. "I'll see you tonight." She walked after Eshe.

Rhys talked to his wife for a long time. Nyx finally sat in the doorway, hat brim lowered, and dozed. When he eventually hung up and walked back over, he looked tired.

"She'll expect us," he said, and that was that.

Nyx rode downtown with Rhys on the beetle-powered train. Like the rest of Tirhan, it was clean and efficient. It came on time. It dropped them off exactly where it said it would at exactly the time the little schedule promised it would. Nyx found it disconcerting.

From there they took a taxi to the suburbs. The cabbie was a lot more personable in the presence of a magician. Nyx made a note of that for the next time she was running around in Tirhan. Might be useful to dress up like a magician, since they all wore some kind of uniform here.

As they stepped out of the taxi and started walking up the street, Rhys said, "What's wrong?"

"Huh?"

"You haven't said a word since lunch."

"Yeah. A lot on my mind."

They stepped onto a porch that looked so much like Khos and Inaya's that Nyx could guess the layout of the house.

"What," Nyx said, "they map out this place like a city of the future?"

"Famous architect," he said. "The neighborhood was originally built for mullahs and the Martyr's closest allies."

"Doesn't look that old."

"It's only been a couple centuries."

"I suppose money does wonders."

"It certainly doesn't hurt."

Rhys palmed open the door. The filter popped.

They walked inside. The floor was gray, spongy organic like Khos and Inaya's house. But the layout was different. They walked into an arched foyer. Straight ahead was a bright, boxy kitchen, and to the left, a strange sunken living area that opened onto the tiled back porch—filtered, of course.

A small, fine-boned woman stood near the desk, hair neatly covered. She was slender and all-right looking, Nyx supposed. Almond-shaped eyes and dark skin, but she didn't have the sort of easy grace that Rhys did. Her fine features and narrow waist made her look pretty sickly, in Nyx's opinion. She wouldn't be any good humping twenty kilos of gear across a war zone, or hauling forty kilos of bursts across the desert during a night raid. Useless in a hard fight.

Just the sort of wife she'd expect for Rhys.

The wife said something in Tirhani.

Nyx glanced over at Rhys.

The wife said, in Chenjan, "You are Nyx?"

"Yeah."

She looked Nyx over disdainfully. "You're much uglier than I expected."

"Quite a relief, isn't it?" Nyx said in Nasheenian.

Her petite little face scrunched up. "I don't know what you're saying," she said in Chenjan.

Nyx pulled off her hat. "Don't worry about Rhys. You got yourself a virtuous man."

"If it's here, it'll be upstairs," Rhys said pointedly.

"Oh, you go right ahead," Nyx said, still in Nasheenian. "I can keep Elhena company."

"Elahyiah," Rhys said. "Come upstairs, Nyx."

Nyx grinned and winked at his wife. "Will do."

He led Nyx up to the bedroom. Nyx hesitated under the archway. Inside, everything was clean and neat. The sheets were white, the pillows were white, the gauzy curtains surrounding the bed were white. Nyx wondered if the wife spent all her time cleaning. She must. It wasn't as if Chenjan wives were officially employed outside the home unless driven to by dire necessity. Rhys wouldn't want that from his little prize.

"So, why just the one wife?" Nyx asked as he got out a footstool and began going through boxes on top of his wardrobe. "You can afford more. Even the Tirhani Book gives you at least four, right? Khos used to talk about how great that would be."

"I find one wife fully sufficient," he said.

"What a rebel."

He pulled a box down and brought it over to the bed. "I do love her, if that's what you're asking."

"Not my business."

"No, it's not."

Rhys pulled open the box and waved his hand over another, smaller box of bug secretions inside. Something rattled. He pulled the lid off. Three sluggish beetles peered out. He stirred his fingers around in the contents, shook his head. "It's not—" then pulled out a small rectangular casing. Inside was a beetle suspended in clear fluid.

"This is it," he said. He waved his hand over the box to lock it and put it away.

He handed her the casing.

It was still warm from his hand. Nyx held it up to the light. Nothing at all remarkable about it. Green beetle in clear transmission fluid, wrapped in wiry strings of organic code. She tucked it away into her breast binding next to the one Alharazad had given her.

"Thanks," she said. "Guess that's it."

"You should take this to somebody you can trust. A lot could happen between here and there."

Nyx shrugged. "A lot can happen crossing the street."

"I'll take you to my transcription office. I have a com. You can translate it and have your answer today."

"This is all I came for."

"It's not any trouble," he said. "I'm curious to know who it was, myself. Her putting out a note on you drove me here. You remember?"

"That so?"

He looked away and started to the door. "Come down. I'll tell Elahyiah I'll be back before dark. We'll have time to take the girls to the festival."

"Your call," Nyx said.

They walked downstairs. Nyx waited in the foyer while he talked to his wife in low tones. The wife raised her voice at one point, and they switched from Chenjan to Tirhani.

Nyx showed herself out onto the porch. As she did, she came face to face with a little girl, Chenjan-dark, with familiar eyes. Out on the sidewalk, a hunched little Ras Tiegan woman held the hand of another dark girl, smaller than the first, with braided hair.

The girl on the porch stared at her.

The Ras Tiegan woman took Nyx in with one long, penetrating look.

Rhys appeared then. He kissed the little girl on the porch, called her Laleh, and told the Ras Tiegan woman to go inside and help Elahyiah with the laundry.

"Yes'im," the Ras Tiegan woman said, and Nyx had her answer about who kept the house so clean. Of course they'd have a Ras Tiegan servant. They were practically Tirhani.

"Your kids?" Nyx asked as the youngest pattered inside with the housekeeper.

"Yes." He pulled on a hat. The day had moved into late afternoon.

Nyx dug around for her goggles. She'd taken to packing them, last few days. "This better not be far."

"It's near downtown. One more ride, then we'll have some new answers to old questions. You owe me that much, at least."

"I thought what I owed you was to go away."

"That will happen soon enough," he said.

They took a taxi to the transcription office, a battered little storefront tucked into a steep, narrow street. The language moved easily from Tirhani to Chenjan as they traveled, and the smell changed, the way it usually did when moving into a Chenjan district. Gravy and curry and heavy incense. They passed prayer wheels hung outside windows, bowls of milk put out for demons. Shadows were collecting along the street. The day was moving fast.

Rhys unlocked the door. As they walked in, they passed a passive wasp swarm. It clung together, a humming nest of bodies, in a far corner. The office was small, little more than the storefront proper. It looked like he had a tiny storage area in back, curtained off. There were three writing stations, two cushions on either side of each low wooden table. Along the wall were jars of bugs, mostly locusts, and transmission fluid. The place even smelled like bugs, some subtle odor, like when you stuck your nose up close to some rotting forest floor at the coast. Thick, musty, death.

Rhys pulled the curtain away from the storage area. The com was there, a hulking console made of various types of scrounged metal and bug secretions. She handed over the mercenary's transmission. Rhys inserted the rectangle into a free slot and held out his hand to her.

"You have the reel Alharazad gave you?"

Nyx handed it over.

Rhys slid it into another open slot. He stirred up the fire beetles at the bottom of the com and waved a hand over the filter. A cacophony of noise and vapors seeped from the filter. Blue and yellow mist colored the dim air.

"The hell?" Nyx said.

"It's warming up. I haven't used it in a while."

Rhys played the transcription. Nyx hadn't heard it the first time.

"We have a death note on mercenaries and bounty hunters accepting notes on Nikodem Jordan, an alien emissary from New Kinaan. Nikodem Jordan is to be kept alive at all costs. These aren't pale notes. Deliver your heads to the Black Stag Beetle hotel in Punjai. Ask for Leveh."

It was a pretty standard black note transmission. The Black Stag Beetle was a regular haunt for black note dealers back then. Now it was the Dire Wind cantina just outside Basra.

Nikodem. Nyx hadn't heard that name since Kasbah invoked it. Hadn't thought much about it. Some days it was just another body. Aliens bled red, just like everybody else. No ships had touched down on Umayma since Nyx sent them home with their sister's head. She wondered how long it would be until they came scrabbling back to Umayma looking for genetic material. Maybe they'd had enough of the planet. Nyx didn't blame them.

"Alharazad's reel should have been preprogrammed," Rhys said. "I'll just activate it and ask it to match up the voice pattern."

"Sure," Nyx said.

Rhys pressed a button. A tinny-sounding belch came from the machine.

"How long's it been since you used this?" Nyx said. He had never been great with a com.

"Matched pattern," said a warm, matronly voice. A stir of red mist filtered up from the tinny speaker. "Voice pattern recognized as that of Shadha so Murshida. Run check again?"

Nyx folded her arms. "One of Shadha's girls," Fatima had said. Apparently Shadha's girls had been running things their own way for a long time. Not terribly useful information, though she could have Suha ask around for somebody called "Leveh" now as well. If Shadha still ran with her, she'd likely be high up the food chain by now.

She turned to Rhys to thank him, and noted that he'd gone very still.

"What?" Nyx said. "You heard of her?"

"Nyx," Rhys said softly.

"Yeah?"

He raised his head, and his eyes were wide, just like his daughter's had been on the porch. "You should go."

"You heard of her?"

"I did business with her last week."

Nyx started. That was a bit of luck. "Where? What business?"

"Bad business," he said.

"I need an address."

He pulled both of the transmissions out of the com unit and pushed them across the slab toward her. "She's selling some weapon from the red desert. Some kind of flesh-eating sand."

"Selling it to who, Tirhan?"

"Yes."

"No shit?"

"Nyx, I don't know that this is the sort of woman you want to go up against."

"What are you talking about?"

"The weapon. Nyx, this is more than cutting off a head. You cut off her head and there will be five more behind her. She had more bel dames with her."

"I know there are rogue bel dames. It's why I'm here."

"It's too big for you."

"It's my country, Rhys."

"Yes, and my father is my father, but it doesn't mean I obeyed him."

"You'd obey your mullahs, though, huh?"

"Nyx," he said, carefully, "there have been times . . . there have been times I didn't obey *God*. I know when something is too much for me."

"That's because you're a coward."

"If you think your Queen is going to look out for you—"

"It's not about that."

"Then what?" he said. He ran his hands over his head. She hadn't seen him do that in a long time. It was a nervous, familiar tic. Comforting. Come home with me, she wanted to say.

"Go home and tell her you couldn't find anything," Rhys said.

"I'm not doing this for the Queen. It's not a note."

He dropped his hands. "Then why?"

"You wouldn't understand. I'm doing this for myself."

"For God's sake, *why*? You're not up for this."

"How would you know what I'm up for?"

"I just . . ." He was looking her over. Her body—not her face. Not her. Just the meat that had failed her.

"I'm not broken!" she said. She grabbed the transmissions off the com and stuffed them away. "Where did you see this Shadha?"

"Nyx . . ."

"Where, Rhys? I won't ask nice again."

"Beh Ayin," he said. "Southeast. I met them at a hotel there. I don't know where they stayed. Probably outside the city."

"That'll have to be enough." She walked into the storefront

proper. She didn't stop at the door but pushed right on through into the street.

Rhys yelled at her from the door. "Don't run off like a child!"

She turned, shouted back at him, "Says the man with the babies and bauble wife living fat and soft in the Tirhani suburbs! You got soft, old man. Coward."

"I never said I was anything else."

She stormed back toward him and shoved her face into his, so close she could smell the spicy Tirhani perfume on his collar.

"No," she said, "but *I* always thought you were more."

Nyx walked off down the street, heading in the direction she hoped was the Ras Tiegan quarter. She supposed it didn't make much difference. The sun was going down. She had a lead on the rogue bel dames. She was one step closer to a bel dame title and averting civil war. Likely not in that order.

All she wanted to do now was get drunk.

24.

Of all the people Nyx expected to be waiting for her back at the hotel, Khos Khadija wasn't one of them. He sat at a sen-stained table near the opaqued window, playing cards with Suha. A ring of lethargic locusts sat at the center of the table. The smell of curried dog wafted up from the room below them. Nyx heard soft, shushing voices speaking muted Ras Tiegan next door.

"Watch out for him," Nyx said as she walked in. "He cheated me out of a basket of scarab beetles the first time we met."

"He says you met in a brothel," Suha said.

"Where's Eshe?"

The radio was on, spewing bubbly Tirhani voices and the green, misty images of some daytime romance. Both beds were unmade. The privy was ensuite, but the door was open, and the little closet-sized room was dark.

"He's hot on some girl at the gym," Suha said.

"Better be a useful girl."

"Maybe so. He said he met some other Nasheenian women—boxers—at another gym. Told him to get in some bag time and find out the names."

"I wish you'd told me more about the note," Khos said.

Nyx took off her burnous and tossed it on the bed. "Why, you looking for work? From the looks of your pretty house, you're not hard up."

"Rogue bel dames are everybody's business," Khos said.

Nyx shot Suha a look.

Suha shrugged. "Figured if he ran off before you got back, I'd kill him," she said.

"Try," Khos said.

Suha leaned back, so her long coat fell away, revealing her duel pistols. "Try me," she said.

Khos looked back at Nyx. "I want to buy you a drink."

"I've never been one to pass up free liquor," Nyx said. She was curious about why he came. Did he miss slumming? "I'm gonna wash up and let Suha bleed you a little more, then we'll get going."

She cleaned up in the privy. When she returned, Suha and Khos had already broken out some bootleg whiskey.

"If you and Eshe go out tonight, add another name to your round," Nyx told Suha as she pulled her burnous back on. "Woman called Leveh. Over thirty by now, I'd bet, but don't quote me."

"Bel dame?" Suha said. Her voice was a little drawl. Nyx didn't blame her. She was ready to go out and get drunk, too.

"Likely. Maybe just a contact," Nyx said. "And watch the liquor tonight. Set down some traps. I don't want a repeat of Punjai."

"Last one," Suha said, and took a pull from the bottle.

"Let's go, Khos," Nyx said.

He pulled his big body from the chair and came after her. They walked downstairs in silence. She let the silence stretch as they entered the street.

"Used to live out here when we first came to Tirhan," Khos said. "Good shebeen around the corner. Unlicensed."

"Shebeen?"

"Like a tavern. Uh, less formal. You'll see."

"Thanks for bringing the whiskey."

"Figured you'd need it. Been rough living in a dry country. You can still get it. Just a lot more trouble."

They stepped into an old Ras Tiegan dive not much better than the hedge witch's hovel in Punjai. The floors were dirt and most of the roof tiles were broken. There was one long counter along the far wall and dirty tables. Nyx set herself up in a corner so she'd have a view of the door. Khos bought the first round.

"What we here for?" Nyx asked, three drinks and a dozen nattering pleasantries later.

Khos shook his head. Nyx realized she missed his dreadlocks. Tattoos were the same, though. She always liked those.

"You should have told me you were looking for bel dames," he said.

"You never asked."

"Wrong. I did ask."

"And you said trouble with bel dames scared the shit out of you and slammed the door. Why is it all the guys I put on my team are cowards?"

"We're less trouble, I'd wager."

"You looking to screw me again?"

His eyes widened.

"Not like that," Nyx said, waving a dismissive hand. "The betraying part, not the fucking part."

"I got a family now."

"So you family guys keep telling me."

"I'm here to help."

"I'm listening."

"I think me and Inaya can help you. Come on back to the house. She . . . she and I don't get on as well as we used to, but you and her are working for some of the same things."

Nyx snorted. "When did Inaya and I ever have anything in common?"

"She does . . . work. I suspect she has something to do with the Ras Tiegan underground. A shifter rights group. You know what that is?"

"Never heard of it."

"She sees and hears things that might help you. I want you to come over and talk to her."

"So . . . why isn't she here?"

"I need you to ask her. I can't."

"What, she doesn't know you know?"

"No."

"What kind of fucked up relationship you two have?"

"No more fucked up than any of yours."

"Why are you really here? Prostitutes not brutal enough for you? Lack of whores in Tirhan?"

His face reddened. "You're never fair."

"Just right."

He started to stand. "I wanted to help."

Nyx sighed. "Sit, sit," she said. "Let me finish my goddamn drink. Should have known you and Inaya wouldn't stay out of the covert business out here. Can't say the same for Rhys."

Khos sat back down, avoided her eyes. "He not what you expected?"

Nyx finished her drink and knocked the glass back on the table. The whiskey burned going down. God, she'd missed it. "No, he was everything I expected," Nyx said. "That's always the problem."

"Maybe you should go after different types of guys."

"Or more girls."

"Or more girls. Though, as I recall, you like the same sorts of girls, too."

"Which are those?"

"The ones who don't want you."

Nyx glared at him. "You want to compare bed partners? I'll have you beat."

"I don't doubt it. I didn't grow up the way you did."

"How's that?"

"With women. It's another good reason to speak to Inaya. Maybe you can figure her out."

Nyx laughed. "Because I'm a woman?"

"What?" He looked genuinely affronted.

"Khos, me and Inaya have nothing in common. When are you going to get that? We have as much in common as you and Rhys."

She did like the fact that he was trying to get her to go home with him, though. It had been a long while since anybody tried.

A few drinks later, they caught the train to the city center. The trains were packed with revelers headed to the waterfront for the festival and fireworks. Getting a taxi wasn't possible, so they walked up into the suburbs, which helped Nyx walk off some of the booze.

The air was cool, but not cold. Still, Nyx had her coat buckled up, and she was winded by the time they came to the top of the hill. Her skin hurt, and her left knee was starting to go out. As she limped along, she wondered if this was how Fatima felt. Broken down old crone at thirty-eight.

"What happened to you, anyway?" Khos asked. "Never seen you look so bad."

"I pissed off the wrong people, that's all. Bound to happen sooner or later."

"Least you're still breathing."

"It's something."

Khos suddenly stopped. "You smell that?"

"What?"

"Smoke."

"There are fireworks at the waterfront, drunk man."

"Not that." They were at the low end of the park, a couple blocks away from Khos's house. The streets were quiet. Most of the houses were dark. Everyone had bled out downtown hours ago. Nyx couldn't help looking across the park, toward Rhys's house.

Khos started running.

"What?" Nyx yelled.

She jogged after him. Her body protested. Half a block up, she realized what was wrong. There was something dark billowing from the windows of one of the houses. Nyx heard the *crack-pop-roar* of a bustling little blaze, still hidden from view.

Khos ran up the steps.

The burning house was *his*.

"Out back!" he yelled at her. "There's a well out back! I'll come help you with the pump!"

He pulled open the door, and a billowing cloud of smoke rolled out. Inside, something roared. She saw a wash of orange light.

"Inaya!" Khos yelled.

Nyx ran around the back of the house, into the garden. The back windows of the house shattered. Behind her, the house bellowed. Her skin throbbed. She rolled and scrambled up in the light of the blazing house. The skin on her shoulder tore, bled. She found the well at the bottom of the yard.

The well was already uncovered. An old bucket pull was set up over it. A large tree stood behind the well, clawing at the sky with branches clotted with tattered leaves.

Nyx put her hands on the edge of the well and looked down. The water was glassy black. She stared at her darker half, gazing up at her from the bottom of the well. There was nothing but water and her reflection and the stir of the water around the rope.

The rope.

She gave a sharp tug on the rope. It stayed taut. There was something on the other end.

The best way to poison a well was to throw a body into it. Nyx cranked the wheel of the pull, grunting with the effort.

She had one long stretch of time to think about who it was on the other end of the rope. Inaya? No . . . She knew how bel dames thought. They would have drowned the children here. Their bodies would be sodden and gray.

Prepare for the worst. Always prepare for the worst, because if you see anything less than that, it will be a prize, a relief.

Fuck, I've gotten soft, she thought, and was reminded of Rhys. She heard something splashing in the water.

Nyx let the lever catch. She leaned over to peer into the well again. There, at the other end of the rope, was the bucket, and a pair of hands desperately clinging to it while a smaller figure shivered inside the bucket. Two cold, wet faces peered up at her, trembling; their expressions shadowed and terrified.

"It's Nyx!" Nyx yelled at them, stupidly, but it was dark, wasn't it, and how could they know her, in the dark? Hell, how would they know her anyway? She'd only seen them once. "I'm getting you up. Come on now!"

She turned back to the lever. A stiff wind buffeted her from behind. She heard a scattering of dead leaves roil along the dirt drive. The wind stirred the tree. She raised her head and saw a hundred cicadas crawling along the trunk, flitting among the branches. As the wind stirred, the cicadas moved as well, flying around the tree like a cloud. She braced herself, squinted, prepared to be swarmed.

But something else happened.

The tree began to tremble. The wind died. The cicadas coagulated into a throbbing mass, then pulled *into* the tree, a tree that was rapidly becoming smaller, condensing. The dead leaves moved along the ground, drawn back up into the tree's branches. They melted together like butter, merged with the cicadas. Nyx had a dizzying moment of vertigo. The world seemed to bend. Something in the air around her twisted, tore, and the tree and leaves and cicadas became a liquid thing, like mottled, melted flesh. Something screamed, something inside the tree; the cicadas, maybe, dying.

Branches flew up, a crown of leaves; branches became hands, the crown of leaves elongated, shuddered.

"Oh God," Nyx said, and the breath left her body. She knew what it was becoming—what the tree, the leaves, the air, the bugs, were becoming.

"Oh God," she said again, because she was suddenly sick, because it was like something in the world had been distorted; something . . . wrong.

As the tree's color paled, the melted shape took on a more human form. The gaping hole in the face—the half-formed mouth—vomited a black cloud of flies, and with the flies came another scream; not from the bugs this time, but a true human scream; the rage and pain and terror of birth.

The figure stumbled toward Nyx, shaking and shuddering, slinging off long strings of mucus and leaf pulp, and the black eyes grew lashes and the irises formed and focused, and the cascade of hair and leaves went black, black and long as Inaya's hair; Inaya's face, round but still slack-eyed, and the fingers at the ends of the new arms were held in tight fists, oozing mucus and blood and something else that had the tangy smell of oak hybrid sap. Flies and leaf pulp, dirt and the shimmering wings of cicadas, stuck to the slick mucus covering her naked body.

The fists reached out, made open hands. Clung to the edge of the well. The eyes focused, and it was something more or less human, more or less Inaya, and Nyx knew her then, really knew her, and she felt a deep cramping in her stomach, sudden nausea. She backed a half step away and dry heaved.

Inaya screamed into the well. As she screamed, a handful of flies escaped from her newly formed lungs.

"Up!" was the word she screamed, or maybe that was just some grunt, some noise, but the next words were her children's names, and not even Nyx could mistake those.

"Are you all right?" Inaya yelled at them, and the children cried up at her.

Inaya raised her head to Nyx—her damp, mucus-crusted head—and her eyes were so very fucking black, and the look on that face, in that face . . .

"Haul them up!" Inaya snarled.

Nyx grabbed the lever and hauled them up like some other woman—someone far younger, far stronger, far less broken and exhausted. Sweat beaded her brow, ran between her breasts, her shoulder blades, long before she was tired or spent. She was shaking at the end.

When the bucket was close enough, Inaya reached into the well and hauled up the girl first—Nyx hadn't understood her name—then Taite. The children hit the dirt and clung to their mother.

Inaya patted them down, asking after hurts. When she was done, she turned again to Nyx, opened her mouth to speak, and stopped. She turned to the blazing house.

"Khos," Inaya said. Then, "Watch the children."

And in a breath, an instant, she blew apart, piece by piece, and each piece disintegrated into another piece, another, smaller and smaller, until there was only a pale mist, a fog, as if she'd transformed into some cheap radio drama, and the mist blew across the yard and into the burning house; a howling, contaminated wind.

The children gathered around Nyx and gazed with her, open-mouthed.

Nyx's mouth was dry. She tried working some spit into it and asked, "She do that often?"

"Never," Taite said, breathless.

"Holy shit," Nyx said.

"Holy shit," the girl said. Inaya had apparently taught her children Nasheenian.

Nyx grabbed them each by the hand. "Let's go," she said, and started walking toward the blazing house and the demon.

When they got to the porch, Inaya was already there, human again, naked. She knelt over Khos as he coughed and spat, his face covered in soot.

"You're a stupid fool," she said.

"What happened?" Nyx asked.

Inaya slowly turned her head, stared at Nyx with her pitch-black eyes. "What do you think happened? They came for you. Looking for *you*."

"Bel dames?" Khos asked, and started coughing again.

"Have you been drinking?" Inaya asked. Her eyes narrowed. "Were you *drinking* while these women tried to tear us apart?"

Nyx looked out at the park. "How many?" she said.

"Six, seven, I don't know," Inaya said. "I saw them coming up the walk. I knew what they were. I hid the children and . . . myself. They burned the house and left."

Nyx felt a sudden, stabbing pain in her gut. "Left and went where?" she said.

Inaya shook her head. "I don't—" She stopped. She, too, looked across the park.

"Rhys," Nyx said, and began to run.

25.

Rhys found the house in disarray. Elahyiah argued with the housekeeper in the kitchen. Something to do with missing laundry. The girls were in the sunken study, in varying states of dress. Slippers and stockings littered the floor. He saw dirty, discarded head-scarves on the porch.

Elahyiah was pulling at an earring. He noted that her pair didn't match. She was barefoot.

Outside, the neighbors' houses were going dark. He heard revelers walking through the park to catch taxis downtown to the waterfront. They would soon find themselves in a deserted neighborhood.

"I'm going up to wash and dress," he said.

Elahyiah did not acknowledge him then, but she came to him in the bathroom as he disrobed. He started the water in the tub.

She stood in the doorway.

"It was old business. It's done now," he said.

"What did you think, bringing that woman into our house?"

"I was thinking it was my house, and I could bring in whomever I please."

"How can you say that? I've heard the stories of this woman. Eight years you lived with her—"

"Six. It isn't as if we were married."

"That's worse!"

"Is it? Elahyiah, please. I don't want to fight over this. She's nothing. She was not a wife, not even a temporary one. You insult me if you think we were anything but employer and employee."

"I did not . . ." She choked on her words.

Rhys slipped into the tub. The warm water felt deliciously good. "I'll be down soon."

"We'll be late," she said.

"We're always late."

"Rhys . . ." She knelt by the tub. "I know it is not my place to ask. I know it is not my place to question, but you did not marry me for my silence."

"No, I did not." Rhys stared at the water coming out of the facet, his own skinny knees poking up from the water. He remembered the storefront back in Nasheen, in the dusty dive in Punjai. Nyx used to keep an ablution bowl near the door. Customers who came to her with bounty business all wanted to wash, after.

"That woman scares me," Elahyiah said.

"I used to be like her," he said.

"I don't believe that." She touched his face. "She is nothing. She has turned her back to God. I could see that in her face."

"Am I so different?" He raised his head. "She stayed and fought. Here I am, hiding in Tirhan."

"Hiding from what? The war? That is not your war, Rhys."

"My father thought differently."

"Mine did not. We came here because we will not fight a war for rich mullahs. This is our life, Rhys. We owe nothing to those broken countries."

"I love you," he said. And he did.

She bent and kissed him, softly. "God made us partners, love."

"I know. I'm sorry. It was disrespectful to bring her here. That life is over." He took her hand, met her look.

She nodded and pulled away. "We're almost ready."

Rhys let himself sink under the water, cut out sound. In the silence, he began to recite the ninety-nine names of God. He had his world back. Nyx would not come to him again. She had too much pride to ask for another favor.

In the warm silence, he felt something slipping away. Some rotten part of himself? Or was it some better part? The part that would fight for something more than a clean house and a well-paying job?

Her work is not honorable, he reminded himself. You are a father and husband. There is far more honor in that.

Rhys took his time and dressed in a clean khameez and bisht. He wore soft sandals. After dabbing on some perfume he opened the wardrobe and pulled a locked box from the top shelf. It was a sand-bitten old box of synthetic gray wood and amber. He ran one hand over it, and thought of the desert.

Four years ago, his wedding day, he had locked this box and sworn not to open it again. But for the last three days he'd wanted nothing more in the world than what it contained.

Rhys passed his hand over it a second time, disarming the spider poised beneath the lid. He opened it.

Inside, two jade-hilted pistols were nestled atop a length of green silk. Underneath were four boxes of non-organic ammunition. He didn't want fever bursts in his house. Metal was expensive, but more stable.

He wanted to touch them. He wanted to grab his belt, get his holsters. Weapons at his hip again, just like the desert. That other life.

And if you pick them up, he thought, you'll never put them down again. They are everything you put aside. Which do you want? You cannot have both.

Rhys closed the box.

He re-triggered the spider with a wave of his hand and replaced the box in the wardrobe.

"Rhys? Rhys, they're starting the fireworks!" Elahyiah called from downstairs.

Rhys shuttered the light, watched the room go dim. The bloody light of the moons poured in from the windows. He faced the mirror next to the door. In the bloody light, with his neatly shaven head, his gauzy bisht, he looked like a dervish from one of his mother's stories.

He started down the stairs.

"Ella? Ella?" Elahyiah's voice again, coming up the stairs. The housekeeper's name was Ella.

Rhys arrived in the kitchen. Elahyiah was struggling with Laleh's headscarf.

"They're too young for them," Rhys said.

"Their cousins are wearing them," Elahyiah said. "They're already teased for not being clean. Let's not give them anything else."

"If your uncle starts in on us again about cutting our girls—"

Elahyiah put her hands over Laleh's ears. "Stop that now."

Souri tugged at Elahyiah's sleeve. "I have to go," she said. "Please, Ma." She squirmed.

"I'll take her," Rhys said. He scooped Souri up and brought her into the privy just off the study.

"Can't go if you watch!" Souri said.

Rhys sighed and turned away.

"Ella!" Elahyiah called again.

"Where did she go?" Rhys asked.

"Into the garden. I wanted to bring lemons for Uncle Shaya's new wife."

"I'll find her," Rhys said.

"Da! I'm done, Da!"

Rhys made sure Souri's underclothes were in order and stepped back into the room. He saw Elahyiah at the counter with her head in her hands. Laleh clung to her hip.

"Elahyiah," he said softly.

She raised her head. Her eyes were wet.

He took her face in his hands and kissed her softly, said, "I love you. Just you and no other. You understand that?"

She leaned her forehead against his, wiped at her eyes. "I'm sorry."

"I'm at fault. Hush, now. I'll find Ella and we'll go to the waterfront? Yes?"

"I want to have fruit cakes!" Laleh said.

He palmed her head. "And you'll have them," he said.

Rhys walked to the back porch, through the filter, and into the dark garden.

"Ella?" he called. Was she out meeting men again? Elahyiah had caught the girl talking to some street boy on the porch once. Ras Tiegan girls were loose as wives' tongues.

"Ella! Do you have those lemons?" He walked past the well, to the little patch of lemon trees at the edge of the yard. He tripped over something in the grass. He looked down. He'd kicked over a basket half-full of lemons.

Rhys picked up the basket. He peered into the darkness of the garden. "Ella?" he said, more softly.

He looked back at the house. The street was eerily quiet. The houses all along the block were still. He saw one light on, high up in a house one street over. Most everyone was already at the waterfront.

Rhys picked his way across the yard, holding the basket of lemons. So quiet.

He paused at the edge of the porch. The bugs. The bugs had gone quiet. No crickets. No cicadas. Rhys dropped the basket. He walked quickly back into the house, through the filter.

Souri looked up as he came in. Laleh was knotting her headscarf. "Da?" she said.

Elahyiah was opening the front door.

"Don't!" Rhys said.

It all happened very fast.

Ella careened into the house, screaming. Behind her were three big women. The first inside grabbed Elahyiah by the hair. The second twisted the housekeeper's skinny head. Her neck snapped. Rhys heard it.

There was a sudden, pervasive smell of oranges.

Rhys choked and raised a hand, called for the wasp swarm at the center of the room.

The girls began to scream.

He felt the filters go down. The constant humming—the singing that sent him to sleep at night—went silent. The house was naked.

The wasp swarm swooped toward the woman holding Elahyiah.

The bel dame holding his wife.

Rhys grabbed Souri with his free hand. She was screaming and screaming.

Something heavy thumped him from behind. A hand went over his mouth. He felt a bug in his mouth. Smelled bug-repelling unguent on his attacker's fingers.

He elbowed his attacker, but there was someone else with her, and they were both on him now. They wrestled him to the ground. The swarm swam lazily away from him, misdirected, confused. He called them in to sting his attackers and asked for a beetle swarm. The nearest was in the garden. He felt them there, but could not call them. Oh, God, why give him any skill at all if it could not help him now?

He choked on the beetle. The poison began to work its way down his throat.

Screaming. His daughters were screaming. Elahyiah.

My wife. The bel dames and my wife.

Rhys tried to heave himself out of their grip. They held firm. The struggle was enough to make him gag on the bug. He swallowed, knowing as he did that he was half a minute away from losing the bugs completely.

"Out, all right? Bring them out!"

A long-legged woman stepped over Souri's sobbing form and crouched next to Rhys. She cocked her head at him, leaned in close. A lovely, clear-skinned face, but something in her was lacking, some light behind her eyes.

"Missed me, black man?" Rasheeda said.

Rasheeda. The white raven had found him.

Rhys pulled against the bel dames again.

"Come now, I was always better at this than she was," Rasheeda said.

They hauled him up and bound him. Elahyiah, too.

The girls they wrapped once with sticky bands and moved outside.

"Where are you taking them?" Rhys said, voice hoarse. The world was muted, dumb. It was like being blind, without the bugs.

"Leave my family inside. They're nothing to you."

"You forget, black man. None of you are anything to me."

"Rasheeda—"

The women dragged him out to the back porch. He recognized one of them now. She was the tall bel dame who'd stood next to Shadha so Murshida in Beh Ayin, the one with the burn-scarred neck. What was her name? Dhiya.

"You're making a mistake, Dhiya," Rhys said.

She turned to him, coolly, said, "You have no idea."

Outside, the bloody moons cast the whole yard in crimson shadows.

Elahyiah and the girls were huddled at the end of the porch. The girls were sobbing. Elahyiah looked over at him. He saw her breathing deep, but she did not cry. She did not tremble.

Two of the bel dames were uncovering the well. They must have broken the padlock.

Dhiya pushed him to his knees. He was just ten feet away from Elahyiah and the girls. He looked over at his wife again. She met his look for one long minute.

Neither said a word.

Rasheeda tossed a loop of something to one of the bel dames. "Rope them up in that," she said. She strode over to Rhys.

"I have some questions for you, gravy eater." She crouched again, cocked her head. "I heard you had a meet with an old friend of ours. I need to know what you gave her."

"She came here for a recording," Rhys said. "I don't have it anymore. She has it." Nyx could take care of herself. He and Elahyiah could not.

"So you gave her everything?"

"Yes. Search the house. There's nothing. She wanted a voice reel we had back when we were hunting the alien, Nikodem Jordan. She needed to match it to the voice of a bel dame."

"And did she match it?"

Rhys paused. Too long a pause. Dhiya hovered behind him. "I don't know," Rhys said. "The reel she got was out of date."

"The reel?"

"She got a voice recognition reel."

"From who?"

A thin line, here. He looked over at Elahyiah and the girls again. Then back at Rasheeda. Hadn't he always been a good liar? "Another bel dame. She's staying in the Ras Tiegan district. You can find her there."

Rasheeda rose. She flicked a hand at the other women.

They rolled out the loop of wire and started winding it around Elahyiah and the children.

"Rhys?" Elahyiah said. Softly.

"I said to leave them alone! That's all I know. I told you where they are. You go ask Nyx if you have any more questions!"

"I already know where Nyx is," Rasheeda said. "There's someone else I came for."

"What are you doing? Rasheeda, that's everything! I'll answer anything! Rasheeda!"

She lolled toward his wife and children. "String them up," she said.

"Rasheeda, Goddamn you!"

Dhiya and one of the other bel dames hauled his wife and children over to the well. They had wound them together tightly with jagged wire, the sort they used on the back fences in the rural areas to keep out stray dogs and giant stag beetles. Souri and Laleh continued to cry.

"Stop this! Rasheeda!" Rhys yelled. He looked up at the neighboring houses, all dark. He heard a soft *whizz-pop*, and a hazy blue glow momentarily lit the yard. Residue from the Martyr's celebration at the waterfront.

The fireworks had started.

"Let's give you a fighting chance," Rasheeda said.

The other bel dames looped the wire through the old tripod bucket pull. Back before the row of houses had running water, the well had served as water source for the house and its nearest neighbors. Most houses in the district had them.

They'd knotted the girls into Elahyiah's arms, wound tight against her body. She clutched them to her. He saw the wire digging into flesh. Saw her lips moving. The ninety-nine names of God.

Dhiya locked the wire into the bucket pull and pushed Elahyiah and the girls toward the well.

"Over you go," Dhiya said, and shoved them over the lip of the well.

Screaming.

Rhys lunged forward. The bel dame behind him cuffed him.

His family hung over the black hole of the well, strung together with skin-biting jagged wire, screaming.

Screaming.

"Rasheeda!"

Rasheeda turned slowly on her heel. "Why don't we play a game? If you can pull them up you can have them."

"Don't do this."

"Who was the bel dame she got the reel from?"

"Alharazad," Rhys said.

"And the woman Nyx identified? Who was she?"

Souri and Laleh were whimpering now. Voices hoarse. Elahyiah dangled over the well, like a strangled butterfly, wings mutilated.

"Shadha so Murshida," Rhys said. "The woman I met with in Beh Ayin."

"Who else knows?"

"No one. She and I heard it. I don't know if she told her team or not. I've told no one."

"Good," Rasheeda said. She took him by the collar, helped him to his feet. His bisht was torn and dirty. "Now you have a chance to pull them back." She pushed him toward Dhiya.

Dhiya held out the limp end of the wire. It fed up into the triangular pull. The wheel lock held it in place and kept his family suspended over the well.

"Hold on," Dhiya said.

Rhys turned to Rasheeda. "You can't expect—"

"Pull them up," Rasheeda said. "Pull them up, and they're yours."

The thin strand of wire was hooked with barbs.

"Rasheeda . . ."

"You say my name like I don't know it," she said. "Come now, easy, isn't it? Just pull them up and over. You're a Tirhani man, hey, a boxer? You boxing magicians. Show us how men care for their families in Tirhan." She reached into her coat and pulled out a gun. She aimed it at Elahyiah. "Or I could shoot them right now . . . the way you shot me and my sisters."

Rhys reached for the wire.

Everything bled out of him. All thought. All reason. He watched his wife, his children, hanging above the well, slowly crushed by their own weight, winding them tighter and tighter in the wire.

Pull them up, and they were his again.

The world was quiet. No bugs. He couldn't sense them or hear them or see them. The occasional orange or blue or lavender firework crested the rise of the buildings, splashed them in the ambient glow. There were no fireworks in the desert. All the light in the sky was there from bursts and munitions.

In Tirhan, all the light was beautiful.

He twisted the wire in his hands, until the barbs bit into his flesh. If he could not pull them up, he would hold them. Hold them until the end of the world.

Rasheeda was watching him. She gestured to Dhiya.

Dhiya walked over to the wheel lock.

Rhys grit his teeth. Dug in his heels.

Elahyiah lifted her head.

The world went blue, then pale lavender as the fireworks fell behind the horizon of the house behind them.

Dhiya released the lock.

Rhys jerked forward. The barbs cut into his hands. He hit the ground, held on. Pain. Just pain. Hold on. Pull.

The girls whimpered. They'd dipped beneath the lip of the well. Their voices were distant, muffled.

Rasheeda walked toward him.

Rhys found his feet. Dug in his heels again. Pulled. His hands had gone numb. He saw his hands, once, rapidly swelling, beaded in blood. Then his eyes were on the lip of the well. He began to recite the ninety-nine names of God.

"Pull," Rasheeda said softly.

He did not look at her. Nothing but the wire connecting him to his wife and daughters. Such a thin wire. His body trembled. He couldn't feel his hands. I can hold them, he thought. How long can I hold them? God, help me. Just for this. I need you, one last time.

But his body shook. His feet began to slip.

He heard something behind him, then. Someone yelling sharply. He saw Rasheeda turn, confused, mouth agape.

He saw her reach for her machete. Heard heavy footsteps. The creak and hiss of blades leaving sheaths.

There was a long, slow cry. A blade flashed. Rasheeda fell onto him. The blade flashed again. Everything moved like a dream. Some bloody nightmare.

He couldn't see his wife.

God, Elahyiah.

The blade flashed again. Rasheeda tumbled into him and fell against his straining arms.

Someone's blade clipped right through the soft fat of Rasheeda's shoulder as she jerked away . . . and neatly severed Rhys's arms at the wrist.

Tension released.

Elahyiah screamed.

Rhys watched, curious, as his still-grasping hands—tangled in the wire—were jerked sharply toward the bottomless mouth of the well.

Rhys fell back, hard, onto his ass. Great steams of blood pumped from his wrists. My blood, he thought, distantly. Beside him, Rasheeda hissed and spat and rolled to her feet, oblivious of the chunk taken out of her shoulder.

Rhys held up the bloody stumps of his arms.

Gaped. Dizzy.

Blood pumped across his bisht. He shoved his arms, reflexively, beneath his armpits and struggled toward the well on his knees. Blackness rode at the edges of his vision. Someone was laughing. His stomach heaved. Fireworks popped.

And the missing sound. The silence.

The staggering, crushing silence.

He staggered toward the well. Blackness ate at the edges of his vision as figures whirled around him. Blades. Blood. He looked up, and from the edge of the blackness he saw a tall, tangle-haired woman raise her machete and cut Rasheeda's head off.

The head thumped onto the bloody ground, still sneering. The eyelids fluttered. Rasheeda's coterie of bel dames began to scatter.

Rhys stared. The tangle-haired woman stood over Rasheeda's cooling body, machete in hand. He knew her. It was not the woman he expected.

Shadha so Murshida was breathing hard, and bloody. Not all of the blood was Rasheeda's. Four more bel dames stood with her. Another chased after those who had fled. Shadha finally lifted her gaze from the body and met his look.

She walked over to him. Blood dripped from her blade. Her face was ghastly.

"Haul them up!" she barked at the women behind her. The women jogged toward the well.

Shadha pulled a length of wire from the ground, knelt next to him, and—to his horror—began to savagely tie off the ends of his bloody stumps.

Rhys passed out. For how long, he didn't know, but when he came to he lay on his side. Flesh beetles lapped at the bloody ground all around him. Shadha stood with a handful of other dark figures. When she saw him, she walked over and crouched next to him.

"Shouldn't have gone that way," she said. "Wasn't you I was after. Rasheeda . . . she gets carried way. She plays her own games. This was the last one."

Rhys stared at the sky behind her. The big bloody moons had risen above the trees. His head felt lighter than air. My hands, he thought, distantly. Stop the blood. Pull the girls out.

"Elahyiah?" he croaked.

Shadha glanced over her shoulder. "We have to go," she said, and stood. "Sorry."

The Nasheenian word for "sorry" translated into Tirhani as something akin to, "I'll do it better next time."

"Please," Rhys murmured, but she was already moving. The women moved with her. And as they pulled away from the yard, he saw that they'd been standing around a dark, crumpled mass.

Rhys struggled up again to his knees. He was going to be sick. He pressed his forehead to the ground. Ninety-nine names of God . . . Prayer. It must be past evening prayer. He hadn't heard the muezzin.

Nyx would come for them. She would come. She would pull Elahyiah and his daughters from the well. She would stop the bleeding. She would pick him up in her strong arms. She would hold him like a child. She would drag his family from the well. She would ask, and he would tell her where Yah Tayyib the rogue magician was hiding. He would tell her about Shadha. Whatever she wanted, whoever she wanted to bring in. He would tell her everything.

They were not all lost yet. Not quite yet.

Please, God, let her come back to me.

His strength gave out. He collapsed onto the dusty ground.

Rhys screamed. He screamed with every sinew and cell of his body. He screamed like a dying man. He screamed and screamed under the bloody lights of the moons, nostrils thick with the stink of his own blood.

He screamed.

✛

Nyx bolted through the park. Ten yards in, her left knee gave out. She stumbled, caught herself on her hands, and kept plodding forward despite her awkward gait and bleeding hands. She cursed her bloody, broken body. She cursed Khos and his drunken rambling. She cursed Rhys and his stupid family. But mostly, she cursed herself. Damned stupid fool woman, dragging her dying hide into Tirhan and pulling bel dames behind her like cats to a carcass. I was careful, she wanted to say. We weren't followed from Nasheen. These bel dames were already here. But if she was so careful, how had they found her once she was here? Who had told them she was coming? And why take out Khos and Rhys? What did they have to do with anything? Why not kill her and be done with it?

The park smelled of smoke and loam. Not all of it was from the fire. She heard the soft *whizz-pop* of fireworks along the waterfront. The dim roar of distant cheering. A whole soft city drunk on the celebration of their Martyr.

As if the world didn't have enough martyrs.

She passed a twist in the path and saw Rhys's house, a gray shadow, across the street. No lights, no fire. Darkness. God willing, they were gone, out celebrating on the waterfront with the others.

Nyx slowed down, tried to catch her breath. She was sweating hard. I'm not broken, she told herself. I'm not broken. Get to the fucking house, woman. Go be broken at the house.

She reached for the scattergun at her back.

Heard something behind her. A wasp swarm, maybe? Some chigger mass. She turned to look.

She remembered, then. You start a fire in the cane fields to flush out the cane beetles.

Old and stupid. She was so fucking old and stupid.

She ducked and fired the scattergun. A burst of smoke. A flash of movement. Turned, too late.

A woman stepped out of the scrub behind her, flashed metal. Someone else surged onto the path ahead of Nyx and leapt over the figure she had caught with her gun. The woman was fast. Bloody fucking fast. She swung at Nyx with some kind of club.

The blow crushed Nyx's jaw, sent her crashing to the ground.

Hot, black pain.

Nyx's scattergun rolled across the ground.

Pain. Nyx choked and spit blood. There was something wrong with her face.

She turned onto her side before they could get on top of her. Yanked at her sword as she rolled to her feet.

Heard a pistol shot.

Fire burned her gut.

Nyx pulled the sword free and swung. Caught a slick-looking kid in the face. Saw the flash of an organic burnous. Turned again, lashed out, working on sound and movement now. She couldn't see much. Her face was hot and black. Blood ran freely down her chin.

Two more shots.

Time was, she thought she could dodge bullets.

Pain shot through her left knee. She went down. Her whole body was on fire. She clawed at the ground with her free hand and lashed out with her left.

A tall, tangle-haired woman stepped forward, came right up on top of her, and slammed Nyx's sword away with the edge of her gun. Pressed the barrel against Nyx's mangled face. So cold it felt good on her burning flesh.

Pulled the trigger.

Click.

She was out.

My lucky day, Nyx thought, distantly. She released her sword and grabbed the barrel of the gun with both hands.

The woman kept hold of the gun with one hand and reached

behind her for a dagger. Nyx brought her knee in and kicked up and out into the woman's groin. The woman caught her leg and twisted, hard.

Pain shot through Nyx's leg. Her body followed the leg, desperate not to break it. She lay on her belly, flopping like a fish, reaching for her sword, bleeding across the gravel while darkness ate at her vision.

It was over in a breath.

A cool ribbon of fire slipped between her ribs. Felt a knee on her back, a heavy body. A knife, clean and neat. Somebody else with half a face stepped forward and jerked her head back by the braids, bared her throat.

The knife cut cleanly across her throat. Nyx had done it so many times she never wondered what it felt like. Her chest was suddenly warm and wet.

Nyx clawed at her head. Sought one of the needles in her hair.

Fuck you you're coming with me you fucking black death one clean cut I have eight more seconds you bloody . . .

But the woman was quick. She yanked Nyx over onto her back and pinned her to the ground beneath her. Held her while she bled out. Stared into her face. Right into her face.

Nyx spit blood at her.

A young woman, a mane of tangled hair. But it was the expression that struck Nyx: the expression on the bel dame's face as the world went wholly dark, as Nyx's hands cooled. Life, blood, darkness.

The bel dame's mouth was a thin line. Her eyes were big and dark and completely blank, like looking into the blackest part of the sky in the desert, that big reach of darkness where there were no stars, just emptiness. Umayma, at the edge of everything.

Nyx choked on a word.

But there was only blood. And blackness . . .

And a desperate, passionate desire to live.

Don't.

That was the word.

Please don't. Not yet.

She had a staggering moment of vertigo. I'm drowning in my own blood, she thought.

Rhys, I'm drowning.

Then it was over.

26.

When Rhys next woke, the moons had moved across the sky. A few lights were on in neighboring houses. He heard the sound of low laughter, felt the muted hum of a wasp swarm. He lay on his right side, his arms . . . the stumps of his arms in front of him. Congealing blood glistened on the ground. Something moved at the ends of his ruined arms. He heard the soft chittering of flesh beetles. The beetles' sticky saliva had sealed his wounds. Had they come on their own, or had he called them?

Then, pain. As if his hands were crushed. Ghostly pain. Hands no longer attached to his body.

Rhys pushed himself up against the side of the well, and rested his head against the smooth stone.

The neighbors. There was a light on in the house nearest him. He knew the family. Their gardener was his housekeeper's father.

Rhys hooked his elbow over the lip of the well and pushed himself to his feet. Did not look into the inky blackness.

He stumbled forward, fell. Reached out his hands to hold himself—

He remembered, too late. He landed on the stumps of his arms. Pain smeared his vision. He screamed.

Blackness.

When he opened his eyes next, a man stood over him. The hulking shape blotted out the moons. A large shaven head, broad shoulders, thick legs . . .

"Khos?" Rhys croaked. He was thirsty. Incredibly thirsty. "Elahyiah. The well. The children."

Khos picked him up.

Rhys was fascinated by the ease of the movement, the massive spread of the man's hands. Khos could squash Rhys's head between those hands.

"Elahyiah," Rhys said.

"Where is she?"

"In the well. They put them in the well."

Khos walked over to the well, shifted Rhys's weight in his arms, looked over his shoulder into the blackness. "There's nothing down there, Rhys."

"Elahyiah. The children."

"Let's get you out of here."

"The bel dames. The bel dames are coming."

"I know."

"Where's Nyx?" Rhys murmured. "Is Nyx here?"

"I'm going to take you someplace safe. The girls? Both your daughters were in the well, too?"

"Yes."

"Your girl, too?"

"The housekeeper . . . yes. In the house. Dead, in the house."

Khos grunted. He walked across the garden and to the street. A bakkie waited outside, spitting dead beetles from the exhaust.

"Nyx?" Rhys asked.

An ugly woman pushed open the back door. Rhys recognized her as Nyx's weapons tech, Suha. Inaya was at the wheel. She turned to look at him. Her face was pinched and drawn. Her headscarf was gone. He saw dirt and soot on her face.

"We don't know," Khos said. He lifted Rhys into the back seat. The flesh beetles fell free of his arms, skittered across the seat.

"Where are the girls?" Inaya said. "Elahyiah? Where are Elahyiah and the girls, Rhys?"

"They're gone," Khos said. He slammed the door.

Rhys let his head drop against the seat. The smell of Suha, next to him, was sour and fermented, old sweat and new fear. She had a custom organic shotgun set with the butt at her feet. She kept her attention out the window.

He listened to Khos and Inaya talking, low. His attention drifted. He closed his eyes, saw the black well again. Dark water. Emptiness. Gaping darkness. The bite of the machete. Screaming. His or the girls'?

He choked on something like a sob. Khos and Inaya's voices swam at the edge of his grief.

"Where are you going?" Inaya said.

"I'm going to look for Nyx," Khos said.

"Don't be a bloody fool. Let me do it."

"You?"

Inaya stepped out of the bakkie, left it running while she crossed to the other side.

Rhys drifted in and out as they spoke.

"They took too many tonight," Inaya said. "I need you with the children. If she's alive, I can get her out of there and back without notice. You can't."

"They nearly took everything, Inaya," Khos said, and lowered his voice to a fierce whisper. "Rhys's family! Gone! Like that. These aren't border toughs. These are bel dames."

"More reason for me to go. Give me a gun."

"Inaya—"

"Don't question me. Not now. You know what I am."

"Bloody fool."

"And you married me. What does that make you?"

Rhys heard the door open and close again. Heard the bakkie grind out of park, and suddenly they were moving. He opened his eyes.

"Inaya?" he said.

"She's looking for Nyx, the fool," Khos said.

"Your children?"

"Safe," he said. "God willing. I left them with my other wife."

"I . . ." Rhys tried to tangle through that. It didn't make sense. "Your . . . other wife?"

"God will keep us safe."

"God did not keep my children safe," Rhys said.

And though Khos did not say it, he saw his answer in the thin, hard line of Khos's mouth in the rearview mirror.

God could only be at one house that night.

He had not chosen Rhys's house.

27.

Inaya went through the garden first, and pulled along the cloak of the night with her. Her body felt weightless, insubstantial, so free. The air around her danced. She took a deep breath, and surrendered herself to her body's promise of freedom.

She became the night.

Deep marks in the ground. Footprints. Four, five women had been there. Likely medium height: one small, heavy in build.

She moved over the well and gazed deeply inside, saw nothing. She passed over an overturned basket of lemons on the back porch, and noted the filter was down, though that would not have stopped her movement through the house. They must have powered down the house before coming in.

A little girl's slipper lay at the center of the living room. The desk had been overturned, its contents rifled and spilled across the floor. The housekeeper's body was sprawled just inside the doorway, like a broken mantid. There were dirty dishes in the sink, avocado peels and bread crusts on the counter. She moved upstairs.

Scarves, clothing, and loose papers littered the stairs. Inside Rhys's bedroom, she found the source. The women had ransacked the room, starting with the writing desk and moving to the wardrobe.

She paused halfway inside. One brown, bare leg was just visible, sticking out from the other side of the bed. She rose up over the bed to get a better look. The woman lay face up, dressed in a tunic and belled trousers. Her face was bloated and discolored.

This was their end, then.

She breathed in for a long moment—like pulling air through her skin—and shifted back.

Painful. Like trying to fit a fire inside a soda bottle. She assembled the pieces of herself and found her footing again on the soft, organic floor. Felt the heavy pull of the world, the weight of her bones, again.

From what was left of the mist, she reconstructed the shotgun. A sleek metal and organic piece not a year old. A present Khos had given her during better times. She watched it take form as she stitched it back into existence.

When she was done, she rubbed herself down with one of the bed sheets and pulled on one of Elahyiah's abayas. She bent and patted down the dead bel dame's body, found nothing. No weapons, no papers, no trinkets. Her sisters had cleaned her out. On the bed near her, she saw a faux wooden box. There was no lock. Inside was a tattered length of green silk and two pistols. Inaya picked it up and dumped it out. A black spider, big as her thumb, skittered free.

Other than the spider, just pistols, dead ammo. She went back to the wardrobe and grabbed a somber blue hijab as she went to search the other rooms.

She found no more bodies. They had even searched the children's room, overturned the wardrobe, cut open the mattresses. Dead and dying beetles littered the floor, released from their broken lamps. What were they looking for?

But she found no more bodies.

No Nyx.

Inaya went back out to the well where Khos had said he found Rhys. The ground was muddy with blood and crushed grass. Rasheeda's body was there. She recognized the sneering radio-star face immediately. Someone had split open the back of that pretty head, though. Inaya kicked at the leaking pieces of Rasheeda's head, and smashed the gray matter into the soil. A single roach encased in an amber-colored sac was visible among the offal. It flexed its mandibles. She crushed that, too, then gingerly picked up half of Rasheeda's skull and tossed it into the well. One less bel dame to keep her up at night.

She stared into the black well again. The wells here were deep, built to tap into the underground river that fed the city's salty sea. The city used up most of the water before it reached the sea, but up on the hill, the aquifer was still deep. The bodies would have been pulled into the sea by now, or caught down there on some rocky protrusion. The bodies could poison wells in the neighborhood if left to rot. She'd need to make an anonymous call to the health authority.

As she turned away, she saw something heaped at the edge of the copse of lemon trees and scrub brush behind the well. She raised the shotgun and walked toward it. The smell gave it away. To her eyes, it looked like a pile of damp rags and brittle bones, but her nose said differently.

Inaya knelt in the bloody grass. Elahyiah's body was bent and twisted in on itself, tangled in wire. Her skin was cool to the touch. Inaya moved the twisted body and found the tangled ruin of one of the children beneath her.

Her gut churned, and she had to look away. Her hands shook. She sent up a prayer to Mhari, protector of women and children. Was it Souri, the broken child? Her skull had been crushed, likely against the wall of the well on the way down. Her tiny limbs bent and broken. Inaya saw no sign of Laleh. From the look of the wire, the body had torn free sometime between falling into the well and getting hauled back up.

They must have been hauled up. Inaya looked over toward

the well, at least a dozen paces distant. Why had the bel dames pulled her out? What game was this?

"El?" she said, softly. She put her fingers in front of Elahyiah's mouth. Waited for breath. If she'd only drowned, there was still time . . .

Elahyiah made some sound. Death rattle, or cough?

"El?"

Inaya began untangling Elahyiah's body from her dead child's. The wire had cut into her flesh, torn long rents in her robes. She'd have broken ribs, likely, and perhaps much worse.

"Come now, we're going to get some help and get you out of here."

"My babies," Elahyiah murmured.

"I'm getting help." Inaya could not take apart and reassemble living things. She could become them, yes, but sentient creatures were much harder to pull apart and put back together than organic tubing and blister shells.

"I'll get us a taxi," Inaya said. "Be still."

Inaya stood, and started toward the front porch to finish the search. Maybe Laleh had run off? But there was nothing on the porch, just the filthy organic sludge of the ruptured bug juice tank that had fed the house's filters.

Inaya slipped the shotgun under her abaya and walked back across the street, toward the park. Some of the revelers had returned now. She didn't need to be seen on the street with a shotgun. A few notes would coax a rickshaw puller from the taxi ranks to get Elahyiah to . . . that other woman's house? Or the true safe house?

Inaya grit her teeth. Desperate times. It was she who had suggested they visit the other wife to secure the children. Khos had not seemed surprised at her knowledge. Had he assumed she always knew? That she wanted it like this?

She pulled the shotgun again as she entered the park. She

paused a moment to sniff the air. Her sense of smell wasn't nearly as good as it was in shifter form, but it was still better than most.

Just smoke. All she could smell was that terrible smoke.

She walked back through the park, taking the same route she had watched Nyx take. What was she doing out here, looking for some bloody mercenary? But Elahyiah had been alive. If Elahyiah could survive bel dames and drowning, Nyx could survive a simple assassination.

Would she have gone around the park? No. Inaya had not known Nyx well, but she had spent a good deal of time with Rhys after coming to Tirhan. She saw the way he looked when he spoke of her. And she knew Nyx had come back for him. Nyx wouldn't have gone around, even though that way was more cautious. Caution had never ruled her thinking when it came to Rhys.

Inaya saw her own smoldering house on the other side of the park. Organic technicians had arrived to put out the blaze. She saw them in their great blue smocks talking on the porch.

She turned around to look into the park. She would have to take the long way.

Inaya walked the path again, slower this time, and watched the ground. As she came within sight of Rhys's house, she saw the blood. Someone had smeared dirt over it. Standing this close now, she could smell it.

She paused, closed her eyes, and took a long, deep breath through her nose. The world hummed around her. Her body tugged at her. That same urge for freedom.

Inaya pushed off the path and into the thick brush and hanging vines. Bugs whirred and buzzed around her.

Just off the path, years of runoff had created a deep ditch, cluttered in forest litter: dead leaves, dead insects, broken carapaces, twisted vines. Thorn bushes grew from it. Inaya hunted along the ditch.

The blue-gray dawn was still distant along the horizon. She saw the boot in the bloody half-light of the waning moons, and paused. She looked along the ditch another few feet.

The body had been dumped in the widest part of the ditch. Dead leaves, dirt, and loam had been kicked over it.

Inaya approached slowly, gun out, listening for others along the path, listening for ambushers; a body for bait.

But there was nothing.

She reached forward. The body had been turned on its side and covered over in a coat. She pulled the coat back. Dirt and loam and dead leaves fell softly to the ground.

Nyx lay curled on her side, face ashen, dirt and blood in her hair. Her jaw was askew, crushed. Inaya saw a thick black pool of drying blood soaked into the front of her tunic. Fire ants swarmed across her torso, her face, but avoided her eyes. Her blank, dead eyes.

Just another dead thing along the road.

Inaya started to reach forward to look for weapons or cash, but hesitated. Expected Nyx to leap up and cut her head off. She pulled her hands back. The bel dames would have cleaned her out, just as they had cleaned out their sister Rasheeda. Inaya covered the body again with the burnous.

She walked onto the path and wiped the bugs and detritus from her abaya, then concealed her gun. She walked back to the street and walked quickly toward the taxi ranks.

Someone had finally called Nyx to account for her crimes.

God leaves no one unpunished, Inaya thought. But her eyes watered, blurred. Nyx was dead. Whether it meant the rest of them were damned or saved now, she did not know.

28.

Inaya pushed through the frame of the door, shepherding Elahyiah behind her. They stumbled into the blasted interior of the main room of the mausoleum. The door was still mostly intact, but from inside Inaya could look out the busted colored glass of the window and into the tangle of the graveyard.

Nyx's big ugly companion, Suha, must have seen her approach. She met Inaya at the door and helped her pull Elahyiah in and off to the next room.

"Are you all right?" Khos asked.

Inside, the mausoleum was dusty and crowded. Inaya coughed.

"God," Khos said. "Did you . . . did you pull her up? Was she in the well?"

"No," Inaya said. She wiped the dirt and dried blood from her forehead. Elahyiah's blood. "She was already up. They must have pulled her up."

"The children?"

Inaya shook her head, then met his look. "Our children?"

"Safe," he said.

She nodded and looked away. A conversation for another time. All she needed now was their safety. She didn't care how they achieved it.

She followed Suha into the second, darker room. Rhys lay on a tattered mattress under the wan light of a handful of dirty glow bulbs. They'd bound the stumps of his arms. She had plenty of morphine and thorn bug juice stored here, but he would need a magician, a very good one, soon.

Suha helped Elahyiah ease down onto the mattress besides Rhys. Elahyiah saw him then, what was left of him, and began to cry.

Inaya wanted to take her up in her arms and comfort her. Say something soothing. But her mouth was dry. She had nothing to give her. Everything felt . . . She wasn't sure, really. She wasn't sure she felt anything at all.

"And Nyx?"

Inaya turned.

Khos watched her, blocking the doorway. Inaya looked at Elahyiah lying beside Rhys. Together, the two bodies looked like casualties of war. A handless Chenjan. A broken, childless mother.

"She's dead," Inaya said. Flat.

"Dead?" Suha said from the other room. She appeared in the doorway. "The fuck you say?"

"Dead," Inaya repeated. "You can look at her yourself."

"You're full of shit," Suha said.

"Where?" Khos said.

"The park. She's dead. We need to focus on staying alive."

"The fuck you think we're doing?" Suha said.

"We'll need to move in the morning and collect the children. We have the insurance on the house and the cache here," Inaya said.

"Rhys needs a magician. Elahyiah doesn't look much better."

"We can take them into town. Nyx is dead. They won't be looking for us."

"Are you so sure of that?" Khos said. Khos moved inside and navigated the tight space, knelt next to Elahyiah.

Suha moved away and squeezed past Inaya and into the

front room. She was shorter than Nyx, but heavier—a bulky Nasheenian woman. She stank like death.

Khos reached out a tentative hand to Elahyiah's forehead. It still surprised Inaya sometimes, to see how gentle he was. The rest, though, there were times . . .

"You're all right now," Khos said. "You're among friends."

"My babies," Elahyiah said.

"We'll look for them," Khos said.

Inaya frowned. But that was likely best, for now.

"Please." Elahyiah reached up and grabbed hold of his collar. "Please, our children."

"We'll keep looking. Hush now. We'll get you a magician." He turned to Inaya. "You speak with her."

Inaya knelt. "We're here, Elahyiah. Rhys is here too." She turned and saw that Rhys's face was covered in sweat. He shivered, opened his eyes. "Elahyiah," he said.

"She's here, Rhys," Inaya said.

Rhys shook his head, squeezed his eyes shut.

"Can't risk taking you to a magician yet," Khos said. "You understand?"

"Do you know any magicians we can trust?" Inaya asked. "Someone we can call on?"

Rhys's eyes were glassy, feverish. "The girls. Where are the girls? Elahyiah."

"I'm here," Elahyiah said softly. She grabbed at his dirty bisht and began to weep in earnest.

"We need one for you first," Khos said. "You'll die here on the table and you'll be no good to anyone. Who can we ask? You must know someone."

When Rhys just moaned, Khos looked up at Inaya. "Do you think we could bribe someone?"

Inaya made a sound of distaste. "Don't be stupid. You want to bring someone here who can be bribed? Stop and think."

"Stop it," he said.

"You asked my opinion. Or have I turned into a Mhorian woman?" It tasted bitter.

Khos's face got dark.

"Tayyib," Rhys said. His eyes were open again. "Yah Tayyib."

"He's hallucinating," Inaya said. She looked for the pack of bugs and drugging agents she'd stowed in the old prayer niche behind them. The images of the Ras Tiegan saints, even in this overgrown, forgotten place, had been defaced and mutilated. "I can give him something more for the pain."

"Yah Tayyib," Rhys said again. "He's in the magicians' gym. City center."

"Yah Tayyib died in Chenja," Khos said.

"No." Rhys pushed the stump of his arm toward Khos. "He's here. We have tea on weekend prayer days."

"It's true," Elahyiah said, wiping at her eyes. "I have met this magician. What of him? Can he help Rhys? Our children?"

Inaya pulled out the thorn juice she'd been keeping to drug her own children. If the bel dames started stalking the mausoleums, crying children would have been deadly. She never thought she would be thankful for Khos's other wife.

"Go to the magicians' gym," Rhys said. "He'll remember you. Tell him what happened. He'll come."

"He'll give us up to them," Khos said.

"No. Go to him."

Inaya pulled the stopper on the thorn juice, brought it to Rhys's lips. He shook his head, pursed his mouth.

"Don't," Khos said.

"He's talking craziness."

She met Khos's look. For a moment they regarded one another. His eyes were narrow slits, the mouth a thin line, and his skin all looked too tight. He was terrified, she realized. Though he did not tremble, and his voice remained steady, she could see the terror in him now. A terror that mirrored hers. God, she thought, dear God in heaven, how will we do this?

"I'll take the bakkie downtown and ask," Khos said. "That may be the only hope we have for the fever."

"A regular surgeon or hedge witch could take down the fever," Inaya said.

"We need to do something about his hands." Khos stood.

"Khos—"

He walked out into the front room. She followed, still carrying the thorn juice.

"Leaving him here risks his death," Khos said.

As they came in, Suha stepped outside. Inaya had not seen the other one, the shifter boy. She wondered if he was dead too.

"Nyx is dead," Khos said. "She was a bel dame. Maybe not the best of them, but one of the toughest. Whoever she had after her is better than she is."

"Which means that if they wanted us dead, they would have done it," Inaya said. Then, low, "I would be like Elahyiah, and you would have no children."

His face looked sad. Stricken. Something knifed through her, then, some sympathetic emotion. How many years had they stumbled through all this together? How much had he given up for this, just as she had? How much had he risked to keep them safe? She'd never considered it before.

"I'm sorry," she said. "You just don't understand. You don't know what it feels like to be—"

"Someone who's lost everything?" he said quietly.

She caught herself, and remembered his other life. As dark as hers, truly? When they came to Tirhan, he had been looking for his son.

"I have not thanked you for what you've done. Or . . . appreciated it. Your son . . . I'm sorry."

"He went to a good Tirhani family. I know I'm not much of a father."

"You're a fine father," she said, and caught herself, shook her head. "I'm sorry."

He reached out, tentatively, gently. "I came here to build my own family."

She flinched from his touch. He pulled his hand away.

"You lied to me."

"I didn't."

"That Mhorian woman—" Inaya caught her breath. It was only the second time she'd said it aloud. The first she'd done only to save her children. She wrung her hands.

"I'm sorry. You don't understand—"

"I understand perfectly well. I understand that you despise me and fear me. That you—"

"What?"

She looked up at him.

"Do you even know who she is to me?"

"Your wife?"

"No. Before that. You said nothing. I thought you knew."

"About what?"

"Inaya, she's the mother of my son, the half-breed boy the underground smuggled out of Nasheen. She isn't Mhorian. She's mostly Nasheenian, and she fled here after I did, to get away from the war. She would have lost her Tirhani visa if I hadn't married her. It was my duty. Any man's duty."

"I . . . why didn't you tell me who she was?"

"You never asked. With all the work that you do . . . I assumed you knew. You always know everything."

"You're a bloody fool."

"I'm the fool?"

"Hey!" Suha yelled.

Inaya turned.

"Get the fuck moving. Work out your shit later. Magicians first. Catshit later," Suha said, moving back into the room from the yard.

Inaya felt heat rise in her face. "What do you know about it?" Inaya said.

Khos met her look. For a long moment, Inaya wondered if the last year had been some kind of bloody nightmare. She wondered if she would wake up tomorrow to a warm house, a content husband, children without a shifter's burgeoning allergies, and an intact house.

"Go," she said.

He did.

Inaya bolted the mausoleum door and turned back inside where Suha sat in a far corner, taking apart her pistol.

"God in heaven protect us," Inaya murmured.

"God ain't got nothing to do with it," Suha said, and spit a wad of sen on the floor at her feet. "Ain't you learned that yet?"

✛

Khos returned on Suha's watch, just after dusk. Inaya heard them come in. Khos carried a red carpet bag in one hand and a black case in the other. The magician walked in behind him.

"Yah Tayyib," Inaya said.

She had never seen Yah Tayyib, but she had heard that Nyx put a knife in him in Chenja. He was a rebel and a traitor to Nasheen, implicated in at least half a dozen deaths and the attempted murder of several of the Queen's magicians. He was a war veteran, and the image of him she had conjured in her mind was one of a stocky, brutalized soldier, one arm the wrong color, an organic green plate in his head, one leaking eye.

But the man in the door was tall and slender and intact. He carried himself aloof and erect, like a court magician. He wore his hair white and long. A beard the same color made a soft point from his chin to the center of his chest, hiding much of the severe expression on his deeply lined brown face. His eyes were two dark pools, the nose mashed, but his hands, his magician's hands, were long-fingered, smooth, beautiful. He clasped them in front of him now as he walked toward her.

Inaya shouldered her shotgun and gave Yah Tayyib a brief bow of the head, proper in Ras Tieg and Tirhan.

"I am Inaya," she said, in Tirhani.

"I know who you are," he said coolly—in Nasheenian.

You have no idea, Inaya thought, with equal calm. "He's this way," she said. She took him to Rhys's side. Elahyiah lay next to him, holding him.

The magician stared down at Rhys and Elahyiah. Frowned.

"We'll need a table. A slab. Elevated. Are there pedestals in here?" he asked.

"In the room in the back," Inaya said. Someone had stolen the urns from the top of them long ago, and no one put bodies on them anymore. The Ras Tiegan mausoleums had been defiled and abandoned a hundred years before.

"And light," he said.

"I can string the globes," Inaya said.

Suha and Khos moved Rhys into the back room. Elahyiah stayed behind, hugging her knees to her chest. Inaya dusted the old globes, smeared them in unguent, and placed them in sconces.

Rhys twisted on the slab. Yah Tayyib put a hand to Rhys's chest to still him, murmured something.

Khos set Yah Tayyib's case and carpet bag on the pedestal opposite.

Suha drifted back toward the door.

"How long has he had this fever?" Yah Tayyib asked.

"Since he came in," Inaya said.

Yah Tayyib rolled up his sleeves and began to unpack his instruments from the carpet bag. "He would have died of infection in another twelve hours."

"I don't have flesh beetles here," she said.

"I did not have time to get a proper match, or a proper fit, but I can get him functional," Yah Tayyib said. He wore a long yellow bisht with a white khameez beneath, and as he brought up his hands, she saw a cicada the color of jade scurry back into the protection of the sleeve now hanging about his elbow.

"Yah Tayyib?" Rhys murmured. His eyelids flickered. He raised one of his stumps. The bandages were organic, but they were bloody. There was more blood than the bugs could eat.

"You have to find them," Rhys said. "Yah Tayyib, my children. My wife."

"Hush now," Yah Tayyib said. Inaya was surprised at the tenderness in his voice.

The magician slipped a dagger from beneath his khameez and cut through the sleeves of Rhys's bisht and khameez, releasing his arms. "I'm going to get you out of immediate danger, do you understand?"

"My children. My wife. There's still time."

"You're going to feel a little pinch now, Rhys. When you wake up, you will be out of danger."

Rhys. Inaya heard the strangeness of the name, then. Rhys wasn't his real name, but some kind of Heidian moniker. It sounded somehow stronger in Yah Tayyib's Nasheenian than it did with a Tirhani accent. Inaya had never thought to ask what it meant, or why he'd chosen it. If he was fleeing to Nasheen, why not choose a Nasheenian name?

"Elahyiah."

"She's fine, Rhys," Inaya said. But as with all the other times she'd said it, he did not seem to hear it.

Yah Tayyib pulled a bug box from his carpet bag. He released a large pincher beetle. The spotted bug crawled along Rhys's bare arm.

"I'll need a basin of water," Yah Tayyib said.

"I can bring you a few bulbs. We have no basin here," Inaya said.

"That will suffice."

"Shouldn't we bring him to the gym? To your work room?"

"I don't want to move him until he's out of danger. And you'll need him serviceable in the meantime. A magician with no hands is not a magician at all. What fool thing did she get you into now?"

But the last was not a question for Inaya. He said it to Rhys, softly, as the pincher beetle bit his naked arm.

"I have syringes," Inaya said.

"Far too primitive. Imprecise," Yah Tayyib said. "And far less controllable." He waved his hand over the beetle, and it obediently crawled back into its box.

"Can I help?" Khos asked from the doorway.

Yah Tayyib motioned him in. "Let the big man help now, child," he told Inaya. "I need someone strong to hold him down."

"I'm—" she began.

"Please," he said. "You are not built like a Nasheenian. Come now, we have little time. Tend to Elahyiah's hurts while I restore her husband."

Inaya went out to sit with Elahyiah.

Elahyiah was feverish, moaning. The light was still bad. Inaya retrieved her water bulbs and began to clean Elahyiah up while she trembled.

"My children," Elahyiah murmured. "My children."

Inaya did not tell her, you are lucky to have your life. Don't beg God for more than that.

✦

It was four hours, and full dark, before Khos emerged from the back room. Inaya had heated up some broth—enough to warm everyone's empty bellies.

Suha slept in the main room, Eshe the raven tucked in the crook of her arm. He had returned after dark. Suha had cradled him and fallen immediately to sleep. He had not shifted. Shifting would mean a staggering desire for protein that they did not have, and a mess of mucus and feathers that would be difficult to clean up. Inaya was already worrying over the broth. They only had three days of supplies here now with so many to feed.

It was Suha's watch, but Inaya didn't have the heart to wake her.

Where would these two go now? Inaya thought. With Nyx dead, what would become of them? She imagined them walking the clean streets of Tirhan, Suha with her mashed-in face, Eshe picking up odd, dubious jobs as a messenger. They would not last long. How many notes could she and Khos spare?

"Did he live?" Inaya asked.

Khos was wiping his hands on an organic rag that ate the blood from his hands.

"I don't know if he has much feeling or coordination in his fingers, but he has fingers again," Khos said. "Not his own. But something. Yah Tayyib did the best he could."

"At least it gives him a chance to rebuild." Rebuild, she thought. Rebuild with nothing. We have *nothing*. The nothingness terrified her.

"Yes." Khos looked out into the main room where Suha and Eshe slept. "No one's on watch?"

"I was waiting for you."

He nodded slowly, his eyes fixed on some far point.

"I don't know where to go now," she said. How much longer until it started to show? Until she was picking dog hair or feathers out of Tatie's bed? "Not Ras Tieg."

"Let's wait for him to come out of it. He'll have his own ideas about what's next."

"His grief should have killed him already," she murmured. And what she didn't say was, I don't know if I can take care of him, too. I don't know if we can survive that. I don't know if we'll survive *this*.

Yah Tayyib stepped into the room. Under the dim light of the globes, he looked ancient, tired. He carried his carpet bag and case, and Inaya saw some kind of roach scuttle up underneath his long white hair. She shuddered.

"There are no longer signs of infection," Yah Tayyib said. "I've had them all eaten or burned out, and stuffed him with enough bugs to clean a corpse."

"Thank you," Khos said.

Yah Tayyib gazed about the little room. She saw him note Suha and Eshe, before asking, "Where's Nyx?"

"Dead," Khos said.

Yah Tayyib tilted his head. "When?"

"Bel dames killed her last night," Khos said. "When they did this to Rhys."

"You seem very certain of that," Yah Tayyib said. "Was her head cut off?"

There was a long, pregnant pause.

Khos looked at Inaya.

She didn't want to say it, but it came out anyway: "No."

"That is . . . odd. Where is she?"

"Where they left her. A ditch in the park," Inaya said, and the image washed over her again: the broken bel dame, one leg twisted, face mashed in, the blood.

"I didn't want to move the body in case someone was watching it," Khos said. "I'm sure a patrol's picked it up by now."

"Bring her here."

"Yah Tayyib," Khos said slowly, "she's a day dead. This isn't a child whose heart stopped on the table."

"She's a bel dame," Yah Tayyib said, and there was amusement in his haggard face. "They are difficult to kill for good reason."

"She's dead," Inaya said, and it came out colder than she meant it to. "There is nothing in this world for her anymore."

Yah Tayyib regarded her, but it was the same way he had looked at her when he came in, as if she were a particularly common insect, nothing more. "Isn't there?" Then, to Khos. "Bring her here. I can't be seen with you, but you can take that ugly woman out there, and the bird. Have him scout the body before you take it to make sure no one's posted a watch. Bring her here."

"She's dead," Inaya repeated. "Like Rhys's girls. He wanted us to drag up his family from the well . . ."

"And if you had reached me twelve hours ago I may have been able to do something with them," Yah Tayyib said sharply. "But what we have for Nyx is a sixty-hour window, and you have already wasted nearly fifty of those hours. If she died at thirteen the night before last, I have less than ten hours to get her heart beating."

"We don't have the tools for that here," Khos said. "I've seen a magician's work room—"

"You would be amazed what I can do with a few bugs and a bel dame," Yah Tayyib said. "Bring her. I will need supplies from my operating theater. It won't take more than an hour. All we need is a beating heart. Her head will do the rest."

"We can't afford—" Khos began.

"No, you cannot. I said nothing of payment."

"But she tried to *kill* you," Inaya said. That's what they'd told her. This was the same man who tried to sell alien technology to the Chenjans and betray his own country. Who could trust this man?

"She has tried to kill a good many people," Yah Tayyib said, "and succeeded in killing many more. Nyx and I have mutual enemies, however. With the bel dames and the monarchy corrupt, there are few people whose motives I know, understand, or trust. She may not be a friend, but her motives are certainly . . . predictable." He took them all in again, one long look. "And to be honest, I do not know how this bunch of misfits will make it without her."

"With her dead we have a chance," Khos said softly. "You put her back together and you put us in danger. Our children——"

"We're going to get Nyx," Inaya said, suddenly, absurdly. Khos and Suha both stared at her.

Suha pushed herself to her feet and grabbed for her pistols. "Let's get the fuck going then," she said.

"I may need another magician," Yah Tayyib said. "Someone who won't be noticed. It will be difficult enough to do it outside of a theater."

"You know anyone?" Suha asked.

Yah Tayyib shook his head. "No one who is discreet. Not in Tirhan. You must know others. Others . . . like yourselves."

"I know somebody," Suha said. Eshe perched on her shoulder. "She was a magician once. She'll work cheap. And I know where to find her."

"Bring her," Yah Tayyib said. "If you trust her."

"Never said I trusted her. But she's what we've got."

Inaya knew who they faced. She knew what they could do. But she had also seen what Nyx could do, and it was far worse.

"Inaya——" Khos began.

"Don't fight me," she said.

He grimaced and walked into the dark with Suha and the raven.

Inaya watched after them. When they were well gone, she said, without turning, "Can you really bring her back?"

"It's possible, if the head is intact. Not terribly probable, but possible. I've brought back worse cases. Under better circumstances, but worse cases."

"Why bring her back?"

"We are not even, she and I."

"What do you mean?"

"That is for her alone to know. God willing."

But Inaya knew better.

God had nothing to do with it.

29.

Rhys woke alone.

The light was a dull orange haze. His body was cold and stiff, a body on a slab. He tried to move. He saw someone's hand on the end of his arm, neatly stapled to his wrist with insect mandibles. The name of the bug flitted through his mind. Flesh roaches. Not to be mistaken for flesh beetles, which repaired skin. He could feel those too, repairing the flesh that bound his new hands to his arms.

They were ugly hands, not as dark as his own, short, stubby fingers. Calloused palms and fingers. Clumsy hands. A laborer's hands.

He tried to move the fingers into a fist. Watched them twitch in response. He let his arm drop. His head swam with the twitter, click, and chatter of bugs. His blood was singing with them. Tiny blood mites to clean the contagion from his blood and scrub the foreign blood from his foreign hands, speeding recovery. The flesh beetles, too small to see, stitching his new tendons and flesh together. And blood boosts—tiny organisms that allowed his blood to transport and his body to absorb a higher quantity of glucose to feed the bugs while they repaired him. He knew them all. They were all a part of him, until he bled or shit or vomited them out when their jobs were done.

Then it came to him, again.

Elahyiah.

Rhys pushed himself up on the slab with his elbows. He stared at the back of the room. What was this place? He remembered seeing Yah Tayyib, Khos, and Inaya. And that woman of Nyx's, Suha. Were any of them real?

He carefully moved his legs off the slab. Where was Nyx? The sleeves of his bisht and khameez were cut, loose. This was Yah Tayyib's work. Where was he?

He turned.

Inaya stood in the doorway behind him, shotgun over her shoulder. She was slim, pale, and in the dim light she looked a decade older, with a haunted face.

"Can you move your fingers?"

"Not my fingers. These are . . . Yah Tayyib was here?"

"Yes."

"How did—"

"You told us about him. We thought you were just feverish, but it turned out to be true."

He let his head hang. "I'm thirsty." The well. The dark well. He started to cry. He didn't know it until he saw the wet on the slab. "Oh God," he said. His gorge rose. He wanted to vomit. "The girls . . . Elahyiah? Where is she?"

"I'm here."

He looked up and saw his wife standing in the doorway. Hair uncovered, filthy. Her abaya was torn. He saw bloodstains, and long, scabbed marks on her hands. But it was Elahyiah all the same.

"God is great," he murmured.

"The girls," Elahyiah said, and her voice broke. "The girls are dead."

Rhys eased off the slab and moved toward her. She pulled away. He hesitated.

"I'm sorry," she said. "I'm sorry." She put her arms around him.

He pulled her to him, tried to flex his stiff, alien fingers. He still had little movement. He buried his face in her hair and tried to cling to her, to find comfort. But there was no comfort there, just terror. She shook and wept.

"I'm sorry, Rhys."

He held her. Her hair smelled of bloody loam. He saw fragments of grass in her hair. Something inside of him went numb.

Rhys turned to Inaya, said softly. "Your children?"

"Safe," she said. "They're . . . with a friend. I hid them in the well when the bel dames came."

"Bel dames?"

"Yes. I . . . saw them coming."

"You saw them?"

"Yes." She would not look at him.

"And Khos?"

"He was out drinking. With Nyx."

Nyx.

Rhys pulled away from Elahyiah. She clung to his bisht.

"Where's Nyx?"

"Dead," Inaya said.

A stab of fear. "That's not possible," he said.

"I saw her body in the park."

He felt winded again, as if a great weight had settled across his chest. He stared down at his new hands. He did not want to look at them, they were so ugly.

"My girls?"

"I searched for them. We'll need to call the city officials, tell them about . . . a contaminated well. You may . . . You may get the bodies back. For burning."

The bodies. His children.

All that he had built. That they had built together. Elahyiah let out another low, long sob.

"Do you think they meant to kill you?" he asked Inaya.

"I don't know. They didn't kill you, either."

No, he thought, just my family. The ones who had nothing to do with this.

"They must have had a reason," he said.

"They're mad, Rhys. They don't have reasons. Even Nyx didn't have reasons."

He heard someone in the outer room, and looked over his shoulder. He expected Khos, or one of Nyx's crew, but it was Yah Tayyib's thin frame that cut the doorway.

Elahyiah pulled herself closer to Rhys and touched her hair. He smoothed it back from her face.

"Here," Inaya said, taking her arm. "I have a hijab in the other room. Come with me."

"Thank you for coming," Rhys said to Yah Tayyib as Inaya led Elahyiah into the other room.

"Khos tells me I owe you for your silence."

Rhys shook his head. "You owe me nothing."

"Then perhaps you owe me something now."

"Who told you I wanted to come back?"

Yah Tayyib smiled. He placed a long-fingered hand on Rhys's naked arm. He leaned toward him. "Dead men are worth nothing. Living men take revenge."

"Do they?"

"I came back from the front alive—"

"For revenge?"

"No. For the future. Because without living people to fight we have nothing but animals slaughtered at God's altar."

"What do you know about these bel dames?"

"I know they are the same ones who crossed me, and a good deal more besides. We'll speak of it later. We have much to do tonight. I may need your hands for this, if we can't find another magician."

"For what?"

"They did not tell you?"

"No."

Rhys heard voices from the other room.

"What did she not tell me?" Rhys said.

Khos's voice, "In here. Watch this end, Suha!"

Khos and Suha entered, carrying an enormous rolled up carpet between them. Someone else came in behind them, a scrawny old woman with a curved spine. A magician. He felt that immediately, though she was dressed like a pauper, and her face . . . her face looked like a battlefield.

"Rhys, off!" Khos said.

Rhys shuffled away from the slab. Yah Tayyib put a hand out to steady him.

Suha grunted with the effort of pushing the carpet onto the slab.

"What is this?" Rhys asked.

Khos and Suha's hands and faces were scratched, dirty. Suha's elbow was bleeding. A raven—it must have been Nyx's shifter—flew into the room and perched on one of the empty sconces.

Khos pulled out a dagger and cut the carpet open.

For a moment, a breathtaking, gut-wrenching moment, Rhys thought they had found one of the children. He gasped. He thought, Yah Tayyib will bring them back. He didn't know how, not in that moment. But in that one knife-sharp moment he believed they had brought him his daughters.

And then the carpet fell away, and the body was too big, coarse. A solid body, filthy, covered in dirt and loam and a burnous stiff with dried blood. It was a corpse. Not his daughters' corpses.

"I need you to help me bring her back," Yah Tayyib said.

And Rhys knew her.

"Fuck you," Rhys said. "Fuck all of you."

He stumbled out of the room, past Inaya and his wife. He needed open air. He wanted the sky.

Rhys tumbled out the front of the mausoleum, and fell knee deep in loam. He turned his face to the sky.

"Damn you. And her. Damn her too."

He could not save his girls. Instead, they would bring *her* back. They always brought the monster back.

30.

She was in Yah Tayyib's operating theater. He held a jar in his slender hands. Inside was a perfectly heart-shaped organ, two fallopian tubes floating out at the ends in the formaldehyde.

"You'll find the other one more useful," Yah Tayyib said. "You wouldn't have been able to carry anything in this one anyhow. Not useful to you, but prized among magicians for its deformity. Our organs grow in two identical halves, did you know that? Only sometimes the halves are not identical. Sometimes, as they grow, they do not fuse. This is what happened to your womb. Closed up too quickly. Not a perfect globe now, but a heart."

She had traded that first womb for twenty notes and a case of Ras Tiegan beer.

The operating theater bled away, and Yah Tayyib's face loomed over her. His beard was white now, like his hair. The eyes were cold and black, hooded. The man who had kept the secrets of a hundred bel dames and a thousand boxers. The man who had built her and betrayed her.

"We are even now, you and I," he said.

✚

Rhys stood over Nyx's body. The body was breathing now, warm to the touch, but she had not moved. Had not opened her eyes. Eshe the raven had curled up in the crook of her arm, despite

Yah Tayyib's protests. When Rhys had come back in and tried to get Suha to move the raven, she had just firmed up her mouth and turned away from him. It was her watch now, and that eased the tightness in his shoulders. Inaya and Khos were speaking in the front room, voices muted.

Yah Tayyib squirted water over his hands from one of the water bulbs. Behdis lingered in the doorway. Rhys wondered, not for the first time, where Suha had dug up this crone.

"Watch her carefully over the next few days," Yah Tayyib said, and it took Rhys a moment to realize he was talking about Nyx, not Behdis. "If she comes back wrong, you'll know it then."

Rhys turned. "Wrong?"

"It's not a perfect map. Sometimes parts of the brain rot, or are reconnected incorrectly." He set the bulb on the other slab. "We brought her back at the far end of her expiration date. She may not wake at all. I've known bel dames who didn't. If she does come back, watch her. She may be different. Dangerous."

Rhys barked out a laugh at that. "Dangerous? She was a kitten before?"

"Just watch her." Yah Tayyib placed a hand on Rhys's shoulder. "It took a group of bel dames to kill her the first time. If she's rotten, cut off the head this time and burn her."

He finished packing his things. Rhys watched him walk into the front of the mausoleum. Heard him talking with Khos and Inaya.

Rhys looked down at the body again. The raven shivered there in the crook of her arm.

"You want me to stay on, case she wakes up?" Behdis asked.

Rhys hesitated. If Nyx turned, Khos's strength and his paltry magician's skills wouldn't do much against her. At the same time, he didn't like this hungry magician. "Can you stay until morning?"

"Yeah, sure. Not long now."

Maybe four or five hours. Rhys supposed he could put up with her that long.

"You want me to sit watch? Want to get some sleep?" Behdis asked eagerly. Her eyes shone.

Rhys shook his head. Yes, he was tired. Bone tired. Yah Tayyib's bugs had cleaned him out, physically, but the rest was still there, waiting. Rasheeda's laughter. The sound of Shadha's machete severing his hands at the wrist. His children's screams. And Elahyiah. God, how would they put this all together again?

"I'll stay awake. I'll call you when I'm ready," he said. He started to rub his eyes, saw the new hands, shuddered, dropped them.

He sat on the slab across from Nyx's body. Behdis wandered into the front. Khos came in after her.

"You holding up?" Khos asked.

"What do you think?"

"Sorry. Elahyiah's asleep. Inaya just gave her some thorn juice to put her out."

"And your children?"

"I . . . they're safe."

"Inaya said the same. You had a safe house?"

"Something like that."

Rhys didn't like the vague response. "You prepared for something like this?"

"You didn't?"

Rhys grimaced.

"You knew her better than anybody," Khos said. "You knew she'd come back someday. You knew this was coming."

"I . . . stopped expecting her."

"You want me to send Inaya in with some thorn juice for you, too?"

"You didn't lose everything tonight, Khos."

"Best I can see, you still have a good wife and a roof over your head."

Then why do I feel so empty? Rhys thought. "You still have your hands. Your children. Your wife."

"Not my roof."

"Is this a contest?"

Khos bared his teeth. "Always is, isn't it? Get some sleep. I can take your watch."

"No, I . . . I will, soon."

Khos nodded. "You do that." He thumped Rhys on the shoulder. When was the last time he'd done that?

The others slept. Rhys swam in and out of wakefulness until the blue dawn. The first dawn was the last thing he remembered before succumbing to sleep.

When he woke, someone was shaking him, and there were voices, loud voices, nearby.

He opened his eyes and saw Inaya standing over him, shotgun over one shoulder, her other hand on him, shaking.

"She's gone," Inaya said. There were dark circles under her eyes. There was bickering in the front room. Khos and Suha.

Rhys pushed off the slab. His new hands ached, and he was incredibly thirsty. Nyx's slab was empty. Only a smear of dirt and loam and dried blood remained, broken carapaces, some dead flesh beetles.

The second sun had risen. It was well after morning prayer. I've forgotten prayer, Rhys thought, distantly.

"We need to find her," Rhys said. He pushed into the front where Suha and Khos were arguing. He turned to ensure that Elahyiah was still asleep, and saw her tossing and turning on the thin mattress. Behdis hovered in the main doorway, peering into the graveyard.

Suha said, "Don't go fucking it up. Eshe's out now. He'll find her."

"If she finds the road and hitches a ride, we've lost her," Rhys said.

"You hear me?" Suha said. "We all run off in five directions we won't come together quick enough to bag her." It was the most Rhys had ever heard her speak.

"Who the fuck put you in charge?" Khos said.

"Nyx did," Suha said. "Last I heard, you family boys were all out of the covert recovery business."

"That doesn't mean we don't know our shit," Khos said.

"Then get your big head out of your big ass," Suha said.

Rhys searched for a wasp swarm, but either his senses were still off or there were none nearby. If I was weak before, he thought, I'm useless now.

Eshe returned a quarter hour later. He led them north across the overgrown grounds of the graveyard. Khos and Inaya had chosen the safe house well. The grounds went on for at least two kilometers in every direction. It was a great place to lose somebody who was tracking you. Or just get lost.

Rhys picked his way through the underbrush with his new hands. Biting insects swarmed them in clouds. Rhys kept them from feeding on their party, but controlling the flight of the swarms proved to be too much. His blood was still humming dully with the bugs in his body as they made the last of the repairs. He had pissed out beady little blood mites half a kilometer back.

Eshe led them up a low rise, through a tangle of violet vines and hoarthorn. Rhys tripped into a small clearing.

Nyx crouched there next to a half-buried headstone, her back to them. She had one filthy hand on the lip of the headstone.

Rhys froze.

Suha held up her hand, warned them back.

"Nyx?" Suha said.

Nyx hung her head. Her hair was a tangle of unraveling braids shot through with broken bits of sticks and leaves. A giant mantid clung to the hem of her trousers. Rhys saw blood running down one bare arm. A new injury? Or was her blood not clotting?

Rhys reached once more to his hip—for a pistol he no longer carried.

We've grown soft and stupid, he thought, and heard his children screaming again.

"Nyx?" Suha said.

Nyx turned.

Her eyes were utterly vacant. No one looked back at them from those eyes. Sweat rolled down her face.

"Nyx?" Rhys said.

And then her arm slid off the headstone and she was on the ground. She started convulsing.

"Fuck!" Khos said. He ran forward and picked her up.

Rhys ran his hands over her. Bugs chittered and sang. He listened. There was something wrong with . . . She'd caught something. The flesh beetles were in stasis while the blood mites fought it off.

"She's sick," Rhys said. "But it feels . . . tailored." My God, Rhys thought, did Yah Tayyib kill her after all?

"That's how she lost her skin," Suha said. "The other magician couldn't get rid of it either. The other magician said it was some tailored bug."

They hauled her through the bush and back to the slab. Rhys and Behdis shot her full of antibiotics with a live syringe Inaya had in her bag. Blood ran freely down Nyx's arm, like liquid mercury. Pooled on the floor.

She wavered in and out of consciousness. She slapped their hands away. At one point, she vomited, and Rhys and Behdis turned her over to keep her from choking on it.

Rhys stood over her. She was slathered in sweat. The syringe wound wasn't healing properly. It still oozed. "We're losing her," Rhys said.

"We can't take her to Yah Tayyib," Khos said. "His place is right downtown. God and everyone will see us there."

"My place," Behdis said.

Rhys looked over at her.

"I got a place," she insisted. "Got what we need there, too. Two more phials of biotics, yeah? We can get that."

Rhys exchanged a look with Khos.

"I'm not putting her up with my children. Not risking that. It's her they're after. I won't put my kids in danger."

"We've come too far to let her die on the table," Rhys said.

"I'll tell her you said that," Suha said, walking in. Eshe perched on her shoulder. Her gun was in her hand.

"We're going to take her into town," Rhys said. "We need to keep her breathing until then. We'll shoot her full of antibiotics and leave it to God."

"I don't leave shit to God," Suha said. "I can carry her."

Suha and Khos carried Nyx outside while Inaya and Rhys woke Elahyiah.

She stirred, still groggy with thorn juice, and clung to him. "Love," she murmured, "I had a terrible dream."

"Come now," he said. "We're going back to town."

"Home?" she asked.

"Soon," he said.

He led her into the yard. Suha was wiping her hands on her trousers. "Body's in the trunk. One of you has to ride sitting on the others in the back. Keep your heads down."

Eshe the raven cawed and made a low, lazy circle above her head before perching on her shoulder.

Suha absently stroked his head. "You coming or not? Let's go."

Rhys helped his wife into the back. He stared a long moment at the trunk, then looked back to the tangled ruin of the mausoleum.

He straightened and asked Khos, "Is leaving the safe house really such a good idea?"

"You got a better one?"

"No," Rhys said.

"Then let's get the fuck out of here before Inaya changes her mind."

31.

They drove to the other side of the city. Inaya watched the tangle of the twisted green countryside spill over into shantytowns and hill houses. Behdis brought them to a pit of a hovel at the edge of the Ras Tiegan district. Inaya would not have let a roach live there, let alone a human being. But this was where Suha stopped.

The house, such as it was, was so small that Inaya and Khos had to sleep out in the yard on tatty old burnouses from the magician's days back in Nasheen. It was a dirty, refuse-filled yard, just like the house, but it was fenced, and there was a tattered awning.

Inaya sat awake with the shotgun on her chest, one hand on the barrel. She stared up at the big black patch of nothing above her, that patch of the sky they called the Void where no stars were visible, listening to Elahyiah and Rhys speaking inside. The sound of Elahyiah crying. She wanted to cry, too, but she didn't have the strength.

She remembered her mother fucking dogs in the street. Her father's desperation. She remembered her brother Taite running away after their mother was taken. Inaya had found him hiding underneath the house eating mayflies, the ones that tasted like strawberries. He hadn't spoken for nearly a year after that. It's what made him turn to the guts and tubes and bugs of their parents' com unit. It was when Inaya started covering her hair and dressing like a martyr's wife. She would not be like her mother. She would not be Other, a monster. She would be just another standard, another good Ras Tiegan matron. So she accepted her first marriage proposal, from a man twice her age with three other wives who had no shifters in his family. His uncle was in politics. He had two nephews working for the police. It was a political family who had hated and despised her for what her mother was, but a standard family nonetheless.

She had tried to bend the world, and change what all of them were. It's not us who are sick, she thought—stirred by the memory of a woman beating her mother with a stick on the street—it's the world that's wrong. The contaminated world they built.

Her children, though . . . Could they really just keep running? Run to Ras Tieg where she and Khos and Tatie would be hunted like animals? And what of Isfahan? How much longer until she, too, began to show the talent? Inaya had known the risks of having children. Known and done it anyway. And God, she loved them. Her breath, her soul made flesh. It made her heart ache.

Khos shifted in his sleep, and began to snore softly.

She could do nothing, she supposed.

But doing nothing . . . that made her as bad as the woman who used to beat her mother in the street. It made her as bad as all the others in Ras Tieg—the ones who passed casually by while shifter children were dragged into smoked-glass bakkies.

Inaya stared up into the night sky.

"I will build a better world for you," she whispered.

She closed her eyes. God, how her heart ached.

✝

In the morning, Inaya woke with the dawn and prayed to Mhari for strength in the days to come, and thanked God for all she still possessed.

Inside, Rhys sat them all around Behdis's little table.

"Where's Elahyiah?" Inaya asked.

"I took her home," Rhys said.

"Not your house?"

"To her father. It's what she wanted. It was Rasheeda who tried to kill us, and . . . that other one who pulled her out. I don't expect it's Elahyiah who's in danger."

Eshe sat next to him, back in human form. His eyes were ringed in dark circles. He sat hunched at the table, squeezed next to Suha. His hands looked stiff, curled into claws.

Inaya rested a hand lightly on his shoulder. He jerked his head up to look at her.

"I'm pleased to see you in human form again," she said.

He frowned.

Khos leaned up against the wall near the back door, arms crossed.

"I wanted to get us all together while Behdis was out," Rhys said. "She has six hours at the gym today."

"Where's Nyx?" Khos asked.

"She was . . . lucid, last night," Rhys said. "Behdis and I pumped her full of antibiotics and cleaned her up. She started screaming at me, but . . ."

Khos grunted. "She must be better then."

Rhys's face softened. "She hasn't said a word since then. She went back under this morning. I called Yah Tayyib to take another look at her, but I don't know if he'll come. I wanted to bring everyone together to figure out what it is we want to do."

"You want to kill her," Eshe said. His voice was oddly monotone. Inaya wrinkled her brow.

"I mean us," Rhys said. "I want to know what we'll do. If you and Suha want to keep Nyx, maybe that's best. I want . . . I don't know if . . ." He sighed.

"You want to know if we're keeping her note or keeping her?" Suha said.

"I think the two of you should go back to Nasheen with her," Rhys said.

"Fuck you," Suha said. "There's a note on her head. She forget to tell you that?"

"Shit," Khos said. "When were you going to mention that?"

"It just came up on the boards," Eshe said. "I found out last night."

Inaya started. "You flew back to Nasheen?"

"Don't be dumb," Eshe said. "I called one of Suha's friends."

"We do got those, you know," Suha said, and spit sen on the filthy floor.

Rhys put his new hands around his cup. Inaya wondered if they would always look that ugly. "There's a bel dame coup. Nyx is supposed to bring in the woman at the head of it. But that's not all."

"It never is," Khos muttered.

"The rogue bel dames are negotiating with Tirhan as if they already run the country. They have a very dangerous weapon, a type of flesh eating sand that they want to give to them in return for their support of their coup."

"You acted as translator, didn't you?" Inaya said.

Rhys nodded.

"You could have told us. You could have warned us there were bel dames in Tirhan," she said.

"I didn't know that meant Nyx would be here too," he said.

"She does always seem to be the catalyst," Khos said.

"You all weren't prepared," Suha said. "That was your fucking problem. Not Nyx's."

"Fuck you," Khos said.

"Why should we be prepared?" Inaya said. "It's not us they were after. Nyx brings nothing but blood with her."

"Yeah," Suha said, and Inaya watched a petulant smile creep across her face. "'Cause none of you got blood on your hands."

"Regardless," Rhys said. "There's very little we can do about it."

"Wrong."

Inaya looked. They all looked.

Nyx stood at the curtain that portioned off the main sleeping area. She was tall and still frighteningly thin. But the eyes were not as Rhys had said. The eyes were hard, glassy, and very much alive.

"There's a lot we can do about it," Nyx said.

Eshe jumped up from the table and ran to her. He flung his arms around her so forcefully that she stumbled back.

"I need a bath and a piss," Nyx said. "But first I need you to tell me where the fuck we are."

32.

"We needed a safe house they didn't know about," Suha said.

Nyx squatted over a pot in the curtained off bedroom while Suha leaned against the wall. The world looked remarkably clear. Rhys and Khos had gone out to pick up some food while Inaya pulled together clean clothes out back.

Eshe banged around in the kitchen and brought her a cold roti and a basin of water.

"Thanks," Nyx said. She tousled Eshe's dark, unkempt hair.

He raised his head to look at her with his black eyes. Yawned. Terrible breath. He needed a cut and a wash.

"You were dead," he said.

"So I heard."

Suha leaned forward. "We need to get out of Tirhan. And this house," she said, low.

"I know." Nyx patted Eshe's head again and dipped her hands into the water. It was warm and clear. She stared into it a long minute. God, her head felt clear. Everything looked so much cleaner. Sharper. Like waking up with a new body. But her poorly matched skin looked just the same, and the reflection staring back at her was as hideous as ever.

"You call Yah Tayyib to bring me back?" she asked. She knew his work.

"Rhys found him. Said he's been carrying on with him for years."

"Fucker," Nyx muttered. She washed her face.

She stripped off her dhoti and breast binding and washed. The water turned brown and crimson. Her hands began to tremble. She had to stop, take a deep breath.

"You need help?" Suha asked.

"No," Nyx said. Her skin felt good. Limber. God, her head was so clear.

"How'd he do it?" Eshe asked. "I couldn't figure it out. I know it's hard to kill bel dames, but you were dead a long time."

"Got a bug in my head," Nyx said. "When I die, it shuts everything down and seals it all up. Have some time to bring me back so long as everything's sealed up." And whatever way it brought her back, it had scrubbed her good with adrenaline and immune boosters. She should have seen the Plague Sisters after the contagion took her skin. They'd have cleared her up with a bug like this. Saved a lot of pain and misery.

But that's what living is, isn't it? Nyx thought, and grimaced. She moved her hand to her throat. Traced the jagged scar. If she'd looked like death before, she looked like a proper corpse now. Her jaw felt a little off, and ached. She wondered if it was healing straight.

"I don't trust these people," Eshe said. "They all wanted you to die."

"They all say a lot of things. What they do and what they say are different things. I wouldn't be alive, otherwise."

"I don't trust the magician, either," Suha said.

"Rhys?"

"He's really fucked up."

"And we're not?"

"Don't know," Suha said, and peered at her sharply. "That other magician, the old one. He said you might be kinda fucked in the head. Said we may not have woke you up in time."

"Maybe so," Nyx said. Mainly, she was thirsty. Pissing out all the shit Tayyib had pumped her full of. And she knew there was some absence. God, what was the absence? Was there something she was forgetting? Something important? Her memory was muddled. Long stretches of blackness. Some things were . . . gone. Others, frighteningly clear. She knew why they were in Tirhan. She knew the bel dames had succeeded in killing her. She knew she needed to return the favor.

"Catch me up," Nyx said. "Need to know what you got up to when I got my head chopped off."

Suha and Eshe filled her in. Nyx tried to eat the cold roti. Her jaw clicked and ached. What she managed to choke down didn't settle right. She drank a bunch more water, and the nausea passed.

Inaya showed up a little later with a clean tunic and trousers and long Ras Tiegan coat.

"Thought you'd hand me an abaya," Nyx said.

"Since when have you presented yourself as a real woman?" Inaya said.

"Good point."

As Nyx pulled on the clothes, she heard Rhys and Khos return. Her mind was tick-ticking away, sorting out what Eshe and Suha had told her. They were a wild, raving bunch without somebody to tell them where to land. And I'm shitty at it, she thought, but we're all dead in an hour if we don't move.

"Get everybody in here," Nyx said, and pushed past the curtain and into the main room. Her hands were trembling. The trousers had pockets, so she stuffed her hands in them.

Khos and Rhys were putting take-out curry containers and wrapped rotis on the table.

"Bad house choice," Nyx said. Rhys raised his head. He had dark circles under his eyes, but what she noticed in that moment was not his weariness but his strange, ugly hands gripping one of the curry boxes. She opened her mouth to say something. Saw the raised pinkish scars around the wrists. Stubby fingers, fat thumbs, wide palms. Not Rhys's hands at all.

"I've made a lot of bad choices recently," Rhys said coolly.

"I want to know how soft you all got, taking us to a safe house with a magician who's likely got bel dames outside right now."

"I can't believe that's the first thing out of your mouth," Rhys said. "Would you rather we left you in that ditch?"

Nyx didn't meet his look.

"Behdis is an addict," Suha said. "She works for the drip. She hasn't come to us with anything from bel dames. She went in to work."

"She go in today?"

"Yeah."

"We don't have a lot of time."

"Why? What's wrong with her?" Eshe asked.

"It took me a while to sort out," Nyx said. "Suha and Eshe told me what happened. They hit Khos's house first, they said. But how'd they know where it was?"

"Fuck," Suha said. "Goddammit."

"Yeah."

"What?" Khos said.

"I gave Behdis your address as a contact for messages. Just tie a string on the gate, then we go find her and pick up her message."

"You bitch," Inaya said softly.

"Real easy way to find out who she was working for," Nyx said.

"And sacrifice my family to do it? You fucking bitch!" Inaya jumped at her.

Eshe stepped between them. Nyx stood a little straighter. Inside her pockets, she had bunched her fists, tried to still the trembling. Her legs weren't the steadiest either, but none of them knew that. "You've fought me before, Inaya. This one will end the same."

"Fuck you!" Inaya said, and stormed out into the yard.

Khos shook his head. "You didn't even warn us."

"The way you didn't warn me when you betrayed me in Chenja? We would have gotten out of there, Khos. You know what they did to me? What they did to Rhys?"

"You nearly cost us everything."

"I cost you nothing. Your marriage was shitty before that."

"Is this your day to burn bridges? After we brought you back from the dead?" Khos said.

"All I asked from you was loyalty. You get what you give. Could have been she wasn't working for them, and you'd still have a house. Didn't turn out that way, that's all."

Khos folded his arms. Nyx was aware of the sheer bulk of him, but her clear head and scrubbed body made her feel powerful for the first time in a year. Let him take a swing. Let him fight her. She was itching for a fight. So long as he didn't hit her in the jaw, or try and knock her off her feet, or . . . well, she'd be fine.

No, you won't, she thought. Her jaw hurt.

"You risked all of us for that fucking magician," Khos said. "You're always risking everything for that fucking magician. What was I supposed to do? Risk Inaya and me and Anneke and all the rest?"

"You left me and Anneke."

"You let Taite die!"

"People die in this business. Or didn't you notice?" Nyx gestured angrily at her neck.

"Inaya wanted you to live, did you know that? I sure as fuck didn't. Rhys didn't. Nobody wanted you back. Because of this. Because you're like this about it. You can't even thank us."

Nyx shot a look at Rhys. He turned away.

"Fuck that," Suha said. "I would have hauled her out the back if you hadn't gotten your guts together."

"This is stupid," Eshe said.

"The only one you ever gave a shit about is Rhys, and it's his kids you killed and his hands you took." Khos said. "You guys should fuck over the corpses and be done with it."

"That's enough," Rhys said softly. He was staring at his hands.

"It's not enough!" Khos said. He crossed the room.

Nyx rolled reflexively into a fighting stance. A shot of adrenaline coursed through her, and the trembling in her hands ceased. She felt . . . more grounded. Suha's hands hovered at the hilts of her pistols. Eshe took a step back and moved to flank Khos.

Khos stopped within her reach and pointed a finger at her. His face was flush. "It was running off like some love struck cunt that got you killed in the first place."

Nyx hit him with a hard left hook. Folks always forgot she was a southpaw, and he was no exception. He tried to block, too late, and she followed it up with a right jab that hit him square in the face. Heard the crunch of bone and cartilage. Blood burst from his nose. He stumbled back and caught himself on the table.

Her hand throbbed. Her knees were suddenly unsteady.

"You need to sit the fuck down," Nyx said.

"You bitch," he said, spitting blood. "You'd sacrifice us for *this*."

"You're right," Nyx said. "I don't give a fuck about your families. I'd sacrifice every damn one of you. You know what I give a fuck about? Two hundred and fifty thousand dead boys at the front. Eighty-four thousand civilians dead in Mushtallah two weeks ago. You see me with a family, Khos? You see me with anything I give a shit about? I lost it all a long time ago, and I wasn't stupid enough to run off and build a new one. We're killers, every fucking one of us, and the killing is going to keep on until the war ends."

"And maybe longer than that," Suha muttered.

"I have a coup to put down and a country to save," Nyx said. "You can hole up here for another couple years sucking off that fat tit until it dries up, but it *will* dry up, because you're sucking on the blood of dead men, and there's only so many of those to go around. What then, Mhorian?"

"Then I fucking kill you," Khos said, spitting more blood.

"Some days I wonder if that's your problem, Khos. You can't decide whether to fuck me or kill me."

Rhys put his ugly hand on Khos's arm. "We have bigger problems, Khos."

"Yeah, and she brought them right to our door!"

"And you let me in," Nyx said, "and bought me a drink."

Khos wiped his bloody face with his sleeve. "You'll do this without me and my family."

"You go out there now and you're as good as dead," Nyx said. "If the bel dames aren't already on point, they're on their way."

"I'm a shifter, Nyx. So's my wife. We'll get out. The rest of you . . . that's up to you." He looked at Eshe. "You can get out too. I'd leave with us."

"Fuck off," Eshe said.

"Inaya!" Khos yelled, and turned to the door leading into the yard. But she was already there, staring in at them, a curious look on her face.

"We're going," Khos said.

"Are we?" she said. Nyx remembered that tone of voice. It was the same one Inaya used back in Chenja after she blew a hole in a gene pirate.

"Stop. Let's go." He stepped away from the table and took her arm.

"Company," Suha said, nodding out toward the yard beyond Inaya. Suha pulled her pistols.

Nyx looked over Inaya's slim shoulder and saw two figures in the yard. She saw them toss the grenade.

"Get down!" Nyx yelled.

Everyone scattered.

Khos grabbed Inaya. Rhys bolted to the front door. Nyx yanked the curtain separating the rooms and threw it over Eshe. She jerked him back into the far corner of the bedroom. Suha was already kicking out the lattice window. Nyx had Eshe halfway bundled up through the opening—cursing and flailing—when the grenade went off.

Nyx let him go and dropped to the floor, hands over her ears. Suha kicked over the flimsy bed frame to shield them from the blast.

The world went quiet—muffled, dark.

Nyx choked on dust and smoke. She opened her eyes—surprised to be conscious—and scrambled for a weapon. The center of the ceiling had caved in. Dust caught the light and held it, blinded her. She scrabbled toward the kicked-out window and caught a glimpse of Eshe running and morphing at the same time across the dirty street. He shook free of his clothes and took flight. Three gunshots sounded, muted to her ravaged ears.

She turned back into the house and grabbed a chunk of broken tile from the collapsed roof.

Suha pushed off the ruin of the bed frame and winced. A jagged wooden splinter had lodged itself in her shoulder. She pulled one of her pistols and threw it to Nyx.

"The fuck I'm supposed to do with this?" Nyx shouted—barely able to hear her own voice. She was a terrible shot.

Suha fired into the haze.

Nyx ducked behind the ruin of the bed with Suha.

They were coming in.

Two came in from the front door, three more from the door into the yard.

Nyx pointed and fired. The gun popped in her hand. If she laid down suppressing fire it might take a while for them to realize she couldn't hit shit, even at this range.

The two at the front backed off from the assault and ducked behind the door. One at the side door rolled in and took up position behind the table. Nyx pressed her back to the ruin of the bed, took a deep breath, turned, and fired off a few wild shots.

Suha waited until she was down, then fired a few more. Yelled something at her.

"WHAT?" Nyx yelled.

Suha signed to her—clenched fist with the thumb sticking out: need ammo.

Pistols like Suha's didn't have more than ten shots a count. Fuck, Nyx thought. How many had she already fired off? Five? Six? She wished she had her sword. Swords didn't run out of death.

Nyx popped off another round.

Suha pushed up after her, popped off two more.

Then, nothing. The hand sign: clenched fist with thumb pointing down. She was out.

Nyx popped out one more. The bel dames countered with a long spray. Another grenade came over the top of their makeshift barricade. Nyx picked it up and huffed it back at them. It careened out through the side door. The women scattered outside.

Suha was patting herself down for ammo. Nyx pulled a couple of tiles into a neat pile next to her. At the end of the world, the war was going to come down to throwing stones. Might as well start now.

The grenade exploded outside. Nyx pointed the gun in the general direction of the other two women and fired the last of her bullets. When it was empty, she threw the gun at the nearest woman. The gun careened into the doorframe and clattered to the floor.

Nyx slid back down and exchanged one last heated look with Suha. Suha had her mouth bunched up. Sweat beaded her furrowed brow. She pulled a curved blade from a sheath at her back. Took a deep breath.

Nyx waited for the bel dames to reload.

The popping stopped.

Nyx and Suha burst over the barrier and rushed the front door. The two bel dames jerked out of their defensive positions and raised double-barreled organic shotguns. They were too fast for Nyx to close the distance and push the barrels away.

This is going to hurt, Nyx thought. And I was feeling so good, too.

Then the bel dame's head exploded.

Blood splattered Nyx's face. For a minute she thought she'd been hit, and clutched at herself for an injury. No pain. Nothing. Just bloody shock.

The second bel dame jerked back. Her shotgun went off. The sniper blast caught her in the throat, tore open a big hole. Blood gushed.

Nyx grabbed the bel dame's shotgun and pushed past the bodies. She crouched in the doorway and did a long sweep of the street. A few curious heads peeked out of nearby windows. When they saw her with the gun, they ducked back in. She'd need to move fast. They'd call the order keepers soon.

She scanned for snipers. Her eyes had always been good, and the bug that woke her body had sharpened them a little more. Nobody on the roofs on the street. Back behind them, though . . .

Nyx crawled across the bodies. Suha was lying on her belly just inside the door leading to the yard. She had the second shotgun with her.

"Ours or theirs?" Nyx asked, but her voice still sounded muffled, even to her own ears. She tapped Suha's ankle and signed when she looked back, asking if the snipers were friendly or not. Suha signed back: two fingers to the temple. Friendly.

Nyx pushed herself against the door jam and glanced into the yard. She'd gotten one of the bel dames with the grenade. The other two were missing. On the other side of the yard, she saw somebody toss a green organic sniper rifle with a single-shot acid burst cartridge over the fence. Then they crawled up over it.

Eshe.

Naked as the day he was born, wandering around in full sun. He picked up the gun and grinned. He yelled something.

"WHAT?" Nyx yelled back.

"Had it in the bakkie!" he yelled.

"Need to put you on point more often!" she said.

Nyx stood. A dog barked, and the familiar yellow mutt that was Khos-the-dog prowled into the yard from the front.

"Plenty of good you did," Nyx said.

Khos-the-dog shivered once, then started to morph. Dog limbs elongated, muscles moved and stretched and tore, and dog hair shook off the melting torso in clumps. In a few minutes, Khos, too, stood naked in the yard, wiping mucus and dog hair from his pale arms and shoulders.

His lips started moving, but all Nyx heard was *bwaaa bwaaa muhhh mwaaaa.*

"WHAT?" Nyx said.

He raised his voice and repeated. "I tracked them as far as their bakkie. Inaya took over then."

"She tailing?"

"All the way."

"Where's Rhys?" Nyx asked.

"Other side of the fence," Eshe shouted. "He's coming around!"

Nyx looked back at Khos. "Bel dames aren't worth interrogating. They won't break. Not even under me."

"I bet I know somebody who is," Suha said.

Nyx nodded. "Drugs first. New safe house. We need to move fast. She won't stay still long."

"WHAT?" Suha said.

Nyx raised her voice and repeated.

"Who?" Khos asked.

Rhys walked out into the yard, picking his way past the bodies. Nyx felt something inside of her ease up. He stopped a few paces away, didn't look at her.

"Need some magician's drugs," Nyx said. "You help with that?"

"WHAT?" he said.

33.

Rhys went home.

The public order police had sealed off the house with tailored organic tape to keep out miscreants and squatters. Too late for that, Rhys thought. He moved his hands over the tape and subtly altered the bugs' coding. They were simple enough bugs that even he could control them. The filter was still down. The house was silent.

He walked upstairs. The house had been thoroughly ransacked. By the bel dames, he assumed, not the police, though he would need to file a report with them shortly. He poked through the house. Found one of Laleh's headscarves. A crudely drawn avocado from Souri's first days learning Ras Tiegan with the housekeeper. He ran the water in the bath and stared at the alien hands that moved the hot water slider. Someone else's hands. Someone else's life.

Instead of getting in the tub, though, he washed himself standing up, as if preparing for prayer. He found some old clothes in his wardrobe. Long trousers, long, dark coat, a short tunic with green trim at the hem and cuffs. He dressed slowly, deliberately. Then walked across his room to the box where his pistols lay. Inaya had told him there was a body in his room, but it wasn't there any longer. Nor was his housekeeper's.

He pulled out the leather holster from his wardrobe and strapped it securely around his hips. Picked up the first jade-hilted pistol. Cleaned and loaded it, slow and deliberate, just as he had dressed. Then the second one. He holstered both at his hips and pulled the coat forward to hide them.

When he stood in front of the mirror, he almost didn't recognize himself. No magician, now. Just some Chenjan refugee. Some mercenary.

He grabbed a hat he found at the top of the wardrobe, pulled the petty cash from Elahyiah's jewelry box, and collected some food from the fridge.

Rhys stood in line for a taxi. He paid nearly half a note more to the driver than usual. He took the train to the southern edge of the city. No one gave up their seat. No one got out of his way. He stood the entire ride.

When he disembarked, he caught the familiar smell of curried protein cakes and gravy. Heard the call to evening prayer roll out over the quarter. As he walked, he saw matrons setting out cats' milk for demons. Heard the tinny whine of someone up on a roof spinning their big prayer wheels. The first sun set, and blue dusk fell over the city.

Elahyiah's father lived in a three-story walk-up above a laundry run by his two wives and children. Rhys ascended the stairs and knocked at the door.

Elahyiah's cousin, Faraz, opened the door.

"I'm here to see my wife," Rhys said.

Faraz was twenty, smooth-faced and heavy-browed. He looked Rhys over a long moment and frowned deeply. "She doesn't want to see you."

"Is that him?" Rhys heard Elahyiah's father, Saman, inside. "Is that him?"

The old man pushed his way to the door. "Come, get out of his way. A man has a right to see his wife. Let him in."

Rhys moved past Faraz and into the cramped living room. The room smelled of tobacco and marijuana and bleach from the laundry downstairs. The women's quarters were curtained off from the main living area.

"Come, sit with us. Have tea," Saman said.

"Thank you," Rhys said, "but I am here for my wife."

"Of course." Saman saw his hands, then. Shook his head. Rhys had not gone up when he dropped Elahyiah off. "Come, sit, have tea."

"Elahyiah?" Rhys said, loud enough to be heard beyond the curtain.

"Come, tea," Saman said.

"I don't want to come back there, Elahyiah," Rhys said. "I do not wish to be rude."

She emerged from behind the curtain. She wore a clean abaya and hijab—both too big—likely her mother's.

"Let's go to the roof," Rhys said. "Do you permit me, Saman?"

"Of course, my son," Saman said. "Come up, come up."

Elahyiah whispered something fiercely to someone behind the curtain. Her mother? Perhaps one of her cousins?

Rhys followed Saman up onto the cool, flat roof. There was a garden there, mostly succulents in pots as big around as Rhys could reach, protected from the worst of the sun by a broad awning that stretched across the roof. The marijuana grew up here, too, and the long, red flowering stalks of sen.

Saman went downstairs to get Elahyiah. Rhys took off his hat in the blue dusk and waited. He waited a long time.

She came up, eventually. In the blue light she looked even more like a lizard, some fragile thing.

She hesitated a few steps away. Lowered her eyes, clasped her hands.

"Elahyiah?"

"I will do as you wish. You know that," she said.

"Don't," he said. He reached toward her with his hand. She flinched. Not my hand, he amended. Someone else's—some other man's hand. Another man's hand, touching my wife. He pulled the hand away.

"I'm sorry," he said. "I don't know how to make it right."

She shook her head.

"I know this place is safe," he said. "You should stay here until the danger's over. But . . . I want to rebuild, Elahyiah. You're my life."

She began to cry.

"Elahyiah?"

She threw her arms around him and wept. Rhys let his arms rest at his sides, uncertain of what to do with his hands. Would she pull away again?

"I love you," she said. "I love you. They took everything. Oh, God is great but so cruel. God is so cruel."

"Hush," Rhys said. He reached a hand tentatively up and cupped the back of her head. "Hush." Something inside of him loosened, some terrible fear. "We'll rebuild our life. You know that?"

"No," she said. She pulled away from him and wiped at her eyes.

"Elahyiah?"

"No," she said. "You did not see your daughter's broken skull. I saw it, Rhys. I saw what . . . I saw. The things I saw!"

"Forget that. It happened to someone else."

"No."

"What can I do?"

She bunched her hands into fists and met his gaze for the first time. Her eyes were hard and bright. He had never seen her look so fierce.

"Kill them," she said. "Kill all of them."

34.

They jumped Behdis four blocks from the gym. Suha stepped neatly out of the bakkie and shoved a beetle down her throat. Nyx opened the bakkie door to shield what she was doing and dragged Behdis into the back.

Behdis put up a lot of fight for an old woman.

Suha locked and closed the door, then casually walked over to the other side of the bakkie. She slipped into the driver's seat, took the wheel, and pulled away from the curb.

Nyx hadn't bothered finding a rental. Rentals, even in the shittiest parts of town, wouldn't allow her to do what needed to be done. Instead, she had Eshe scout out places while they cleaned Behdis's ruined hovel of drugs, weapons, and food. He found an old abandoned warehouse along the far bank of the viscous inland sea. Nyx left Khos at the house to wait for Inaya.

"You want in, you share the safe house. You want out, get the fuck out of my face," she'd told him. "I'll send Eshe back for you in an hour."

It was just posturing. He had a good nose in shifter form, and he could sniff them out pretty quick if he had a mind to. Of course, if it came down to that, she had no trouble killing him.

Nyx and Suha hauled Behdis downstairs to a former ice room, tied her to a support beam, and beat the shit out of her.

When they came upstairs, they were splattered in blood and vomit, and about all Nyx knew was what Behdis had had for breakfast.

"She's old," Suha said. "I told you she ain't gonna talk. The bel dames can do worse to her."

"Then we starve her out," Nyx said.

Suha pursed her mouth.

"Cut her loose and lock her up. Let her dry out. We'll have a name in thirty or forty hours."

"Nyx—"

"Give me a better idea."

They sat upstairs and played cards for an hour, then sparred, barehanded, for an hour more.

Nyx felt faster and stronger, but it wasn't until she really started moving that she realized how slow and sick she'd been. Suha blocked her first three punches, but the next two landed, and she forced Suha back across the grimy warehouse floor. And though they were both pulling their punches, Suha had the ghost of a bruised eye and Nyx's nose was bloody by the end of it.

Suha bent over, breathing heavy. "Fuck, woman, what did that magician do to you?"

Sweat dripped from Nyx's chin. She wiped her face with her discarded coat. She needed a wash. "Don't know," she said. "Still don't have the power, though. No muscle behind it."

"It'll get there," Suha said.

A black raven cawed and swooped in through the warehouse door. Suha straightened, and Nyx finished wiping herself down while Eshe shifted.

She tossed him her coat to clean himself off.

"They coming?" Nyx asked.

Eshe shook his head. Long strings of mucus dripped from his arms. She wished he'd shifted downstairs. Raven feathers stuck to her sweaty legs.

"Khos says he's going home to his kids. Not like I begged him or nothing," Eshe said.

Nyx thumped him on the shoulder. "Come on and get something to eat, then. It's just us."

"That white bitch says she trailed the bel dames to the train station," Eshe said. He bent over the hoard of supplies they'd gotten from Behdis's house and then pulled on a pair of dirty, too-big trousers. "They got tickets to Beh Ayin."

Beh Ayin again. But why?

"Rhys still not back?"

"No."

Suha stretched out on the floor. "He's likely making up with his wife. Don't expect him."

"We don't need him," Eshe said.

"Don't know if you knew, but I'm not good at pulling magicians out of my ass," Nyx said, "and we'll need one."

"He's a shitty magician anyway," Eshe said. "I don't know why you ever signed with him."

"I do," Suha said. She put her hands behind her head and grinned.

"Thought your tastes ran different," Nyx said.

"Doesn't mean I don't know a pretty thing when I see it."

"Let's eat," Nyx said, searching for an easier subject.

They ate on the floor.

"You think you can open a line to Anneke?" Nyx asked Suha.

"Anneke? That mercenary you used to run with back in Nasheen? The one with all the kids?"

"The same."

Suha shook her head. "Can't get you a secure line."

"Doesn't need to be secure."

"What the hell you want to talk to some old mercenary in Nasheen for? Can't help us out here," Suha said.

"Remember the guy who built the boat?"

"The guy . . .?" Suha said.

"You know, that story. With all the animals."

"Noah?" Eshe suggested, using the Ras Tiegan name.

"Close enough. When did God tell him to build a boat?"

"Um. Before the flood?" Eshe said.

"Exactly," Nyx said.

✚

Nyx sat on the loading dock and watched the blue dawn come up. Somebody was playing a call to prayer on a radio, pumping it out over the sea. It carried with the wind. Nyx was finishing her second whiskey. Eshe had bought it from a Nasheenian merchant in the Ras Tiegan district. She watched the boats out on the sea, shuttling goods between Shirhazi and the southern cities. Suha came up, hollow-eyed and stiff in the shoulders.

"She's yelling," Suha said.

"Just yelling? Or asking to talk to me?"

"Just yelling. Cursing Shadha so Murshida, mostly."

"Then let her be. Wait until she asks for me."

Suha sat down. Eshe slept inside, curled up on a dog-hair mattress they'd pulled out of a nearby trash heap. "What if she's telling the truth? What if it's just Shadha behind it? Just Shadha and those thugs?"

"If it was just Shadha, she would have killed me. No, somebody else wanted me alive. The same person who's been playing cat and roach with me from the beginning."

"Is that who Leveh is?"

"No. It's whoever Leveh and Shadha work for. I want the name. I think she has it."

"And if she doesn't?"

"Then we killed some old bitch for no reason," Nyx said. "Wouldn't be the first time. Want a drink?"

Suha drank.

Behdis started crying for Nyx ten hours later.

Behdis was crammed into the far corner of the room, hugging herself with her skinny arms. A long trail of blood oozed from beneath her ass, pooled into the drain at the center of the floor.

As Nyx stepped inside the old ice room, she saw the glistening stir of maggoty venom worms thrashing in the blood, fine as silver thread, drunk on their own death.

Behdis was shivering so hard she knocked her head against the wall.

Nyx crouched next to her. The old woman's eyes were glazed over.

"I want to know where they are." Nyx held out a phial of venom. Just the phial. No needle.

Behdis's eyes focused. Her gaze rolled toward the phial. Hungry, terrified gaze.

"Who's leading this, Behdis? I know it's not Shadha's idea. Who got her started? Was it Fatima?"

"Kill me," Behdis said. "Kill me."

"You're dying now. A lot slower than anything she'll do to you. And a lot messier. You know how this works? That venom feeds the worms that keep you high, the buzz that burns out your senses. Now the worms are dying, bleeding black pus and shit into your body and starting to claw their way out your ass. Ten more hours and they'll be crawling out your mouth and nose, too, pouring out every orifice looking for food. If you don't bleed to death, you'll die from the toxins they're excreting in your blood. Good stuff, yeah? Is that how you wanna die?"

"Please kill me," Behdis sobbed.

"I can do better. I can bring you back. But I want to know who wanted me alive."

"Shadha wanted you dead," Behdis spat, and her eyes were wild and yellow. Nyx held her ground. "She should have killed you. I told them! I told them!"

"Why didn't she kill me, Behdis?"

Behdis whimpered. "Please kill me."

Nyx stood, turned away. "Another ten hours," she said.

Suha looked away.

"No!" Behdis shrieked. "No! She'll kill me!"

Nyx kept walking.

And then:

"Alharazad! Alharazad! She wants you alive! Oh God, kill me! Please kill me!"

Nyx felt her gut go icy. She turned. Saw Behdis spitting and slobbering.

"Kill me! Kill me!"

Nyx walked back to her, crouched next to her.

"Alharazad?" Nyx said.

"She wants you alive. I don't know! That's what I heard. I heard it. I don't know! Please kill me."

Nyx broke the cap on the phial. Pulled out the syringe.

"Noooo!" Behdis shrieked.

"Where are they in Beh Ayin?" Nyx asked.

"I don't . . . Beh Ayin? I don't know! Please, I don't know!"

"Who's protecting them? I need to know where they are, Behdis, or you're going to die very badly."

"Please," Behdis sobbed. "Please. Ask Alharazad. She knows. She knows everything. Kill me, please!"

Nyx filled the syringe. She met Behdis's eyes. "I am," she said, and plunged the syringe into Behdis's thigh.

Nyx stood, tucked the syringe into the pocket of her tunic. "Cut her down," she told Suha.

Behdis's head slumped. She started convulsing.

"Where are we dumping her?" Suha asked.

They loaded the body into the bakkie and dumped it on the far eastern side of the inland sea. The drive back was quiet. Suha drank whiskey straight from the bottle. Nyx concentrated on the road.

They picked up Eshe at a boxing gym in the Ras Tiegan quarter. His face was still forgettable and Ras Tiegan enough to not get him much notice, and he was good with the handful of girls whose fathers allowed them to take up boxing, generally because they were showing some interest or affinity for working with bugs.

Eshe slipped into the back seat.

"Nyx?" Eshe asked after a long minute.

"Yeah?"

"You think God wants me to go to war?"

It was just after midday prayer. Suha had made her stop on the way there to pray. Nyx watched him in the rearview mirror. He was sitting up straight, hands in his lap, gazing at the window with brow furrowed.

"I don't know what God wants, Eshe."

"The mullahs say they know what God wants," Eshe said. "You believe them?" He met her look in the rearview mirror.

Nyx looked back at the road. "The mullahs can't figure out what they want for dinner," she said.

"I've been thinking about the war. It's not so different from what we do."

"It's a lot different," Nyx said.

"How?"

Suha snorted.

"It just is," Nyx said. "Who said what we do is like the war?"

"I was just thinking it was."

"We kill a few people to stop a lot of people dying," Nyx said. "Wars kill a lot of people to keep a few people rich."

"You think God likes what we do? You think that's why God brought you back?"

Nyx sighed. She wanted to say, I don't give a fuck what God thinks, but snatched the whiskey bottle from Suha instead and took a long pull.

"God didn't bring me back," she said. "Yah Tayyib did. There's a big difference."

They drove to the edge of the quarter. Suha got her a line to Anneke.

"The fuck you up to out the fuck there?" Anneke said over the hissing, spitting line.

"Need a favor," Nyx said.

"Ohhhhh fuck," Anneke said.

Nyx returned the rented bakkie and bought a new one—new to Nyx, anyway—from an orange vendor in the Mhorian district. They picked up some supplies. A table slide, enough food to last a week, some household goods she and Suha could convert to explosives, deadtech bugging devices, and homemade security traps.

They started cleaning up the top floor of the abandoned warehouse. The corner storage room had easy access to two fire escapes. Nyx found more mattresses in a dump heap in the Heidian district that still smelled of cabbage. She splurged on new sheets, a short sword, and a full-sized scattergun that she immediately converted to a portable sawed-off.

Then she sat at her worktable with Suha and started putting together explosives.

She was due to pay a visit to Yah Tayyib.

✛

It was a gorgeous day in Shirhazi. Clear lavender sky. The air didn't smell like rotting shit—a nice change. Nyx figured the place could almost be pleasant if the wind kept up.

The magicians' gym downtown was typical of Tirhan. She swore some of the inlay was real gold. A swarm of locusts blackened the dome. The whole gym was surrounded in a filter, a filter that wouldn't take kindly to a Nasheenian woman's blood code.

The power supply wasn't hard to find. Tirhan was a soft country, drunk on love of itself, and the power station was just a little one-room checkpoint tower near the entrance where the magician in charge of feeding and directing the bugs kept the primary bug nest pumping out bugs with the right instructions.

She walked right up to the guard tower, and said she had a delivery in her broken Chenjan. She haggled with the actual guard on duty for a couple of minutes while she planted the mine.

Nyx kept hold of her package, and found a good, unguarded entrance on the other side of the building to wait.

The mine going off was a small sound, a muted boom. Then the filter popped and blinked out. She walked right in. She thought of babies and candy, and that made her think of Mercia with her sweet stick, running through the streets of Mushtallah.

Babies, indeed.

She walked into a broad reception area and asked the woman in Tirhani if she spoke Nasheenian.

The woman said she did. Nyx said she had a delivery for Yah Tayyib. Behind the reception desk, Nyx saw the most amazing thing—a big shimmery display board with the names of magicians on it. And the call patterns for their offices.

Sweet fuck, Nyx thought. Yah Tayyib was on the third floor, room 435.

The receptionist told her to leave the package.

"I'm sorry," Nyx said, "it's from another magician. Yah Rhys. I was given explicit instructions to deliver this to Yah Tayyib. I'll either need to drop it in his rooms, or you'll need to call him out."

"I'm sorry—" the receptionist began, and then seemed distracted. There would be some kind of emergency call on her console by now. Somebody had probably sent a swarm as well. It wouldn't take long to get the filter back up. She didn't have much time.

"Listen, I can see you're busy," Nyx said.

The receptionist's brows were knit.

"You're new here, aren't you?" Nyx said.

The receptionist raised her eyes, gave a guilty smile.

"It's no problem," Nyx said. "I'll just take this to 435, all right? Third floor. I've visited him before. Old friend, you know? Nasheenian." She winked. It felt totally unconvincing.

You're going to get your ass thrown out, she thought.

But there were more people coming in now. Nyx could see sweat on the woman's brow. She was reaching for her transceiver. "All right. Just hurry down, please," she said.

Nyx headed left.

"Mother?" the receptionist said.

Nyx felt her heart squeeze. Dammit. Did she look that old?

"The lifts are the other way," the receptionist said pleasantly.

"Of course. Yeah," Nyx said. She went to the lifts, but walked right past and went up the stairs. She had never used a lift before, and didn't like the look of them.

The room was easy to find, but when she knocked, no one answered. It was locked, but not filtered. Odd. She supposed the filter outside kept out most folks. She checked the hall, then jimmied open the door with a couple of hijab pins. Old Chenjan trick. Easy to crack a place with low security.

The door opened. She stepped into a dimly lit room and shut the door.

She noticed the sound first, the low hum.

"Fucking shit," she said, and grabbed for the door again.

A wasp swarm engulfed her. She shut her mouth and covered her ears.

"Nyx?"

The swarm abated. When she looked up, Yah Tayyib was standing in a doorway leading into another room.

She looked around. Stone slab for a desk, some antique books, a couple of bugs in jars.

"Seems kind of a shitty time to decide to kill me," Nyx said. She spit out a wasp.

"They wouldn't have killed you," Yah Tayyib said. "What are you doing here?"

"Alharazad," Nyx said.

Yah Tayyib drew himself up a little straighter, sighed through his nose. "Yes," he said. "Come in. Rhys has been looking for you."

He motioned her into the next room.

"Rhys?"

It was his operating theater. At the center was a great stone slab. The walls were lined in jars of organs. Flesh beetles squirmed around in the bowl of the sink at the head of the slab. There was a dead boy on the slab, his chest pinned open. The head was in a jar of solution sitting on a counter at the back. Roaches busied themselves at something in the boy's chest cavity.

"I'm interrupting?" Nyx said.

"Always."

Nyx sat on a stool on the other side of the body. She watched Yah Tayyib as he began to work again.

"You said Rhys was looking for me?"

"He left a call pattern. It's on my desk."

"Why'd you bring me back?" she said.

"I thought you knew."

"I'm too tired for games, Tayyib."

"You and I have a mutual enemy," he said.

"Alharazad."

"Just so." He picked up a scalpel and cut something out of the boy, some fleshy bit, and placed it in a jar of solution.

"When did she turn?"

"Decades ago, when the first of the aliens visited. She saw them as a threat to Nasheen. Their meddling with the world, she believed, would ruin everything we created here. It is the world that makes us unique, and it is the world that keeps us bound here. Ships don't stay long on Nasheen. When they do, the bugs of our world eat out their innards and leave them stranded. Just as they did to those who first fell from the sky. She approached a good many of us with her concerns. She even tried hijacking a vessel herself with several of us using tailored swarms." He waved his hand over the body, and four roaches crawled out. He pulled a handful of flesh beetles from the sink and drove them deep down into the boy's guts.

"You were working with the aliens, though," Nyx said.

"I've worked for many sides, when I believed one was working harder than the other for what I wanted."

"And what did you want?"

"What you want. An end to the war."

"Shitty way of going about it."

"You think so?" Yah Tayyib washed his hands in the sink. "Alharazad has moved many of us around on her chessboard for decades. I no longer wanted to be moved. I acted on my own. Perhaps my judgment was misguided——"

"Misguided?" Nyx said, "You wanted to teach Chenja how to breed monsters to kill our boys."

"No." He dried his hands on his apron. "I wanted an end to the war. That would only happen if both sides had the ability to annihilate each other. I realize you have no love of history, but we have warred a good deal longer than any realize. Disagreements between our people go back to the days before the beginning of the world."

"There was nothing before that."

"There was the moons."

Nyx waved a hand. "Old stories. You can't expect to believe anything that old."

"We bickered on those moons a thousand years while the magicians worked to make this world habitable. Yes, a good deal was lost, and much that remains is myth, but there are seeds of truth to every myth."

"So what stopped the war? Coming down here?"

"No. It ended before that, when both sides got perilously close to losing everything. They developed a weapon so powerful it had the ability to completely annihilate the other. There was as much spying and espionage then as now, and it didn't take long for both sides to gain this power."

"You thought Chenja and Nasheen would stop fighting just because they could both breed mutant armies?"

"I hoped it would give them pause, yes."

"I've been thinking some about that."

"Thinking? Not killing?"

"There's been some of that too."

"Ah, well." Yah Tayyib sighed. "What are you here for, Nyx?"

"Just verifying some information," she said, sliding off the stool. "What I'm about to do is a big deal. I need to make sure I'm not full of shit."

"That's rather . . . prudent of you, isn't it?"

"Yeah, trying something new. You die once and suddenly dying again seems kinda redundant, you know?"

"I do."

"Gotta go," Nyx said. "Your filter's gonna go back up in five minutes."

She walked to the door.

"Nyx?"

She turned.

"I would have let you in," he said. "Go to a call box next time instead of blowing up a filter, would you?"

She shrugged. "Habit." She walked back out to his desk, fished around for the call pattern Rhys had left. Found the card. Stared at it a long moment.

"Hey, Tayyib!" She called into his operating theater.

He walked back into the doorway. "Yes?"

She tapped the card. "You know any good magicians want to help me kill some bel dames?"

"I wondered if you'd ever ask," he said.

"Why'd you bring me back, really?"

"Perhaps because I know you're the only person foolish enough to attempt to murder half the bel dame council," he said, "including the only other woman to try it."

"I like that reason better. Meet us at the train station at eighteen."

35.

Khos drove Inaya to a four-room, three-story walk-up at the edge of their former district. There was nothing left to salvage from the old house. Inaya mourned the children's projects, the certificate of merit she had received from the Ras Tiegan ambassador (she loved it for the irony, if nothing else), and the big stone tub upstairs, the one with the clawed feet.

As they mounted the steps, Inaya prepared for the worst. The woman who opened the door was a fleshy matron about Khos's age, handsome, Inaya supposed, but not beautiful. She felt oddly relieved at that. Her dark abaya did her no favors—they generally didn't, with fleshy women. Her eyes were blue, like Khos's, but her complexion was Nasheenian.

"You must be Inaya," she said, and held out her hands the way one would to a sister.

Inaya took them, hesitant. The woman's hands were warm and rough. Inaya guessed she was a weaver. She had done work like that herself back in Nasheen.

"Mam! Mam!"

Isfahan pushed past the Mhorian woman and clung to Inaya's leg. Tears came, unbidden, and Inaya scooped her up into her arms. "Hello, love."

Inaya moved into the room, past the Mhorian, and found Tatie playing at stones with another young boy on the floor. He was too young to be Khos's original half-breed boy. Had he fathered another? Or was this woman simply as loose as a Nasheenian?

The flat felt cramped and depressingly empty. Kitchen, bedroom, and a curtained-off living area to make it two rooms. She didn't see a privy, and wondered if they had a shared one down the hall.

Tatie looked up at her as she entered, brow furrowed, frowning. But he did not stir until Khos came in. Then his face lit up, and he ran.

Khos took Tatie up into his arms. Inaya had to push down a spark of jealousy. At least they hadn't both clung to the Mhorian.

"I'm Batia," the Mhorian said.

Inaya nodded. She mustered up some semblance of manners. "Thank you for taking us in. There wasn't much to salvage at the house." She did not say that she knew her husband paid for the cramped little flat. This is her home, Inaya thought fiercely. It's not her fault Khos kept her from me. Don't punish her. She's trying to make her way, just as you did.

They had stored all of their relevant documents in a safe deposit box downtown. So they had all of their travel documents and visas, the certificate of insurance, all of the vital bits and pieces of organic paper and official recordings they needed to rebuild their lives here in this little flat.

Inaya looked over at Khos. He was beaming. Tatie had his arms wrapped around him. The Mhorian, too—Batia—she corrected herself—was beaming also. So happy. Happy to be alive, to be together. Lovely little family.

"Mam, come see my drawings!" Isfahan said, clapping her hands.

Inaya set her down and let her lead her behind the curtain to a little sleeping area. The children had hung up drawings along the wall in the corner where they slept.

"This is you," Isfahan said, pointing to a drawing of a great green blob. "This is Da"—pointing to some kind of four-footed animal—"and this is us and Batia"—pointing to a stick figure with a brown scribble for an abaya holding hands with two smaller figures colored over in red. Most Nasheenians and Chenjans didn't encourage drawing living things. Seeing this Mhorian-Nasheenian encouraging it in her children gave Inaya pause.

Inaya frowned. Next to this drawing was another of a big square building bleeding jagged orange and red edges . . . and beside it, a swirling green monster hovering above the blazing house. Am I really just a big green monster? she thought.

She squeezed Isfahan close. The girl pushed her away. "Mam, look, look—" and she showed her more drawings.

That night, Inaya and Khos slept together with the children in the curtained off sleeping area while Batia slept alone in her bedroom.

Inaya lay awake long after the children slept, listening for footsteps on the stairs. Pistol shots. Grenades.

Khos said softly, in the darkness, "I thought you would change your mind."

"I thought you were asleep."

"You want to go with her, don't you?"

"I don't know. I don't know what I want." Not this, Inaya thought. She thought of her life before. Scrubbing floors, taking Tatie back and forth to the madrassa, staying up with her children when they were sick, ferrying information to the rebels, unable to act on it. Crippled, torn. "I love my children," she said.

"You have a great gift."

"A curse."

"A gift. Don't let all those catshit Ras Tiegan politics cloud that."

"They . . . do you know what they do to people like me?"

"I wanted to protect you."

"I know."

"But you're very good at protecting yourself."

Inaya absently stroked Isfahan's head. Isfahan stirred in her sleep, pressed her warm body against Inaya's.

"You should have told me properly about . . . Batia," she said.

"I know. I thought . . . I didn't know what to do about it."

"You always did hate conflict."

"Always running away from it. Always end up back in it. I've loved our life the last four years."

Married life.

"I . . ." she hesitated. "I thought I would too."

"What do you want?" He shifted onto his side, propped himself up on one elbow, and gazed down at her. She stared up into his graven face. A handsome man, big and kind. I blame him for my unhappiness, she realized. He's not the cause of it. He never was. I've done this to myself. She had tried so long to do what was expected of her. Married the right sorts of men. Tried to be the right sort of wife.

"I think . . ." she said. "I think . . . this is not the life for me." She let out her breath. It was like cutting open a rotten wound and draining the pus. Pain. Then relief. What would God think of her? Turning away from her husband, her family? You're already damned, she thought.

Khos brushed her hair away from her face. So gentle. "I love you," he said. "Always did."

She took a deep breath.

"I can help build a better world for them. Especially if both are . . . are . . ."

"Shifters," he said.

Hearing it out loud hurt.

"Yes. I'm afraid, Khos. I'm afraid of myself all the time."

"I'm sorry about Batia."

She reached out, pressed her hand to his cheek. "I forgive you," she said.

He pulled her into his arms.

+

Inaya packed her things an hour before the blue dawn touched the sky. She wore one of Batia's full hijabs, and gloves.

She woke Tatie and Isfahan. Khos was already up, packing rations.

"Mam," Tatie said, "I'm tired, Mam."

"Why are you dressed up?" Isfahan said.

"I need you to know something, love," Inaya said, and looking at her daughter in the blue dawn reminded her of her mother coming to her in the darkness, smelling of dogs and offal, saying, "They've come for me. They'll come for you, too."

"I need you both to know that I love you very much. I'm going to do some important work. But it means I may be gone for a while."

"How long, Mam?" Isa said.

"I don't know. You'll be big when I see you again, though. Batia and Da will take good care of you while I'm gone. I want you to be polite to her. You promise?"

Tatie looked at her suspiciously. "When are you coming back?"

"She's your second mam. You know, like your friend Akhshan has. You know Akhshan's two mams?"

"My friend Riara has four," Isa said. She held up three fingers.

"That's right," Inaya said. "That's right." She took Isa's hand and kissed it. Tears were spilling down her cheeks, soaking her veil. "It will be just like that."

She hugged them both, so tightly that Tatie started to squirm.

"Get some sleep now," she said.

She kissed them again and pushed past the curtain into the main room. Khos stood in the kitchen.

"I called Rhys," he said. "Nyx put them on a train to Beh Ayin last night. You should be able to meet them at a hotel called the Petit Bijoux."

"Beh Ayin?" She frowned. Sudden understanding dawned. "The magistrate," she breathed.

"What?" he asked.

She shook her head. "Nothing, I . . . I know where they are." She took the food he offered and pressed it into her pack.

"Are you ready?" he asked.

She nodded. "You watch after them. You promise me."

"I love this life, Inaya. I'd give everything for it."

Including me, Inaya thought. Yes.

He walked her to the door. She hesitated on the threshold. God, give me the strength for this, she thought, and sent out a prayer. Keep them safe. Please, God, in all your infinite mercy, keep them safe.

She stepped into the blue dawn.

Khos shut the door behind her.

The morning was cool, almost cold. She looked back once. Once was enough to nearly lose her resolve. She did not look back again.

36.

The train to Beh Ayin was crowded. Nyx had expected something a little more posh, considering the Tirhani streets, but Beh Ayin was out in the contaminated wilderness. The train practically hummed with filters. There were filters over the doors coming in, and none of the windows opened. Everything was slathered in bug-repelling unguent.

Sitting on the sterilized seats made her skin itch right through her clothes. She ended up sitting on her coat.

They were a motley crew, so Nyx had split them up into a couple of groups. She got enough attention on her own as it was. Yah Tayyib and Rhys shared a compartment in first class. They looked the most like they belonged there, and Yah Tayyib could afford the ticket. Nyx rode in third class with Eshe at the back of the car. Suha had her own seat at the front of the same car next to some fussy old Ras Tiegan woman. Most everybody in third class was foreign, and there wasn't enough room for them.

Nyx walked up through second class and found it was less than half full, and every passenger a neat little Tirhani. She convinced a suspicious porter that all the privies were full in second and she'd piss on the floor if she didn't get by.

She knocked on Rhys and Yah Tayyib's compartment door.

"Come," Rhys said, in Tirhani.

Nyx rolled the door open.

Rhys was alone, sitting against the window with a tattered book in his ugly hands. He wore trousers, and she couldn't help but look at the outline of his long legs. Outside, the verdant Tirhani jungle whooshed past: huge amber trees and ropey vines as wide as her arm. A giant suckered insect of some kind thudded on the window, then flew off.

"Everything all right?" he asked.

"Yeah," she said, rolling the door closed behind her. "Just kinda crowded back there. Wanted some air."

He closed the book. She'd assumed it was the Kitab, but no, it was some poetry book.

She sat across from him, near the door.

"Hungry?" she asked.

"No." He opened the book again.

She fidgeted. They had packed a few weapons in the cases at their feet, but mostly the cases were full of bugs. Useful things Yah Tayyib and Rhys said might help secure a safe house in Beh Ayin.

"Thanks for coming," she said, lamely. It felt stupid the moment she said it.

"I'm not doing this for you," he said. "I'm doing this for my wife."

"Right. I know. I—" she stopped. Chewed on her words. This was always where she pissed people off. It wasn't a great time to do that. He wore his pistols at his hips again. His hair had started to grow out. Her gaze moved across his clear, pretty face, the broad shoulders, slender chest, and settled there on the ugly hands. The too-big, short-fingered stevedore's hands. Dead man's hands.

She pulled her gaze away. "You call that woman you know out here? The one you told me about?"

"Tasyin doesn't know where they're staying. But she did infer that they're coming to an agreement soon. A day or two. Not much more. We'll have to work fast. If they get the weapon . . . I don't know."

"Maybe they'll sell it to Nasheen and Chenja at the same time. Save us some trouble."

Rhys shook his head. "Still doesn't take care of the coup."

"No. That one's up to us, whether or not they make the deal."

They sat in silence a good while longer.

"Tayyib go out for food?"

"Privy. The train makes him sick."

"Hrm," Nyx said. She sighed and stood. "Well, that's enough air, I guess."

"Nyx?"

"Yeah?"

"Make me a promise."

Nyx hesitated. Felt herself fidgeting again. Fuck, what was wrong with her? "Sure," she said, "if I can."

"I need you to promise that no matter what happens, you won't look for me. You won't come for me."

"You think I would?"

"If you needed me. The way you needed me this time."

"Rhys—"

"I want your oath, Nyx. I want a bel dame blood oath that when I leave here you won't look for me again."

Give it to him, she thought. You owe him that.

"I do this and we're even," she said.

He didn't answer.

Nyx pulled the dagger at her hip. It was small enough that it hadn't raised too many eyebrows on the train. She made a smooth cut across her thumb. Blood welled up. She stood, reached out and pressed her bloody thumb to his forehead, left a smear of red behind.

"I swear I won't come for you. By God, even. You want my bloody print on paper? You want witnesses? Want me to wait for Tayyib?"

"No," he said. He kept his dark eyes locked with hers while he wiped the blood from his forehead with his sleeve.

"Good enough?" she said.

"Good enough," he said, and went back to his book.

Nyx grit her teeth. "That's it? The best you've got?"

He didn't answer.

"Why did you come, Rhys? Why go to all the trouble?"

"I told you. My wife asked me."

"Fine."

He closed the book, raised his head. "What did you expect me to say, Nyx?"

"That you missed it. All of it. Not the worst parts maybe, but the good parts. If you didn't, you'd be back there with her instead of me."

She rolled open the door and stepped into the hall. *Fuck him and his—*

Yah Tayyib stepped out of the privy in front of her. She sighed and made to push past him.

"Didn't go as well as you hoped?" Yah Tayyib said. She wanted to punch the smirk off his tattered face.

The train suddenly spasmed. Nyx lost her footing and jerked forward, smack into Yah Tayyib. He flew back. The whole train juddered. Screams.

Then Nyx was tumbling. Loud voices. More screaming. Noise. Darkness.

The world stopped moving.

Nyx's stomach heaved. She vomited.

She was tangled with a crush of others. When she put out her hands, she found bare earth. The stink of her own vomit made her move. Push through the debris.

Nyx scrambled for a twisting sliver of light among the wreckage and slithered free. Her head spun. She clambered up on top of the twisted car and stared out at the jungle. Her hands and knees were scraped and bloody. She turned and looked behind her.

The first class car had split open on the track. She staggered off the car and back toward the rest of the wreckage. Bodies littered the jungle floor. The car had split open and let them tumble down the slight rise of the track and into the jungle. Beyond the strip around the tracks, the free contaminated world buzzed and whirred.

She crawled over the wreckage, onto the track. Most of the rear of the train had tumbled off, but nothing had broken open. Most folks would probably be alive. The front half was in worse shape. Much worse. The front three cars had carved out a long swath of jungle ahead of them.

"Nyx!"

She turned. Yah Tayyib was upright. Blood streamed from his face.

"Tayyib? I need to find Rhys!"

Yah Tayyib started climbing toward her. Other passengers began to move and moan. Nyx pushed past a few as they staggered around looking for belongings. A high, keening cry cut the air. Then another and another as the survivors picked through the corpses.

"What of Suha and Eshe?" Yah Tayyib asked as he came up next to her. She climbed on top of the shattered hull of the overturned first class cabin and started pressing her face to all the opaqued windows.

"They're at the back. They'll find us," she said. "No damage back there."

The porters were calling people together to comb the wreckage.

Nyx crawled across broken windows and twisted metal. Bug swarms were gathering above them.

"We need to move soon," Yah Tayyib said, staring at the swarms.

"Where?" Nyx said. "Into the jungle?"

"We're only a few kilometers from Beh Ayin. It's dangerous, yes, but not as dangerous as staying here."

"Nyx?"

Rhys's voice.

She looked down the pitch of the tracks. He stood straight in his tattered coat. He was missing a boot, and she saw his hands were scratched and bloody.

She crawled down from the wreckage and walked toward him.

"Yah Tayyib's right," Rhys said. "We need to move. The bugs are going to pick this place clean."

They found Suha and Eshe bruised and shaken, but alive. It took another half hour to recover their bags and get Rhys some new boots off a corpse. By then, the swarms had darkened the sky.

"Come, come," Yah Tayyib said.

"Where do you think you're going?" one of the porters called. The porter had gathered a few dozen survivors in the ruins of the train. More were climbing along the rear of the train, pulling people from the cars.

Nyx didn't even look back at him. She handed Eshe a jar of unguent. "You slather yourself in that. It's a long hike. Won't be pleasant."

Yah Tayyib looked back up at the sky as they pushed into the jungle.

"They're dead, ain't they?" Suha said.

"Without a half-dozen magicians?" Yah Tayyib said. "Yes." He led the way deeper into the contaminated wilderness.

37.

Within an hour, cysts had appeared in the warm, moist crevices of Rhys's armpits, the kink of his elbow, the soft flesh behind his ear. He could convince some of them to burst and expire through will alone, but the rest he cut out. It always hurt worse if you let the little ticks and midges grow and split open on their own.

Yah Tayyib kept away the worst of the bugs—the hulking, skittering shapes that paced them as they walked along the tracks. They had moved back onto the train tracks after they cleared the wreck. They moved steadily east now in the faltering daylight. Getting caught out in the jungle overnight wasn't . . . promising. The bugs out here were far too big and far too wild for Rhys to control. He felt them, yes, though not as keenly as Yah Tayyib felt them. Every few minutes, he was able to call in a dragonfly swarm to eat the lesser biting bugs that plagued them—the ones Yah Tayyib did not have the stamina to bother with.

Rhys brought up the rear of their little processional. Suha walked ahead of him, hands moving to her pistols every time something in the undergrowth shuddered and hissed. He didn't bother telling her that the bugs would be too fast and too well-armored to kill with regular bullets. They had few enough bullets as it was to go bouncing them off mutant scarabs and horned beetles that likely weighed a hundred kilos.

Ahead, Yah Tayyib paused. Rhys saw a large, dark shape moving along the tracks ahead.

"You want me to shoot it?" Eshe asked.

"Low on ammo," Suha said. "Save it for when we need it."

When. Not if. Rhys appreciated her sense of the inevitable.

Nyx pushed up next to Yah Tayyib. Rhys moved next to her to get a better look.

"What the fuck is that?" Nyx said.

It was a centipede, six meters long, gnawing on some dead creature run over by the last train that had come through. The centipede's head was as big as Rhys's—the torso about matched Eshe's in breadth.

As Rhys watched, it lifted its giant head from its meal and turned its antennae toward them.

"Please tell me I can shoot it," Eshe said.

"Save the bullets," Nyx said. "Tayyib?"

Yah Tayyib shook his head. "It's not responding. They're very wild out here. Very contaminated. Not everything responds."

Nyx looked back at Rhys. She had fished a hijab out of the wreckage, and wore it pulled forward to get some relief from the sun pounding down on her uncovered face.

"Any ideas?" she asked.

"Eshe has a good one," Rhys said. "It's not as well-armored as the beetles. But then, the bullets might just antagonize it."

"If it's angry, it will charge," Yah Tayyib said. "Are you keen on wrestling with a giant centipede?"

"It would be a first," Nyx said.

Rhys snorted. He didn't think it was a laugh until it came out that way. Nyx looked surprised, raised a brow.

"You want to help?" she asked.

He shook his head. "You're on your own."

"Maybe we can just wait," Eshe said. "Or go around?"

"Fuck that," Suha said. She pulled her pistols. "Fine. Let's do it."

Nyx raised her scattergun, and the two of them stepped up

in front of Yah Tayyib. Rhys shook his head and stepped up with them.

"You game, gravy?" Nyx said.

"Somebody here actually needs to hit something," he said.

"Might be I'm a better shot these days with all that good bug juice Tayyib gave me."

"Then I'll know for sure it's the End Times," he said.

Rhys pulled his pistols. They felt strange in his new hands. Not quite alien, but . . . different. Somebody else wielding all that death.

They started forward together.

The centipede's head bobbed back and forth. Its legs rippled. The first three meters reared up at them. Rhys realized what a massive reach the thing would have.

He fired first.

The centipede's head jerked back. Rhys saw a satisfying spray of blackish blood. Then it hissed. The massive jaws worked, and then it was coming straight at them.

Six meters of centipede was a lot of bug.

They opened fire.

It kept coming.

Rhys stepped back. Nyx started reloading her scattergun. Suha swore.

Rhys aimed again at the head. The centipede reared up again and lashed out with its broken, oozing head.

Nyx swung her scattergun, caught the thing in the jaw.

Rhys fired three more times, point blank. The head dropped—right onto his shoulder. He went down under the smooth, bloody carapace.

"Fuck!" Rhys yelled. Blood and bug offal splattered his face. He tried to push the bug off him. The long, velvety legs—long as his hands—twitched.

Nyx was making some kind of sound. Rhys tried wriggling

out from under the centipede. He managed to clear his head.

Nyx was laughing.

"For God's sake!" Rhys said.

Nyx laughed. She, too, was covered in blood. She bent over and helped him up. Her shoulders still shook.

"Oh God, you should see your face," she said. "You should see it."

Rhys tried to wipe some of the blood and offal from his coat.

"Let's keep moving," Yah Tayyib said. He came forward and patted Rhys on the shoulder. "Very nice shooting."

"That's about all we got, though," Suha said, unloading her clip. He watched her count the remaining bullets. Three still in the clip. Rhys had two left in each pistol. He wasn't sure about Nyx.

"Let me kill it next time," Eshe said as he stepped over the twitching ruin of the centipede. "Knives don't run out."

"I'd love to see you wrangle the next one," Rhys said.

"Wanna fight me for it?" Eshe said, slyly.

As they walked, the bugs got bolder.

Suha started throwing stones at some of the shiny scarab beetles—tall as Rhys's knee—that poked their heads up out of the underbrush.

These were easier for Yah Tayyib to turn away, but it meant the midges and markflies and mosquitoes and other biting insects got worse.

They stopped three times to slather on more bug unguent. Rhys's thick hands were already littered with bites. When he handed Nyx the bottle of unguent, he saw a bruise on the side of her face big as a thumbnail, and a long smear of some dead bug that had tried sucking her face off.

In truth, he was more worried about the scarabs.

"Think I could get anything for the shells?" Eshe asked as they walked. Nyx was passing around the last of their water. "Real pretty."

"You get close enough to take a shell, it'll take your arm off," Rhys said.

"Yours, maybe," Eshe said.

"They're carrion eaters. Those jaws are designed to strip flesh from bone."

"It can try," Eshe said. His knife appeared in his hands. A slim blade about as long as his arm from wrist to elbow.

"Careful you don't cut your arm off with that," Rhys said.

"I know which end's the pointy one," Eshe said. He glanced at Rhys's hands. Rhys waited for a follow up about clumsy fingers. It didn't come. Maybe the boy was smarter than he pretended. He'd have to be, to survive this long with Nyx.

They trailed the others.

"How'd you end up with her?" Rhys asked.

Eshe eyed him sideways. "How did you?"

"Seemed like a good idea at the time."

"It was like that," Eshe said, and nodded. He sheathed his blade.

Rhys slapped at a mosquito—big as his thumb—that had settled on his left wrist. He sent out another call for a dragonfly swarm. There were none nearby. He tried again, a stronger message this time. Something tickled back in response. Some errant swarm. He told them to find others like them and bring them to him.

"So," Eshe said, nodding toward Nyx where she walked ahead of them with Yah Tayyib, just out of earshot, "you two ever . . . you know?"

"Why does everyone ask that?"

"Just seems like a normal thing to do," Eshe said.

"Maybe in Nasheen. I'm Chenjan. The world doesn't work that way. We have morals."

"I have morals," Eshe said. "I've prayed three times today. I haven't seen you pray once."

Rhys frowned. His chest tightened. Guilt? Anger? He wasn't

sure. Something he didn't feel comfortable naming, not yet. "It takes concentration to keep the swarms from overtaking us," he said.

The boy looked dubious.

Rhys watched Nyx walking ahead of him. She was an intimidating figure, even now, twenty kilos lighter than when he'd last seen her. Broad in the shoulders, the hips. When she sparred—

He shook his head and looked away, back out into the brush. He missed his lemon trees. Elahyiah. The girls playing with ladybugs in the yard. It was just . . . How long ago, now? The pistols at his hips felt heavy. He missed the gauzy bisht, the . . .

Another biting bug attacked his neck. He smacked at it. The dragonfly swarm finally arrived. They began to swim and dart above him. Eshe breathed a sigh of relief.

Rhys was covered in dried blood and crushed beetle carapace. His hands were heavy. His fingers were slightly numb at the tips. He hadn't prayed since the morning before, and he hadn't missed it. It was not the Kitab he brought with him to Beh Ayin, but a book of poetry called *The Caged Unbeliever*. Chenjan poetry—old—from before the war. Like most works written before the war, it was in the prayer language, which was why he could make any sense of it at all.

Why had he brought that instead of the Kitab?

"We got movement!" Suha yelled.

Rhys turned. The day was moving into dusk. He saw a low purple haze along the western edge of the horizon. As he watched, a dozen giant scarabs burst from the undergrowth and charged up the cleared bank of the train tracks toward them.

Rhys fired. It took two shots just to stop one of them. Two more shots for a second, and he was out. Suha's guns clicked immediately after his. Nyx's scattergun didn't faze the incoming wave of insects. She stopped to reload as the first wave broke.

Eshe pulled his knife. Rhys drew a dagger from his boot.

Yah Tayyib turned toward the bugs and drew his hands up and across his body.

A massive black swarm of locusts rose from the scrub brush along the tracks and created a wall between them and the scarabs.

"Move, move!" Nyx yelled at Rhys and Eshe.

Rhys didn't need a second prompt. He ran after her and Suha up the tracks. Yah Tayyib followed after them. Rhys glanced over his shoulder. The locust swarm was holding, but the scarabs were simply chewing their way through.

"The fuck longer is it?" Suha yelled.

Rhys shook his head. His breath came hard and fast. Yah Tayyib wasn't as fit, and lagged behind. Rhys eased up his pace, held out a hand.

"Come on!" he said.

Yah Tayyib took his hand.

They brought up the rear of the group as the train tracks wound around a low rise. As they rounded it, Rhys was blinded by the setting suns. The big orange demon hung bloody red in the dusky sky. Above it, the bigger blue sun still raged, just visible now that the light from its companion had begun to wane. The whole world went lavender.

Rhys caught his breath, and choked on a giant mosquito. He coughed and spat.

Ahead of them—not a kilometer distant—the sheered, broken hilltop of Beh Ayin gleamed in the dusky sky.

"That's it!" Rhys said. "That's it!"

Nyx and Suha and Eshe paused ahead of him. Nyx followed the line of his arm and grinned.

"Fuck me," Nyx said.

A dark shape blackened the sky. It came in so fast Rhys blinked and Nyx was suddenly gone, sprawled on the other side of the tracks.

Rhys scrambled after her, but Eshe was quicker.

The black shape circled once, then rushed back at Nyx with a high-pitched buzzing that hurt Rhys's ears. It was a massive hornet, big as a dog, like nothing Rhys had ever seen.

As it dove, Rhys watched Eshe draw his dagger and leap at it from the height of the tracks.

The hornet dropped like a stone.

Nyx was scrambling back up the hill.

Rhys ran down. They met over the body of the hornet. Eshe's big knife spouted from the insect's armored head. Eshe still had both hands on the hilt.

"The fuck is that?" Suha called.

"Are there more of those?" Nyx said, rubbing her shoulder.

"I very nearly had it," Yah Tayyib said. He placed a slender hand on the hornet's abdomen. "I nearly controlled it." Rhys heard something like awe. Tried to imagine the kind of damage Yah Tayyib could do with a hornet that size.

The stinger on the hornet's abdomen was as long as Eshe's knife. Eshe pulled the knife free of the head and pointed it at Rhys.

"That's the pointy end," Eshe said.

38.

Nyx soaked in a tub of aloe and bug balm from the local hedge witch—they called them mendicants, here—and wished she was back in the desert.

It was a lot safer.

"Hey, hurry up in there!" Suha yelled.

Nyx hosed herself off in the tiled shower. Rhys had found them a hotel at the lower end of the city, right up against the filter. When she sat out on the balcony, she could hear the bugs outside hissing and chittering. She wasn't sure how many of them were going to sleep tonight with all that racket going on. Not her.

She opened the door for Suha and finished dressing while Suha disrobed.

"How you holding up?" Nyx asked. She had washed out her hair. It hung clean and ropy across her shoulders. She started braiding it, using the bronzed mirror over the stone sink as a guide.

"Weird question," Suha said from the tub.

"Guess so," Nyx said.

"Nyx?" Eshe's voice.

"What?" Nyx yelled back at the door.

"Inaya's here!"

"Who?"

"Inaya! That white woman!"

"You're kidding me," Suha muttered.

Nyx pulled her hair back into a tail and opened the door. Eshe had already cleaned up. His hair was damp and shaggy around his ears. She was starting to get used to it.

"Where is she?" Nyx asked.

"Downstairs. They wouldn't give her the room number. I came down."

"She alone?"

"Yeah."

"Say why she's here?"

"No. Just wants to talk to you."

Nyx padded barefoot down the smooth steps. For all its proximity to the filter, the hotel was clean enough, and nobody asked her to cover her hair. It was something.

Inaya waited in the latticed archway separating the reception counter from the waiting area. She was dressed like a good Tirhani matron, and carried a large carpet bag in both hands.

Nyx hesitated along the stair, looking for some sign of Khos. Nothing.

"What you doing here?" Nyx asked as she came into the foyer.

Inaya looked oddly relieved to see her. "You're alive," she said. "I heard about the train."

"Terrorist bomb, they're saying. Didn't know you Ras Tiegans had that big a grudge with Tirhan, still."

Inaya's face twisted. "They murdered thirty thousand people when they claimed this region. Whole towns. I do not begrudge the people here. They are colonized."

"Careful where you say that," Nyx said. There was no one at the front desk, and Beh Ayin seemed like a laid-back frontier town, but Nyx didn't trust Tirhanis much more than Chenjans.

"It's not about that anyhow," Inaya said. "Or, it is, but not in the way you think. Can we speak privately?"

"Come up." Nyx brought her upstairs to the room she shared with Eshe and Suha. They'd split up the rooms for privacy and sanity. Rhys and Yah Tayyib slept next door.

It was a small but clean room, two single beds and a low couch, tea table, and the balcony. Nyx went right to the windowed doors leading out onto the balcony and pulled the curtains.

"Where's Khos?" she asked.

"With his wife. And the children."

"His other wife?"

Inaya nodded. "It's a long story. I came here to help you."

"Why?"

"I have some information you might need."

"And you needed to bring it to me in person?"

"Yes. It's the sort of information I'm not supposed to have."

"This should be good." Nyx sat on the edge of the bed.

Inaya sat across from her on the divan. "I work for the Ras Tiegan underground."

"A spy? Khos said as much."

Inaya looked surprised. "Did he?"

"Close enough. What do you know?"

"I found out our embassy is paying a significant amount of money to a local magistrate in Beh Ayin."

"Not so strange. Bribe?"

"Yes."

"She harboring your rebels?"

"It's a he. And no, I don't think so. The Ras Tiegan government doesn't support the rebels."

"Not officially."

"No. Not ever. They're the same group arguing for shifter rights within the country. The government would never support them."

"You think—"

"Ras Tieg would be *very* interested in whatever weapon your bel dames have to offer, and they couldn't parley officially with bel dames without angering the Queen. If there are as many as we suspect, they'd be expensive to house and feed, and even more expensive to keep the local government quiet about them."

"You have an address?"

"Better."

"Better?"

"It's nearly Offsday, by the Ras Tiegan calendar."

"What the fuck is that?"

"It's our prayer day." Inaya smiled, and Nyx understood her then. She remembered this little woman picking up a shotgun after Khos tried to hustle her to safety back in Chenja. "I know where he goes to church."

"How are we running this?" Rhys asked.

"Clean and neat," Nyx said. "Like always."

She felt better leaning over a schematic, even if the best they could find was a dodgy little portable slide with a ripple in the organic screen. They had spent three days scouting out the church, and now they were running out of time. If they didn't move now, the bel dames would. After three days of scouting, they would know Nyx was coming. Nyx had what she needed to put something together, but the others still balked.

"I have been party to the end result of most of your plans, Nyx," Yah Tayyib said. "Perhaps we should try something a bit more realistic."

"There's very little chance he knows we're here," Inaya said. "And he certainly wouldn't think we're coming for him."

"He won't. They will," Suha said from her post at the window. She spit sen on the floor.

"I'm counting on that," Nyx said.

Inaya wrinkled her nose and handed her a cup.

Suha snorted.

"Are we just going to blow up half the country?" Rhys said. He sat on the divan in their room eating curried rice from a take-out container.

"You have a subtler way, Rhys?" Nyx said. "You told me they're close to a deal. We don't move now and we may not get another chance."

"Fool's errands," Yah Tayyib said.

"*You* got a better idea?" Nyx said.

"I don't like shifting," Inaya said. "Too much of this plan relies on that."

"I don't like dying," Nyx said. "Sometimes we do shit we don't like."

"It's a big building," Eshe said. "If we had a week or two more to scout it out—"

"We don't," Nyx said.

"I say we just snipe the fucker and see who claims the body," Suha said. "That's clean and neat."

"Listen. He eats and sleeps and probably fucks in this church," Nyx said. "And if we snipe him and leave him they'll likely burn him inside it. It won't draw them out. Only we can do that. Every day but prayer day, the place is a fucking fortress. We got one day. Tomorrow. Or we wait another nine days until it comes around again. We want to risk nine days? Anybody?" Nyx looked around at them all in turn.

No answer. Blank faces.

"We want to move," Nyx said, "we move first. That train took out the tracks. It's going to be days before anybody else comes into town. Or goes out of it." She glanced at Inaya, realized she hadn't bothered asking her how Inaya had gotten in without a train. She could do that, and a lot more, of course. Which was why they needed her for this. "They won't be looking for or expecting visitors. We got lucky. They could have had a woman at the station waiting for us. Instead, we came around the back. We're low and quiet now. We have the edge. It's a slim edge, but an edge, and we won't have it much longer."

"Let's do it," Eshe said.

Suha threw up her hands. "I'm up half the night on gear grab and then you got me on a bug hunt? Shit, Nyx."

"You sleep in the morning before your hunt," Nyx said.

Yah Tayyib rubbed at his temples. "I find it difficult to believe I am going along with one of your schemes."

"Oh, come on, you've been wanting to fuck up all those big, bad bel dames a long time," Nyx said.

"I will not deny that."

"Let's go, then." Nyx slid the schematic closed.

Suha gestured to Eshe, and the two slipped out to start pulling together gear. Nyx was on munitions duty, but that would wait until they had the raw materials.

"I will retire for the night," Yah Tayyib said.

Inaya stayed to speak with Rhys for a time. Nyx drew out some simple explosive designs on the slide while they talked. It'd been a while since she put anything custom together like this, but even the simplest stuff could be effective. Especially when nobody was expecting it.

She poured herself a finger's length of whiskey. They may have been out of guns and ammo, but Eshe never failed to find some bootleg whiskey at every town they visited. Some days Nyx wondered if it was why she'd hired him in the first place.

When she looked up, Inaya was closing the door, leaving her alone with Rhys.

She got back to the whiskey.

He stood. "I'm not a great sniper," he said.

"I know." She raised her head. He had cleaned up some, and looked human again. "But they don't. They'll think that's where I put you on purpose."

He turned toward the door. Paused. "Why did you agree to take this note?" he asked.

"Just wanted to do it."

"You just got it into your head to go after rogue bel dames?"

"So full of questions. Little late for that, you think?"

"No," he said. He sat across from her. Put his big ugly hands flat on the table, just like a polite Nasheenian. Some habits were hard to break, she supposed. "Eshe said you talked to the bel dame council."

"You two getting on real well, then, you and Eshe?"

"Look at me."

"Fuck you," Nyx said. "I'm not some fucking Chenjan harem girl. You want to issue commands like I'm some dog, I'll cut your goddamn hands off again." She finished the whiskey in the glass. It burned.

He sat back. Pulled his hands off the table.

"I forget, sometimes."

"That I'm not a dog?"

She chanced a look up now, careful. She was always curious about what she'd see on his face. Always half-hoping he would look at her with something other than contempt and disgust. But his face was oddly taciturn now, resigned.

"I forget you're Nasheenian," he said.

"Your mistake," she said. Angry, again. Why was it that's all she could say to him, ever? Angry, bitter words to a man who had followed her through hell for six years.

"Yes."

They sat in silence for a while. Nyx figured he was trying to wait her out. Two could play that. And she was better at it.

"What did they promise you, I wonder?" Rhys said. "What could they give you that would possibly bring you out all this way?"

Nyx tapped her finger on the slide, chose a different trigger.

"The Queen couldn't make you a bel dame again, but the bel dame council can, can't they? If you do them a large favor. Hunt down their rogues."

She stopped her tapping.

"Don't lie," he said. "You bring them the rogues and they make you a bel dame, right? That's it, then." He let out a long breath. "We are so stupid. My God, you're not doing this for Nasheen at all. Not for your brothers or any dead boys or that squad you burned yourself up for. You're giving it all up. All of us up. To be a bel dame again. A government-sponsored murderer."

"Being a bel dame is an honorable thing," Nyx said. She tossed the slide onto the table, met his look. His face was hard and bitter, like the flat silty beach surrounding the inland sea. "Isn't that what you're always going on about, how I'm so dishonorable?"

"Ah, of course. Because what those bel dames did to my family was quite honorable."

"Those are rogues, not real bel dames."

"You did worse to other families when you were a bel dame."

"I never—"

"I know what bel dames do, Nyx. Wrap it up with pretty words like honor and sacrifice and it's still just hunting and killing children." Rhys shook his head. "I should have listened to Khos."

"I've never lied to you about what I do."

"Catshit."

"You've gotten a dirty mouth since we got on that train."

"It is catshit, Nyx. You lie all the time."

"I got lots of reason to do what I do. Just 'cause I don't tell you all of them doesn't mean I'm a liar."

"So the bel dames did send you."

"You know," Nyx said, "I thought fucking would loosen you up a little. But you just act more and more like a cat in heat— rubbing your ass up against everything until it gives."

"You didn't get anything from that transmission you couldn't have figured out on your own in the local gyms," he said.

"What happened to your family wasn't my fault. Rasheeda would have found you regardless. You were the one who shot her."

"To save your life."

Nyx rubbed her face. The air around them was cool, but humid. She listened to the chittering bugs beyond the filter. Her skin prickled. She searched for some way around what he had said, found some words, half believed them:

"You were saving your own ass," she said. Even to her ears, it sounded lame.

"Why would I save myself, Nyx? Do you know what my father called me when I . . . he called me infidel. When I refused . . ." He hesitated.

"Refused what?" she said, low.

"I didn't get exiled for protecting a relative," he said. "I got exiled because I refused to go to the front."

Nyx sat back in her seat. It was a little like being punched. "What are you talking about?"

"God called me to the front. Like he called you. And your brothers. And every Chenjan man but the first born."

"You were first born—"

"My father insisted I go."

"But disobeying your father, that's—"

"Disobeying God, yes."

"And . . . Wait. Hold on. You? But you're . . . you're . . ."

"That's what he called me. Does it make it so? I don't know. But every day I spent in Nasheen I wondered if I would have the chance to make it right, somehow. I knew I didn't deserve this life, even before Rasheeda took it."

Nyx shook her head. She heard the midnight call to prayer roll out over the city for the Chenjans and Nasheenians. Tirhanis didn't have a midnight prayer. It sounded soft and low, muted. A flicker of a call, a whisper, then stillness. Those waiting for it would hear it. To the rest, it was just the background noise of a frontier city at the edge of the world.

Rhys stood. "I should go."

"Yeah," Nyx said. For a long moment, they faced one another across the table. Time stretched. She wanted to offer him a drink, but was afraid he would take it. She felt her heart beat just a little faster. Infidels did all sorts of . . . Oh, fucking stop it, she thought. This is Rhys. But then why was he still looking at her?

"Good night," he said.

"Yeah, go," Nyx said. "No, wait."

"Yes?" His gaze was comforting, still, even after all the blazing, angry words and blood.

"If I wasn't . . ." She stopped. Started over. "If I was something else . . . Not a monster. If I could be . . . something else . . ." She huffed in a long breath. "If I wasn't . . . what I am . . ."

Something softened in his face. Big, dark eyes, the ones she had wanted to look at her forever. The beautiful but unskilled magician she had hired and kept safe in Nasheen, only to smash apart his life when he no longer needed her.

"If you weren't what you are, and I wasn't what I am, we'd both be dead," Rhys said. "And we would have nothing to speak of."

"The good ones all die at the front," Nyx said.

"Yes. They submit to God. And they die for it. But after, they find a place at the feet of God in paradise. I suspect my wife and children will find that place also, but not me. Not after all I've done."

"I don't believe in God, Rhys. When I died . . . everything just stopped. There was no hell. No God. Just . . . nothing."

Rhys shrugged. "Perhaps this is your hell then."

"I don't want to be a monster anymore."

"I can't help you with that, Nyx. That's something you have to work out on your own."

"I was always better with you around," she said.

"No," he said. "You are much worse."

He left her. When the door closed, she had trouble finding her seat. Her hands trembled. She poured herself another drink. Felt hollow, adrift.

Being a bel dame had made her strong, honorable, powerful. Without it, she was nothing, wasn't she? Just some monstrous bloodletter. A murderer.

She didn't know how to be anything else.

39.

When the great red stone Ras Tiegan church at the center of Beh Ayin was converted to a mosque, the remaining Ras Tiegans who did not convert to the Tirhani faith moved into the original stone church built along the edge of the filter back when Beh Ayin was a true colony. It was a squat little building with a standard ambulatory and radiating chapel on the east end, probably about a hundred feet from base to blue tiled roof, best Nyx could guess. She knew the parts and pieces only because the Ras Tiegan districts in Nasheen were generally dirty and poor enough that she frequented them. She'd killed some people in Ras Tiegan churches, and found the standard structure pretty useful for planning assassinations.

The bell tower sounded just as she and Inaya crunched up the gravel walk onto the church grounds. Eshe was perched on a mossy standing-stone property marker nearby at the edge of the old graveyard. Like most folks on Umayma, it had taken the Ras Tiegans a while to figure out that burying their dead was a bad idea. The tumble of headstones and broken, X-shaped markers in the yard made it clear nothing had been buried in the contaminated dirt for several centuries.

A few pale Ras Tiegans stood at the entrance to the church, greeting patrons as they arrived. It was still a little early in the day for Nyx, and she was nursing a slight hangover.

"How much did you drink last night?"

"Not enough."

As they approached, Nyx saw that everybody entering the church was pale as piss. The women wore standard Tirhani abayas and headscarves, but there were no multiple wives here.

"Welcome, child," one of the robed clerics—priests, Nyx amended—said in Tirhani as they walked up the broad stone steps. He held out his hands to Inaya.

She took them both in hers and bowed her head. "God bless," she said.

"And God bless you. You are a visitor to Beh Ayin?"

"My mistress permitted me to come and worship during our stay."

Nyx didn't trust her Tirhani enough to say anything, which was probably best. She could follow along well enough to pass. "Indeed," the priest said, and looked at Nyx. "All are welcome here, even unbelievers. Please let us know if you have questions about the faith. We encourage all God's children to seek the True Path." He looked Nyx over again. "She will need to cover her hair, however."

Nyx was already looking past him, into the nave. She wore long trousers, and had buttoned up the collar of her coat to hide the rusty scar on her neck. "I need to check my weapons?" she asked, in Nasheenian.

Inaya began to translate.

The priest raised a brow. "Oh, I know Nasheenian," he said. He switched to it and said, "We have seen a few of your kind come through over the years."

"Not for a good long time, I expect," Nyx said.

His eyes narrowed, and she wondered if she'd fucked it.

But his expression cleared, and he smiled thinly. "No, not for some time. We are, indeed, at the edge of everything. But yes, we would appreciate it if you checked your weapons. The hair, first, however."

He walked inside and returned with a long scarf. Nyx wound it around her head.

Satisfied, the priest said, "This way, please."

He took her inside to a small alcove while Inaya engaged the other priest. Nyx glanced over her shoulder and saw Eshe fly in through the unchecked door. He went straight into the rafters above the doorway and settled in the darkness.

Nyx checked her scattergun. She pulled out the short knife at her hip, but the priest merely smiled and waved his hand. "No need," he said. "Personal tools are allowed."

Nyx nodded. People who thought you couldn't do much with a little knife deserved whatever was coming to them.

Inaya met her in the nave. Men sat on the left side of the church, women and children on the right. Nyx hadn't expected that. She needed to be on the left.

Inaya met her look. "There are worse things," she said, and found them seats on the far right, toward the middle.

The church wasn't anywhere near full. Capacity was probably three or four hundred, and by Nyx's count, maybe thirty men and forty women were in attendance. It was still a half hour until the service started, but it seemed a pretty poor showing, even by Nasheenian standards.

Nyx wondered how good the chances were that somebody else spoke Nasheenian. The priest's knowledge had given her pause. At this point, though, if she needed to give Inaya any more instructions, she'd done a poor job in planning, and they were fucked anyway.

She took a breath and straightened in her seat. The benches were cold stone padded in dog hair, and about as comfortable as they looked. A stone basin filled with water stood in front of the apse. She watched as a half-dozen young boys in long blue robes began to transverse the ambulatory and light the tall candles under the bug globes. The smell of amber incense tickled her nose. She turned to see another boy wandering down the nave, swinging a sieved incense burner in front of him. She supposed it improved the smell, at least. The stone building was crude, without water cooling or conditioning, and that meant that in about an hour, they'd all be sweating and stinking and ready to claw their way out of this oven.

Nyx waited a few minutes more while others began to funnel into the church. Then she stood and made her way to the far left transept. She had to go all the way around the men's side to do it, but no one stopped her. She slipped into a small priest's hall that ran the length of the building, and neatly stepped into the side door they had spotted from the outside. She pressed herself into the doorway—flat as she could make herself—and started working on the lock.

"Help you, matron?"

Nyx gave the lock a final nudge. Heard a satisfying click. She slipped her tools back up into her sleeve and turned. A fresh-faced young Ras Tiegan boy stood a few feet away with a puzzled look on his face.

Nyx stepped away from the door, looked up at the lintel. "Sorry. Looking for the privy. Up here?" She pointed further along the hall where the stairway went up.

"No," he said, then—something, something—"quarters"—something—"women's privies"—something, something—"you new?"

"Sorry, my Tirhani's not good," she said. "Show me?"

The boy still didn't look quite convinced, but it got him away from the door. He led her across the nave and into the opposite transept and another long corridor.

"Down here," the boy said. Something, something "service."

Nyx ducked down the hall and paid her respects to the privy, then made her way back to her seat.

"That's him," Inaya said, nodding to a slender, high-browed

Ras Tiegan man stepping up behind the basin in the apse. He wore a fine red coat over loose trousers and a gauzy bisht, an odd pairing of sensible Ras Tiegan attire and traditional Tirhani garb.

"Welcome," the magistrate said. "Please be seated while we open today's prayer."

Inaya bowed her head. Nyx bowed hers, too, but kept her eyes open. She noted Eshe fluttering in the rafters, making his way to the nave.

The magistrate began to recite some Ras Tiegan prayer about dust and honor and forgiveness.

As he spoke, two figures turned down Nyx's aisle. Nyx raised her head.

A tangle-haired woman sat next to her. She casually draped her arm over Nyx's shoulder and leaned in. In her other hand, she held a slim pistol. She gently pushed it into Nyx's side.

Nyx's whole body tensed. Inaya's head remained bowed.

"Let's get up before the sermon starts. Ras Tiegan sermons are pretty boring," Shadha so Murshida said.

This close, Nyx realized how young she was. Twenty-five? Twenty-six? Barely older than Nyx was when she got tossed out of service. Her dark hair was a matted tangle, tied back from a hard, flat face that looked a tad Ras Tiegan. It was the eyes Nyx remembered, though. Those flat black eyes that had held hers while her life drained across the park.

"Don't you know you're supposed to cover your hair in church?" Nyx said.

Nyx saw two more Nasheenian women, wearing long coats and trousers, sit down behind them.

Inaya looked up now, and the color drained from her face.

"I've been kicked out of a mosque or two," Shadha said. She had a hard, smoky voice. Nyx might have found it sexy under different circumstances. "Need a couple churches to complete the set. C'mon now, let's get upstairs. Seems we have a lot to talk about."

"Don't know if talking is what I had in mind," Nyx said. It took a lot of effort to look away. She watched the magistrate finish his prayer and then introduce the high priest. Adrenaline made her blood sizzle. Everything looked especially clear and sharp, the way it did back when she was Shadha's age and the whole world was a big black pit she needed to fill with blood.

"C'mon," Shadha said, squeezing her shoulder hard enough to hurt, pushing herself up against her. "We've spent long enough running around after each other. Let's make up."

"If you think I'm above killing you in a church, you don't know much about me."

Shadha twisted the gun into her hip. Old wounds throbbed. She'd been shot there a couple of times, and didn't fancy getting shot there again. "You think I'm not keen on shooting you right here, you don't know *me* very well. I thought you'd know exactly what I'm capable of by now."

"You're the only person ever killed me," Nyx said. "Good execution, piss poor follow through."

"You assume killing you was the end game. Come upstairs, Nyx."

"I think we can finish this here."

Inaya made a noise of distress.

Shadha leaned in and whispered in Nyx's ear, so close her warm breath tickled her neck. "There's a fat little raven up there in the rafters I have a mind to eat tonight. You want to find out if I'm a better shot than you? This is a Ras Tiegan church. We're authorized to kill shifters on sight. You know that?"

"We'll go up," Inaya said.

Nyx frowned.

"Up it is," Shadha said. "Come now, let's not interrupt this fine sermon."

Shadha pushed them out the far side of the aisle and brought them around behind the seating area to the men's side. The two other bel dames flanked them.

They walked into the far transept and up the long corridor toward the stairwell the Ras Tiegan boy had said led into the "quarters." Nyx deliberately didn't look at the door she'd picked as they passed. It was still possible that Suha and Rhys were dead upstairs, of course, but Nyx had bet against that. Yah Tayyib's position was better, but not perfect. Every plan had its drawbacks.

Nyx hesitated at the bottom of the stair. Inaya bumped into her. "Nyx?" Inaya said.

Easier for Inaya to go up, maybe. She had more faith. And she hadn't died once already.

"Up," Shadha said, and prodded her with the gun.

"You shove that thing at me one more time and I'm taking off that hand," Nyx said.

Shadha twisted the barrel into the small of Nyx's back. Hard. "I think you should leave the dismemberment to me," she said. "Up."

Nyx mounted the steps. At the top was a short hall and a single open door. She stepped into the room. The "quarters" were above the nave, and looked ornate enough to be the head priest's quarters. Not typical of most Ras Tiegan churches, but when Nyx had looked over the schematic from the local archives, it was the only quiet corner aside from the cellar where anybody would be bedding down. Bel dames wouldn't like the cold and damp of the basement. She sure didn't.

Two massive stained-glass windows flanked the room. A large desk sat between them. Along the edges of the room were two covered divans and upholstered chairs. They looked out of place against the stark stone. But what looked even more out of place were the dozen bel dames waiting there.

Nyx recognized a few of them from her days running notes for the order. There was Maysun so Nadar and her blood sister Sadira; Almira Sameh with the deformed hand she refused to fix; Zayda ma Sara, nearly forty now, with the complexion of rocky dirt; and Raja Halah, who'd been a kid when Nyx first took her own vows. But the rest were new faces—young, tough, barely blemished faces that reminded Nyx of the boys she saw come off the front after their first day in the trenches. A little shell-shocked, sure, but pleased and cocky to be alive. When you survived your first battle, you thought you were invincible. Time eventually cured you of that.

Shadha moved past her and into the room.

"You all know Nyx," Shadha said. She sat on the edge of the desk, pistol still in hand. She was a small, broad-shouldered little woman, but the power was there. The way she walked, stood, sat—cocky little woman, just like her friends.

Nyx and Inaya moved to the center of the room. Inaya was trembling a little. Nyx didn't blame her.

The two bel dames behind them shut the door.

Nyx glanced at the windows. Five paces left, six paces right. There were benches under both windows. Two bel dames sitting on the left, three on the right.

"So you don't want to kill me," Nyx said. "What next?"

"Now I pay off your informant. It was a good plan, Nyx, but bad follow through. Curious as to who turned?"

"Somebody always turns," Nyx said.

Shadha gestured to the tall bel dame next to her. The woman walked to a small door leading into the chamber opposite, the one further down the hall.

Another woman led Suha and Rhys inside. Nyx wanted to feign some outrage, but had a tough time with it. What was the point? Somebody always turned. The women in this room knew that. They expected it.

Rhys was missing his pistols. Suha still looked armed.

The bel dame who led them in pushed Rhys onto the divan near the door, right in front of the window nearest Nyx.

Suha came in with her eyes down. "Let's get this the fuck over with," she muttered. "I ain't here to parade around."

"No. Not at all," Shadha said. She grinned.

So fucking cocky, Nyx thought. Was I ever that cocky?

Suha didn't walk in any further.

"They kept you armed," Nyx said. "Shows a lot of trust, I'd say."

"More than you should have given her," Shadha said. She pulled a stack of notes from a drawer in her desk and passed them to Suha. "You can go," she said.

Nyx watched Suha leave. Kept quiet. Too quiet, maybe? But the fight had gone out of her. This was easier.

Inaya glanced up at her. Nyx gave a little shake of her head.

Shadha sat back on the desk.

"Now we deal," Shadha said.

"With what?" Nyx said.

"You probably know who wants you alive. It's not me."

"Alharazad," Nyx said.

"Very good. You got Behdis to squeal? I know my girls didn't. This is Alharazad's operation. I just cut off the heads. You understand that, I know. Here's the deal."

"No," Nyx said.

"You haven't even heard it yet."

"I'm not a bel dame. Why recruit me?"

"Because Alharazad likes what you do," Shadha said. "You're worth more to us alive than dead. You got nothing to lose, you know. Queen put out a note on you and your team, finally. Took a little urging from Alharazad, but it's done now. Wonder why your girl turned? 'Cause there's a note out on her, too—and your shifter. Bet she didn't tell you that, did she? You guys cross that border, and you're fucked. You got nowhere to go."

"There's always somewhere to go."

"True enough. It's your choice. You know what happened to that magician who got you out? Yahfia? They sent Yahfia to the front. Revoked her privileges. And look what happened to gravy's family over there. Running with you's a death sentence, Nyx. They all know that. It's just a matter of time before they stab you in the back."

"You want me to wait for you to stab me instead? Seems to me you weren't so great at it last time."

Shadha's jaw worked. Hurt pride, perhaps? "The point wasn't to kill you, like I said. I could have done that easy. I had orders to come back and reanimate you. This discussion would have gone a lot smoother then, I think."

Inaya was looking at Nyx again. Nyx glanced over at her, shook her head. "Listen," Nyx said. "I'm here for the sand. You all can walk away from this. I just want the weapon."

Shadha grinned. "Stubborn till the end. You've got nothing to go home to, Nyx."

"Neither do you."

"I will. All of us will. We're getting back to the good old days, Nyx, back when bel dames—"

Nyx sighed. "Hate to tell you this, Shadha, but I'm not going to sit here and let you roll out your grand plan. I realize it makes you feel all rich and important, got a famous rogue bel dame in here you're giving ultimatums to in front of your cronies, but I got shit to do, and I'm looking for the dragonfly, not the midge. You got the weapon or not?"

The grin on Shadha's face wavered. For the first time, Nyx saw a stir of doubt. "Maybe you need some time to think about it. We've got a great cellar," she said. She slid off the desk.

Paused.

"I just got one question," Shadha said. "I got your turncoat.

I got your boyfriend. I know the raven's shut up downstairs in the nave. But where's your magician? The real one?"

Inaya looked at Nyx again. Nyx could feel her quaking like a leaf.

Nyx turned to Rhys and gave him a little two-fingered salute. The windows shattered.

Two giant hornets careened into the room, buzzing like a freight train. The bel dames scattered.

Nyx spun, crouched, and lifted up the back of Inaya's abaya. She pulled her scattergun free of the belted harness at Inaya's back.

Inaya yanked open the front of her abaya. The already loosened buttons popped free. She stepped out of the abaya. She wore a tight tunic and trousers beneath—and over that, Nyx had strapped her with enough explosives to take out a small army.

Fitting, since they were standing right in the middle of one.

Inaya grabbed the detonator at her hip.

Nyx fired at the two bel dames at her left and pulled another pistol from Inaya's rear holster for Rhys. She sliced his bonds with her dagger and leapt up onto the bench and over the jagged window. The roof there came right up to the window. She reached for Rhys's hand.

The bel dames pointed and fired at Inaya.

Inaya hit the detonator, and, simply—burst. Green mist exploded from the head of the tunic. The pile of clothing and explosives fell neatly to the floor as a dozen bel dame pistols went off.

Rhys grabbed Nyx's hands with his thick, rough fingers. She had a strange moment of dissonance, then braced herself against the lip of the window and yanked. Rhys kicked over the top of the window and tumbled after her.

The explosion knocked them both back. She lost hold of Rhys and tumbled down the slick tile roof. Grabbed the stony overhang. Hung a moment, suspended over a two-story drop. Then fell.

She landed on her side with all her limbs tucked in. The fall knocked the breath from her body. Shattered glass and bits of stone rained on her from above.

Nyx tried to suck in some air.

Suha already had hold of her arm. "Let's go, let's go!" Suha said, tugging her up. But Suha had had plenty of time to make her way down, and Nyx's exit was a lot rougher.

Nyx fished around for her scattergun.

"Rhys?" She turned and saw him limping toward her. Saw his ankle rapidly swelling. He had the pistol at his hip.

"I'm here," he said. "Let's fucking finish this."

The church's congregation was pouring out the front of the church, wailing. Nyx avoided the crowd and went to the door she'd opened on the north side of the church and stepped right back into the empty hall leading into the high priest's quarters.

She was catching her breath now, drawing deep. Suha had both pistols drawn.

"Tayyib still out there?" Nyx said.

"Until the local magicians realize he's cut a hole in the filter and sucked in some giant hornets, yeah," Suha said.

They pounded upstairs.

Nyx went in shooting.

The bel dames were sprawled across the room in various states of death, dying, and shell-shock. The air was heavy and clotted with dust and smoke. Nyx shot the nearest bel dame in the face, not sure if she was alive or dead and not caring. The windows had completely shattered. The one at the right had taken a good deal of the wall with it. Most of the roof had collapsed, but the floor was intact.

"Shadha's mine!" Nyx said, pushing her way through the rubble. Suha was firing off rounds into broken bel dames' heads.

Rhys was working his way around the other side, doing the same with a sort of slow, steady determination that reminded Nyx of a boy who'd spent six months cleaning his friends' guts off his gear and who'd just taken his first batch of Chenjan prisoners.

Nyx mashed in a couple of familiar faces and went digging for Shadha near the desk. She pushed past piles of broken blue tile and shattered glass and found Shadha behind the desk. She'd been impaled by a jagged shard of glass, and had dragged herself away from the front of the desk to a protected little alcove near a broken shelf. She lay in a bloody pool, panting.

Nyx pushed her scattergun into Shadha's sweaty face, made her look up at her.

Not so cocky, now.

"Where is it?"

"Here," Shadha said. Snotty bubbles appeared under her nose. She hacked and coughed and struggled again with the jagged shard in her chest. Touched it with already bloodied fingers. She bared her teeth. "You set it free. It's hungry, now."

"Nyx!"

Suha was moving toward her across the rubble, fast.

Something hissed.

Nyx swore. She shot Shadha in the face and leapt on top of the desk. Suha jumped up with her.

"Fucking shit's eating me! Fuck!" Suha started pulling up her tunic.

Nyx saw something moving along Suha's bloody arm, like a swarm of maggots.

Suha started scrubbing at it with the tunic.

"Rhys! Rhys!" Nyx reached toward him. He was standing over the body of a tall, twisted bel dame with burn scars on her neck. Broken as a rag doll. "Rhys, goddammit, get up here!"

He turned.

The hissing, spitting sound grew louder. Where had it been?

Locked in the desk? One of the big cabinets near the door? Everything was broken and busted in. They'd blown the room and started cutting people up, and now it was out.

Rhys turned toward the sound of the sand.

"Here! Rhys, get the fuck up here!" Nyx said.

He stared at the body of the bel dame. Blood spattered his hands. His face. He left the corpse and waded toward them across the rubble.

Something spat at him. A spray of fine gray mist. He jerked away, startled. Smacked at it like he would a mosquito, a biting fly.

Nyx looked around at the bloody ruin of the tower. It feeds on blood, Rhys had said. But none of them were wounded. Did that make a difference?

She watched him smacking at the dusty air. He started coughing.

"Rhys?"

She jumped off the desk.

"Nyx!" Suha yelled.

Nyx took hold of Rhys by the collar and hauled him to the desk. A blistering rash had opened up on his cheek where some bel dame's blood had splattered him.

She pushed him onto the desk. "Get it off, Suha! Wipe it off!"

A raven cawed.

Nyx saw Eshe circling. She felt something biting at her blood-soaked trousers. She sat up on the desk and pulled them off, threw the bloody trousers onto the hissing floor.

The few living bel dames were screaming now. Weird, high-pitched cries.

Nyx started pulling off Rhys's blood-soaked clothes and feeding them to the spitting, hissing sand that popped and cackled around them.

Suha's arm was a red rash. She, too, had stripped down to her dhoti and breast binding. She scrubbed at Rhys's face until he pushed her away.

"Fuck!" Rhys said, crouching at the edge of the desk. He was nearly naked, stripped down to his small clothes.

Nyx heard someone on the stairs.

Yah Tayyib carefully moved into the doorway. His face was unreadable. For a moment, Nyx expected him to cackle madly and tell them this had been his plan all along. It seemed like a pretty good one. Leave her and the rest to starve to death—naked—amid a stir of dead bel dames contaminated with flesh-eating sand.

Instead, Yah Tayyib raised his arms and called a swarm of locusts.

The locusts descended from a clear sky. They were a black plague so massive Nyx lost sight of everything—Yah Tayyib, Rhys, the desk, the bodies. The world was a buzzing, chitinous mass of death. Suha grabbed at her. Nyx grabbed for Suha, and a moment later Rhys's strong, slim arms encircled Nyx's torso, and the three of them clung together in the merciless swarm. Nyx dared not open her mouth. She breathed slow through her nose. She felt Rhys's heartbeat—strong and fast—against her shoulder.

Then the swarm was gone, just as suddenly as Yah Tayyib had called it.

Nyx tried opening her eyes. The light was back—orange, warm. Suha and Rhys pulled away. She stared out at the ruined tower. The corpses had been picked clean, leaving behind piles of soft white bones and tattered clothing.

Nyx let out a breath.

A few locusts still fluttered among the rubble. She flicked one off her arm.

Yah Tayyib leaned wearily against the doorway. His face looked haggard.

"You look ridiculous," he said, and collapsed.

Nyx scrambled off the desk. She picked her way back across the ruins, and found Yah Tayyib partially supine, wedged in the doorway. She had to climb over him and kneel on the other side.

"You all right? Tayyib?"

His eyelids fluttered. "Yes," he muttered. "Yes, of course." He opened his eyes and gave her a long, piercing look. "Listen, now," he said.

"Oh, shut up," Nyx said.

He winced and tried to sit up a little straighter. "No. The only time you ever listen is when you think you're losing. Listen now. You've squandered your talent."

Nyx sighed and stood. "Oh, just die already."

"No, I won't," Yah Tayyib said. He used the lintel to help pull himself up. One hand clutched at his side, but Nyx didn't see any blood. No sign of visible injury. "I've done some terrible things, I admit that."

"Finally."

"But I did them to free Nasheen."

"Let's not argue about this again."

Suha was pulling her clothes back on. Rhys was already half-dressed. Pity, Nyx thought.

"Would you listen?" Yah Tayyib said.

She folded her arms and regarded him. The room was cold. She realized how strange she must look, mostly naked, her mismatched skin and bizarre corpse scars fully visible. Nothing he hasn't seen before, she reminded herself.

"We need to get moving, Tayyib. Likely order keepers on the way, and I don't want to answer all the questions they'll have about this catshit."

"Promise me something."

"I don't promise anybody anything."

"Let all of this go."

"Tayyib—"

"Goodbye." But he didn't walk into the hall. He started walking into the ruined tower.

"Hold on. What about the locusts, Tayyib? The locusts ate the flesh. The flesh holds the sand. Where are they?"

He turned. The ghost of a smile touched his face. "Let go," he said.

Four giant hornets buzzed through the broken roof. Nyx jumped back into the hall.

The hornets gripped Yah Tayyib by the back of his coat and picked him up neatly into the air. He caught hold of their slender feet and they buzzed up and away into the bright lavender sky.

"Holy fuck," Nyx muttered.

Rhys shook his head, awestruck. "I can't believe he managed that."

"What the fuck was that?" Suha asked.

"What is it always?" Nyx said. "Tayyib fucking me over."

"He did say you were even," Rhys said.

Nyx looked over at Rhys. He sat on the edge of the desk, his dark, dirty hands gripping the lip of it.

"We should go," Rhys said.

Nyx kicked at one of the piles of bones and clothing at her feet. "Why can't you do shit like this?" she said.

He slid off the desk. "If I could do that, I'd be king of Chenja."

40.

The evening call to prayer rolled out over Beh Ayin, low and comforting and just a little too loud for Nyx's aching head. She sat on the balcony with a fifth of whiskey, watching bugs incinerate themselves on the filter with a hiss and pop and spray of gray ash.

Eshe had his feet pulled up under him. He was eating cold curry, something Inaya had cooked the night before.

Suha offered Nyx a sen cigarette.

Nyx shook her head.

Suha lit up, and leaned over the balcony. "Risky, Nyx."

"Always is."

They sat outside in silence for a good while longer. "You know I can't go back to Nasheen," Nyx said.

Suha nodded. "All our names are on the bounty boards now. Load of good Fatima did sending us to Alharazad. You think she knew?"

"Not likely," Nyx said. "Fatima had an interest in us catching the bad guys."

"Fuck 'em," Eshe said.

Nyx snorted. "Easy enough to say, Eshe. Harder to do." She looked over at Suha. "I want you to have the storefront."

"They'll have tagged me. I won't get in through that filter in Mushtallah."

"Records were all purged during the burst. They'll have to refile you. Under whatever name you want."

"What, you think nobody will know me?"

"You think I registered your employment with the local under your real name?" Nyx said. "You think I'm stupid? I been doing this a long time, Suha. You should stop by and clean it out at least. Lot of good gear still at the storefront."

"What about you?" Eshe said.

"I've got my shit in order," Nyx said. "The flood, remember?"

Suha finished her cigarette and patted Nyx on the shoulder. "I'm getting out of here tomorrow, then. Eshe? What you think?"

"Don't know," Eshe said.

Suha shrugged. "Your call." She went inside.

Nyx looked at him. He gazed out over the balcony.

"Suha wouldn't be such a bad employer," Nyx said.

"Where *you* going?"

"Can't tell you that."

"Why?"

"You know why."

He rubbed angrily at his eyes with the heels of his hands. "Fuck you."

"Fuck you, fuck me, fuck everybody," Nyx said. "Doesn't change it." She felt a lump forming in her throat, and swallowed another mouthful of whiskey.

"You never gave me a good answer," he said.

"About what?"

"About what makes us different than everybody at the front. 'Cause I didn't see anything different."

"That's up to you, Eshe. I can't make your decisions for you."

"God says—"

"God says a lot of things, depending on who quotes Him."

Eshe chewed his lip. "Inaya said she's going to Ras Tieg."

"Yeah?"

"She said there's a rebellion there. A shifter rebellion."

"That so?"

"She's going to help."

"Huh."

"That's like what we do, isn't it?"

Nyx considered that. Maybe it was, if they were trying to upset the status quo instead of maintain it, but all that catshit back there was about stopping the coup and keeping the war machine running. Put some more weapons into Tirhani hands. Or whoever Tayyib was working for.

"It's probably better than what we do," Nyx said. Maybe then he could know, for certain, that he was one of the good guys. Nyx supposed he might find some comfort in that. For however long it lasted.

"You think I should go with her?"

"Your decision, Eshe."

He finished the curry and tossed the box over the railing. Some local bug pack below hissed and chattered. He stood. "When are you going?"

"Morning, likely. Heard the trains are running again."

He nodded.

Then he lunged toward her.

She jerked back, startled. He wrapped his arms around her and held on tight, buried his face in her hair. Then, just as suddenly, he pulled away and left her.

Nyx rubbed her eyes. Long day, she thought. Long fucking day.

✛

Nyx drove them to the train station the next morning. They all sat together on the train this time. Inaya and Rhys on one seat, Suha and Eshe on the other, Nyx across the aisle.

At the central station in Shirhazi, Inaya and Eshe bought tickets for Ras Tieg. When it came time to walk away, Eshe just firmed up his mouth and told her goodbye. She wished him luck.

No tears this time, no embarrassing display of emotion that left her befuddled and reeling. No, he acted just like a boy headed to the front. Just the way she'd taught him to.

Suha made a couple calls. Nyx and Rhys walked her back out to the taxi ranks.

"Azizah's cache isn't too far from here," Suha said. "She's got a way to get me back into Nasheen. Get me some new papers."

"You clean out that storefront," Nyx said. "I don't want any of those fire-happy bel dame apprentices to clean it out first."

After Suha got into the taxi, Nyx turned to Rhys. She gestured to the next taxi. "Yours, gravy," she said.

He did not smile, did not react. Just watched her with his big, dark eyes. She was reminded then of the first time she saw him—years ago, an age ago, when he was just a dancer and she was some arrogant bel dame on the run—saw him across a smoky, crowded gym while her ruined body healed and her bloody bel dame sisters sniffed her out. He was the most beautiful thing she'd ever seen.

He still was.

"Don't come for me again," he said.

"I won't," she said. "You get on back to your wife."

He stepped into the taxi. She slammed the door behind him.

41.

Rhys took the taxi as far as the edge of the Chenjan district. As they came up on Elahyiah's father's block, he told the taxi driver to slow down.

"It's just here," Rhys said, but as they arrived at the walk-up, Rhys let the driver continue on by while he gazed up at the shuttered windows.

"Where is it, huh?" the driver asked.

"Never mind," Rhys said. "Never mind. Keep going."

"Where?" The driver asked.

"Back to the station," Rhys said.

✛

Rhys jumped out of the taxi and pushed his way back through the blue arches of the station, favoring his twisted ankle. Polite Tirhanis moved aside. Some made shocked noises, but no one swore or caught at his coat. Tirhanis—always so polite.

He followed the signs for trains to the coast. There were six of them leaving in an hour—two to the southern coast and four more to the eastern.

Nyx hadn't said where she was going, but he had a good idea.

Rhys hobbled along the train platforms, looking for Nyx's familiar broad torso. The arrogant stance. The peculiar cant to her head as she pretended to understand somebody talking to her in a language she couldn't even name. He looked for her brown coat, buttoned all the way up even in the heat to hide her scars. He walked and walked until he reached the third to last platform where he caught sight of a lone, familiar profile waiting at the other end of the platform.

He stopped in his tracks. Passengers moved politely around him, a ceaseless tide. He watched her pull something from her coat and stare at it a long moment. Then her head came up, and she was looking out at the incoming train, taking a step back from the edge of the platform.

Rhys pushed his hands into his pockets. Realized what she was looking at.

She'd stolen his book of poetry. When had she lifted that?

He watched her step into the train. Willed her to look back. One look. Just one.

Nyx disappeared into the car.

Rhys let out his breath.

He waited until the train pulled away from the station. Watched it move past him. The windows were opaqued. He wondered, briefly, if she saw him. Wondered if she cared.

She would sacrifice everything, he reminded himself. You won't. That's the difference between you.

But in that moment, as he watched the train disappear toward the eastern coast, that knowledge gave him no comfort.

42.

Getting back into Nasheen, as a Nasheenian woman, alone, wasn't so tough. She knew just as many organic forgers as Suha, and she knew the best way to get into Nasheen was at the coast. Taking a boat back, though, was the tough part. Nyx spent the whole trip sick.

When she stumbled onto dry land, she was on the Nasheenian coast, and though she hated the coast, it was a lot better than being on the actual ocean. They asked for her papers. They checked her blood, her sex, checked her papers again.

"You're traveling alone?" the customs officer asked.

"Yeah," she said.

They noted that down.

She was pretty sure she knew why.

Eshe would thank her someday, after he stopped hating her.

She bought a sun-sick, spitting bakkie off a dog vendor and kept half her cash stuffed in the seat, and the other half in her dhoti. She drove the bakkie into the wastelands. She had trouble finding the place. She didn't remember the last time she'd driven a bakkie on her own. Since long before she got sick, she supposed. There was freedom on the road, a rush of adrenaline, speeding through the desert, wearing nothing but her dhoti and binding. The sand gummed up the corners of her eyes. The heat sucked her dry. She felt clean, free. So bloody fucking free.

She wound up the pitted drive and saw Alharazad's half-buried derelict rear into view. She half-expected a couple of bel dames on watch, maybe a sniper on the roof. But that wasn't Alharazad's style.

Nyx ground the bakkie to a halt and stepped out. Her burnous billowed behind her. She left her goggles inside. She stood a moment behind the bakkie door, taking in the derelict, the opaqued windows.

She kept one hand just behind her, within reach of her scattergun, as she approached. Dead cicadas littered the walk. Some of the kill jars on the porch had recent additions: a couple of hooked-nosed plybugs, an enormous butterfly the size of her head, a mutant owl bug with long stalks for eyes.

Nyx knocked at one of the windows. As she waited, she took another look around the yard. The weather had turned, and the heat was bearable. At night, the bugs in the jars would be lethargic.

She saw her, then, coming down from the shallow rise that looped behind the house. Alharazad wore a green organic burnous and goggles. Three bug cages hung from the end of a pole slung over one shoulder. Her windswept hair was knotted at the back of her head.

Alharazad trudged toward her, weaponless. Spit sen.

"I suppose you're here to kill me," Alharazad said.

"What fun would there be in that?" Nyx said.

Alharazad stepped onto the porch and pushed in the door. Unlocked, unfiltered. A perfectly insecure door.

Nyx followed her inside.

The marijuana plants were gone, replaced by what looked like opium seedlings and cardamom. New season, new crops. It reminded Nyx of Mushirah. They would be planting saffron and ambergrass this time of year.

Alharazad stacked the bug crates on the table. Kept her goggles on.

"I don't believe you won't bring in this note," Alharazad said.

"There was never any note on you. Besides, I'm retired," Nyx said.

"I don't believe either of us is retired."

"I've already died once. Didn't like it much. I don't think you'd like it either. Everything stops."

"That so? A lot like living in the desert, then." Alharazad pulled off her goggles, regarded her with bloodshot eyes. "What you here for, then? You want my head, you'll have a hard time getting it."

"Why didn't you take mine?"

Alharazad grinned and spit. She began pulling the bugs from the cages. She slipped them into the kill jars she kept on the floor. "I don't like waste. You wasted a good many women out there, from what I hear."

"I figured some of them were likely mine anyway."

"Been thinking of babies, have you? Your genetic stuff belongs to the bel dames. What they do with it isn't your concern."

"But some were, weren't they?"

Alharazad smiled. She set the now empty cage back on the floor. "When you can't get the real thing, you settle on an imitation. But blood codes don't make good bel dames. Hardship does. I always did prefer the real thing."

Nyx shrugged. "Sorry. Politics aren't my thing."

"Let me tell you something, girl. I've been bringing in black sisters and terrorists, aliens and gun-runners, since long before you were born. It's not the first time I had a bel dame squeal my name to some mark."

"It was Behdis who squealed, not Shadha. She didn't start talking till she knew we were on to her."

"Behdis? Interesting. How long did it take you to get that?"

"About twenty hours of detox."

Alharazad clucked her tongue. She walked over to the ice box, pulled a bottle down from on top of it. "Whiskey?"

"I ain't staying long."

Alharazad poured herself a glass. "Probably a good idea. Let me tell you about women, Nyxnissa so Dasheem. There are hot young things from the front—crazy, bloodthirsty, good at butchering. Your Rasheeda is like that. Good tool, when used right. It's when you lose control of her that she becomes a threat. I put Shadha on the council myself. You figured that out?"

"Sounds about right."

"Wasn't so bad. She needed direction. I was happy to give it. Then she comes to me about the Queen. She tells me about black deals with interstellar gene pirates. She tells me we're giving the monarchy to a magician. She tells me the Queen's looking to end the war with a Tirhani treaty. Imagine that? Chenja and Nasheen, signing a truce in Tirhan? That fucking bloated body? Nothing but rot, there. And you know what I realized, Nyx? You and I have seen the whole bloody world. The best and worst of it. We've given life, and taken it. That Queen? That woman we swore to? She's done none of that. She sat behind a filter from the time she's born. You ever seen her hands? Not a scratch. Not a callous."

"You wanted Shadha to take the fall for the bel dame coup. You didn't think it would succeed?"

"Succeed? We're bel dames. We ruled the world once. We could do it again. And we would have."

"But?"

"But not her."

Nyx snorted. "You aren't serious."

"You would have done the same. The council's clean now, Nyx. And there's a huge power vacuum. Who do you think they'll call in to fill it? Not you. Not the rogue bel dame who poisoned the Queen's heir and killed one of her messengers. If you can't play nice, I make sure you can't play at all."

"Who did you get to contaminate me?"

"We all have a price. Even Yahfia, your little lost magician."

"That explains why I could guilt her into getting me out of Faleen, then."

"Yes, her conscience did get the better of her in the end. You heard the Queen shipped her to the front for that little bit of mercy?"

"I did."

Alharazad opened the other bug cage. "And now I'd suggest that you get in that bakkie and get on the road. You don't have a lot of time. Someone will figure out your papers are forgeries eventually. How long do you have, you think?"

"You said to me you can't kill people," Nyx said. "You gotta kill ideas. We killed an idea out there. You think another bel dame is going to follow you against the Queen? Not so long as they remember what I did out there."

"What did you do, Nyx? Who's to know?"

"You forgot who I was working for," Nyx said.

Alharazad peered at her. "You were running rogue on an ear worm from the Queen."

"I was running for Fatima Kosan. I was working for the bel dame council, Alharazad."

"Catshit."

"Truth."

Alharazad waved a hand. "Easy enough to fix."

"Is it? I figure if you had a mind to kill me, you'd have done it already."

"Maybe I have other plans for you."

"Might be I have some for you, too." Nyx moved toward the door. "See you around."

"Here," Alharazad said. She picked up a jar, and handed it to Nyx. Inside was a dead dragonfly, perfectly still, perfectly preserved. "Take it."

"Why? Something to remember you by?" Nyx threw it back at her. Alharazad caught it.

Nyx walked outside. She started the bakkie and then turned it around in the tight, sandy drive.

Long way back to civilization, but she was breathing. That was something, and more than it felt like she'd had in a long time.

43.

Nyx washed her hands in the ablution bowl next to the door. She was surprised that this close to the Drucian border, all the cantinas still had ablution bowls. She had a special fondness for border town cantinas, and this one was no exception. She paid for a bottle of whiskey and a pinch of morphine from the barkeep, then hauled her duffle bags outside under the awning.

She had sold the bakkie to a cancerous creeper three blocks back and used the cash to buy some clothes better suited for the milder weather on the coast and the Drucian interior. Out here, the world was still a dusty desert, but she could see the dark outline of the mountains in the distance. Cooler weather. Fewer people. Fewer bugs, too.

A sun-sick bakkie chugged up to the bug feed station outside the cantina. A dark little woman jumped out. She wore goggles and a headscarf around her narrow head. Pistols were visible at her hips, and the stock of a shotgun poked up through her burnous. To the casual eye, she looked like a Chenjan, but when she spoke, her Nasheenian was pure.

"You ready?" Anneke said. She hadn't aged a day. Why was she the only one who looked like she'd rolled out with the Queen's reward for a dead alien just yesterday?

"Let's do it," Nyx said.

Anneke picked up one of the duffle bags, and they walked out to Anneke's waiting bakkie. Loaded up Nyx's things.

"What did you do with all your gear?" Anneke asked.

"Saving it for a bloody day."

"Thought you were getting out of those."

"You never know."

"Heh. Yeah, that's it, I guess. You never know."

Nyx rolled down the window. Anneke started the bakkie and drove south, toward the smoky mountains of Druce.

The desert rolled out ahead of them. Anneke drove around a big sand drift that was eating at the road, and then it was east, southeast, where the sun would rise tomorrow but right now it was getting dark, so dark, and Nyx couldn't help looking back over her shoulder at the sunset—the bloody, gorgeous dying of the world.

"It'll still be there," Anneke said.

"Yeah, I guess. Just wondering how I'm going to pass the time."

"Rumor has it you're a bad shot."

Nyx grinned. "That so?"

"Figured somebody oughta do something about that. You being unemployed and all, you got plenty of time. Don't know how you stayed alive so long, not knowing how to fucking shoot."

Nyx laughed, and it broke something up inside of her. She laughed so hard that tears bunched up at the corners of her eyes. She wiped them away.

"Thanks for coming out here."

"I needed a little excitement. Always knew you were good for that, boss. So how's it feel?"

"What?"

"Being a wanted woman."

"Fatima might still be able to get me cleared, yet," Nyx said, but even saying it out loud didn't sound convincing. Get her pardoned by the Queen? No. Not even the bel dames had that kind of power. She had fucked herself by killing that messenger. How many years until she didn't look guilty? Until Fatima called?

Until she could take a shit without expecting some bel dame to shoot her for slaughtering a dozen of their best?

There was something on the radio. Talking heads. Politics. First Families with rich, privileged voices.

"Listen to that," Anneke said. "They totter on like nothing's changed."

"It hasn't," Nyx said.

"You never did believe in anything," Anneke said. "Not God. Not the bel dames. Now you're all nagging on Nasheen. We got a word for people like you."

Nyx stared out the window a good long time, watched the deep amber dunes turn to black as they entered the blasted desert that stretched from the eastern edge of Nasheen to the Drucian border. Chenjan bursts and ancient magicians' blights had swallowed this part of the desert. She saw the cratered remains of old, nameless cities. The air tasted of tar and ashes.

"I wasn't worth bringing back," Nyx said.

"That so?" Anneke said. She spit sen, rolled her shoulders. "Lots of boys weren't worth killing, either. But it ain't up to you."

Anneke changed the radio to a new station, something with a southern cantina beat and high, clear vocals. The old mercenary raised her rickety voice and started to sing along.

"All you do is learn how to fight a war," Nyx said. "Nobody ever teaches you how to stop."

Nyx leaned out the window and watched the big orange demon fall below the horizon, saw the whole world go blue-violet. It was, she decided, very beautiful. Like a Chenjan magician she once knew.

Some things were worth coming back for. Even way out here, at the end of the world.

✦

ACKNOWLEDGEMENTS

Compared to writing *God's War*, writing *Infidel* was a cake walk. Despite the fact that I was finishing various drafts of *Infidel* while *God's War* was being edited, dropped, shopped, re-sold, and edited again, the first half went pretty smoothly.

Many thanks to my agent, Jennifer Jackson, for keeping things moving on the business end with *God's War*, which allowed me to actually write this damn book. Though I suffered my fair share of Book Depression when *God's War* was dropped and re-shopped, things would have been far, far worse if I had to deal with the nuts-and-bolts business end of shopping a book while . . . you know, *writing* a book. So thanks, Jenn.

My first readers had the unenviable job of reading through the original second half of this book (as well as all the rest), which, to be honest, kind of sucked. Thanks to David Moles, Patrick Weekes, and Miriam Hurst for bearing with me (and David in particular for assuring me that I didn't need to TOTALLY start over). Your fried grasshoppers and chocolate-covered crickets are in the mail . . . .

Once the big stuff was addressed, my beta readers were invaluable in helping ensure that there were as few discrepancies between *God's War* and *Infidel* as possible, always a tricky undertaking when you're doing series books. Thanks to Jayson Utz and Matt McDaniel for their last-minute read through. In particular, many kudos to Dave Zelasco, whose attention to "bugs, guns, and whiskey" helped me iron out a lot of discrepancies regarding those particular items. As ever, any of the crap that's been left in is my own damn fault. But be assured that there is much less of it thanks to these folks.

For final editing and copyediting, many thanks to my editor, Ross Lockhart, and my copyeditor, Marty Halpern. Special thanks to Ross and David Palumbo for putting up with my strong opinions on book covers, too. And, lest I forget, thanks again to Jeremy Lassen for originally purchasing these books in the first place.

As ever, my parents—Terri and Jack Hurley—have been endlessly supportive of my work, even if it's not exactly Oprah Book Club material. Thanks for being my biggest fans.

Thanks also to Jayson Utz for being a great partner. Living with a writer is tough. We stay in a lot. We snarl at our neighbors a lot. We watch too many episodes of *The Twilight Zone*. And we have these really annoying things called deadlines. Jayson has endured all of this and far more with a tremendous amount of love and good humor.

Finally, thanks to all the other writers and readers who have supported these bloody little books. I can't promise you all a happy ending, but I do hope you continue to enjoy the ride.

The Big Red House
Ohio
Spring, 2011

ABOUT THE AUTHOR

Kameron Hurley currently hacks out a living as a marketing and advertising writer in Ohio. She's lived in Fairbanks, Alaska; Durban, South Africa; and Chicago, but grew up in and around Washington State. Her personal and professional exploits have taken her all around the world. She spent much of her roaring twenties traveling, pretending to learn how to box, and trying not to die spectacularly. Along the way, she justified her nomadic lifestyle by picking up degrees in history from the University of Alaska and the University of Kwa-Zulu Natal. Today she lives a comparatively boring life sustained by Coke Zero, Chipotle, low-carb cooking, and lots of words. She continues to work hard at not dying. Follow the fun at www.kameronhurley.com

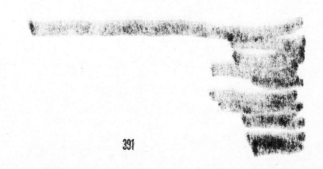

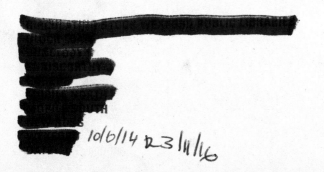

10/6/14 ₹3/11/16